Uprising

Book One of the *Fitzjohn* Duology

J. E. Rizzo

Literary Wanderlust | Denver, Colorado

Uprising is a work of fiction. Names, characters, places and incidents are either the product of the author's imagination or are used fictitiously, and any resemblance to actual persons, living or dead, business establishments, event or locales is entirely coincidental.

Published in the United States by Literary Wanderlust LLC, Denver, Colorado. www.LiteraryWanderlust.com

ISBN print: 978-1-956615-64-7
ISBN digital: 978-1-956615-65-4

To Noble Steve,
the father who believed
in healing through everyday magic.

Prologue

FOBBING, ENGLAND
APRIL 1370

My head is full of wool, raw and fluffy from the shears, not yet beaten into submissive yarn. I sigh, on the contented brink of another slumber. Then something sparkles in the dark. It fades but soon regains its strength, pulsating and throbbing.

I open my eyes, then wince and shut them again. A gasping moan escapes my lips.

"Hush, sweeting," someone murmurs. A cool cloth comes to rest on my forehead.

I exhale.

"Tha's better, yes?" The mysterious voice again.

I attempt a nod and clutch my aching skull.

"Don't move. Just stay calm," she says. It is a woman, I'm sure of it. The voice is deep and melodic, yet decidedly feminine.

I crack one eye and curl my fingers over the homespun blanket, inhaling the smell of a thatched roof. The coverlet is yellow, the wattle-and-daub walls white, trimmed with brown. I am home in my bed.

My vision is blurry as I open my eyes wider. A small figure, worn with age, rests on a stool beside me, but the lines of her face swim and I can't recognize her.

I try to sit up, and the cloth slides down my front. With a light *tsk*, the woman reaches to take it, then places a palm on my brow.

Her fingers are dry and calloused, but they brush away my tension, a rigidity I carry in my bones—worry over being scolded, or laughed at, or whispered about—if only for a moment. Smells of brackish marsh water breach my senses. Salt and grime, and chamomile.

She dips the cloth in a shallow basin beside her feet, then wrings it out. As my vision comes into focus, I remember her.

"El...El..." I stutter. "Ella?"

The woman laughs. "No, sweeting. Eldridge." Humming a light tune, she returns the cloth to my forehead. It smells of lavender, plus something sweet and tart.

Eldridge, the village wisewoman. Healer, recluse, conjuror, witch. Necessary, yet only for the desperate. Most give her tumbling-down hovel a wide berth.

"Did Maman call for you?" I ask.

Another laugh, the sound like river rocks shifting in the tide. "No, child. I saw the two of you piling out of the church, she 'bout to clop you round the ear. I stopped her and made her put you to bed."

I gape. I've never seen anyone *make* my mother do anything.

Eldridge tilts her head, listens. In the dining chamber, located below us on the cottage's first floor, Maman picks up a chair and slams it down. She's not cleaning—she doesn't—just taking her anger out on furniture.

Her anger with me over what happened this morning at church. Another one of my episodes. A spell. A slip. An episode of what, slipping into where, I cannot say. I don't understand what happens to me. No one does. But I sense the villagers, along with my maman, have some ideas. None of them kind.

Eldridge stares at me, and my mind races. What should I say? I almost burst out with *Are you really a witch?* but resist the urge. That would be rude; I can imagine Maman's chastisement over such a blunder. *That's my daughter for you, always blurting out whatever's in her head.*

I've never smelled a witch, of course, but I can't imagine they'd smell like the woman sitting before me. Eldridge's scent is safe, like the forest or marsh. I sniff again, and she leans closer. Can she read minds? I hope not.

In the end, "Thank you" is all I manage.

She sits back on her stool, silent.

A bright fire crackles in the hearth, and with the shutter closed tight, the chamber is warm. Too warm.

I wriggle my arms out from under the coverlet, watching Eldridge all the while. I half expect her to object, to scold about evil miasmas lurking about. But she doesn't, so I sigh, letting the cool air kiss my bare forearms.

Something soft brushes my wrist, and I give a little shriek, lurching up onto one elbow. A furry lump is curled at my side: an animal no bigger than my two fists. Its yellow-red fur is like the burning dawn, and it has a scrap of fabric wrapped around one leg. The white linen is stained with red.

"What?" I peer at it.

"The little Groom boy brought it for you." The creases of her mouth deepen as she grins.

"Geoff Groom?"

She nods.

"I've never spoken to him. No one—" I shut my mouth with an audible click. *No one speaks to me.* I push the ricocheting words away.

She gives a little shrug. "Truth be told, Geoff gave the creature to *me* this morning, just before I saw you at the church.

He'd snatched it from a couple bullies who were torturing it in the village square. They hurt the poor beast, as you can see." Eldridge touches one of the kitten's minuscule paws. He flexes his claws, each the width of a hair. "A good lad, Geoff. Better'n most, I'd say."

I have no idea what to say in response. Geoff isn't cruel, unlike most of the village's children. He doesn't taunt me or refuse to look at me, but we've still never had a real conversation. He's always either working in the stables with his father or on their tiny plot of land, allocated by the earl.

I swallow and nod toward the kitten. "Will it be all right?"

Another shrug. "Time will tell. It always does." She reaches down to soak the cloth in the dish, swirling it through the herbs floating on the water's surface.

"What are those?" I point at the green leaves. "I recognize the lavender, but I've never seen leaves like that and can't define the smell, much as I like it. It's not bay. Bay leaves only have one point. Sage leaves don't have those sharp ridges." I tick off the different herb names on my fingers. "Agrimony leaves do, but they're sharper. I suppose it could be—"

I glance at Eldridge. Her brows are lifted, but an odd light dances in her eyes. Recognition? Acceptance?

I clamp my own mouth closed. *There she goes, blabbering again.*

Eldridge looks down at the water, then back at me. "Lemon balm," she says. "Like plants, do you?"

I nod.

"Ye've much experience with them?"

I shake my head.

"Seem to know a great deal about them."

I shrug. The truth is, I know nothing about plants. I like them but have only seen the herbs I mentioned once, while spying on Master Cook last week. But once is all it takes for me to remember some things forever.

Eldridge keeps staring, and as is so often the case, my mouth begins to run before my brain gives its consent. "I do like plants. A little, I suppose. I like watching Cook, and I like the plants in the forest and the marsh. The happy ones are the best, but the others are fine too."

Her briny scent intensifies, becoming earthy like lichen creeping up the rough bark of an aged tree. "The happy ones?" she asks.

I bob my head.

"How do you know if they're happy, sweeting?"

"They tell me."

Eldridge leans over to pick up the kitten with one hand, checks his wound, then hands him to me. "How do they tell you?"

I twist my mouth in surprise. "Well, with words, of course."

The moss of her eyes brightens to the radiance of a clutch of ferns. "What else talks to you?"

"Just Maman, sometimes."

She smiles.

I fiddle with the edge of the coverlet. "There are the smells." My lips tingle. Why, *why* did I say that?

"The smells," she repeats. I nod but keep silent. "Tell me, Blanche Fitzjohn."

The sound of my surname, the one Maman and the duke made up for me, strangles my courage. I look down at the cat again, straightening his bandage.

"Is there something more you want to say, Mistress Fitzjohn?" she asks.

There is, but I can't. The name ricochets through my mind. Fitzjohn. My ears ring, as if Eldridge says it over and over, chanting. Like the other children do in the town square. I've never liked my name, surname *or* given name, truth be told. Maman named me Blanche after my father's wife—an awkward choice to say the least. But as is the case for most infants, I had no say in the matter.

I watch Eldridge from the corner of my eye as the kitten falls asleep on my chest. If I tell her about the smells, will she think I'm mad? Will she tell Maman?

I'm not normal, but Eldridge isn't either. If there's anyone who can explain these strange odors, it's her. What if...what if she smells them too?

I take a breath. *Have you ever smelled someone's mood?*

The words dance on my tongue, but when I open my mouth, "Teach me to grow herbs. To heal with them" is what comes out.

Eldridge sits back on her stool. She settles herself against the silence, making friends with it. The only sounds are the crackling fire and raindrops drumming on the shutters.

Fingering the end of her thick, ash-colored plait, she tilts her head for a full minute. I begin to think she didn't hear me.

"How old are you, Blanche Fitzjohn?" she asks at last.

"I celebrated my eleventh saint's day in October." As a mere girl of humble origins—despite the Plantagenet blood in my veins—I don't know my real date of birth. So, like every female I know, I count each year of life at the passing of my saint's feast day.

"Ye're still a child, but you must understand." She widens her eyes. "A healer straddles useful an' evil. Or at least that's what people think. If a woman knows too much, if she's too skilled, it brings danger." Dropping her voice to a whisper, she leans in and one corner of her mouth turns up. "You know some fools in this town name me a witch, do you?"

I don't allow myself the barest nod, not the flick of an eyelash. Of course I've heard them call her a witch, but I don't care.

My disregard for the villagers' opinions should frighten me. Instead, I'm emboldened. "I can smell people's moods," I say without the slightest hesitation.

Eldridge doesn't look away. She asks me for details about the types of odors and when I notice them. I tell her everything, my coiled tension releasing as I settle the kitten, still sleeping, on my lap.

I tell her I can see in dark shadows without a candle. "And I can hear travelers riding from miles away," I boast. Eldridge's mouth forms a perfect oval, but she closes it with alacrity and gives a satisfied nod. "Sometimes," I finish lamely.

My fingers flutter, almost flapping. Eldridge clasps them in her own. She doesn't squeeze, doesn't press down to still their movement, like Maman would. Instead, she circles her thumbs over my palms, her touch featherlight. Then she moves up to my wrists, rubbing where my pulse beats. It slows as, again, a pressure gives way, like a kettle steaming from its boil. Relief floods me.

"The sight is a gift, child," she whispers. "Don't let anyone make you feel guilty for it. Not for any of yer many gifts. You hear me?" She waggles one crooked finger.

I draw in a ragged breath, wet with emotion, but nod.

"Ye're special, Blanche."

I stare at her, mouth working. *Odd. Too much. Different.* Those are the words used to describe me, not special. The kitten wakes and meows, the sound so high-pitched I might have mistaken it for a baby bird. I clap a hand over my mouth, unable to bear his sweet innocence.

Eldridge chuckles. "And I told Geoff Groom ye'd be the one caring for his kitten."

"What? Why?"

"You need each other." Her eyes gleam.

"Me and the kitten?"

She strokes its head, silent.

"Did Maman see it?" I ask.

Eldridge snorts, then coughs and straightens her thin shoulders. "No." She takes in a sharp breath. "I'd recommend you keep it that way, sweeting."

I give her a tight smile. "I shouldn't keep the cat. What if I can't help it?"

"You can help it as much as me, Blanche Fitzjohn. Leastways, that's what I told Geoff Groom."

"I—"

"Come to me hut tomorrow, before dawn," she breaks in.

I stare at her, but nod, lips parted.

Eldridge screws her mouth to one side. For a moment, I worry she's changed her mind. Until she grins wryly and says, "Best not tell yer mother, yes?"

Chapter One

MAY 1381

Rows of hanging herbs sway as wind penetrates the flimsy wattle-and-daub walls. Their eerie shadows flit like purple damselflies over the crocks and vials crammed into baskets or strewn across shelves and tables.

Pressed against the door, Cecily Baker watches Eldridge reach beneath the thatched ceiling. Eyes never leaving Cecily's, Eldridge grasps a bundle of tansy, instinct and experience directing her hands through the dozens of herbs. She places the yellow flowers on the table, still watching our visitor. Cecily shudders. I hear the crackle of her tunic, the brush of hair over her shoulder.

Eldridge's fingers freeze over the button-like blooms. "Are you sure?" she asks.

A hank of tawny hair slips from Cecily's coif as she nods. I glance up, taking in her hazel eyes, wide as a doe before its archer.

Eldridge rips a generous quantity of flowers from their stems, releasing the fragrance of sweet camphor. It tickles my nostrils, making my eyes water. She deposits them into the mortar, motioning for me to keep grinding. The tansy's yellow infuses the green of yarrow and hellebore, lightening its fine powder to gray in the predawn light.

Cecily darts forward and places a lumpy fabric sack beside me. The smell of bread, sweet and yeasty and no doubt freshly baked, wafts up. Her payment. When I take it, my hand brushes Cecily's. I feel a small burn on her finger, likely from working in the bakery with her father, mother, and siblings. The calluses lining the pads of her fingers don't touch mine, but I sense them, their soreness. Cecily is tired. A soft, golden light pulses around her hands, her head. It's not just from kneading dough or heaving bread loaves in and out of the massive oven. She hasn't slept, maybe in days.

She flinches at my touch.

Eldridge takes the mortar and tips the powder into a small cloth bag before depositing it into a kettle of wine. "Drink it every day," she tells Cecily, placing the kettle in the fire, "for at least five days. Or"—she nudges the kettle further into the glowing embers with one bare toe—"until it starts working."

"How will I know?"

Eldridge scoffs. "When you bleed."

Cecily's rosebud lips work open and closed, soundless.

"This is dangerous, girl, make no mistake."

Cecily presses to the door, white hands like two starfish against the plank. "What d'you mean?" she asks. "I—"

Something darts from behind a basket of dried lavender and swishes past Cecily's feet. She squeaks like a mouse, then clutches her breast and glances at the shadow now retreating behind my tunic's hem.

"No, Rhead," I whisper. "Bad boy." I step to the side, and my yellow-red cat glares at Cecily, golden eyes glowing in the firelight.

Eldridge chuckles but doesn't answer Cecily's question for several minutes, until the kettle starts to boil. From her place at the door, the girl smells like grain spoiled after an inattentive farmer doesn't store it properly over a wet winter. Doubt.

I can identify everything in this hut with my eyes shut tight. Anyone else would find it impossible to discern anything from the hovel's overflowing cookpot of smells: herbs, animal hides, pickled vegetables, and woodsmoke, to name just a few. Still, the girl's changeable moods are easier even than that. The young are always that way, and the very old.

Eldridge grabs a towel and removes the kettle, pouring the wine into a small pottery crock. "If the bleeding gets heavy, send for me."

"I canna tell me mum, nor me da," Cecily rushes. "You canna tell them." Her gaze rakes over Eldridge and me in turn. With a start, I realize it's the first time she's looked at me, really looked, in two decades of acquaintance. "They've enough to worry about."

I don't need to ask her for details. Cecily's parents are villeins, and as their daughter, so is she. They belong to their manor lord. For the citizens of Fobbing, that lord is the late Earl of Hereford's widow, the Countess of Hereford. She owns Fobbing and its surrounding land, and its citizens owe her fealty, labor, and rent. Well, most of its citizens. Maman and I are free, not villeins. We don't pay rent for our small cottage and don't have to work the countess's land. That's why they hate us. One reason why.

Eldridge adds two pinches of clove, one of pepper, and a dribble of honey to the hot wine. I listen to the honey sinking into the liquid, popping and hissing as it melts.

In addition to the work and taxes owed their manor lord, earlier this year the king and his council demanded villeins pay a poll tax of one shilling per person over fifteen years old, to help finance the ongoing war with France. The villeins don't want to pay. Many can't. Cecily's father, Thomas Baker, has four children over age fifteen and three below. He may be considered fortunate for a villein—he has a high-paying trade and a good number of acres—but being one of the richest villeins in a community still doesn't mean much. The last time the royal tax collector visited, Baker's four adult children hid in the woods. By underpaying the tax, Baker was able to keep his family fed through another winter.

Eldridge closes the crock and swirls it in one hand. "Then come yourself." She tosses her ash-colored braid over one shoulder. "Or don't, but know you could die."

The blood drains from Cecily's face, and a fine sheen of perspiration glistens on her brow.

I see Rhead slink under the wall, leaving the hovel without a backward glance. Reflex makes me strain to hear Geoff's sharp whistle, but I stop. It's unlikely he's nearby. His work in the countess's stables starts before dawn, and he'd be punished for abandoning his post. Rhead must have simply heard a rodent or something else to hunt.

With no land of his own, Geoff is a laborer. The lowest of the low. Without leased land, laborers can't improve their circumstances through hard work and can't leave for higher pay elsewhere. Not since King Edward, my grandsire, passed laws forbidding any villein from leaving their manor or demanding higher wages.

Earnings are thus stagnant, even as expenses continue to rise. Everyone, even landless laborers like Geoff, is expected to pay the king's poll tax, no matter that their wages haven't increased in thirty-five years. Fobbing's streets teem with a hum of whispered, seething protest, like a fire licking at heels or a caustic smoke curling around frayed tunic hems. They're tired of subservience, tired of paying for the ceaseless war with France. No one speaks to me about it, of course. I'm the daughter of the enemy. But I hear them nonetheless.

Cecily reaches a trembling hand toward the crock. "I won't have a bas—" Wide hazel eyes flick to mine. She takes the crock, looking down as the aroma of spoiled milk fills the small space. Embarrassment is another scent I know well.

Eldridge nods before ushering Cecily through the door. We watch her hurry away, pink dawn spreading above the distant trees. Rhead hides in the hedgerow, watching her pass the church. I hear his breathing, the twitch of his whiskers. Padded paws step easily, leaving no indentations in the sandy soil as he makes to follow the girl home.

"Blasted beast," I mutter.

Eldridge exhales.

"Aren't you afraid?" I ask. "If something goes wrong, everyone will know you gave her the herbs."

She chuckles. "Cecily will be fine. I was just trying to scare her."

I gape. "How d'you know she'll be all right?"

"I've seen it."

"Seen what?"

Peering at me, she shakes her head. "Nothing."

I close the door, and she returns to the table to tidy away the spices and remaining herbs.

"Women like you and me..." she trails off.

I eye her sideways. "Yes?"

Silence.

After eleven years of tutelage, Eldridge has taught me to heal agues and set bones, to deliver babies and help nursing mothers with infants that refuse to suck. But there are some things she's still unwilling to divulge. Sometimes I suspect she enjoys the mystery. Other times, I worry she doesn't trust me with the truth.

"You said 'Women like you and me.' What did you mean?"

"Nothing." She slams a pottery crock on the table. "Cecily will be fine. Of that, I am sure."

Without Eldridge, my existence would be intolerable. We have a commonality. I sense it; I know it's true. But she won't discuss it. I've asked if she smells people's moods dozens of times—no, hundreds.

I take a step closer. "You saw her future, didn't you?" Eldridge's thick plait swings when she shakes her head. I try again. "I know the truth. I can see it in your eyes—have seen it before, when you talked to Master Thatcher's new wife. You knew something about her future."

She retreats to the other side of the hovel.

"Do you think I'll ever have visions?"

Silence. I decide to change tack.

"If you see the future, surely you've seen mine. Tell me about it."

Her gaze flashes in the firelight, and for an instant, I see words forming in her mouth. I rise on my toes, body angled toward her. I've asked so many times, but now the answer feels urgent, pressing.

Before my eyes, her cheeks suddenly go hollow and lean, and dark smudges press beneath her eyes. Her hair appears no longer gray, but white.

The change is gone in the same instant it appeared, but something constricts my chest. I give a little cough.

"The sun's coming up," Eldridge says. "Ye'd best get home before yer mother awakens."

Chapter Two

I enter our cottage through the kitchen, intending, like always, to dash up the stairs, rip off my work tunic, and jump into bed before Maman wakes up. Today, however, a hand snatches my wrist before I move an inch beyond the back door.

"M'lady wants to see you."

I turn to find Ceira Cook's beady, mud-colored eyes glaring at me from over her hooked nose. Wife to Master Ilbert Cook, who prepares our meals, Ceira cleans the cottage and helps Maman dress every day. Cook's teenage son, Hamish, cares for our chickens and dairy cow, housed in the crooked outbuilding behind our cottage. He also works in Fobbing Manor's kitchens, where he sleeps. His father and Ceira sleep in our dining hall. Hamish's mother was Cook's first wife, who died in the pestilence that swept through Fobbing ten years ago.

"I need to change, Ceira."

She narrows her eyes and grinds her teeth.

"Mistress Cook, I mean." Ceira only recently married Master Cook, and I'm not used to the change yet. Neither is Hamish.

The maid shoves me through the tiny door between our kitchen and dining hall without another word. I try to snatch at my shabby tunic's hem to keep from tripping, but when I right myself, my eyes widen and my jaw drops.

Maman should still be in bed. Instead, she stands before me in her best cream-colored undertunic and dove-gray surcoat, fashionable white tippets flowing to her knees. Silvery blonde hair peeks from the edge of her wimple, and her gray eyes flash. A silver ring, the one memento that remains of my father—other than me, I suppose—glints in the light.

Even in the face of my shock, I only glance at her.

The chamber is crowded—too crowded—and a young man steps forward. I stare at his long, straight nose, so like mine that I fight the urge to touch two fingertips to my face.

"Blanche! Qu'est-ce que tu portes?" *What on earth are you wearing?*

Maman's words burn like a slap, and I look down at my homespun tunic, spattered with marsh scum and mud. Before making the tincture for Cecily, Eldridge and I spent the predawn hours foraging in the tidelands. I hide my hands in the folds of my apron, hoping she doesn't notice the soil and sand caked under my nails.

"I'm sorry—" I blurt.

I sense rather than see Maman's flinch. I can almost hear her silent reprimand. *How many times have I told you? Women don't yell.*

I swallow convulsively and watch the stranger standing before the room's central hearth. He smells clean, like Castilian soap. Confident.

Towering above my diminutive mother, the top of his red velvet chaperon brushes the smoke-stained ceiling, even though his clean jaw makes it clear he's no older than fifteen. An ornate doublet of crimson brocade stretches across his chest, decorated with costly buttons marching up the middle. The garment is also secured with an intricate black belt. In the back of my panicked mind, logic insists that he couldn't possibly need the buttons *and* the belt.

I recognize his heraldic badge, entwined esses stitched in gold thread, on the hem of his chaperon. He's a Lancaster, like my father.

I search his face. The crystalline blue eyes aren't unkind, and the corner of his mouth twitches as he takes in my shabby garb. His auburn hair shines in the morning sun, streaming through the cottage's open front door. My stomach heats up and churns like Eldridge's kettle. Why would a Lancaster come here? Fobbing, a small coastal village where the Thames meets the North Sea, is beneath anyone's notice except the Herefords, the nobles who own the manor, its land, and its villeins. My father's never even been here.

I clutch my hands at my waist in a failed attempt to keep them still.

The young man sweeps a courteous bow, as if he's in the king's receiving chamber at Westminster, instead of our little cottage's dining hall.

"Blanche," Maman grinds out, "may I present Henry of Lancaster, the Earl of Derby."

My brother. Well, half-brother. I try not to stare.

Heir to the Duchy of Lancaster and destined for power, like our father. He would never speak to me in public; I'm sure I don't matter to him. Still, he fascinates me. I've never met any of my half-siblings, not one of my father's four legitimate children nor his four other illegitimate offspring.

"Je...Je...Je m'excuse, mon seigneur..." I stutter, adding a clumsy curtsy and gazing down at my bare feet, caked with mud. I continue in French. "...for my appearance. You see, I was unaware of your visit and was working in the garden." I clench my fingers together until my knuckles glow white, desperate to hide my flapping hands.

"You look delightful," he says in English. I give a little start. Most noblemen, descended from the Normans, detest the Anglo-Saxon language. He gives me a warm smile, and an absurd flush of pleasure heats my face even as my neck begins to itch.

I long to dip a finger beneath my collar and pull the rough fabric away from my skin. An itch of discomfort races across my shoulders and down my spine, like a pervasive rodent. I suppress a shiver and a grimace.

"I'm pleased to see you." My brother is speaking again, in English, and I blink, trying to refocus. "What do you grow?"

"Oh, Blanche...grows..." Maman stammers. Her English has never been good. "...all...herbs." Her pale skin turns bright red, and she looks at her feet.

"Wonderful." He smiles, open and unabashed, certain the world will mold to his whims. The way all powerful, lucky men smile.

I'm not powerful, nor a man, and I am certainly not lucky. My stomach does a flip.

Out of the corner of my eye, I see movement. The second man, standing at Henry's left, shuffles into the light, assailing my nostrils with the pungent odor of rose oil laced with ale. He's not tall, no more than myself, but he is broad and muscular, with a plain face and flaming red hair. About thirty years old, he wears a tunic and hose of less expensive fabric than Henry's, but still of good cut and quality. His mouth bends in a petulant scowl, eyes downcast.

From the open door, one of the men's destriers bugles. Another horse stomps its hoof.

When my gaze flicks toward the sounds, I spy another figure on the dusty road outside my house. Geoff.

As one of the Dowager Countess's many villeins, he has no doubt been tasked with tending the gentlemen's horses. For once, however, Geoff is ignoring the beasts. Instead, he stares at me, lips pressed into a tight line and eyes searching, almost frightened. Icy water rushes through my veins. With anyone else, I'd turn, avoiding such a look, but not Geoff.

His brown eyes open wider.

Before I can consider how to respond, a yellow-red blur darts between Geoff's legs, bolting through the open door and into the chamber. Rhead has returned from escorting Cecily home, hopefully without terrifying her. The cat streaks into the room and hides beneath the trestle table. My half-brother chuckles, but Maman's eyes flick toward the swishing tail, then back to me. Gazing up at the ceiling and flaring her nostrils, she exhales a puff of air like an angry warhorse.

"Sortez ce chat d'ici," she growls. *Get that cat out of here.*

The shorter, red-haired man gives a little grunt, too low for anyone's ears but mine, and points at Rhead before moving toward him. His scent intensifies until the sour ale is like vinegar, and my guts knot.

He makes to grab Rhead, but the cat dashes away just in time. The red-haired man's fist, bigger than both of mine put together, slams into the trestle, knocking it over. The sound sends a painful jolt through me, and I cover my ears. He sneers, and his scent changes again, to that of sweaty children playing in the village courtyard. I can almost hear their gleeful cries. I imagine it smelled that way when Geoff rescued Rhead from the bullies who tried to kill him.

"Care to join in the fun, Derby?" the strange, red-haired man says over his shoulder.

Before my half-brother can respond, Geoff strides through the front door, picks up the cat with one fluid movement, and cradles Rhead against his plain, dirty surcoat. He looks at me, widening his eyes. I give a slow blink, just once, and he blinks back. We stare at each other, the air thick like congealed soup.

"Blanche."

My half-brother is speaking again, yet I can't look away from Geoff.

Geoff leaves with the cat purring in his arms, his vast shoulders casting a momentary shadow across the doorway. At last, my cat safe, I tear my eyes from them both.

"This"—Henry gestures to the red-haired man, who steps back to my brother's side as if he didn't just try to kill my cat—"is Sir Thomas Prescott."

Sir Thomas gives a sharp and succinct bow before looking into my face. His eyes, in contrast to his fair hair and skin, are black and cold as steel. When he moves toward me, I instinctively back away, heart pounding in my ears. The smell of ale and roses is so pervasive that my throat constricts, as if I've ingested glass. I try to swallow, to clear the blockage, but I cannot.

I ball my hands into fists, digging them into my thighs through the homespun tunic, willing them not to shake. But the trestle table presses into the backs of my legs, and I have nowhere to go. Flicking my gaze to Maman, I can't miss the warning in her eyes. But it's difficult to stop, so very difficult. The putrid aroma, and that awful feeling that something's wrong. Something I can't identify.

I must silence this, must calm my body. If my mind and body take me away, Maman will beat me bloody.

There's more than that, too. My brother is watching, and he'll tell my father if I make a fool of myself. I yearn to be the woman my father expects, what he wants. Accomplished, educated, attractive. What every eldest daughter should be. But above all, I want to be normal. *Normal.*

I inhale and close my eyes, letting my mind carry me the half mile to my marsh. Over High Road to the wharf, then down the ridge's steep slope to the Thames.

Scents of river and sea flood my nostrils. In my mind's eye, I watch the tide overtake the sand and grass. Above me, thick clouds form a canopy to shelter me from the weak, gray morning light. The salt and damp smells join with the tall green grass, soil, and bark. I inhale it all, each color and texture of my home unique and recognizable, catalogued in my mind.

"Mistress Fitzjohn."

At Henry's words, the tidelands' aromas rush away, leaving me back in my cottage's dining hall.

"I'm pleased to deliver a message from our father." His eyes cut to Sir Thomas. I can't smell Henry's mood—Thomas is too pungent—but I sense something unpleasant in the set of his mouth. "I'm here to announce your betrothal to Sir Thomas. You're to marry in one month's time."

I gawk. Sir Thomas clears his throat. The sound is like a stone mason chipping away inside my ears.

Henry goes on, his tone flat. "Our father bids me to tell you that Sir Thomas is high in King Richard's favor and is to be made Constable of the Tower. You shall become Lady Prescott and move to London."

There's a scratching behind the kitchen door. Ceira—Mistress Cook—and her husband must be listening in. Outside the front door, Geoff shuffles his feet and Rhead leaps down from his arms. I feel my throat swelling.

"Blanche," Maman says. "Answer Lord Henry. Thank him."

Sir Thomas coughs, and Maman emits a nervous giggle. The two noises are small, my rational mind knows this, but in this moment their dissonance is like the collision of two ocean waves in a windstorm.

"M...m...my lord," I manage. "I am honored, truly."

Another giggle and a cough.

My hands flap, but I hide them behind my back. I take another gasping breath, and Maman's angry glare presses into me. "But I cannot possibly leave my mother." My words rush out, high-pitched and juvenile.

Outside the cottage, the noblemen's destriers snort and shake their bridles. Geoff speaks to them, his tone harsh. Sir Thomas coughs again.

My throat tightens. I can't swallow, can't *breathe*. I close a hand over my neck.

"Our father will be pleased by your devotion to your mother." Henry's voice smiles.

I wheeze. I am going to die. A vision of Eldridge's face, irregularly shadowed and bruised beneath the eyes, swims before me. The distorted way I saw it only this morning.

"But don't fear," Henry continues, his own face flashing in and out of my sight, "she will be cared for."

Sir Thomas wrenches my hand from behind my back. His fingers are smooth and cold, and I try to recoil, but he holds me fast. Before I realize what's happening, he plants a kiss on my knuckles. My hand, so overwhelmed and unpredictable, begins to flutter.

It's only a slight tremor at first, but Sir Thomas drops my fingers as if I'm sick with the pestilence. The increasingly thick smell of rose oil and ale makes my ears buzz.

Sir Thomas's almost inhuman eyes, so black that they have no differentiation between pupil or iris, are small and marble-like, reminding me of the sharks I once saw on Geoff's uncle's fishing boat. Sounds roar in my ears, screaming of death, and above them all, I hear Eldridge. She's not here. She never comes to my home anymore, but I hear her all the same. Her voice is shadowed, like her face in my vision. Clouded by cobwebs of age. And death.

My hands flap against my chest, then come together. My mind closes. Once overloaded from smells or sounds or information, I can't control the reaction. It doesn't matter that Henry and Sir Thomas are here; nothing matters. My body takes over. Or my mind takes over my body. I don't know which.

Chapter Three

I don't see my brother and Sir Prescott leave. I don't see anything when my senses take me over. But after I wake late that afternoon—tucked into my bed, just like the day I met Eldridge—Maman tells me they hurried away after my "fit," to stay the night at the Countess of Hereford's manor before riding back to London. The countess is Henry's mother-by-law, as he's married to Mary Hereford, one of England's wealthiest heiresses. He's always welcomed at Fobbing Manor, unlike me.

"You'll stay here until you're prepared to write to Lord Henry and apologize," Maman says, a vein throbbing at her temple. In the chamber's afternoon light, tinted lavender and blue like an old bruise, Maman looks older than her forty years. Her skin appears translucent, and a stark vein webs up her neck to her bony jaw like a jagged scar. "And you'll write to Sir Prescott."

"I won't, Maman." I cover my eyes, trying to blot out the light streaming from the open window, pulsing with the beat of my heart. My eyes burn, my throat is parched. All of me aches.

"You will. He already doesn't want to marry you," she continues. "I heard him say it to Lord Henry. He thinks you're mad. Even worse..." Her voice drops to a whisper. "He called you a witch."

I groan and sit up. Maman sits at my bedside, arms crossed and lips pressed into a thin line. Over her shoulder, I catch a glimpse of Geoff in the corridor. He smiles at me for a moment before looking down at Rhead, who is marching his front paws on the homespun coverlet. I let my outstretched palm settle on the cat's fur.

Geoff steps into the room. "I brought him for you. Now you can rest, Dandelion."

Maman glares at him. She doesn't speak much English, and he doesn't speak French, but she knows his nickname for me—Dandelion—and as always, she does not approve.

Splotches of red bloom in his cheeks.

After I nursed Rhead back to health, Geoff started visiting us both whenever he could get away from his work. We soon discovered our shared passion for the marsh and woods surrounding Fobbing, and for animals.

One day, Geoff found me sitting in the weeds, weaving yellow dandelion flowers through my hair while Rhead played with one at my feet. He has called me Dandelion ever since, and throughout the spring, it's become his habit to leave the yellow flowers for me. Most often on our doorstep, but sometimes in the outbuilding, in my foraging basket, even at Eldridge's hut. Maman used to switch him with a reed for it when we were children. Now, I suppose, he's too big for that. I'm a tall woman, but Geoff towers over me, much less Maman. But that doesn't stop her from scowling, or Geoff from being afraid of her.

Stepping back, he closes the door with a cough.

I pull the coverlet over my eyes.

"You must write to Sir Prescott immediately. Or, better yet, I'll go to St Michael's and ask Master Adam to write for you. Sir

Prescott may not like a wife who can read and write, and your apologies will be more effectual coming from a man."

"That's stupid."

"Blanche," she hisses. "Keep that mouth of yours shut, for once."

"I'm not writing to anybody. And if you have that doughty old Master Adam write *for* me, I'll send my own letter refuting any agreement you faked."

"Blanche, how you grew to be such a fool is beyond me. Your noble father supported you and gave you his royal blood..."

"I've never met him—"

"And I'll say nothing of my own struggles to raise you right," she traipses over my statement almost before I've finished. "I worked to give you a proper upbringing and education, to prepare you for one thing. A good marriage. And now it's here, a better match than I could have hoped for. But you—"

"I refuse, yes." My voice is muffled from beneath the coverlet.

She stands and Rhead leaps down from the bed to hide. Maman ignores him, tapping something metal against the doorframe. I pull my head out from the blanket to confirm my fears. It's a key.

"You'll stay here"—she taps again—"until you come to your senses."

"Geoff and I—"

"That boy is a peasant," she snaps. "Landless. The worst sort, if there is such a thing."

"He's my friend."

"He *was* your friend. Now he's nothing. You're not to see him. In fact..." She strides back across the room and snatches a tankard from the sideboard. I hadn't noticed until now, but it's full of bright yellow flowers. Dandelions.

"Did Geoff bring—"

"You're not to see him anymore, Blanche. Much less accept these *weeds* he's always leaving around." With a jerking movement, she tosses the flowers out the window and clops the empty tankard back on the sideboard.

"How dare you?" I swing my legs over the side of the bed. Rhead's paws emerge from beneath the mattress's coarse ropes to bat at my ankles. "I will see him, Maman."

"No. You'll see no one."

"Then Eldridge. I must see her. She's expecting me."

"Absolutely not."

My chest constricts. Eldridge will know what to do, how to escape the clutches of my impending betrothal. I've seen her fix any number of the villagers' problems. Cecily's unexpected pregnancy, another woman's unrequited love, a goodwife's infertility. There must be a potion, something she can do. Maybe if I drank a combination of stewed herbs, I'd become terribly disfigured. So unattractive that Sir Prescott would refuse to marry me, and my father would let me live out my days in Eldridge's hovel.

Maybe Eldridge could create a disguise and I could run away. My mouth goes dry. Adventure is one thing in a book, or in a puppeteer's portrayal in the village square. It's another when it comes knocking at your doorstep, disemboweling your life and all your plans.

I don't want to run away. I want to stay here with Eldridge. And Geoff. No matter what Maman says, she can't keep me from them.

"You're not to see her again." Maman's shrill voice pulls me out of my reverie. "I command it. She's made you a village outcast, and Sir Prescott already thinks you're a witch. He can't find out you've been gallivanting around the marsh with that recluse. Not ever."

I open my mouth to argue, but the slam of the chamber's heavy oaken door, followed by the metallic click of the lock, drowns out my words before they're even formed.

I count her light footsteps on the stairs. After the ninth and final one, I haul myself up, ignoring my aching limbs, and hurry to the chamber's solitary window. The bedchamber is on the second floor, above the kitchen, but that's never stopped me from climbing out before.

Rhead slinks to my side, watching with globe-like eyes as I pull my homespun tunic over my chemise. I comb my fingers through my matted tangle of brown hair, trying to tame it into a plait. I give up. It doesn't matter what anyone thinks of my appearance. All that matters right now is getting to Eldridge.

She'll know what to do. She always does.

I place both hands on the windowsill. Rhead leaps up between them and jumps out.

"Blasted cat," someone squeaks.

When I stick my head out the window, I find Ceira Cook sitting on a stool below my window, sewing.

"Mistress." She nods to me as if doing so costs her one year of life.

I boost my weight onto my hands, about to haul my knees onto the window ledge.

"Don't even think about it." Her voice is like a blacksmith's ancient machinery, squeaky and oily at the same time. "I've me instructions from m'lady. You come one bit out that window and Master Cook is to beat you with a spoon, she said." Ceira grins, displaying a row of tiny, decaying teeth.

My stomach twists. The last time Cook hit me with the spoon, I had welts for a week. "God's wounds..." I slump back inside the window, ignoring Ceira's shocked intake of breath. At least my cursing got the result I was hoping for.

Rhead jumps back inside the window and I spend the next few hours slumped beside it, the cat curled in my lap. I tune my ears to what's happening outside, but no one approaches. Geoff doesn't return, Eldridge stays away, and my brother and Sir Thomas must be feasting at the manor house. The only human sounds are Ceira's mumbled complaints as she maintains her vigil beneath my window.

Cook brings me a bread trencher of greasy stew, but I ignore it.

Once it's dark outside, Maman returns to find me back in bed, covered with blankets. Ceira undresses her for bed and leaves, given firm instructions to keep up her guard beneath our window.

"You know you don't have a choice, Blanche," Maman says, locking the chamber door behind Ceira's departing back. She tucks the key inside her chemise and strides to glance out the window.

After another minute or so, I hear Ceira below, her breath a soft whistle against the evening breeze. I should be surprised Maman would make her servant spend the night outside, but I'm not. To my mother, Ceira is just another villein. Useful, yet disposable. Here for one purpose: to serve the nobility, which Maman pretends to be a part of. Maman gives a satisfied nod, then shuts and latches the window's shutter.

When she joins me atop the rickety mattress, I roll over to face the door.

"My favorite," she mutters through clenched teeth. "Taut silence."

I hold my breath. Maybe if I pass out, she'll abandon me and I can at least die in peace.

"Blanche," she hisses. "I know you're not sleeping. Turn around and look at me."

I say nothing and don't move.

"I'm your maman, am I not? You must do what I say. Look at me when I speak to you. Now."

The mattress creaks on its ropes as I roll over.

Her eyes sparkle in the dim light and she smells like a smoldering fire.

"Don't you see?" Her breath makes the little hairs around her face tremble. "After your marriage, you won't carry the name of bas—*illegitimacy* anymore. You'll be Lady Prescott, the wife of a knight. A *landed* knight, Blanche. Sir Prescott has property, and he's to be made Constable of the Tower." She starts to grind her molars; the sound, punctuated by the *drip, drip, drip* of water in the corridor—a pervasive leak we can't seem to fix—makes my skin teem with invisible life.

"I told you, I won't marry him."

She lifts one hand to her forehead and closes her eyes. "Oh," she groans. "I feel so faint, Blanche. So faint." There's no glowing evidence of pain or sickness around her. I know she's fine, but when she speaks, her voice is low and tremulous. "Blanche, this is what your father wants. He arranged this because he loves you."

"He doesn't love me. He doesn't even know me." I lose control over the quaver in my voice. "He arranged this to get me off his household accounts. This is about settling a debt, not fatherly love."

"He—"

"He didn't even bother to come himself. He sent his son instead."

"You—"

"I've *never* seen him, Maman. Not once in two and twenty years. I know he's the most powerful man in Christendom, but doesn't it bother you that he's never laid eyes on me, his eldest child?"

Maman's burning smell intensifies until my skin prickles, and her pale eyes flare.

She draws a shaking breath. "Go to sleep, Blanche." Each word is enunciated with deliberate care, as if I'm an idiot. "We will be busy tomorrow. There is much I must teach you about living at court, about being a married lady. You must—"

"You never married," I interrupt. Drawing back, she blinks.

I can't believe I said it. *I actually said it*. I've always wanted to but was too afraid. Did an opportunity for marriage not arise? Or did she think that someday the duke would return to her?

I drop my eyes from her glare and pick at a wrinkle in the sheet. Since I can remember, Maman's spent every free moment in relentless, cruel pursuit of my education. Never talked of my father's absence, only of my lineage, my future. She took me to St. Michael's and forced the priest, Master Adam, to teach me to read and write. Every afternoon, she droned on—about how the king structures his court, how the late Queen Philippa, whom Maman used to serve, appointed her servants. As she spoke, she smelled of fruit left to rot in a courtyard in high summer. She doesn't yearn for me to marry and become a lady because she loves me. No, she loathes me—I smell the filth of it—but my future success at court is the only way she can recover from her past failures.

"Your father expects you to be a good wife." Maman sniffs. "Do that, and maybe then he'll love you."

I flop back to face the door and squeeze my eyes closed. Maman huffs, but within five minutes, her breathing smooths and changes to soft snores.

Unlike me, she always sleeps heavily. Most nights, I lie awake for hours, listening to our cottage's three resident mice scrabble through the walls. A small rodent population, thanks to Rhead's dutiful efforts. When it's so cold that the mice are silent, I still can't calm my mind. The names of long-dead Plantagenet princes and kings parade through my brain in ceaseless and monotonous succession, and catalogues of the king's servants mock my search for rest. Despite my efforts to ignore Maman's lessons, I think I've absorbed quite a bit. My knack for details is more of a curse than a blessing.

Maman sleeps on for half an hour. I lay still, staring at the bolted door. But I don't see it. I don't see anything. I'm busy feeling each blade of straw in the mattress, poking my torso, my left arm, my cheek. There's a worrisome cluster beneath the crook of my neck. If I shift the wrong way, the mattress will creak. But if I move forward as I straighten, I just might be able to get up without making a sound, and, most importantly, without shifting the bed beneath me.

I ease my head from the pillow and move my weight onto my elbows. At the clump of straw, I ease my torso forward and sit up in one fluid movement.

All is silent. I fold the coverlet down to reveal my shabby homespun tunic instead of my sleeping chemise. Maman's a fool if she truly thinks Ceira will sit out in the rain all night while her mistress sleeps. And I'm not going to lay here, locked in my bedchamber, when there's a perfectly good window to climb out of.

I swing my legs over the mattress and step onto the cold floor with one swift, light movement, praying it won't make Maman's body shift. The linen sheet crackles with the sudden removal of my weight, and the mattress's straw seems to buzz like a pack of bees. I cringe and glance over my shoulder. Maman's childlike hand is tucked beneath her cheek and her eyes are closed. She's still snoring. For a moment, I see her as she must have been when I was born, when she and my father were both nineteen. Beautiful, with delicate, elf-like features and white-blonde hair. So different from my own broad cheekbones and long nose. Maman tells anyone who will listen that I look like Old King Edward, my grandsire. Although I've always thought a king's blood is too good for my veins, after seeing my half-brother Henry, I think she might be right.

I creep to the window on bare feet, thankful for my years of foraging in the marsh with Eldridge. She didn't just teach me to identify and use everything we found but to be adept and light on my feet, soundless and stealthy.

I raise the window's latch. The shutter squeaks, but Maman doesn't wake. I lift my nose to the night air. Raindrops patter on the thatched roof. Even in the darkness, I can see Ceira's gone. Taken cover inside, driven by exhaustion and the weather, and her certainty that a young woman would never be so foolish as to sneak out at night in the rain.

With an abrupt and shadowy flash, a small figure leaps from behind me and onto the sill. I clutch my chest, then let my shoulders slump with a shuddering exhale. Rhead's head swivels like an owl's. I grin, raising a finger to my lips in a silent signal. I could swear he nods before leaping out the open window without a sound.

I reach between my legs and pull the back hem of my tunic to the front, tucking it into my twine belt. In a moment, I've made myself an odd pair of hose where once I had a skirt. A part of me wishes Maman would wake and see me, just to witness her horror.

I press my palms to the windowsill and boost myself up. Without voluminous skirts, I'm able to crouch in the tiny, rectangular space without trouble, like a yellow bunting preparing to take flight from an oak.

The bedchamber is the only room on the cottage's second floor, nestled into a thatched gable, its two walls built with dark beams, wattle, and daub. On the building's outside, one of the wooden beams stretches from the base of the window to either side. I ease myself out the window to stand upon it. It's slippery with rainwater, but my toes are rough from running barefoot through the woods and marsh. Fingers clinging to the wattle branches, I shimmy my bare feet to sidle along the beam. Bits of daub flutter to the ground at the house's corner. Although I'm directly above the kitchen window, I doubt Cook and Ceira will notice, even though they're both surely still awake. As always, they'll be too distracted by their interminable tasks, their minds fogged by exhaustion.

Still clinging to the building's side and facing the small toft of land at the cottage's rear, I balance on my toes and close my eyes. I will my body to think it's on a flat surface, to believe I have the necessary traction to jump. This was much easier when I was a child. Now, my calf muscles scream, and for a moment I think my legs might buckle. Before they can, I press my palms against the wall and spring like a frog through the night air.

Wind whistles in my ears. The moisture clinging to it—I remember in the dim recesses of my thrilled mind that it's still raining—beads on my lashes and in the tangled hair around my face.

I land with a thud on the outbuilding's roof, a crouching structure built of earth and branches. One of my feet has almost made a hole in its thatch. Beneath me, our three chickens cluck and the dairy cow backs into a wall.

"What was that?" Cook asks from the kitchen.

I force my body flat against the roof. A light sound makes me flick my eyes to my right. Rhead's golden stare watches me through the rain.

I grin at him.

"That foul beast," Ceira responds. "The cat."

"Aye."

Cook shuffles away from the window, grumbling about how much work he still has. I exhale and move like a crab along the small width of flat thatch. Rhead follows. Once up and over the roof's seam, I start the steep descent down the roof's other side, which slants all the way to the ground. I go feet first, hands grappling and slipping on wet thatch as I half climb, half slide the rest of the way.

Chapter Four

My feet squish in sticky mud as a sheet of rain breaks free from the darkness and pours over the already sodden landscape. We run, Rhead's yellow-red fur spiked with wet and my hair a frizzled and wild halo around my face. The wind whips and stings my skin, but I cover my mouth to stifle my giggles when we careen past villeins' cottages, headed toward the edge of Fobbing, where Eldridge lives.

At the Bakerscroft, however, I pause and dodge into a shadow, panting. Rhead takes a few more steps, but freezes when he notices my absence.

"Psst," I hiss and pat my knee from behind the building's thatched eave. Rhead looks left and right, clearly annoyed, but trots back to meet me.

The Bakerscroft is home to Thomas Baker, his wife Avice, and their many offspring. I'm sure Cecily's taken Eldridge's potion by now. She's likely in pain, bleeding, and alone. I take one step toward the croft, then stop. Although many laborers and other members of the villeinage are still awake, I should be home, tucked in my bed beside Maman. If I'm seen, what excuse could I give for being out?

Cecily and I are not friends. I can't claim to be making a routine, albeit late, social call. Like most in the village, Cecily only deigns to speak to me when she needs an herbal remedy or a wound dressed.

I peek from my hiding place. Rain sheets down, soaking the croft's whitewashed walls and solitary window. All seems quiet within, but a crunching footstep makes me shrink further back.

Two men approach from Fobbing Hill Street. When they turn right onto High Road, I see one has rounded, hulking shoulders, and the other is tall and stringy. Even through the spitting rain, I recognize Thomas Baker and his friend, Wulfric Plowman. Their stumbling gaits and the stiff reek of ale make it clear that they've been drinking together at the White Lion Tavern, just down Fobbing Hill.

"...poll tax. How're we supposed to pay?" Baker mumbles to Plowman.

"No choice, I'd say."

"No choice?"

"King's orders."

"Humph." Baker kicks a stone with his boot.

I try to force myself to turn and run. Baker and Plowman have no idea I can hear their conversation; listening feels wrong. *Take care with yer gifts, Blanche,* Eldridge often says. *Private words are meant to stay private. Nothing good comes of hearing what you shouldn't.*

"King's orders..." Baker spits into the rain and pulls his hat brim down tighter. "Fie! More like Lancaster's orders."

Plowman grunts.

"Well, I won't pay," Baker continues.

"Won't pay? How d'you plan on that?"

The two men stop in front of the Bakerscroft. At my feet, Rhead swishes his tail silently back and forth and stares up at me. I don't dare move a muscle. My opportunity to flee has passed. I cling to the Bakerscroft's walls, not daring to breathe and shrouded in darkness. My fingernails dig into the flaking daub, and before I can stop it, a single pebble dislodges itself from the wall and clinks to the ground.

It seems impossible that anyone—other than me, of course—could hear the sound through the pattering rain, but Baker's head tilts and his eyes slice toward my hiding spot.

Plowman follows his glance, but Baker claps his friend on the shoulder. "Don't worry, man. We'll talk about it tomorrow. It's late..."

Plowman nods and slumps away. My tension uncoils slightly, but then Baker pivots on his heel and glares right at me.

"Mistress Fitzjohn," he grumbles. "Good evening."

I try to hide my startled flinch with a nonchalant shrug.

Baker's hazel eyes, the same color as Cecily's, are hooded and tired. A pervasive light shines around the left one; he's suffered from inflamed boils in the lids for years but refuses to let Eldridge treat them.

"Good evening, Master Baker," I say loudly. "How's your family?"

The smell of decaying garbage fills my nostrils when he narrows his eyes. "Fine," he says at last. "Fine, though you have no right to meddle."

"I wasn't meddling, I—"

"I canna stand around chatting, mistress," he interrupts. "There's work to do. The king's taxes won't pay themselves." His smell intensifies to the point that my eyes water. I try to take a step back, then remember I'm flat against the wall.

He disappears through the front door without another word and starts banging pans and other utensils around the bakery at the front of their residence.

I should leave. If Baker sees me lingering, he could become angry and go tell the Cooks I'm not where I should be.

Instead, I sidle up to the bakery window.

Cecily's hazel eyes are etched in my memory. She faces a terrible choice. Bear a bastard and face a lifetime of shame, bringing a new mouth into a household that can barely feed its current residents. Or drink a potion that might kill her.

I stretch my neck, inching my nose closer to the window.

Blood's metallic scent drifts on the oven's fumes from the rear of the croft, where there's likely a bedchamber. I exhale a sigh of relief. It's a small amount, maybe nothing more than a regular monthly menses. Eldridge was right. Cecily will be fine.

I trot away, Rhead by my side. I suppose I'll never know if Cecily would have accepted my help, had I offered.

Just before the wharf, I skid to a stop in front of St Michael's, peeking around the wattle fence at the squat church. Its brown stone glistens in the rain. The building crumbles at the edges, the sprinkling of headstones in the yard like crooked teeth in an old crone's gaping mouth. About a quarter mile beyond, Eldridge's hovel sits in dense fog.

Without warning, the small hairs on my nape stand, and I turn to scan the handful of nearby cottages. My sharp eyes take in the shadows, the corners, the dark alley. I find nothing, no one. Cloaked in dark mist, Fobbing appears calm and peaceful. I look back at the church, but can't shake the feeling I'm being watched.

I spot Master Adam's stooped figure walking from the decaying church to the shallow latrine pit beyond. When he reaches his destination behind a scrubby copse of trees, Rhead and I dash through the gate.

In less than a minute, I dart around Eldridge's hovel, a crouching structure with wattle-and-daub walls rounding to a makeshift thatched roof. I push the panel of wood that serves as a door, but it doesn't budge.

"Eldridge," I call, voice low, "are you already asleep?"

She doesn't answer.

A drop of water slides from the overhanging thatch and slithers down my spine in a cold rivulet. My skin contracts.

Rationally, I know Eldridge might simply be abed, but something about the stillness feels...unnatural.

"Eldridge!" Voice climbing, I rattle the door on its leather hinges. It's bolted from within.

I swallow my panic and sniff the space between the wall and the door. The hovel's familiar smells pour through the infinitesimal opening, and I draw them into myself, searching, desperate. Woodsmoke, bacon, and above all, herbs. Still, I sense a kernel of truth. There's no Eldridge. No earthy flavor of tilled soil. No salty, brackish water laced with calming chamomile. Only stark absence in tonight's wet air.

I almost trip over Rhead in my rush to get around the building. I try to peek through the solitary window, but the shutter is closed. Again, secured from the inside.

My thudding heartbeat threatens to crack my sternum as I run eastward. Half a mile away, Fobbing Manor overlooks the village. The estate consists of a large central keep built in the traditional style—undercroft storage below with a great hall above, and the lord's chambers atop that—and is surrounded by several outbuildings, including a kitchen, bakery, and stables. I head for the stables.

Sturdier than any village residence, the building's dry warmth makes my wet skin pebble. Rhead shakes droplets from his fur and stretches luxuriously before scanning the building's dark interior with orb-like eyes. He stalks off with his tail held straight up like a flag, then leaps after a mouse scurrying along the floorboards. I ignore him and hurry up the hayloft ladder.

Three grooms sleep in the loft, but my shoulders relax a fraction and an imaginary fisherman's hook pulls me to the one farthest away. As I move closer, I smell him—saddle leather and sugar. Geoff wears his usual threadbare tunic, and his surcoat, made of matching brown homespun, is folded neatly beneath his head.

I drop to my knees and shake his shoulders. "Geoff," I whisper.

He opens his eyes, then jumps and covers himself with a bunch of hay. I lean back on my heels and frown. His legs and feet are bare, yes...but I've seen this before.

For almost a year after Geoff and I became friends, I would pull him out of bed nearly every morning to race together through the marsh, collecting reeds at low tide or catching fish at high.

In those days, Geoff slept on his single-room croft's floor alongside his parents. My nerves smart at the memory. The family had a mere half virgate, fifteen acres—the smallest parcel of land of any villein. Geoff's father, Ceadda, was a groom at the manor and his mother, Hawise, a laundress. As villeins, the couple—along with their only child—were obligated to work three days a week, plus plow, sow, and harvest a set amount of the Hereford's acreage each year. That left little time for working their own land. Their food cabinet was never full, their purse always empty.

In the summer of our twelfth year, excessive rains and cold weather brought an even worse harvest than normal. Geoff's stomach grumbled whenever I woke him, but he refused to talk about it. That rainy, cold summer led to an outbreak of pestilence in the fall. Eldridge and I tried to save Hawise and Ceadda, but once the black wave takes hold, there's not much any healer can do.

After Ceadda died, Lord Hereford demanded a heriot from twelve-year-old Geoff: a forfeiture of the household's finest beast. Geoff had no suitable offering, and no money to make up the difference. The family had slaughtered their dairy cow that summer, desperate for sustenance, and their sheep had died in the pestilence. He had no choice but to give up the fifteen acres and the croft.

Geoff has slept in the hayloft ever since, a landless villein. Even so, he's expected to pay the king's one shilling poll tax. I've no idea how he'll do so, but like his growling stomach the year of his parents' deaths, he won't discuss it.

My throat is thick as I continue to stare at Geoff. At two and twenty, he's a man now, all long legs and broad shoulders. I raise my hands and gaze at the clumps of hay crumpled in my fists. Lost in my memories, I've drawn the hay around myself, just like Geoff. A flimsy lace barrier.

He scrambles to his knees, eyebrows almost to his hairline. "What?" His eyes flick to the two sleeping grooms. "What're you doing here, Dandy?"

"It's Eldridge." I speak English to him, as always. Although French is my mother tongue—Maman is from Hainault and my father is descended from the Normans—Geoff and most of the other villeins hail from Saxon bloodlines.

He sits up. "Is she sick?"

"I don't know." My voice hitches. "She won't answer the door."

With a grunt, he reaches for his felt boots and dingy hose. When he stands to pull them on, though, he flushes crimson and jerks his chin to the ladder.

"Go down," he whispers. "I'll only be a minute."

Chapter Five

When we arrive back at Eldridge's, panting after the half-mile sprint through the dark, I'm numb with terror. I press a hand to my chest, unable to ward off the feeling that there's a gaping hole there and my tender heart is exposed.

Awareness floating just above, I watch myself pound on Eldridge's door.

"Eldridge," I shout. Damn the parish priest to hell, I don't care if he hears me. "*Please.*"

Nothing.

Without hesitation, Geoff draws me away and lowers his right shoulder to barrel through the door. Its leather hinges rip, and the wooden strip barring the other side splinters. Once inside, Geoff falls to his knees to keep from ramming through the opposite wall.

I almost climb over him in my haste. Puffs of dust cloud the air, and I cough, waving my hands. Geoff stands and brushes his tunic.

All goes still. Across the small room, Eldridge lays in her bed. The homespun coverlet is pulled to her chin, and she holds it gently. Her face is unlined and peaceful, yet tinged with gray, like I've always imagined the stone statues in a great city's cathedral.

Silence roars in my ears. I see Geoff's mouth move but can't understand his muffled tones. I kneel at her bedside.

"Eldridge," I whisper. She doesn't move. I jostle her shoulder. It's cold to the touch. "Eldridge, can you hear?" My voice echoes as if from the end of a long corridor.

Her fingers still hold the blanket. They're longer and more elegant than I remember.

The corners of her mouth aren't turned up—I've seen enough of the dead to know they don't smile—but her expression seems like she's about to, as if caught in a pleasant dream. Her thick, ash-colored plait rests over one shoulder. I touch it, remembering all the times she braided my own, steady fingers working through the knots.

Geoff places a warm, heavy hand on my shoulder. "I'm sorry, Dandy."

I don't speak.

"What do you think it was?" he asks.

I'm silent for another three heartbeats, still staring at Eldridge. "She seems to have gone in her sleep," I croak. "I...I don't think there was any pain."

"How d'you know?"

"I don't see any remnants of it." I try to stand but stumble. He grips my elbow. When I look at him, his raised brow makes me jerk away, face heating. Even he doesn't know about the odd things I see when a patient is in pain, the whispering plants, the odors I've learned others can't sense. No one knows now that Eldridge is gone. And I'll never know if she sensed them too.

He squeezes my bicep with gentle fingers. "We need to move quick."

I look up. "What do you mean?"

"The villagers. Once they hear...they'll..." His brown eyes search mine. "She'd want you to have the medicines, Dandy, and anything else."

Understanding creeps through like daybreak, and I give a single nod. The villagers will take everything of value and burn the rest, keen to wash the village clean of her existence.

"And we must bury her," he continues, "tonight. Before they..."

I gape. "You don't ever think they'll take her body?"

He lifts one shoulder. "They think she was a witch." He glances in the direction of St Michael's, where Master Adam is likely preparing for sleep. "There's no point asking that old sot for a place in the church yard."

I scoff in agreement.

"Is there a spot she'd have liked"—he jerks his chin toward the woods—"in there?"

—

Standing just inside Eldridge's ruined door, Geoff glances at the wobbly table beside her bed. I've collected an earthenware basin, a pitcher of water, and herbs. My knife, a ball of twine, and a needle rest on a nearby chair.

"Need help, Dandy?"

I look at Eldridge's body, still lying beneath the coverlet. I'm neither small nor delicate, but Geoff's assistance would be welcome. I stand taller than every other woman I've met, and am at eye level with most men, but Geoff towers above me, with broad shoulders and strong hands. Still, something makes me refuse. I need to do this alone.

I shake my head, and Geoff leaves.

I fill the basin with water, sprinkling its surface with dried lavender and rosemary.

A healer straddles useful an' evil, Eldridge told me the first day we met. *If a woman knows too much, if she's too skilled, it brings danger.* I can still hear her voice. It was smooth, calming, even in her old age. *You know some fools in this town name me a witch, do you?*

Standing over her supine figure, I hear her laugh in my right ear. I jump and look down, half expecting to see her smile. She doesn't. She's still dead.

Dead.

For over a decade, we've foraged in the woods and the marsh, tended her herb garden, and answered the villagers' calls for healing and midwifery. Maman tried to stop me, but she never could bend me to her will.

Still, watching Eldridge's face—her corpse's face, I remind myself with a jolt—I can't help but feel cheated. Eldridge taught me to bruise fresh herbs in the mortar, extracting their juices with the pestle before boiling them over a fire. She showed me the signs that the cooking process was complete, and how to skim the juice before adding oil as a preservative. There are dozens of ointment recipes I've memorized at her side. I know how to save a woman during a difficult labor. Most difficult labors, that is. No healer can save everyone from the peril that is childbearing.

But I'll never know what she would have said about Sir Thomas Prescott. I'm certain she wouldn't have wanted me to marry him. I heard her voice, her screaming in my head, when I met him. And if I told her how he smelled of violence, how it emanated off him, Eldridge would have agreed that I couldn't go to the Tower of London to become Lady Prescott.

But what would she have recommended I do instead? Refusing a father isn't simple for any young woman, but for me...

My father is the son and uncle of kings. Among the wealthiest men in the world. This is a man with authority over all of Christendom; what chance does his own daughter have to escape it?

Although I had utter faith in Eldridge's wisdom, now that it's gone, I'm at a loss.

An ache courses through my limbs, and I crouch at her bedside for a moment, dropping my head into my hands. In the end, I know my grief isn't for the lost lessons of a master healer or soothsayer.

My own mother treats me like a hardship, the consequence of a teenage mistake. Sometimes I think Maman hates me, and not because I'm a bastard, but because of...whatever it is that makes me different. My sensitive hearing, my ability to smell people's moods, my *inability* to conform to society's expectations. But those things were why Eldridge accepted me. She didn't guide me *in spite of* my differences, she did it *because* of them.

The realization wrenches me, and pain slashes through my chest. Eldridge's death was unexpected, unshriven. The worst kind. She hadn't gone to church, so I'm not sure she cared, but Master Adam says that if a person doesn't confess before death, entry to heaven isn't guaranteed. That's why the most devout seek daily confession. Passing on while sleeping, with a dirty soul, means an eternity in purgatory.

It was Eldridge who taught me to prepare a body for burial.

Geoff sharpened my belt knife before he left, and I use it now to cut the seam of Eldridge's white chemise, from the hem by her swollen ankles to armpit, along the sleeve to the cuff on both sides. I tuck the cloth into my basket.

I wash her face first, the finely drawn nose and hairless brows, the creases at the edges of her eyes and mouth. I free her hair from its braid and comb it with my fingers, letting it fall in generous waves over her shoulders. I sit her body up to scrub her back; her delicate skin flakes onto the wool.

The gentle whorl of her ears, like seashells. Her collarbone, the columns of her neck, her breasts. Her soft belly, swollen and creased. There's an irregular, broken scar running from hip to rib. I trace it with my fingertip, listening to the faint brush of skin on skin. It sings, like Eldridge herself used to when we foraged for medicines and food. I didn't know about the scar, nor the pocked remnants of some childhood disease on her arms.

It seems too intimate seeing these things without her permission. Eldridge already suffered death, an unexpected one at that. It seems unfair that after death we must submit to the will of whoever finds us, like a wayward leaf in the wind. It should be a spouse preparing her, or a sister. Someone familiar with the private, slanting curves and bumps of her body.

If I die tomorrow, who will wash me? Maman would refuse. The knowledge makes me shiver.

I empty and refill the basin before washing her legs and feet. Eldridge only wore shoes in the winter, and the water is brown by the time I'm finished. I untuck the sheet from the corners of her mattress; although old and patched, it's clean. It smells of Fobbing, of salt and sandy soil. I remove the pillow from under her head, and easing my arms under her shoulders and legs, I shift her downward, centered over the sheet. I stagger beneath her weight, that of a lifetime gone too soon.

Folding the sheet over the body, I thread my needle. I've never been an accomplished needlewoman, much to Maman's chagrin. I excel at stitching only two things: wounds and shrouds. I sit on a stool, beginning at the feet. My stitches are straight and even, and I work without stopping to stretch my back or rest my eyes until I reach her sternum.

I stand and place the needle on the shroud, but it slips, dangling over the mattress from its thick twine. I ignore it and reach for the herbs.

Chamomile, lavender, thyme, rosemary, angelica. I tuck them into the shroud with trembling fingers.

I try to pull the shroud closed over her face. I know Eldridge isn't here. Other than the gentle whiff of chamomile from the burial herbs, she is gone. There's an absence of her, an inescapable and persistent itch between my shoulder blades. And yet, I open the shroud and gaze at her one last time.

A pit hollows just below my rib cage. Releasing the shroud, I drop my face into one hand, frozen.

I don't want to continue, but there's no choice. I reach down, searching blindly for the needle, still swinging from its thread. It pricks my finger, and I lift my hand, gazing at it.

A single bead of red wells on my forefinger, suspended. I don't know how long I watch it, waiting for it to drip down my ridged skin, standing transfixed for a heartbeat...a minute...ten?

Eyes burning with unshed tears, I wipe the blood on my tunic, sit back on my stool, and sew the fabric into a careful line from chest to head.

I take up my knife again to sever the twine.

Chapter Six

Geoff takes Eldridge's medicine chest—filled with herbs, a mortar and pestle, and a tiny notebook of her drawings—to my cottage's outbuilding. Maman never goes there.

In the middle of the night, before anyone in the village knows Eldridge is dead, he carries the shrouded corpse under the dark tree cover to the woods beyond. There, we dig a grave beneath a massive elm.

"We used to collect elderberries here," I say. Geoff doesn't pause his digging, but I know he's listening. "I remember asking her what medicine we'd make from them. She said, 'Elderberry cordial.'"

He chuckles, but my throat tightens.

By the time Geoff judges the hole deep enough, there are only a few hours until sunrise. Geoff tosses his spade aside and jumps in.

When he gestures for the body, his eyes shine in the moonlight. I force myself not to back away, to *run* away. *He's alive*, I tell myself. *Alive*. Geoff isn't going anywhere. But the sight of him at the bottom of a grave...

I shiver, clutching my tunic and squeezing my eyes tight.

Eldridge is gone. All I have now are Geoff and Maman. There's my father, of course, but he's back in London, or Scotland, or any number of places other than here. I may never meet him, regardless of whether I agree to marry Sir Thomas Prescott.

Behind my closed lids, I see Sir Thomas's pale face and black eyes. I smell him, the sickly-sweet rose petals and sour ale. My heart, still searing with pain, thuds an erratic rhythm. Like a caged bird, its wings beat against my ribs, begging for freedom.

If I refuse Sir Thomas, what will become of Maman? Will my father, in his anger, withdraw his financial support?

I could sell herbal remedies and take payment for midwifery services; with Eldridge gone—a gasping sob catches in my throat—the villagers will need a new healer. I could, I think, support myself. But not me *and* Maman. She's used to a certain level of comfort.

I must be a good daughter, must take care of Maman and do what the Duke of Lancaster requires. I'm not stupid enough to think he loves me, no matter what Maman says. But if I do as he bids, maybe someday he'll see me as a beloved daughter, like his others.

I ease my arms under Eldridge's shoulders and knees, scooting her to where Geoff waits. Her corpse seems even smaller than she was in life, and it isn't difficult to lower it into his waiting arms. Without delay, he places her on the grave bottom's damp soil, climbs out, and fetches his spade.

The first thud of dirt is like a thunderclap. I'd lifted my own spade to help, but at the noise, I stumble backward. I lean on its handle and hunch over.

"Dandy." Geoff touches my elbow. "You all right?"

I nod and make a feeble gesture for him to continue, all the while hardening my mind and heart to what I must do.

It's faster to fill the grave than it was to dig, and it seems like only minutes before a mound of freshly tilled soil rests on its surface.

Geoff steps back, and together we fold our hands and bow our heads. I'm not sure Eldridge would have wanted me to pray for her, but I don't know what else to do. I try to beg the saints to accept her soul, but my thoughts return to how I will manage without her, what I will do without her guidance. My prayers do nothing to assuage my misery, and I shiver.

My voice breaks the silence. "I'm going to accept Sir Thomas."

Geoff turns. His eyes flash in the silver light; his brown hair flutters in the wind. His mouth in a tight line, he looks away, back. Then away again.

"Geoff?"

His gaze snaps to mine. "He's vile."

I look down and swallow the words *I know*. I twist my tunic in my hands. "With Eldridge gone, I…" I look up. His features haven't softened. "I don't have a choice. You know that."

"Everyone's got a choice. There's always a choice," he spits back.

"Lots of people are at the mercy of others, Geoff, including me." I shake my head. "You're a man. I'm…I'm not free to…."

"Am I so free?" he says, voice uncharacteristically shrill. "I'm a villein, Blanche, a *landless* villein. Me father was a groom. Me surname *is* Groom. I'll never be anything else. I've no choices." He gestures, long arms taking in Lady Hereford's land, beyond which he's forbidden to travel. "I could've been a squire, or even a knight, if I'd been born right." He swats a branch.

The unfairness of his situation, and my own insensitivity to it, make my eyes burn. What Geoff said is true. He's just as stuck as me. Geoff isn't like most other villeins. Although he had no formal education and can't read or write, he's unusually clever and highly skilled in the training yard. If his parents had been landed gentry, I can only imagine how high he might have climbed.

"Ye're the daughter of the richest man in the world. You can do whatever you please. Yet, you bow to him and agree to marry a brute. Because he'll make you a *lady*, with a nice clutch of dower lands."

Insulted, I jut my chin toward him and glare. "Is that what you think? That I'd marry Sir Thomas for his title?"

"Yes."

"Eh bien, alors tu es un imbécile," I snap. He stares at me, hands bunched at his sides, but says nothing. "Alors?" I prod.

"Dandy. I've no idea what you just said."

"What?"

"French. You spoke French."

"Oh. Right."

"I hate it when you do that."

"Sorry. Well, anyway. I called you a fool."

"Really?" He leans back.

"Yes."

There's an uncomfortable pause. A minute passes, but he stays silent. My mouth works open and closed.

I plunge forward. "My father might be rich, but do you really think he shares anything beyond the cost of our upkeep? Do you think he sends me some kind of allowance that would enable me to be an independent woman of means?"

"You could charge fer yer healing," he offers.

I rest fists on my hips and prepare to say something else, anything else. "I'm a woman, Geoff. A woman—whether queen or peasant—is really just a villein. We belong to someone. First our father, then our husband. Then, our children. We aren't free. Not ever."

He watches me for a few heartbeats. Then his features smooth. "But, Dandy..."

My breath catches, and I look at my feet, unable to meet his gaze. So much has changed; I'm a woman now, and he's a man. I should demand he call me Blanche. Or Mistress Fitzjohn? I bite my lip. Soon, I'll be Lady Prescott.

"Dandelion," he says, insistent.

I refuse to look up, suddenly absorbed with the dirt under my fingernails.

"Forgive me," he says. "I was too harsh, an' right after...after Eldridge..."

Something shifts, like summer's green leaves transforming to autumnal gold. Speaking with Geoff about my marriage hurts like I'd never expected, a deep ache. The moon thrums, and an owl, perched in a nearby tree, shifts as she searches for prey. My temples throb.

"It seemed..." he begins again. "It seemed he didn't want to marry you, after you..." I glare and cross my arms before lifting my face. He continues: "I thought perhaps you could get out of it because..."

"Because of what?"

"Because, ye're..."

"What, Geoff, what am I?"

His mouth opens like a fish above water, and he doesn't bother to shut it. In the tree, the owl flaps its wings and leaps into the air.

"Ye're..." The tips of Geoff's fingers flutter. "Well, I don't know what you are, Dandy. Ye're just...yerself. And I thought—"

"You thought he wouldn't want me?"

His face falls. "He's not like you, Dandy. That's all. He's not a good man. I heard him talking, when it was just the men..."

He drops his gaze, and his cheekbones redden.

Neither of us seems to know what to say next. After a full minute of silence, he lurches forward and grasps my shoulders, crushing me to his chest. "Blanche, just consider."

I gasp and have to steady myself. But within seconds, tears come to my eyes, along with a calming release of tension. I grip his forearms, inhale his familiar scent. He's always smelled of horses, with a hint of bread dough and sugar from the manor kitchens he's constantly raiding. There's something different tonight. I sniff. It's crisp, yet soft. Evergreens in winter, covered with fresh snow.

He buries his nose in my hair. "You could refuse," he says, voice a gentle rumble against my face, "and stay with yer mother. She'd be angry, yes, but she wouldn't throw you out. They can't drag you to the church. For a marriage to be real, you must consent."

Consent. The word ripples through me. It makes me see that I want more from Maman, from my father, but most of all from Geoff. I need something I can't identify, something I can't express.

"If I marry Thomas..." My muffled voice breaks. "It will make the duke happy. He'll..." I tense, regretting my words.

"He'll what?"

I can't answer, can't tell him that by marrying Sir Thomas, I hope to earn my father's love. To replace...something.

The moon moves behind a cloud, and the trees shift, branches releasing a shower of rain. Geoff drops one hand to the small of my back and lifts the other to my cheek. His palms are warm, and I slide my own to clench his upper arms. When my fingertips brush hardened muscles, I almost snatch my hands back. Before tonight, I still thought of Geoff as a child, the lanky villein who could ride any horse, no matter how fierce. Now...my mouth goes dry, but I can't resist running my hands up the length of his arms, letting them rest on his shoulders. The skin beneath his tunic is damp with sweat.

Corded muscles tense and stretch beneath my fingers, sending little jolts through me. He stoops, chin brushing my temple.

I touch the notch of his throat with my fingertips. He freezes. Tiny curls of dark hair peek above his collar, tickling my fingers. He lets his face linger on mine, and I feel him inhale.

A pleasant warmth spreads through my belly, then down. Something's happening, something I don't understand. I should run, should leave. But I don't. Another breeze drifts through the tree branches, and he pulls me closer, pressing me to him.

I feel him, *all* of him, from feet to chin, in a way I never have. A tingling, heavy warmth settles on me, and I feel Geoff's own need pressing against my belly.

It should make me uncomfortable, but I find myself pressing back, wanting more. Wanting it all.

I'm not well-versed in what happens between a woman and a man—that's one area of my education Maman neglected—but I'm not completely ignorant. I know Geoff and I stand on a cliff, gazing into a deep ravine. One more step, and we'll both be lost.

I'm still touching his throat, suspended in our odd dance beneath the shuddering tree branches, when he bends further. I close my eyes and focus on the sensation of his stubbly chin against my face. He exhales, and a shiver runs down my spine.

"Dandy..." he murmurs.

The owl swoops to snatch a mouse from the forest floor in sharp talons. Her screech is like a battle horn, ricocheting with painful deliberation in my skull, joined by the mouse's squeal. My eyelids snap open.

I step out of his embrace and snatch my hand from his throat as if burned. Geoff's scent shifts to the tangy sap of a winter forest. Together, we listen to the owl careening through the trees.

"You really mean to do this?" he asks after a few moments. "Marry him?"

"Yes."

I sense rather than see him nod.

"It's late," he says. "Let me walk you home."

—

News of Eldridge's death travels through the village with dizzying speed. Her hovel is burned within a day. The smell of ash follows me wherever I go, and I'm left numb and unable to fight. With emptiness ringing in my ears and no appetite, I accept my impending marriage.

The next four weeks rush past with Geoff avoiding me and Maman refusing to speak Eldridge's name. She doesn't, however, stem her constant flow of criticism. My voice is still too loud, my breasts too small, my arms too long.

Maman summons a dressmaker, and I'm fitted for a set of new robes in loathsome colors like pale blue, buttery yellow, and a blushing pink. I convince the dressmaker to include a brown surcoat without Maman's knowledge.

I pack my things.

On the day I'm to leave for London, I'm waiting on my cottage's front stoop for our armed guard when Geoff arrives, leading a glossy mare by the reins, her coat shimmering in the early morning light.

"Mistress." He nods.

My face heats. Since that night in the woods, I've spent every night in a wakeful state of suspended remembrance. His solid body beneath my fingertips. The feel of his arms, his neck. The damp sweat beading on his skin. It hurts to remember, makes me ache from my limbs to my belly, between my legs. But I don't want it to stop. I want to keep remembering, even if it's painful.

"Geoff." My voice quivers. "I've missed you."

He shrugs. I want to scream, to demand he tell me what I'm supposed to derive from such a stupid gesture, why he's avoided me for two fortnights. Instead, I choose a more sensible topic.

"Who is this beautiful creature?" I wave to the horse.

"She's for you, actually."

"For me? Has the countess sent her for my journey?"

"No." The notch of his throat works up and down, and I hide my hand behind my back, fingertips burning with the memory of touching him there. He avoids my gaze. "It's a gift from yer betrothed. Yer wedding present."

"Oh." I force myself to step forward and place a flat palm on the horse's withers. Her flesh ripples. She's sorrel-colored—a shining light-red chestnut with a white blaze on her face and white stockings halfway up her legs. "She's a spectacular beast."

"Indeed. And she's a right good temperament for you, Dandy." He coughs. "Mistress, I mean. She's calm and steady."

I smile. Geoff knows that although I enjoy horses' company, as I do most animals', I'm not always comfortable in the saddle. I can ride; Maman insisted I learn, but I require a gentle mount.

As I scratch the horse's ears, she dips her head and swishes her flaxen-colored tail. I touch her muscular cheek, and one enormous eye, brown laced with green, swivels my way.

"Maybe Sir Thomas isn't so bad, if he's sent such a gift."

Geoff shuffles his feet and looks down, making me think I shouldn't have said that out loud. He clears his throat again. "Aye," he says at last. "I've never seen such a fine horse for a lady. Small yet sturdy, and firm enough to get the job done."

He rubs a square-shaped palm down her leg from the shining red to the white sock beneath. The calluses on his big fingers rub against the silky coat. His hands are raw, not only from constant manual labor but from fighting in the training yard. It's expected that all men—peasants and nobles alike—be ready for battle at any time, given the threat of invasion from France and the fact that the king's government cannot afford to protect the coastline.

My lips quirk. "Well, I trust you. You love nothing more than a beautiful horse."

Again, he doesn't answer, just straightens and runs his hand down the horse's neck, feeling for flaws. He shakes his head and smiles.

"I'll call her Rosemary," I say.

Another groom strides up with a shiny palfrey for Maman. She insisted on the finest horse Lady Hereford's stables could spare, and we'll have an armed guard of five men, sent by the duke. My trousseau, along with my meager possessions, is packed onto a cart. Even Rhead is safely stowed in a woven carrier beside my trunk of gowns. Early this morning, before Maman came outside, I hid Eldridge's medicine box behind the trunk, packed with her mortar and pestle, her notebook, and all the herbs and cuttings I could fit.

I catch a man-at-arms glaring at the cart containing my mewling cat. Rhead isn't happy about his traveling conditions and is unafraid to voice his dissent. The man looks away, chastened by my reproachful glance. Inwardly, however, I pray Rhead will fall asleep, lest the men and Maman lose their patience and release him.

Maman seems to read my mind. "You should leave him here." She steps daintily onto the mounting block. "There will be plenty of cats at the Tower."

I sniff but don't respond. Her horse is much larger than mine, but she needs no assistance. Maman is an excellent horsewoman, something she reminds me of whenever possible. Her small frame sits elegant and regal in the saddle as she heels her horse forward. She claims my father, the Duke of Lancaster, fell in love with her the first time they rode together in a royal hunt with Queen Philippa's falcons. They'd both been nineteen. Maman was such a talented sportswoman—she says—that the duke refused to leave her side from then on. Until I made my presence known, of course.

Geoff eases Rosemary to the block. I can feel Maman's disdainful glare as he holds the bridle for me.

"Just remember, dinna pull her reins," he says. "Ease up and she'll thank you for it. And talk to her. She'll trust you more."

I manage a grateful smile. Maman rides to the men-at-arms, flirting under the guise of discussing the journey, and I press down my heels and lift my chin, keen to appear confident. But when I look down at Geoff, my courage rushes like air from a blacksmith's bellows. My stomach churns and my heart flips.

"Geoff," I whisper, leaning down. "This is goodbye. Maybe forever."

Geoff squares his shoulders, and his brown eyes meet mine for what feels like the first time in years. My face burns with fresh heat, but I don't look away. I can't.

"Dandy." He keeps his voice low. "I want you to be happy. I hope Sir Thomas is a good husband. If he's not—" He compresses his lips.

"If he's not," I say, "there's nothing I can do. I'll be his property."

"You can always count on me help." He reaches into his pocket and pulls out a single yellow flower. A dandelion.

I gaze at it for a suspended moment. When I look back at him, his mouth is flat but his eyes are soft.

Geoff won't be able to help me. He'd face harsh discipline—beating or disfigurement—just for leaving the countess's estate. But I say nothing, just take the dandelion and tuck it into my belt pouch.

"Dandy," he murmurs a second time.

There's only one choice, only one thing I can do. I turn Rosemary's head and follow Maman's palfrey toward the London Road.

I don't look back. Even though I know I'll never hear Geoff call me Dandy ever again.

Chapter Seven

LONDON, ENGLAND
7 JUNE 1381

After two days of hard travel, we arrive at my father's London residence, the Savoy Palace.

I want to cower beneath its splendor. The walls are almost four feet thick, made from Kentish maidstone, and the sprawling complex is so enormous that it can house over one hundred and fifty knights and their retainers, hundreds of servants, and legions of clergy and financial clerks. Of course, right now, my father is in Scotland with his fighting men, so the place is minimally staffed.

Flemish tapestries cover every wall, and acres of rose gardens meander with perfectly planned spontaneity along the Thames River. Right after we arrive, I disappear among the flowers, intent on losing myself—and Maman. After two days of her constant companionship, I'm desperate for peace and solitude.

While walking past a latticed fence covered with yellow roses, I hear a male voice: "They say the king wants to renovate Westminster."

My scalp prickles with annoyance—so much for privacy—but instinct makes me hide behind the lattice. I peek out to see a young gardener with buck teeth and enormous ears speaking to a scullery maid.

The maid sets her fruit basket on the path, then knuckles her back and stretches. The gardener's eyes widen as her very large bosom swells. "If he does," she says, "I reckon it's the duke's fault."

"D'you really think he wants to take the throne?" he asks, words slurring slightly. He stands on his tiptoes for a better view.

I suppress a groan. Even in the face of my impending nuptials, I'd been looking forward to my time at the Savoy. In my father's own home, I'd reasoned, I wouldn't keep overhearing frustrated gossip about him, like in Fobbing. It appears I'd been wrong. The palace's gilded corridors and pristine gardens couldn't be more different from Fobbing's shabby dirt roads and dusty marketplace. The duke's servants, however, seem just as eager to complain as Masters Baker and Plowman.

The girl shrugs. "He sure acts like it. Look at this place."

The gardener's eyes follow her gesture as she waves toward the palace's central keep, before returning to her breasts.

"Lancaster thinks that just because his father was king, he should be king too."

Silence falls between them.

"Well, what do you think, Gardener?" She bunches her skirt in her hand and twitches the fabric his way.

He takes an enormous gulp of air, eyes dancing with the effort of finding something to say. "I think," he answers at last, "young King Richard doesn't have the coin to fix up Westminster."

"That hasn't stopped him in the past." She makes a show of moving her fruit basket to her other hand, preparing to leave.

The gardener grabs her arm. "You don't think he'll levy another tax, do you?"

She twists out of his grip. "Nay. I don't think the king will." She leans in to his ear, dropping her voice so low that only I would be able to hear. The skin on the gardener's neck pebbles under her breath. "It's his ministers. Lancaster will stop at nothing to bleed us dry of every coin."

He watches her saunter off, swinging her basket and singing a maypole song. Once she disappears around a bend, he sighs and abandons his spade and bucket to wander in the opposite direction.

Geoff's face swims before my eyes. He couldn't pay the first poll tax, and now there's talk of the king levying another one? The last time the tax collector visited, Geoff hid from him, along with Cecily Baker and her siblings. I don't think he can get away with that again. The collector promised that next time he'll ask the countess's steward for the household ledger, which lists all her villeins.

Something niggles my mind, and I turn to wander in the same direction as the scullery maid. That girl and the gardener aren't villeins. They don't belong to a manor, but to the growing citizenry of Christendom's large cities. Yet they still owe payment of the king's taxes, and just like the villeins, they can't afford them.

Just like Geoff.

I touch my belt pouch and lean into a yellow rose, preparing my senses for its almost overwhelming sweet scent. But when I inhale, my brow furrows. Flavors of a grass-covered field fill me, the clean scent of nothing more than fresh air and the bittersweet tang of soil. Dandelions.

As I revel in the rose's uniqueness, a new thought blooms. Tomorrow, I'm to marry the Constable of the Tower of London, whom my brother said is high in the king's favor. I'll become Lady of the Tower, courtier to King Richard.

A wife can influence her husband, Blanche. And all courtiers can influence the king. From the lowliest knight to the Duke of Lancaster himself. Maman's words seemed stupid at the time. I'd only been half listening when she told me. Now, I turn them over in my mind.

If the king and his advisors understood what life was like for the commoners, would it change their minds? Could I make my husband see a different perspective than his own?

Geoff lost his parents in the pestilence, only to surrender his home and future in the aftermath. All because he couldn't pay a heriot. Now, he's grown into an intelligent man. After Fobbing Manor's improper feed storage led to moldy oats, he convinced the countess's steward to build granaries on stilts and ventilate the buildings, forestalling the same disaster from repeating in the future. He's also a talented fighter. Strength and skill, combined with a knack for predicting his opponent's next move, have made him virtually undefeated in Fobbing Manor's training yard.

But these qualities can only take a laborer so far. The feudal structure keeps Geoff low on the ladder. Destitute, homeless, stuck.

There's so much potential in people like him, wasted. Ten years ago, when his parents died, the earl could have granted mercy. He could have given the young villein time to pay the heriot or waived it entirely. Had he, I'm certain, the investment and foresight would have reaped future benefits. Master Miller's son, Aelfric, who was ultimately given the land, would still have had his original allotment to farm. There's enough land for everyone, especially after the population was depleted in the plague's first wave thirty-five years ago. But the nobility seem intent on giving the bulk of the land—and therefore the wealth—to a tiny percentage of the country's citizens.

If I'm a good wife, I can wriggle into Sir Thomas's trust. He could influence the king. Once Richard hears how his people suffer under his taxation, he'll reverse his decisions and promise not to take such punitive measures in the future. I am the person to educate him in this; I have lived among the villeinage. I've healed them, heard their woes, befriended them. Well, two of them, at least.

By marrying Sir Thomas, I'll help Geoff, even if he'll never know it nor ever see me again.

—

The next afternoon, I walk down the Savoy Chapel's central aisle, stiff and awkward in a golden-yellow undertunic. Maman laced its sleeves too tight, and I almost trip on the bright green outer tunic's matching tippets that hang from my elbows. My headdress's thick white veil covers most of my face—a style I detest—along with my hair, which is tightly braided and coiled about my ears.

I walk past enormous stained-glass windows stretching from floor to ceiling. My stomach twists in knots, and the memory of Fobbing's church—St Michael's—flashes before my eyes. Its dirt floor had patches of grass and moss in the corners, its windows were nothing more than unglazed holes cut haphazardly from the stone. Here, the stained glass is designed into decorative scenes of the Duke of Lancaster fighting alongside his father and brother in France and Nájera. It creates patchwork blankets of colored sunlight across the stone floors, and my feet, slippered in cream silk, are tinted red, then green, and at last blue on my walk toward the altar. It is like magic, unlike anything I've experienced, but it makes me sick. I want to rip off my veil, to declare myself a fraud and insist I have no idea what I'm doing here, how this happened, or what I'm supposed to do next.

But I can't. Ahead of me, Sir Thomas waits beside the duke's chaplain. I remember the servants' conversation yesterday. By marrying Sir Thomas, I'll have influence. I can help Geoff.

The belt pouch I concealed beneath my surcoat bounces against my hip, and I smell a tendril of clean earth waiting in an untouched field. The sensation gives me a little boost of courage and determination.

But when I meet my betrothed before the altar, my nostrils flare with disgust. His scent hasn't changed. The pervasive odors of rose oil and ale make my head swim. Shuffling my feet to step away, I steal a glance at him from beneath my lowered lashes. Although no taller than me, my new husband's shoulders are muscular, his biceps like small hams. I swallow and squeeze my eyes closed as fears of my wedding night threaten to overwhelm me.

I must not succumb to my mind. It will overtake me. I can feel Maman's glare weighing on me, her words this morning stifling my breath more than my tight tunic. *If you have a fit before Sir Thomas says the words,* she warned, *he may refuse to go through with the wedding. Let that happen, Blanche, and the duke will never forgive you.*

I smell the reek of overheated garbage—disdain—intermingled with Thomas's rose oil and ale. I grip my hands at my waist until they ache. They must not flap. I resolve to breathe through my mouth. Hidden by the veil, no one will notice me gaping like a fish, and I find myself surprisingly grateful for the blasted fashion.

He takes my hand to recite the Latin vows. My stomach knots, before sinking to my feet. His fingers are long and elegant, the skin soft and delicate, nails manicured. I can't reconcile this in my mind. Sir Thomas is a knight, an experienced warrior and the new commander of England's greatest fortress. He's fought in the training yard, the jousting lists, and in battle with the Scots, yet his hands are smooth and pampered as a duchess. My own hand is rough and calloused; I worry it might chafe his. The scent of roses strengthens, and I close my eyes once again.

Every instinct tells me to run. Someone speaks, in the recesses of my thrumming mind, a voice remarkably like Eldridge's. *Resist,* the voice demands. *Say no, Blanche. Do not marry this man.*

When Friar William Appleton, my father's cleric, asks for my consent, my ears buzz and my tongue grows thick. I push Eldridge's voice away. I've made my decision; there's no going back. I nod and give a feeble "I do."

By the end of the Mass, my hands shake with effort, but I retain control. From the first row, Maman breathes a sigh of relief. My father's mistress, Lady Katherine Swynford, stands beside her.

Lady Katherine is the woman the duke chose to love instead of my mother, and whose illegitimate children he adores. When he's not on military campaign, the duke, Lady Katherine, and their four children live together as a happy family. She manages his estates and those of Lord Henry, his son, even though he is married to Constance of Castile, his second wife after Blanche of Lancaster's early death.

I met Lady Katherine last night when we arrived, but Maman has known the lady for years. They served Queen Philippa—my grandmother—together. Until Maman was sent to the country, to be hidden, that is.

Maman cuts her eyes to Lady Katherine and scowls. I find the lady kind and gracious, but Maman's disdain is clear. I can't say I'm surprised. Lady Katherine is fashionably small-boned and delicate, like Maman, but in the set of her shoulders and the tilt of her chin, there's a self-possession that sets her apart. I haven't seen many confident women in my life—such qualities are discouraged—but I think that's the best way to describe her. And no wonder. I've never seen a more lovely woman. Her skin is creamy and smooth, with a permanent rose blush across her nose and cheekbones. Her lips are round and pink, her laughing eyes a golden amber, and through the back of her sheer veil I can see two auburn braids hanging down her back, each thick as my wrist.

Thomas yanks my hand. The ceremony is complete, so I let him lead me down the aisle and through the chapel door. Once in the courtyard, I step away and tear at the front of my veil, trying to pull it up and over my face.

Our horses stand saddled and ready. Rosemary is dwarfed by Sir Thomas's destrier—a dun-colored beast with angry eyes. When it bares its teeth to my mare, her eyes flare and she shies away.

I glance at Maman while still struggling with my veil.

"Stop it, Blanche," she hisses.

The sheer fabric tears. Maman twists it out of my grip and hides it in her skirts before anyone can notice. I'm just glad to have it out of my face. "Will there be no wedding dinner?" I ask.

"No," she says. "Sir Thomas wants to return to the Tower."

Joan, my new serving woman, whom Lady Katherine presented the night before, approaches with my woolen cloak and helps me with its lacings. Maman kisses me on both cheeks, then I kneel for her blessing.

She's never been a gentle mother, but when Marie de St. Hilaire lays her palm on the crown of my head, an unfamiliar ache throbs in my chest. She doesn't love me, but I'm used to life with her. Despite her threats, I know I'm the stronger of the two of us, both in will and physical power. I haven't been truly afraid of her in years.

Now, I don't know what I'm riding toward. The thought of going to the Tower of London, for my wedding night no less, turns my bones to ash. Maman has refused to tell me anything about what will happen—only that Sir Thomas will know what to do and that I must obey him.

She removes her hand, and I stand to curtsy.

"I should curtsy to you," she says, gaze cool and assessing. "You're a lady now. You outrank me."

She turns on her heel and walks back into the palace without another word.

Lady Katherine steps forward. She smells of rosemary and sage. "Good luck, Lady Prescott." My cheeks go cold at the sound of my new name. Something flashes in Lady Katherine's gaze, but it's gone in a moment. "Your wedding gift from the duke is packed among your things. I hope you will treasure it as he does you."

"I doubt he treasures me for myself as much as the prospect of having me off his hands," I mumble through tight lips.

Lady Katherine gives the most ladylike chuckle I've ever heard, and the scent of mint wafts from her headdress. Then, unexpectedly, she leans forward to place a lingering kiss on my cheek. "Take care, child," she whispers in my ear. Her gaze flicks over my shoulder to Sir Thomas, and I'm surprised as the scent of rotten pears wafts from her. Fear. She looks back to me and manages a tight smile.

Sir Thomas grasps my elbow and urges me toward the horses. There, he cups his smooth palms and laces his fingers together to make a step for me to mount my horse. Joan settles my skirts about me while Sir Thomas mounts his destrier. Then she climbs into the cart carrying my possessions. Sir Thomas signals for our little party to depart, and I raise a hand in farewell to Lady Katherine.

Chapter Eight

8 JUNE 1381

The afternoon sun slides behind ominous clouds, and Sir Thomas urges his horse to a brisk trot, leaving the cart. My heart flutters with worry for Rhead and Eldridge's medicinal chest, but I only have one choice: follow my husband.

We ride along Fleet Street, and Sir Thomas raises a thick arm to gesture to a grand house. "That's the London home of Henry, Earl of Derby."

"My brother?" I ask.

He glances over his shoulder. His face is inscrutable, but I think I see mockery in his raised brow. He says nothing.

I stare at the back of his green surcoat, the Flemish wool trimmed in beaver. His bright red hair whips out from the bottom of his black velvet chaperon. As we jostle along, the quick pace shifts me in my saddle, making it impossible to find a comfortable position. Still, I try to make conversation. "I must thank you for the gift of my horse." I know it's not ladylike to shout, but he's so far ahead that I have no choice. "She's an ideal mount."

He nods but says nothing.

I straighten my spine and make a silent list of ingredients for a soothing salve. After the journey from Fobbing, my backside is chafed with sores. Marigold, lemon balm, primrose, and mallow. Yes, that will make me feel better. Years ago, Eldridge and I made a similar ointment for Geoff after he fell from a dappled gray.

What would Geoff say if he saw me now, bouncing along in my saddle, beholden to the whims of a man who doesn't care whether I am in pain?

Geoff's tenderness that night by Eldridge's grave already feels like the lush residue of another lifetime, one I naively thought challenging. Now, from where I sit, riding into an uncertain and frightening future, that past appears simple.

I know what's expected of me tonight. Thomas will take my maidenhead, and although it might be painful, I must not complain.

As I think about it, I feel myself detach, like when I discovered Eldridge's body last month. I watch myself ride Rosemary, approach London's city wall. I watch Thomas's rigid posture. But in an instant, the view shifts, and Geoff rides before my mare, tall and powerful atop one of the countess's shining palfreys.

With a jolt, I'm forced back into my body, a rush of sensation lurching me from the top of my head to my toes. My lips tingle and my hands grow warm and sweaty, not with nerves, but something else...anticipation, excitement. I fidget with my reins as I remember him pressed against me in the darkened woods. My fingers itch, reliving the feeling of his corded muscles, his wiry chest hair. His dirty skin mingling with my own, the smell of us like loamy earth. The corners of my mouth threaten to turn up in an absurd grin.

I was raised to believe all virgins are consumed with fear on their wedding night. Now I know the truth. I don't know when or how I gained this knowledge, but I'm certain that if it was Geoff taking me over the threshold of our new home...I'd hardly be able to wait for the click of the door's latch.

I give my head a shake. I didn't just marry Geoff. My wedding night won't be with him, but with Thomas.

I moan and squeeze my legs to urge Rosemary on. I must stop this. Geoff's a memory. A precious, pivotal part of my life—my dearest friend, now that Eldridge is gone. But I must look forward, not back.

My new husband must hear my choking sob, for he swivels in his saddle. "Are you uncomfortable?" he asks.

I blink, surprised by his concern, but squirm beneath his dark gaze, the first time he's looked into my eyes today.

"We'll be there soon," he says, gaze unwavering. "Then you can rest."

His voice is almost gentle, and my knotted muscles relax a fraction. But those eyes. Black as jet. Such a strange, unnatural contrast to his fair hair and skin.

I know it's not right to flinch away from Sir Thomas because he looks different. My whole life, I've existed on the fringes of society. I know how it feels. But when I meet a person, I'm hit with an onslaught of smells and characteristics. Cataloguing them in my mind can be difficult. If they have opposing features—say, light hair and dark eyes—I can't rectify it.

Of course, if Thomas had been welcoming and kind, if he didn't smell like violence, things would be different. Someone could have purple eyes and green hair for all I care, if they're good-natured and accepting.

There's just something *wrong* about Sir Thomas.

A rumble of thunder pulls me from my bleak thoughts. Thomas glances up at the darkening sky. "Looks like rain." His tone is gruff again, and my shoulders tense.

"I don't mind a little rain," I say. "I—"

"This is Ludgate." He points to the city gate ahead. "Welcome to London."

Ludgate, the westernmost gate in London's wall, is marked by an enormous tower that ascends to dark storm clouds, a statue of the king nestled in its arch. The carving is new, its paint fresh and vivid. On either side of the gate, London's city walls, enormous and foreboding, stretch into the distance.

"It must be fifty feet tall..." I breathe.

"Wait until you see the fortress."

A smile pulls at his lips, but I can't tell why. I never could read a person's intentions by their facial expressions alone, and my husband is too far away for me to smell him. Still, a life led in the shadows of society, facing daily ridicule and criticism, makes me doubt his urge to grin is based on endearment or my charm. It's more likely caused by scorn for my naivety and rural upbringing.

Even if Thomas was right next to me, I'm still not sure I could tune my senses into his moods. London's odors press like a boulder on my chest. To each side of the dirt road run ditches overflowing with refuse that ranges from broken pottery to human excrement. Not far away, a man relieves himself directly into one. I cover my mouth with one hand and gag, then turn my watering eyes back to the city gate—anything other than the piles of stinking shit covered with flies.

Once through the gate, people—more than I've ever seen in one place—move in every direction like bugs. There must be over a hundred of them. To our left, a woman carries an enormous basket of filthy rags and shouts to a boy down the road. Beyond her, two women haggle over the price of thread while stepping out of the way of Sir Thomas's horse. He seems to view the pedestrians as a mere annoyance.

Houses and businesses with thatched roofs jut out at unnatural angles, packed in like sheep waiting for the shears. I hear a splash and look up to see a woman has just thrown a pan of liquid from an upper story. I hope it was washing water. From other windows, servants beat rugs with sticks or shout across the narrow streets to friends and neighbors. On an adjacent alley, a small boy snatches a man's purse and runs away. The man yells and tries to give pursuit, but the pickpocket disappears into the crowd.

Horses, dogs, and cats weave among the people, and cows meander on tethers with their owners. One man prods a gaggle of geese with a stick, herding them away from wild pigs with beady black eyes that remind me of my new husband. I resist covering my ears as the cacophony—shouting people, honking geese, and slamming windows—threatens to overwhelm me.

When I tear my eyes away from a pig nosing through a pile of refuse, a moment of panic blooms. I've lost sight of Thomas. I swing my head left, then right, and heel Rosemary in the ribs, trying to catch up. The mare, unused to the city, shies away from the crowds and balks, refusing to move.

My mouth goes dry. I cling to my reins, lest I drop them, even though they shake in my cold hands.

How will I find my way alone through this quagmire?

On my right, a filthy man with one hand grasps my foot where it rests on my stirrup.

"Fair lady," he wheezes, "spare a coin for a poor old cripple?"

With more strength than I would have thought possible, he yanks on my ankle. I slip, almost tumbling out of my high cantle saddle onto the cobblestones. My hands start to flap.

"Filthy wretch!" I recognize Thomas's voice as he maneuvers his horse between me and the beggar. He must have doubled back to find me. I don't have a moment for relief.

Easily controlling his horse with his knees, he drops his reins and snatches the crippled man by the collar to haul him backward. With his other hand, he draws a dagger from his boot and holds it to the man's throat. A bead of ruby-red blood blooms where he presses the tip to the beggar's skin. Shock stills my hands.

"Sir Thomas, no!" I cry.

He sneers and tosses the beggar to one side like a sack of feed. The man hits the cobblestones with a thud and doesn't get up. Sir Thomas sheathes the blade and grasps Rosemary's bridle. "Come along, wife. Don't dawdle."

Pulling the reins over Rosemary's head, Thomas leads her for me. I look back to where the beggar lies motionless, blending into the filth. His fellow Londoners let unseeing eyes drift over him, as if he's transparent.

Jostling in my saddle, I close my eyes, trying to slow my pounding heart and quickening breath.

Eldridge would have stopped, would have gotten down to help an injured man. But Eldridge wasn't married. I am, since about an hour ago. I belong to this man. I'm like chattel, as Geoff is to the Countess of Hereford. There's no going back.

Thomas guides my horse, so I only need to hold on to the leather cantle and keep my eyes squeezed tight. But the beggar's form, lying slack on the city street, is burned on the insides of my closed lids.

We turn right. I want to pinch my nose to block out the smells of stagnant water, unwashed linens, and rotten food. Instead, I envision my marsh. I watch the tide come in on the Thames and smell the grass and sand. Sediment scratches my fingers and knees. Soil gets beneath my fingernails as I care for my plants, and their stalks, both spiky and smooth, brush against my skin as I trim and prune.

When we make a left, I sway in my saddle but am happy to sense the crowds of people and animals thinning. Then I smell it and hear it: the river.

I open my eyes. The Thames, the mighty pulse of London, rushes and gurgles, and despite my apprehension, I smile. The sun has come out and the storm clouds have dissipated. Graceful swans glide upon the water's surface, and the most magnificent barge I've ever seen, gilded in gold, slips past them. My husband tosses Rosemary's reins back over her head, and I gather them into shaky fingers. The mare gives her head a relieved shake.

I take a deep breath. "It is lovely," I say.

"Yes."

"I've never seen a swan before." He eyes me, and I assume I spoke too loudly. I lower my eyes and voice. "What beauties they are."

"Yes." He flicks his reins. "And headed the right direction. The Constable of the Tower gets any swan that swims under London Bridge." He grins, revealing a front tooth jutting over its neighbor at an unnatural angle. It's the type of feature that's memorable and charming on a charismatic, funny man, yet repugnant on a brute.

When I'm silent, he looks back, expectant brows lifted.

"I had no idea the constable had such privileges," I say, unsure how to respond.

"Oh yes. I also get any animal that falls off the bridge. And dues and taxes from various city travelers."

"Do many animals fall off London Bridge?"

"Yes." His chest swells with pride. "And I get anything that falls into the Tower's moat."

I shiver, but I've always thought any conversation better than silence, so I ask about his family.

"One sister, Libby," he calls over his shoulder.

"Where does she live?" I ask.

He scoffs. "In Suffolk."

I'm glad he's faced away and can't see my embarrassment. He goes on to give a brief listing of our servants at our Tower residence.

"There's Cook, and a serving boy, Bart. Meggy the scullery maid, my squire Lem, and your woman, whom you know."

"I wouldn't say I know her. We only met yesterday."

He doesn't respond.

"When—" I begin, but can't finish my thought. The sight of an enormous structure spanning the river stops me, and I gape, pulling Rosemary to a halt.

Thomas looks back and laughs. He waves a hand at the monstrosity. "London Bridge."

"How long is it?" I ask, incredulous.

"Almost a thousand feet long," he says, "and twenty feet wide."

Over one hundred houses and businesses line it on both sides, except for the center, where a wooden drawbridge stretches, a chapel built to one side. Each building is several stories high, and a few climb to six floors. Hordes of people hurry across the drawbridge, riding horses, carrying children in their arms, or herding animals.

"It's one of the city's major shopping streets," Thomas says. "It is there, wife, that you will find the finest haberdashers and glovers." He looks at my gray riding gloves, the same ones I've used for four years, his mouth twisting in a grimace.

I can't think of anything to say; I'm too dumbfounded by the floating city he calls a bridge. I watch a man push a handcart of vegetables across the drawbridge. He tilts his head to glance at the bridge's gatehouse.

My eyes follow, and I gasp. "Sir Thomas..." I wave a searching hand his way. "Are those...are they—"

Sir Thomas releases a harsh bark of laughter and reins in his horse. Drops of spittle fly from his tongue and land on my face. I don't even flinch. I can't tear my eyes away from the bridge. Five severed heads are mounted on spikes on top of the gatehouse, and as I watch, stomach roiling, enormous black ravens peck at their sightless eyes, lips, and ears.

Rosemary stops to crop the grass beside the road, oblivious. It's the first time I've been jealous of a horse.

Thomas nods toward the bridge, then eyes me. "That's what we do with traitors in London."

Hot acid rises in my throat, but I swallow it down and follow his horse for another half a mile, riding in silence until we reach our destination.

We stop to watch the late afternoon sunshine warm the Tower of London's limestone walls. Screams ring in my ears, like at my wedding. I shiver as if a sluice gate has diverted the river's icy water into my veins.

Rosemary shies away, snorting.

"What's wrong?" Thomas's sharp voice jolts me back.

The screams fade, and I lower my shaking hands to calm my horse. A deep inclination urges me to let her run, to give Rosemary her head and go home. With all my being, I don't want to be here.

I take a ragged breath, forcing such fantasies out of my mind. I need to focus on the truth, on my reality. My father expects me to be a good wife, and I won't embarrass him. I used to belong to him, now I belong to Sir Thomas. As such, I'm a servant to this place, to London's Tower.

"Nothing." I scramble for an excuse. "It's just...I've never seen anything so marvelous."

It's partly true: the Tower of London is unlike anything I've ever imagined, standing sentinel on the Thames, its water gate situated directly on the outer ward. It's not a single tower but an impregnable complex built of multiple towers and buildings, surrounded by two crenelated walls. Nestled within them is the White Tower—four turrets of snowy stone with a massive box-like keep between.

As Thomas nudges his horse into a brisk trot, I shade my eyes against the sun glinting off the towers' golden weathervanes, fashioned like crowns above domed gray-blue turrets. Beyond the drawbridge stands a semicircular barbican.

Thomas stops to point out the structure. His lips pull into a taut grin. "Listen," he says.

For a long moment, I hear nothing but the rush of the Thames and the constant thrum of people's voices. Then, a foreign sound erupts from the crenelated barbican, a roaring beast. My horse quivers beneath me, and the hairs at my nape stand up.

"A wolf?" I struggle to control Rosemary as she whips her head to show the whites of rolling eyes.

He laughs. "I'm sorry," he apologizes. I jerk my head to look at him, surprised by his gentle tone. Then he pats Rosemary's glistening neck, and I realize he's speaking to her, not me. "This is the Lion Tower," he continues. "The king keeps his menagerie here, including three lions."

"Must we pass through?" I grip my reins with white knuckles.

He leers and urges his mount into the stone gatehouse and across the drawbridge. The warhorse is trained to be unafraid of loud noises, but Rosemary shivers and refuses to cross the bridge. I give her a sharp jab with my heels. It's not something I enjoy, but there's no choice; without it the mare will stand here all night.

My mouth is dry and brittle, and when we pass through the stone gatehouse, I look over my shoulder. The cart carrying my belongings, and Rhead, is nowhere to be found. I pray they will bring him to me before letting him loose. With lions housed in the entrance tower, heaven only knows what else this place holds.

The lion roars again, and Rosemary rears. I grip her mane to keep from sliding off her rump, but a soldier has to jump forward and snatch her bridle, urging her across the drawbridge. I make the mistake of glancing at the filthy castle moat, lazing below us, stagnant and brown. The massive ditch of the Tower's moat, over sixteen feet deep, has only three sides. The fourth is the Thames itself. The moat's water flows from it. The river—my river—has made this thing. The Thames has always been my refuge, my solace. Now, it's my jailer.

The reeking refuse and excrement make my eyes water, and I remember what Sir Thomas said about owning anything that falls in. That's not necessary for me. I already belong to the constable.

I manage to raise my head from Rosemary's neck to survey the top of the Lion Tower's expanse of white stone. The lions must be housed beneath us. Rosemary's red-gold coat shivers with every step. Beyond the Lion Tower, we must cross a stone bridge. The soldier, a man in his middle years with a grizzled beard, glances up.

"'Tis Middle Tower, m'lady," he explains. "And beyond that, Byward Tower."

I nod, eyeing the archers lining every wall, sentries atop and below each turret.

Away from the Lion Tower, Rosemary's shivering ceases, but her steps are still hesitant, and when the soldier leads us beneath the portcullis, it's as if each sharpened spike swivels to point at me, sneering.

The soldier hauls Rosemary by the bit across another crenelated stone bridge to the Byward Tower—the entrance to the outer ward.

From the outer ward, I can already see the second, higher wall, and the gate through which we'll likely proceed, housed in yet another tower. It's like a small city, people swarming every which way like bees serving their queen. There are soldiers, but women and children as well. Some lead animals—horses and livestock—while dogs and cats dart underfoot.

Closing my eyes, I let the soldier lead my horse down the path to the next gate. I focus my senses, letting the multitude of sounds narrow. All I hear is a hum like a thousand bees. I clench my jaw until my teeth chatter. The place smells of death. Not the sweet rot of the Thames, but that of darkness and despair. Many people have died here, and many more will in the future. I sense their pain. Women, children too. What enemy would kill the innocent?

In the darkness of my closed lids, I pretend I'm a bee, the hum of my hive the only sound I feel or care about. I wish I were one of them—a busy worker bee, only concerned with laboring for some foreign queen. I long to be a nameless soul, unexposed to the fear and the unidentifiable suffering around me.

Upon seeing Sir Thomas, everyone stops to bow or curtsy, and they favor me as well. I grip my reins until my hands shake. My husband appears to enjoy their obeisance.

Pathways and gravel roads lead to various buildings, towers, and a chapel across the Tower Green. In the midst of it all sits the White Tower. Archers line every wall, and sentries stand at the top and bottom of each turret. To my right, yet another curtained wall encloses a space behind the White Tower.

There is some greenery, and I detect the scents of soil and grass. I suspect there's a garden nearby, beyond the right-hand wall.

We circle the White Tower to the opposite end of the inner ward. Sir Thomas gestures at an imposing tower built into the inner wall and gives a rare, joyful smile.

"Constable Tower," he says.

Chapter Nine

Thomas spears a slice of mutton and deposits it into his mouth, chewing as he pierces me with his black gaze. We sit, silent but for his jaw's bone-wrenching *pop, pop, pop*, for five minutes. I clasp my fingers in the folds of my satin surcoat to hide their trembling.

At last, he wipes his fingers on the tablecloth and stands. I swallow my terror and take his outstretched hand. His twisted scowl tells me he feels—and disapproves of—my shaking, but I cannot help it, and when he leads me up the two flights of winding stairs, my knees almost buckle.

He opens the third floor's single door into a cylindrical bedchamber. Inside, we find my serving woman, Joan, already putting away my linens. She curtsies, folds her hands before her, and bows her head.

With a rush, I recall something Maman said right before my wedding, and my stomach drops. "Remember what I taught you about managing a maid," she'd said. I stayed silent because I had no idea what Maman was talking about. I must have successfully tuned that lady lesson out. "A good maidservant can be your greatest ally," she continued, "and spy."

I drew back, shocked. "Why would I need a *spy*?"

"But make no mistake," Maman continued, ignoring my comment. "She's not your friend. Don't coddle her, but of course you must be kind. A disgruntled maid can undo even the most powerful lady. Of course, don't let her boss you around. Still, you must take her suggestions from time to time. Don't be cruel. Just firm."

I gaped, unable to sort through her jumbled load of contradictions.

When Rhead darts around Joan, the sight of my cat sends a brief shot of warmth through my chest. My mind snaps away from Maman's confusing advice, and a smile tugs at my features.

Sir Thomas sneezes, then hooks one hand under Rhead's belly. In one fluid movement, he tosses the cat down the stairs. I give a little squeak but say nothing. Now that Rhead knows my location, he'll stay close by.

"I'll leave you with your woman now, to prepare for bed."

After he leaves, Joan, a petite woman with dark eyes and a plain but strong face, helps me out of my wedding garments. When she leans over to pluck at my sleeve's lacings, I flare my nostrils and inhale her scent. She smells clean, of nothing more than high-quality soap and a hint of lavender. No disdain, no anger.

She loosens my yellow tunic, and I sigh with relief. The bodice and sleeves have pinched all day, after Maman laced me in this morning. *Tighter is better*, she's always said.

Before Joan removes my belt, I slip a small fabric envelope from its pocket and fold it in a tight fist at my side. She carries the pouch across the room.

"Please—" I begin. She turns and blinks at me. I've no idea how to interact with this girl, my new servant. But this is important. I force myself to try to tell her what I need. "The belt pouch. It...it must be kept safe."

"Of course, my lady." With an encouraging smile, she hangs it on a hook by the door. "It will be right here. Sir Thomas left these hooks for your things, so your pouch won't be disturbed." She pats it with one hand. I try not to wince.

Joan smiles again, but like a frightened rabbit, I say nothing, just gaze around my new chamber.

Night has fallen. The one arrow slit lets in scant moonlight and the fire is low in the hearth, but my eyes don't need much to see details. There are fresh rushes on the floor, and a simple tapestry covers the wall, depicting knights on the battlefield. The bed, a four-poster with a feather mattress drooping on its ropes, dominates almost the entire space. Green curtains of a fine, if old, velvet fabric drape the sides of the bed, which is covered by a green-and-gold damask coverlet.

Joan removes my tunic, pulls my bridal chemise over my head, and ties the cream-colored ribbons at my throat. "It's a lovely garment for a bride, my lady," she says.

My tongue is thick and my heart pounds with dread. Somehow, I manage a gurgle of agreement.

"Sit, my lady. I will brush your hair."

I lower myself to the stool and stretch a trembling hand to the sideboard, where someone has placed two ewers, one of wine and one of ale, along with two goblets.

"Wine, my lady?"

I nod and, as she faces away, open my clenched fist to lift the envelope's flap. The rich scent of herbs drifts on the air. I close my eyes for a moment and draw in a ragged breath: powdered cow parsley, artemisia, juniper, licorice.

I prepared the herbs from a recipe I found in Eldridge's notebook, marked with a red ribbon. Had she known I'd end up an unwilling vessel for Sir Thomas's seed?

For a suspended moment while Joan's back remains turned, I gaze at the open envelope. My goal is supposed to be influence, to ingratiate myself to my husband and help people like Geoff. A pregnancy is surely something he seeks. All men want heirs. Producing one is, according to Maman, a wife's primary duty, and I want to be a good wife.

But I've seen too much of motherhood while caring for my patients.

Five years ago, when Eldridge served as midwife for Emmote Thatcher, I assisted, against Maman's fervent wishes. The babe was presenting feet down. Breeched, Eldridge called it. Eldridge knew how to fix it, but Emmote was tiny. When standing, the top of her head barely reached my sternum, and her hips were narrower than many children's. Try though we did, we could not turn her unborn baby. There was just no room. Finally, the young mother began to bleed. So much blood, almost unnaturally red and reeking with the metallic, burning tang of the forge. It was more than Eldridge and I could staunch.

At the time of her death, Emmote and I were both seventeen. Though we weren't friends, we had grown up together. I knew she was excited to have a baby. It's what she'd always wanted. And I knew she loved her husband, Brim Thatcher, just as he loved her. On that day, I promised myself I'd never become a mother.

Joan hands me the wine and takes the hairbrush from the stool's edge. I shift my weight, knocking the brush to the wooden floor. I flinch as it clatters. When Joan bends to retrieve it, I dump the herbs in the wine and swirl the liquid until they disappear.

Brush in hand, she begins to undo my straight brown tresses from their plaits, and I gulp down the wine, hoping to hide my true purpose behind a veil of virginal nerves. Joan rubs lavender oil through my hair. It's cut blunt at my shoulders, but she says nothing about the unusual length, to my relief. After Eldridge died, Maman refused to help me plait my tangled mass, so I had to cut it short.

When the door opens, I jump, and Joan sinks into another curtsy. Thomas stalks into the chamber and gestures for her to leave. I clasp my hands in my lap. Glancing at my white knuckles, his face gives a little spasm, a vein throbbing in his temple. In the same manner he waved Joan out the door, he gives a rigid signal with one arm for me to move to the bed.

I stand, knees stiff. In a moment, I've passed a lifetime and become an old woman. I trip over my own feet and hobble toward the mattress, stopping before it while still facing away.

"Well?" he says, voice harsh and angry. "What are you doing? Get in bed!"

I face him. "Sir, I..." I know the basics of the sexual act between animals, having seen horses and cows do it on the countess's farm lands. But I don't know the specifics of how it works between humans. I take a deep breath and, as usual, blurt out the first thing that comes to my mind. "I don't know what to do."

His face falls, and he pinches the space between his eyes. He's fully clothed while I'm in a thin chemise that barely covers my figure. I shiver. The air is like ice; the window is uncovered and little warmth emanates from the hearth. Lowering his hand, he starts to unlace my chemise. I gasp in horror when he pulls the fabric off my body, leaving me naked. He tosses the garment onto the rushes.

I try to hide my nakedness, but he grabs my wrists and pins them at my sides. Instinctively, I pull away. He twists his grip, strong hands chafing.

"Stop, wench," he says through gritted teeth.

I open my mouth to say *no*, but stop. I do remember what Maman taught me about this. *A woman must give in to her husband's will, always. Within the marriage bed, and without.* I'm supposed to let him. I must. With an effort, relying on strength pulled from deep within, I let my body go still, limp in his grip.

His eyes rake me from chin to feet, and he flicks the ends of my hair with one hand. His frown deepens before his gaze returns to my breasts. "Well, I might as well tell you I didn't want to marry you," he says. "But even I can't claim you're unpleasant to look at. Mad, maybe, but you're well formed." Gripping both of my arms again, he holds me slightly away from him. "Nice breasts. Not too large. I only like a fistful."

With a detached air, he cups one, tweaking the nipple with his thumb before squeezing the flesh like a piece of fruit.

I gasp. "You're hurting me, sir."

"Get on the bed," he barks.

I do, blood thrumming in my ears. He removes his boots and hose. He doesn't hurry, seeming to enjoy seeing me cold and vulnerable. My skin raises into gooseflesh. At last, he tosses aside his mantle, hitches up his tunic, and clambers on top of me. His fingers pinch my thighs as he tries to wrench them apart, yet I resist. I haven't forgotten Maman's instructions, but now my body has taken over my mind. I don't want to open myself to him. No matter how much I *think* I must submit, I'm finding the physical reality is another thing.

He shoves his face into mine, and my naked chest heaves, tears threatening behind my eyes.

"Listen, you little witch," he whispers. "I don't want you, I told you that. But if you fight me, I'll make you regret it."

"Ah!" I cry out and wrench my back into an arch as he thrusts his fingers inside my most secret place. I begin to weep. "Please, husband. Please stop."

He curses and removes his hand, then reaches down to touch himself. He pumps his hand on his groin in jerking, frustrated movements and grits his teeth. The smoke of fire floods my nostrils, along with the harsh, metallic tang of garlic. I squeeze my eyes shut and pray for the moment he'll be done with me.

My hands flutter at my sides; I cannot survive much more. He shifts his weight to straddle me and pins my wrists with his knees.

"Don't do that." He points at my flapping hands. "Don't you ever fucking do that in front of me, do you hear?"

I tremble and tears flow freely down my cheeks. I taste the salt and snot on my lips, but I can't wipe it away—my hands are trapped beneath him.

"I won't be saddled with a madwoman," he says, still stroking himself. "I don't care whose bastard she is."

My wrists burn with the pain of his weight, and my hands flap, swinging up to brush his shins as he continues to pump with his fingers. He shifts to kneel on my hands, and I hear the bones crack and pop. I grit my teeth. Much longer and he'll break my fingers.

"God's a fucking whoreson," he breathes. I gasp, unable to believe someone would say something so terrible.

He rolls off the mattress, landing on his bare feet among the rushes. He pants with rage and jabs a long finger in my direction. "This is your fault. You've bewitched me, haven't you? You fucking slut of a witch."

He strides to the sideboard, pours a goblet of ale, and downs it in one gulp.

I don't move or speak. I remain on my back. *Breathe...slow your pulse.* I pray he'll go to sleep and leave me alone.

He downs all the ewer's ale before stumbling back to the bed. I've pulled up the covers and closed my eyes in mock sleep, ignoring my aching wrists and hands. Thomas seems unconcerned about my well-being. Climbing into bed, he rolls over, and soon he snores.

Many minutes later, when I'm sure he slumbers, I rise and fetch my chemise from the floor. I cautiously open the chamber door to find Rhead on the spiraling stairs. As he pads inside, I remove a scrap of paper from my belt pouch.

I sit by the hearth for a long time, Rhead curled in my lap and the paper clutched in my fingers. It's a scrap of parchment from Eldridge's tiny book, but something keeps me from unfolding it. My new husband's nearness, or the depressing, dirty damp of my new home, or maybe just the melancholy that's settled over me. Still, deep into the night, with the flames flickering to nothing, I open it.

Geoff's yellow dandelion flower, the last one he gave me, tumbles out of the parchment to rest, dried and flat on my palm. I close my eyes and breathe the rich scent of tilled earth, the buttery flavor of the yellow flowers. Springtime rain soaks them. Sunshine, hot and dry on summer's stagnant air. Fall's crisp breezes spread the tufts of seeds for next year's crop.

Dandelions are resilient, useful. Geoff once told me they grow throughout Christendom wherever they're planted. Eldridge used them in herbal remedies and Cook in our meals. They don't need a home, don't need stability. They grow where they are planted, then change and float away on the wind.

Tears threaten at the back of my throat, in my nose. I refuse them. Somewhere outside, on the expanse of green I noticed outside the Tower grounds, or in the private gardens adjacent to the royal palace, I imagine an abundance of the yellow flowers. In a few weeks, their tufts will turn, as if by magic, to fluffy white clouds. Change is everywhere.

—

The next morning, Joan grabs my hand and eases it forward for closer inspection.

"My lady!" she gasps. My fingers are bruised and swollen with bracelets of purple, gray, and blue encircling both wrists like unwanted decoration. "What happened? Did he—" She squeezes her lips together and glances at the closed door, through which Thomas disappeared five minutes ago.

In some ways, a maid is no different from a lady. Neither has any say over men's actions. I can't question my husband; Joan can't chasten her master.

This marriage was supposed to bring power and influence, to give me a proper surname and a place in the world. Instead, I'm beholden to a cruel man who verbally and physically abuses me. I've become a lady, an elevated social status to which my mother aspired but never achieved. Yet, I'm more caged than ever, taken from my home and sequestered in this Tower. Stuck in a reeking city full of overwhelming sights and sounds.

I suppress a grunt deep in my throat and gingerly flex my fingers. "I'll be all right, Joan. Could you fetch my medicinal chest?"

I wince. *Don't ask her to do things, Blanche,* Maman's voice scolds. *Tell her.*

Joan removes Eldridge's wooden box from under the mattress and sets it on the coverlet, then opens its leather fastenings. When I lift the lid, she gasps and leans in like a child on Twelfth Night. The first tray is fitted with twenty small compartments, each containing a different dried herb. Beneath it is another tray, the same size. Years ago, Eldridge told me that her father, a carpenter, had made the chest, complete with a secret compartment for her recipes. I always marveled at the idea. Not only did Eldridge have a father who was involved in her daily life, but he knew and loved her enough to make such a precious gift, something she'd treasure for her entire life.

My hands, swollen and awkward as a toddler's, fumble to remove the top tray, and I wince when a finger catches its handle. Joan lunges forward to remove it for me, along with the second tray. She places them side by side on the bed. As I locate dried mallow and marigold, she removes Eldridge's stone mortar and pestle from the box's bottom, placing them on the coverlet. I exhale, relieved to find the tools unbroken after my journey.

When I extend one bruised finger to touch the pestle's cold stone, a flash of energy surges through my skin like a lightning bolt. I jerk my hand back .

Chamomile and briny saltwater tickle my nostrils. I look around. "Eldridge?"

"What are you looking for, my lady?" Joan asks. "Who—" At the last word, she gives a little start and purses her lips.

There's no one, just me and Joan. Eldridge is dead. She can't visit me here.

I give what I hope passes for a smile. It feels like a grimace. "Nothing. Thought I heard someone, that's all." I shrug one shoulder, hoping to seem casual. "Is there any aloe to be found at the Tower, Joan?"

"No, my lady. I asked last night."

I raise a brow.

"I know it's sometimes helpful for brides...after." She takes a deep breath. "But I did bring you this, my lady." She withdraws a small pottery crock from her apron pocket and lays it on the coverlet beside my chest. "Goose fat may also be useful."

I smile. "Are you schooled in the healing arts, Joan? You can't possibly be old enough for children of your own."

"No, no." When she smiles, her dark eyes light up. I see that, despite her plain clothes and severe white coif, she's quite lovely. "I have many younger siblings, and as the eldest, my mother taught me what I need to know. Then, the serving woman I trained with schooled me on what herbs a lady might require."

"Are you from London, Joan?"

"Yes, Lady Prescott."

I feel myself blush.

For so long, I've wanted a name, a *real* name. Now that I have one, it feels like a curse. I long to press cool fingers to my hot cheeks but can't draw attention to my discomfiture, not in front of Joan. She's pleasant and thoughtful, and good at her job. Still, I can't forget Maman's words. Lady's maids can be spies. This girl might report my failings to Thomas.

"My father is a lawyer," Joan is saying as she returns the trays to my medicine chest. If she noticed my unease, she's chosen to ignore it. "I didn't want to marry, so I apprenticed with the maid of a merchant's wife, who happened to know Lady Swynford. As you know, she hired me for the duke's daughter. You, my lady."

I straighten, holding onto the mortar. I'd forgotten Joan was hired by Lady Swynford, my father's mistress, the woman he undoubtedly loves, even though she's not his wife. While I would have preferred to interview my own maid, I must admit Lady Katherine has more experience managing staff than me. Furthermore, she was kind and gracious when we met at my wedding, even after Maman was unforgivably rude. Surely, I can trust a servant chosen by Lady Katherine Swynford.

Joan takes the mortar and grinds the herbs to a fine powder, then deposits a generous scoop of goose fat to mix with the herbs. I wash my hands while she works, taking care not to cry out from the pain.

"Can you leave the goose fat in the chest?" I blush again. Stop asking. Command her. Be a lady. Kind, yet firm.

It's hopeless, I know. Maman should have married a knight, not me. I'm like a blind man attempting archery.

Again, Joan doesn't seem to notice my struggle. She deposits the crock in the chest with nothing more than a bobbed curtsy.

When she smears the herbal salve on my bruises, the rub of her work-worn fingers reminds me of Eldridge administering similar ointments to childhood injuries. I close my eyes and breathe through my nose.

"I think the light blue woolen gown today," she says, "with the long hanging sleeves."

I smile and nod.

She laces me into the gown more loosely than Maman ever did. Maybe having a maid isn't so bad after all.

I pull on a surcoat and black hood, glancing out the arrow slit. Dark gray clouds boil in the sky, and the crown-shaped weathervanes atop the White Tower's turrets spin and twirl in every direction.

My toilette complete, I head down the spiraling staircase, careful to keep my hands concealed beneath my sleeves. "Joan," I call over my shoulder, trying to keep my voice commanding yet pleasant, "I'd like to see the Tower kitchen's gardens, please. I mean...no please. Just...show me the gardens...today."

I grit my teeth, and a drop of sweat runs between my shoulder blades. I've failed again. I don't sound like a lady. At this point, I'd settle for passing as a merchant's wife. Anyone with the vaguest inkling of how to employ a servant.

At home in Fobbing, I refused Ceira Cook's help whenever possible. I can dress myself—I've done so for two decades—and can handle my own hair, if it's kept short. I'm also more than able to find the Tower gardens on my own. That's what a nose is for.

What would Eldridge say if she saw me with Joan? What would *Geoff* say? I suppress a groan. My best friend—who I'll likely never see again—would call me ridiculous. He'd say I'm trying to be something I'm not, and rightly so.

Joan clears her throat. "My lady? There's no need for you to see the gardens. You're not responsible for them."

"I know." I descend the last two steps to the dining hall, then straighten my shoulders. "I would like to find a space to grow my own plants."

Lord, I sound almost more demanding than the Countess of Hereford herself. But that's what I wanted, isn't it?

My head aches and it's not even midday.

Joan says nothing, just bobs a curtsy before grabbing our cloaks.

—

The Tower's main gardens border the outer ward, beyond the White Tower and its kitchens. There are thatched livestock sheds and grazing spaces beyond, along with a buttery, a bakehouse, an alehouse, and a dovecote.

Joan takes me to Master Gardener, a rotund man with three sprigs of blond hair sticking straight up from a head that's red as a strawberry.

"I'm pleased ye've an interest in our gardens, m'lady." Master Gardener waves both arms toward the vegetables as we make our way down the narrow pathway separating two plots. Pride shines on his face, glistening in the blustery wind.

"This is very well done, Master Gardener," I say. "Could you show me the herb garden?"

He beams, almost grabbing my hand to pull me to the plot to our right. "Here they are, m'lady."

I nod, keen to show my approval, but what little hope I had for a sanctuary within the Tower, or a resource for my healing, ebbs away. The garden consists of a few rows of shabby plants. Unlike the vegetable gardens, which are robust and well-kept, this space is neglected. Weeds threaten to overtake the herbs and choke off new growth. No one has bothered to clear the ground after winter.

Walking ahead, Gardener is pointing out plants and listing their names to me. "There's dill, of course," he says. "And borage." He points at an anise plant. I refrain from correcting him.

"Lovely, Master Gardener."

Joan whispers in my ear. "I've been told the servants charged with tending the herb garden were sent away, sometime last year. Not enough funds to keep them."

I give her a tiny nod of appreciation.

"And also, m'lady, there's a good deal of herbage growing on Tower Hill. It is, by rights, the constable's property."

My heart gives a little leap. "Really? That's excellent." I grip my hands beneath my breasts, hoping Gardener doesn't notice they're trembling, just the littlest bit. "Tell me, Master Gardener, would it be acceptable to you if I worked in this herb garden some days? I've brought herb cuttings from Essex."

His face appears pleased, but I'm not sure he's sincere. My request is an odd one, and he might worry my husband will be angry if he allows it.

"The Tower is a busy place, and I imagine you could use the help," I continue.

"Yes, yes, of course, m'lady, that will be most welcome," he says at last, bowing.

"Do not worry," I add. "I'll tell no one. That way, when the constable comes to inspect your work, he will praise you."

Gardener beams.

Chapter Ten

9 JUNE 1381

When we return to Constable Tower's grim structure, our serving boy, Bart, bursts from its door.

"M'lady!" He gives a sloppy bow. "A visitor for you, m'lady."

"Who?" I ask, dreading his response.

His beady eyes dart to the door, then back. He lowers his voice. "It's the Earl of Derby, m'lady, Henry of Lancaster."

A sharp intake of air whistles through my front teeth. Although I looked forward to grabbing my cuttings and returning to the garden, I can't refuse an opportunity to speak to my half-brother Henry, the one sibling—of eight—I've met. Plus, I'm obligated to see him. Not only is he family, he's one of the most powerful peers in England. Society's rules would demand I give him my cloak and shoes if he asked.

I press my palms to my dirty and wrinkled clothing, heart beating a nervous rhythm. I haven't seen Henry since the day he came to Fobbing with news of my betrothal. On that morning, he emanated the confident aroma of fine Castilian soap, flavored with the delicate pepper of curiosity as his pale eyes took in my shabby garb and bare feet.

I stride inside with alacrity to find the fifteen-year-old earl in the dining hall. He bows and I respond with a deep curtsy, grateful Maman insisted I practice the skill every day. He seems even taller than the last time I saw him in Fobbing, with handsome features and a sprinkling of reddish facial hair dusting his upper lip.

His blue eyes sparkle, his smile smelling like the cloves, anise, and cinnamon of mulled wine. Being near him is like holding a steaming mug of it between my chilled palms on a winter day. I take a step closer.

"Mon seigneur," I say, "comme c'est agréable de te voir." *How lovely to see you.*

"I came to welcome you to London, my lady," he answers in English.

I silently chastise myself for forgetting he seems to prefer English to French. I'm glad I practiced speaking the language so often with Eldridge and Geoff.

At the thought, a sharp lump forms in my throat. Then I smell chamomile and brackish water. For a moment I think Eldridge has walked through the door, that she's come to the Tower of London to see me.

Fool. Eldridge is gone.

Beneath my hanging sleeves, I pinch my swollen wrist, hoping the pain will force me back to reality, away from my dream world. It doesn't; I still smell her. *Dead*, I think. *Eldridge is dead, and I'll never see her again.* I'll never see Geoff again either. I must stop remembering them both. It's time to look forward, not back.

The smell fades.

I gaze at Henry's auburn hair, shining even in the dull light. With difficulty, I swallow and glance at the door, desperate to leave Constable Tower's dark and shabby confinement right after returning. "It is quite fine out. Shall we walk on the battlements?"

Henry arches a ruddy eyebrow and looks over my shoulder to the unglazed arrow slit. The wind pulls at my hood. I smile and shrug. He laughs and offers me his arm.

As we walk out the door, I gaze at him through my lashes. The resemblance between us is impossible to miss. Every detail of my bone structure is mirrored in his: long nose, high brow, full mouth. His auburn hair differs from my brown, and his eyes are blue like a fine topaz, while mine are like the mud beneath our boots. Still, I think most would recognize us as siblings in a moment. A thrill races up my spine.

"And how do you find London, Lady Prescott?"

The name makes me shiver. I hope he doesn't notice.

"I...I..." I can't think what to say. Fobbing's villagers ignored me, so my conversations up to this point have been limited to Maman, Geoff, and Eldridge. "I'm not sure, my lord." I pull at my cuff with my fingers. How do courtiers converse? "There are fourteen rats living in Constable Tower, which is surprising...but I'm pleased to see they're well-fed," I say at last, proud I didn't just blurt out my first thought. I regret Maman wasn't here to witness it .

He makes a choking sound that shifts smoothly into laughter. "I'm...well...fourteen, you say? Are you sure?"

"Oh yes, I'm quite sure. I can hear them in the walls and floors."

"And well-fed?"

"Yes, remarkably so."

"Perhaps you should tell your cook not to leave food about."

My brow furrows, and I peek at him through my lashes. Is he mocking me?

"I'm sure London is overwhelming," he continues. "It is, after all, very different from Essex."

"Indeed, my lord."

"And please, when we are alone, call me Henry. We're brother and sister, are we not?" he says. A warm tingle starts in my belly and spreads through my chilled limbs. "I must confess, sister, I've always wanted to meet you. You're..." He gives me a crooked smile. "You're named for my mother."

My face tingles with embarrassment.

"It's not a common name," he continues.

"No, it's not."

"But it is lovely."

I blink, then make a vague hum I hope passes for assent. I've always loathed my name, but am quite proud of myself, again, for denying the first thing to pop into my brain. I must write to tell Maman.

I pat his arm. "You were quite young, when she died. Were you not?"

"Yes." He looks out over the inner ward. "I don't remember her."

We pass a few moments in silence, watching the servants, soldiers, and nobles bustling around the White Tower. I marvel at the warm presence of him, leaning against me as I grip his arm.

I know he won't call me his sister in public. Around anyone else, I must refer to him as "my lord." But for me, this private relationship is enough. I pat his arm again. "If I will call you Henry, you must call me Blanche."

He grins and we walk on, watching the Tower's ravens gather in the grass of the outer ward, beneath our vantage point.

"Fierce beasts," he observes. "Fascinating."

"I like them as well," I say, "but I hope Rhead avoids them."

"Rhead?"

"My cat." I smile, somewhat sheepishly. "I'm very fond of him."

"Yes!" he cries. "Rhead..." He scrunches his nose in thought. "Red, in the Old Tongue, yes? He must be that little flame-colored cat, the one that burst into the chamber when I visited you in Fobbing?"

Nodding, I try to suppress my grin—it can't be ladylike to show all your teeth—but fail.

"Your mother was not happy."

I can't help but laugh, and he joins me, the heady scents of anise and clove intensifying.

"You brought him with you, all the way from Essex?"

"Yes."

Henry nods his approval. "Well, I can understand that. I have several dogs I'm rather partial to."

We take a few steps in companionable silence before he speaks again. "Tell me, Blanche, how goes your marriage?"

He says it with the ease and confidence of someone long accustomed to commanding attention. Anyone else would find such a question awkward, but in Henry's world, his comments are always applauded, all his queries answered.

I open my mouth, but no sound comes forth. I long to tell him the truth—that my new husband almost broke my fingers and called me horrible things but was ultimately unable to consummate our union. I know I cannot. Wives—good ones, at least—don't tell such secrets. The last thirty-six hours have shown me it's unlikely I'll succeed in being a good wife, but I'm still determined to try.

My silence stretches on. At last, I say the only thing I can think of. "The duke's gift to me for my marriage was most generous. The little silver spoons are lovely. There are twelve in all, with matching saucers. I would like to write to him, but I don't know how to reach him in Scotland."

Henry glances at me with surprise. "You can write?"

I nod and lift my chin in preparation for the onslaught of opinion. Most men aren't only stunned to learn I can read and write, they're angry.

But Henry's wide mouth stretches into a grin. "Excellent," he says. I blink. "More women should learn. Should I have daughters, I plan to make sure they do." His expression grows dubious. "Your husband, however...I'm not sure he'd share my opinion." My cheeks sting in the cold air, but he continues. "Our father thinks well of him. Sir Thomas is high in King Richard's favor."

He looks behind us to where Joan follows, too far behind to hear, then releases my arm to check down both sides of the curtained wall.

"Sometimes the king's choice of friends is mysterious indeed." His voice is low in the whistling wind. "My father, despite what everyone says, is hopelessly loyal to Richard. He will be loyal to anyone the king favors." Henry's words flow so fast that I can hardly keep up. "But I disagree. The silver spoons and saucers weren't the only gift our father sent for your marriage, Blanche. I imagine he and your mother didn't share with you the details of your dower agreement?"

I shake my head, heart thrumming in my ears.

Henry leans in closer. "Sir Thomas gets one hundred pounds a year from the incomes of two manors. A profitable income for him, in addition to what he already has from Suffolk. Plus, he's been made Constable of the Tower. God's knees, he's the most powerful man in London, but for the king!"

He pauses, looks behind us again, and lowers his voice. "Sir Thomas has gained much through this marriage, but I'm not sure he appreciates it. Your husband..." He grimaces. "Well, sister, if you need me, you know where to find me."

I draw a rattling breath. It surprises me to learn what I've brought Thomas—money, land, power. Yet he treats me like I'm a burden, like Maman did.

There's something beyond that. I'd assumed my father arranged my marriage to get me off his household ledger. With a knighthood and property, Thomas was a good candidate. But according to Henry, Sir Thomas has other qualifications: he is one of the king's favorites. Could this be my father's way of currying favor with the king?

Although I've never believed my father loves me, I didn't think he'd use me as a pawn in his politics either. If what Henry is implying is true...

With a jolt, I remember that Henry is the Duke of Lancaster's son. If I can't trust my father, can I trust Henry?

My fingertips tingle, and I withdraw my hand from the crook of Henry's elbow. He glances at me but says nothing as we walk on.

Once back at Constable Tower, I glance at Joan. Even with my limited experience, I know any decent lady's maid serves as chaperone to prevent gossip. Still, a shiver grips me.

Earlier, I'd worried she was Thomas's creature, tasked with reporting my misbehavior. What if the truth is more complicated? Could Joan be in the service of my father, through Lady Katherine, his lover?

My concoction of herbs—parsley, artemisia, juniper, and licorice—prevents unwanted pregnancies, and my maid will almost always be there when I take them. I can't hide the nightly ritual from Joan forever, and I don't know what's more terrifying: that the young woman might tell Lady Katherine, who would tell my father, or that she might tell my husband.

—

Henry departs, but the weather is so foul that I can't go back to the herb garden. Plus, my hands are too swollen and painful. I succumb to my uselessness and sit staring out of my chamber's arrow slit. Is this what married courtiers do all day? I watch the White Tower's weathervanes spin in the wind, while behind me, Joan straightens the room. Her palms brush the bedspread, trying unsuccessfully to press out its wrinkles. The fabric of my gowns crackle as she refolds them, and the bristles of a broom scrape the floorboards as she sweeps. I don't tell her that one of the Tower's many rats is watching her from a crack in the wall.

She picks up the empty water basin and leaves, no doubt to refill it.

I look down at my bandaged fingers and think of Eldridge's gnarled hands, swollen and blue-veined as I washed them for burial. She never complained, but working in her garden and foraging must have been painful. I'd never thought about it before.

Geoff's hands couldn't have been more different. I close my eyes, envisioning his long, thick fingers and rough, square-shaped palms. My ears ring with the sound of his calluses on Rosemary's coat the morning I left for London. What is he doing now?

I'm resting my palm on my belt pouch, inhaling the calming scent of dandelions, when the door opens. Joan's light footsteps tap as she carries the basin to the sideboard. It thumps, the water lapping against the stoneware's edge.

"My lady?"

I tear my eyes from my fingers. There's nothing I can do for Eldridge, nor Geoff. I'll never see my teacher again, and Geoff is just as lost to me.

Joan stands with hands folded and head lowered. She's run out of chores, and now I must be the boss of her. A full minute passes while I wonder what I can have her do. My head is starting to throb in time with my hands.

"Gather some old goblets and bowls," I say at last, "and fill them with water, please." Blast. I cough. "Fill them with water. For my herb cuttings."

I manage to resist another *please* while Joan helps me deposit the cuttings into shallow pools of water. We set them about my chamber. There's not much sun from the one cross-shaped arrow slit, but it's all I have. I have no private space, no stillroom, and nowhere to build one. This will have to do.

Thomas dines with the officers of the king's guard, so I eat alone in our small first-floor hall and go to bed after drinking the herbal concoction of parsley, artemisia, juniper, and licorice. The wine tastes like deceit, but I don't feel guilty.

I lay awake, dreading his return. At last, in the early hours of the morning, his boots drag up the spiraling stone steps. When he opens the door, the stench of ale and roses floods my nostrils. I stuff the sheet in my mouth to stop my gagging. I'm careful to keep my back to him and pretend to sleep. He stumbles to the bed and stops, inches from where I lie.

He watches me. I hear every breath he takes. In and out. In and out. The air brushes the exposed curves of my cheek and neck, which ripple with gooseflesh. But in the murky darkness of our chamber, made more so by his drunkenness, he thinks I'm asleep. Shuffling to his side of the bed, he falls into it and starts to snore.

I roll onto my back to stare at the tester. His disinterest can only last so long. Eventually, he'll force himself on me. At the thought, my skin seems to retract into itself.

The herbs are my only weapon against what he seeks.

—

The next day, I awaken to find a dim and cloudy dawn creeping through the chamber's arrow slit. A shuffle and an angry grumble draw my attention, and I rise to find Thomas ripping up a green shoot of hyssop.

"What are you doing?" I screech, leaping from the bed to stand barefoot before him.

He throws the ruined hyssop into a bin on the floor, to join the crumpled remains of my other herbs, all lovingly cut and transported from Fobbing.

I hold my ears against their screams. They call out, desperate for me to save them.

"Why?" I cry, hands waving. I clasp them behind my back.

"I told you," Thomas growls, "you're a madwoman, and I'll have none of your witchcraft." He jabs a sharp forefinger into my breastbone.

"Thomas! They're herbs. For healing agues and migraines. Your own fortress has a garden where they grow them. It isn't witchcraft, it's herbalism."

"Yes." He slams an empty crock down after tossing its water in the rushes. "The Tower's gardener keeps the herbs, *not* the constable's wife." He picks up the bin. "How am I to be respected if you're digging in the dirt?"

I try to snatch the bin from his long fingers, but my own are still bruised and swollen. Changing tack, I reach inside to pull the greenery out.

He swings a closed fist and cuffs my left ear. I stumble as a painful ringing reverberates from bone to nerve endings. My clumsy fingers drop the plants, and I fall among the floor rushes, limp as a poppet. Sir Thomas steps toward me, and I instinctively cover my face with my hands in a futile attempt at protection. He grinds what remains of the plants to pulpy destruction in the rushes. I hear their cries as I watch his boot, mere inches from my face.

I press the heels of my hands to my eyes to stem the tears, determined not to show weakness. But it's too late. He knows he can dominate me, that I have no power to usurp his authority over my new life.

He moves toward the door, golden spurs jangling against the floorboards like a court minstrel. I lay on the floor, watching the metal shine against the rushes and filth.

"No plants." He wrenches open the door. "I have enough to deal with today, what with the news from Kent and Essex."

I force my streaming eyes to focus. "Essex?"

"Yes." He leers down, pleased to know something I don't. "Just after you left your *home*"—his mouth twists around the word—"the king sent a commissioner to Essex to examine the inhabitants of three villages, including Fobbing."

Blood roars in my injured ear. Thomas knows any bad news about Fobbing will hurt me, and he's relishing it. I push away my disdain, determined to find out what's going on in my home. "Why?"

"You've heard of the poll tax?"

The scent of mold tickles my nostrils; he doubts my knowledge. I lift my chin and nod. He takes a breath, but I interrupt him. "Set forth by Sudbury, Archbishop of Canterbury. To finance the war. One shilling for every person over fifteen years old."

Thomas's jaw drops, but he snaps it shut with a click. I find myself looking forward to the day he learns I can read. "Indeed. But the damned fools insist they can't pay."

"Of course they can't," I spit, still crouched on the floor. "How could any peasant pay such an exorbitant sum?"

Thomas lurches forward and presses his face into mine. "So, you think like them, do you? Are you a villein after all? Have I bought a nag for the cost of a prized filly?"

It takes every ounce of my strength, but I draw on it and say, "I'm the daughter of John of Gaunt. Noble blood runs in my veins." I hope Thomas can't sense my hesitation. My blood is tainted. I'm a bastard, not a noble princess descended from William the Conqueror. I've never claimed to be something I'm not. Until now.

Thomas barks a tight laugh. "You're a bastard, wife. You're nothing."

I wrinkle my nose. "Why did the king send a commissioner?"

"The peasants lied about the size of their houses."

Everyone knows that, I almost say. "And?"

He stands with his boot just beside my hand. I watch the leather, praying he doesn't stomp on me and break my fingers at last. "They chased the commissioner out of town, pelting him with rocks. So, Richard sent someone else. The peasants attacked that man with clubs and swords. They beheaded three royal clerks, poked their heads up on sticks, and paraded them around town."

A shocked little choke erupts from my throat, and I cover my mouth to stifle it. "No, surely not!" I say through my fingers.

"It's true. There have been similar attacks throughout Essex and Kent. Some say your little friends are marching on London. Maybe they'll come for you?"

Without another word, he strides through the door and slams it behind him.

Chapter Eleven

10 JUNE 1381

When Joan arrives to help me dress, I'm still weeping on the floor. She carries a purring Rhead.

"Oh, my lady," she murmurs. Rhead leaps from her arms to land with a soft thump beside me. I don't need to tell Joan what happened. The evidence is everywhere.

Wordlessly, she clears the empty bowls and mugs and sweeps the ruined plants toward the grate while making disapproving clucking sounds with her tongue. She helps me sit on a stool and gingerly inspects my ear for damage.

"It isn't that bad," she says as Rhead jumps into my lap.

"The blue gown again," I say to her after she bathes my throbbing ear with a cool, wet cloth. "I need to go into London, to an apothecary. I must replace these plants."

—

It's a clear and sunny day, but as Joan leads me through the outer ward to the Middle Tower, her pace quickens. Once we reach the semicircular Lion Tower, she's almost dragging me across the stone building. She's not fast enough, however. Before we get to the drawbridge, one of the lions, located below us, roars. The stones beneath our feet rumble, and Joan squeaks. I'm panting by the time we cross the moat to safety.

"My lady," she gasps. "I'm sorry, I just—"

"I understand, Joan. I don't like them either." I let her take my arm and lead me away from the Tower at a more leisurely pace. "Have you ever seen the lions?"

She shakes her head so hard she almost dislodges her coif. "I'll never, never go down there."

"Are we allowed?"

She sucks in a tiny breath and holds it, but gives a tiny nod.

We continue in silence through the busy London streets, moving in the opposite direction of the Strand, where I was married at the Savoy Palace. Joan informs me our destination is Aldgate. There, London's best apothecary keeps his shop.

When we turn right off Thames Street to make our way to Tower Street, the traffic thickens. Heaps of refuse line both sides of the street. A pig roots through it, its snout releasing foul scents into the air. I gag and cover my mouth. The streets are crooked like drunks making their way home after hours, and the buildings sprouting like weeds around them are no better. It makes me dizzy, and I stop in my tracks, swaying.

Joan grasps my arm. "My lady, are you all right?"

I shake my head. She rummages through the pouch at her waist. I've closed my eyes, but I sense her holding something near my nose. Lavender oil. As I breathe it in, my racing heart slows, and my ragged breath evens out.

I open my eyes. "Thank you, Joan."

"Here, my lady." She shakes a few drops on each of my sleeves. "Hold the fabric to your face. I fear you'll need it soon."

Although I didn't think it possible, there are even more people crammed into this space than on my wedding day when we came in through Ludgate. More pigs dart here and there, there are more horses, more pedestrians. Joan touches my shoulder when she sees me staring at the pigs. "Don't get near them, they're wild."

At last, we're on Aldgate Street. Another scent tickles my nostrils; like steel, but tinged with rot and decay. I see its source in moments. Ahead, a butcher eviscerates a cow at the front of his shop, nestled in between a peppery and a tannery. Not convenient for the peppery, but fortuitous for the tannery. The cow's blood trickles down the sloping street beneath my feet. I smell its progress as it bumps past each knob of cobblestone.

I gag again, the smells emanating not only from the butcher but from the neighboring tannery, twisting my insides into knots. I ram my sleeve to my nose, desperate for the refreshing scent of lavender, but it does no good. Joan drags me along until we're moving at a run beyond the shops into a small, slanting alley. I vomit what little my stomach contains until I can only dry heave.

Joan pats my back. "There, there, my lady," she murmurs. "We'll go home the long way. Although I don't know how we'll avoid nauseous smells in this city..."

"This place...this place is..." I can't finish my sentence. I squeeze my eyelids shut and try to envision the marshes. The way the little birds danced along the trickles of water in the sand at low tide, how Geoff and I would hide in the tufts of coarse marsh grass.

"Don't worry, my lady. You'll get used to it with time."

I lean against a building's cold stone, beads of perspiration gathering on my forehead. I don't know if I can ever get used to this.

When we return to the main street, I breathe through my mouth and refuse to look at the butcher or tannery. Joan leads me to a neat and tidy shop on the opposite side of the street. A sign hung above its door reads *William Burton: Apothecary*.

Joan falls behind me as I push open the door. I blink. The shop, with only one small window facing the street, is dark, and it takes my eyes a moment to adjust.

"How can I help you, my lady?" a male voice calls out.

He stands on the far side of the room, behind a long, polished wooden counter. He is tall and spindly with a fair, square-shaped beard. Atop his close-cropped sandy hair, he wears a brown felt hat, and his face is pale, with a tint of pinkish-red on his cheekbones.

When we approach the counter, his long, brownish fingers are sorting through a collection of bottles and vials. Behind him, and on each of the four walls, floor-to-ceiling shelves hold similar vessels, each containing herbs or other medicines. I inhale and close my eyes as rosemary, saffron, and a dozen other alluring scents permeate my awareness. I see colors among them—pink, red, and bright yellow tendrils that float like particles of dust in the streams of sunlight. The colors entwine in my hair, luring me in. The herbs whisper to me; they ask me not to leave.

In my mind's eye, I crouch beneath the opposite counter, or dart into the small opening that no doubt leads to Master Burton's storeroom and workshop. If I hide here and make myself useful, maybe he'll let me stay. I could care for his plants and mix his customers' medicines. I'd never go back to the Tower. Joan could tell Thomas that I was eaten by a wild pig in the street.

"My lady," the man says again. I'm looking in the other direction, at the rows of glass vials. Despite my acute senses, I don't hear him at first.

He clears his throat. "Mistress?"

I turn my head.

"Welcome, my lady," he says. "How might I help you?"

"Master Burton, I assume?" I move closer and rest my hands on the counter, pleased, for once, to not be embarrassed by my dirty fingernails.

"Yes, I'm afraid." He gives a tight bow. "At your service."

"I am Lady Prescott, of the Tower."

He straightens. I give a little cough. I'm unsure of how to proceed without people avoiding my gaze or passing judgment due to my bastardy.

"I'm new to London, Master Burton, and need some cuttings for my garden, in addition to some lesser-known medicinal ingredients for my stores," I say. His mouth opens a fraction, but he closes it quickly. "I'm willing to pay for the plants," I add, handing him a scrap of parchment that lists my needs.

He scans the paper, then raises a brow. His tongue darts from his mouth to wet his lips. The movement makes a crackling sound, and my swollen ear rings once again.

I'm nervous. Mine is an unusual request, and he doesn't seem to want to comply. Yet, he's conflicted—my husband is influential.

"Of course, my lady," he says at last.

With another bow, he retreats through a small door behind the counter.

Although we must be left waiting for a while—my list was long—for me the time passes like the flick of an eyelash. I peruse the shelves, my excitement growing as I select additional roots and herbs for my stores. Burton's stock is beyond anything I'd hoped for, and it makes me stop worrying about news of the rebellion in Essex. Left alone—but for Joan, with whom I'm feeling more comfortable by the minute—I don't hold back a grin as I bask in this one benefit of life in a large city.

I also have more money to spend on herbs than ever before. As a part of my marriage agreement, I have a monthly stipend for my personal expenses, one of the few pleasures derived from my marriage. Most women would use the funds for gowns or headdresses, but I'm quite pleased to spend my coin on herbs. I have more clothing from my trousseau than I need.

By the time Burton emerges from the little door, both my arms and Joan's are full of my additional purchases. She gives no hint of annoyance.

Burton carries a wooden box full of plant cuttings. Leaning over to inspect them, I resist the urge to clap my hands like a child. Without hesitation, Joan proceeds to package each cutting in bits of paper coated in wax before wrapping them with strips of linen.

Burton gives me the total for my purchases, and I argue. "That can't possibly be enough, Master Apothecary. I must pay you for the plants' worth."

He shakes his head, his smile now genuine and appreciative. Begrudgingly, I pay him. He bows and I bob a curtsy.

"My sincere thanks," I say, feeling giddy. "I assure you I'll be back soon."

—

An hour later, I'm kneeling in the dirt of the Tower's garden. I'd be delighted at the prospect of planting my new herbs, if only I could stop worrying about Geoff.

I try to remind myself he'd never rebel against the king's rule, nor that of the Herefords. But how will he ever pay the poll tax? Geoff, and many of the other villeins, are running out of options.

I can't imagine anyone in Fobbing parading severed heads through the town square. Not the miller, nor the farrier. Not even Thomas Baker. Still, my husband said it happened. My mind keeps pacing around one fact: Geoff was tired of subservience to the Herefords. Everyone was.

But villeinage is a life sentence. There's no escape. Is there?

Running away was easy in the days immediately after the Great Pestilence's first wave, thirty-five years ago. But King Edward enacted laws to make it nearly impossible. For a year and a day, a runaway villein can be caught and returned to his master for punishment. Most lords give the captor a reward and take a hand or an ear from the villein. If the runaway isn't captured, manor lords will punish their family members. Brothers and fathers, even wives, sisters, and mothers can be fined or disfigured. Because of this, most villeins have stopped trying to run, unless they are single men with no living relatives. Like Geoff.

A life without freedom, without the ability to make choices, is no life at all. I know that as well as any villein. From what Thomas told me, it seems the people of England are starting to realize that. But at what cost?

Joan calls to me from beside the nearby dovecote, where she sits on a stool with a pile of mending. "My lady, don't kneel in your gown!"

When I glance at her, I catch sight of Master Gardener limping out of the kitchens. His beleaguered gait is pronounced, and agony emanates from his contorted face.

"Master Gardener!" I call.

He turns, and his pain-laced features stretch into a grin. "M'lady! Good morrow to you."

I hurry his way, then notice a soft glow around his knees. "Are you well, Master Gardener? Forgive me, but I can't help but notice your limp."

Sometimes when I see the glow, it's muted, like a persistent but minor toothache. Other times, such as during Emmote Thatcher's breech birth, it's like lightning consumes the patient and refuses to let go. No matter what, the glow always means one thing: pain. In Emmote's case, the brightest I've seen, the result was a terrible, bloody death.

When I first sought Eldridge's tutelage, she warned me never to speak of my abilities to anyone, and she modeled this belief in her own behavior. She never explained her powers, even to me. Consequently, I'll never know if she also saw these lights, or if her plants spoke to her.

"I thank you for yer concern, Lady Prescott," Gardener says. "A flare-up of me gout, I'm afraid." He makes an obvious effort to smile, but his discomfort turns it into a grimace.

"Ah, I'm sorry, Master Gardener. Have you tried any curatives or treatments?"

"Bit here, bit there, but nothing seems to work."

"Have you used colchicum root?"

"No, m'lady...not heard of it." He sounds doubtful. Whether he's unsure he can trust me, or he's hesitant to believe anything will alleviate his pain, I can't know. My guess is the former.

"I have some in my residence. I'll fetch it. Where will I find you upon my return, Master Gardener?"

He gapes at me like a fish, and I stifle a giggle.

"I'll find you." I cup a hand to my lips. "Joan," I call across the gardens. Everyone within earshot turns to look, but I lack the grace to care. "I need to see to Master Gardener."

Joan stands and trots my way.

As I hurry home, I'm so excited about the prospect of working with my medicines, nothing can dampen my mood. Not the soldiers carrying great stacks of arrows up to the sentries, nor the boys polishing armor and mending chain mail. When I burst through my residence's door, I wave away the servants' questioning looks and go upstairs to fetch my medicinal storage chest.

I have no trouble finding the colchicum root and am already grinding it in my mortar when Joan emerges through the door, panting from exertion.

She takes the mortar and pestle, allowing me to dig through my storage for a suitable receptacle for the powder. Once I have the crockery bowl, Joan carefully scrapes the precious medicine into it, under my close supervision. I cover it with a strip of fabric tied tight by a length of twine, both retrieved for just this purpose from the chest.

I bustle back down the stairs, calling over my shoulder for Joan to bring the chest. I feel quite commanding, like a real lady. Together we march out the door, down the inner ward's wall, and to the gardens.

I'm not surprised that Gardener has disappeared.

"I'm sure he's hiding from me," I mumble.

"Well, my lady, if he doesn't want the help..." Joan's look is hopeful, and she glances back toward Constable Tower.

The cook and his assistants' eyes widen when I sweep into the kitchen.

"Master Cook," I say, "I'm seeking Master Gardener. Have you seen him?"

Cook's eyes cut to the larder. "I don't right know, m'lady..."

I could swear I see him wink, but his face is so old and drooping that it's difficult to be sure. Still, I nod and stride to the door of the larder, which swings on its hinges in a draft.

When I open it, I find the largest larder I've ever seen, and I stand goggling for a moment, cold air wafting from the stone slab shelves. They stretch from a counter up to the top of the high ceiling, piled with vegetables of every sort, from carrots and potatoes at the bottom to lettuce and greens above. There are no berries, as it's only June, but my mouth waters at the thought of the precious scents of fruit that will no doubt flow from these shelves in the months to come. Strings of braided onions dangle from the top shelf, tied by their plaits, and dried cooking herbs hang from the ceiling beams beside them.

Also dangling from the wooden ceiling are hooks with joints of every cut and type of meat in Christendom: pork shoulder, beef ribs, legs of lamb, pork butt, strings of ducks, a goose hanging to dry, and rashers of bacon. Butter churns and laundry equipment are stacked neatly in the corners, beneath counters holding a multitude of every type of container imaginable. I count five different types and sizes of stone mortars, each with its own pestle. Beside them, in wooden and stone bowls, bread dough rises under patterned strips of cloth.

The smells and sensations wrap around me: earth and yeast, joined with the constant threat of decay. My mind stores them away, these new things in my new home. In contrast to Constable Tower—filled with scents of anger and violence—these smells are familiar. Friendly, welcoming. I understand them, unlike my husband and his expectations, which are laced with hatred.

In one corner leans a broom, a pile of dust and crumbs scraped neatly before the bristles, abandoned by some scullery maid. Was she pulled to another task?

Or perhaps she was hurried out by Gardener himself. His stooped figure hides among the pork and beef, pretending to inspect the vegetables.

"Ah, I've found you!"

He jumps. "M'lady, I was just...just...counting carrots!"

Without preamble, I pull a butter casket from beneath the central table. It scrapes on the floor. Under normal circumstances, the sound would grate at me, but I'm too filled with the rush of hope and urgency that comes along with healing.

"Joan, get a cup of ale," I say over my shoulder.

I look at Gardener and point at the circular seat, my every gesture brooking no refusal. He huffs, then settles himself with a grimace. The cook watches through the open door with keen interest, as do half a dozen scullery maids.

Joan arrives at my shoulder with a cup of ale. I remove the twine and fabric from the little pot of powdered colchicum root and sprinkle the light brown powder into the liquid. It floats on the surface for only a moment, disappearing with a swirl of the cup on the table's surface.

I hand the ale to Gardener. "Drink. All of it."

"Does it taste bad?"

I resist commenting on men's inability to grow up. Gardener is no different than Goodwife Smith's eight-year-old son, Roger, when I healed his constant cough.

He grimaces, accepting my silence as affirmation, and swallows the ale down in three gulps. His grimace deepens.

"It's bitter," I say, "but it will help."

He looks up at me like a petulant child and makes to stand. I press my forefinger into his chest and push him back down. He's forgotten that I am, for all intents and purposes, his lady, and scowls. He's on the brink of revolt.

"Stay here and rest, at least half an hour. You should start to feel better. Shall I get you more ale?" My tone is no different with Roger Smith.

Master Gardener nods grudgingly. Joan bustles away to fetch more ale.

"The powder will prevent further attacks and relieve the pain. You'll need to take it every day."

He sighs and his shoulders slump, but he settles himself on the cask.

"Don't let him move for at least thirty minutes," I order a maid with wispy red hair and beady gray eyes. She bobs her head furiously.

Chapter Twelve

Back at Constable Tower, Joan hurries me to my chamber. "What's wrong?" I ask.

"Your surcoat is filthy." Her tone is gentle but firm. "And you have grime caked under your nails. We have to get you changed before anyone sees."

She washes the soil off my skin and scrapes the dirt from beneath my nails. I'm starting to like having a maid.

My husband's voice echoes up the stairs as he yells at Bart. Apparently, someone is at the door. My hands and ear start to throb. Joan scurries to hide my soiled gown inside a chest.

"I'll take care of this while you eat," she says, patting the chest.

"I'm grateful for your help, Joan. I'm not the easiest lady to look after, with my curious habits." I smooth Rhead's fur as he sleeps in my lap. Joan smiles and curtsies.

After securing my wimple, Joan gives my shoulder a light squeeze. When I face her, she steps away and looks at her feet.

I go down the stairs but pause outside the dining hall's closed door.

"Un grand honneur, mon seigneur," Sir Thomas says, continuing still in French: "I apologize for the fare. We had no idea you were joining us."

I glance down. I'm attired in a dark green surcoat, which covers a cream-colored undertunic. Both are fastened with a simple leather belt. I hope it's fine enough for this visitor.

"Don't trouble yourself, Sir Thomas," an easy and lilting voice assures in English. I'm surprised for only a moment. Nobles usually prefer to speak among themselves in French, so their Anglo-Saxon servants won't understand, but I recognize my half-brother's voice. Warmth spreads through my chest, and I hurry to push the door open.

"My Lord of Derby," I say in English, sinking into a deep curtsy. "What a pleasure to see you."

Henry raises me with both hands and kisses each of my cheeks in turn. "Lady Prescott, I hope you don't mind my rude intrusion. I was in the area, and was so hungry for supper I couldn't bear the ride back to the Strand."

"You are always welcome, of course." I glance at Sir Thomas. His upper lip curls with disdain as he takes in my simple garb. "Please," I say, gesturing toward the trestle table at the center of the rush-strewn floor, "sit."

I hope Henry doesn't notice my trembling hand. I've never played hostess. Maman taught me, but of course I only half-listened.

The three of us take our seats as Bart serves a charred beef roast with undercooked vegetables. His form blocks my view, and it isn't until he steps aside that I see the chamber is crowded. In addition to Bart, three other men, dressed in Lancaster livery, line the chamber's walls, waiting to serve. I shouldn't be surprised—it's not unusual for an earl to bring his own servants.

Before I look away, one of the men shrugs a shoulder the slightest bit while holding his hands clasped behind his back. I stifle a gasp. The tall frame, broad shoulders, and haloed outline of unkempt, floppy hair are familiar as my own fingers.

Lord Henry raises a hand, and Geoff steps forward, his shoulders blotting out the firelight. I drop my hand to my belt pouch. I can almost smell the stale sweetness of the dried dandelion flower stowed inside.

Geoff hands the earl a knife for his supper, and our eyes meet. The corners of his mouth quirk up, then he slides back into place along the wall.

Now that I've seen him, my eyes pick out every detail of his face. The strong lines of his cheekbones and nose, the deep cleft in his chin. He wears the red-and-white livery of the House of Lancaster. I've never seen him dressed so fine. He smiles. I widen my eyes, willing him to give some sign of why he is here.

"These events in the east," Sir Thomas is saying. I wrench my attention back to the table. "What do you think of them, my lord?"

"We need to send another representative," Henry says. "Before they march to London."

"You think they could make it to London?" Thomas laughs. "Impossible!"

"It's only thirty miles," Henry counters. "Why impossible?"

"They're peasants. They've no horses. If they did make it, it would take them weeks. But, mark me, they'll descend into chaos and disband before they make it ten miles. They have no military experience."

"True," Henry muses, twirling the knife between his fingers. "But they're united in purpose. That can mean more than experience."

Thomas presses his lips together, considering. "They won't know how to fight, if it comes to it. They're simpletons."

"The peasantry *does* know how to fight," I say. Sir Thomas throws me a glare, and my lips part.

Wives should be seen, not heard. I push Maman's voice away. Now that I've blurted out my opinion, I might as well finish the thought. I glance at Henry, who watches me, eyebrows raised. Not with surprise, but interest. "On the coast," I say, refusing to let my voice quaver, "all men are encouraged to learn, given the threat from France."

"Very true, Lady Prescott." Henry spears a piece of the beef roast.

I try to take a drink—to avoid Thomas's glare—but find my goblet empty. Bart must have neglected to fill it in the confusion of Henry's unexpected arrival. I raise my cup with an encouraging smile.

When he darts forward, my long sleeve slips to my elbow. Joan left my wrists unwrapped because they're no longer swollen, and the colorful blotches seem to glow unnaturally bright in the dark chamber. Henry sets down his knife, eyes narrowing as he takes in my purple fingers and the bracelet of bruises encircling my arm.

He turns to Thomas, eyes sharp and predatory. I freeze as the serving boy fills my goblet.

Henry looks back at me. "What happened, sister?"

Stunned by his use of the familial term, I almost drop the goblet. For a moment I can't speak, and just emit an unattractive grunt. "I fell," I say at last. "On our lodging's stairs."

I've never been able to lie. Maman always says my face is like a window with no shutters.

Henry smells like a smoldering fire—anger—but somewhere else in the room, I smell something violent, like a festering wound. I glance at my husband, whose face is impassive. He chews his meat as if nothing has occurred.

Henry faces him. The Earl of Derby is only fifteen, but he is tall for his age, already built like a man. Of more significance, he's the future Duke of Lancaster. In time, he will be among the most powerful men in the country and the wealthiest. His jaw is set and a vein throbs in his neck. The look he gives Sir Thomas says one thing: *Don't harm her again.*

Geoff takes one step away from the wall. His breath seems labored, and he grips a knife at his belt.

I clear my throat. Thomas will be angry if I speak, but I must change the subject. "What do you think the peasants will do next, my lord?" My voice is small, like a child's.

They look at me, surprised. In the midst of their anger, they've forgotten I exist.

"I know what will happen next," Sir Thomas rumbles, tossing me an irritated look. "The king will send troops and crush them."

"Troops?" Henry chuckles. He swirls his goblet and watches the amber liquid. "What troops, Lord Constable? My uncle just set sail with a third of the king's forces to the Iberian Peninsula, to fight Henry of Trastámara. The second portion of the royal army is in Wales, with the Earl of Buckingham. The rest of the king's soldiers are with my father, fighting the Scots. We are defenseless."

My stomach drops, but after Thomas's glare, I know better than to join the conversation again.

"How can a few hundred peasants threaten us?" Sir Thomas cries.

"A few hundred?" Smiling, Henry eviscerates carrots and potatoes between his molars. "Try a few thousand. That's what my informants tell me."

I gape. Thomas spears another piece of beef and cuts it with abrupt, aggressive movements. I lay down my knife, unable to consider another morsel.

After the meal, Thomas invites Henry to his solar for a glass of hippocras. When my brother accepts, disappointment consumes my husband's face, and the smell of vinegar brings tears to my eyes.

I stand at the foot of the stone stairs and listen to the solar door closing, then lean against the wall, knees turned to water.

Geoff is here in London. In my home.

I need to talk to him, to touch him. Without that, I can't believe he's real.

I whip around and run right into his solid frame.

"How did you sneak up on me like that?" I ask, inexplicably annoyed.

He gives a wolfish grin. "It wasn't hard. You were busy listenin' to whatever's going on upstairs."

"You frightened me. But...but..." I shake my head. "Never mind. Geoff, why on earth are you here?"

He laughs. "Aren't you happy to see me, Dandy?"

At the sound of the nickname, my mouth goes dry. "Of course, of course!" I show my teeth, hoping it looks like a smile.

He pulls me to his chest in a bear hug. At first, I'm stiff and resistant. But when I feel his strong arms, I relax and let him hold me. I bury my nose in his tunic and inhale the familiar scent of horses with the earthy tang of soil and sugar. Beneath it, I pick out the same smell as the night we buried Eldridge—sharp pines covered with snow.

Begrudgingly, I pull away. "Why are you here?"

"You know Henry married the Countess of Hereford's daughter, Mary de Bohun?" he asks.

"Yes, of course."

"Well, Mary just joined her husband's household at Monmouth Castle, in Wales. She's finally old enough. One of her grooms fell ill right before she was set to leave Essex, so her mother sent me in his stead."

"To *Wales*?" Somehow, I can't imagine Geoff so far from home.

He grins. "I never made it there. We broke our journey in London, at Henry's residence. The earl saw me there in the training yard, practicing with me sword, and he took me into his own household. I'm to stay with him an' be a part of his *personal guard*." His chest heaves with excitement.

"His personal guard?" My voice ricochets off the stone walls. I lower it. "And you'll live in the city, away from a manor?" His hair flops when he nods, eyes wide. "Then that means..." I enunciate each word with care. "That means you're free, doesn't it?"

He squeezes my elbow. "I think so, Dandy. I think...I think I'm a free man at last."

I drop my voice to a whisper. "Did he give you papers of manumission?"

"No," he admits, then shrugs. "The earl dinna say as much, but it seems to be understood."

I worry at my lower lip and look down at my slippered feet. If the countess gets word of this, she'll send Geoff straight back to Fobbing. She'd meant for him to belong to Henry's Welsh manor, and without papers of manumission, he's still a villein for a year and one day.

Still, when I tilt my chin to his glowing face, I can't help but smile. "Oh, Geoff. I'm so pleased for you." I try to grip his hands, but wince when his rough fingers brush my bruises.

The joy drains from his features, and he growls deep in his throat. "Yer bruises—" He turns my hand in his to examine the fingers and wrist.

I pull away. "Don't ask me about it. There's nothing you can do."

The intense, festering smell returns. "Did *he* do this to you?"

"I fell, Geoff, that is all."

"You don't fall. Yer the least clumsy person I know." He bends down so we're nose to nose. "I'll speak to the earl. There must be something more he can do."

I've backed against the damp wall, but he's followed me step for step, hunched over with his nose pressed to mine.

The air changes, and what was a cold, drafty castle becomes warm, uncomfortably so. Geoff's mouth opens, and I see his tongue, pink as he leans against me. It darts out to lick his lips, making them dark and slick. I stare, then swallow. My legs and arms are heavy.

I think he must feel my heart pounding a sharp rhythm. In the silence, I feel the beat of his pressing against my breasts. Our rhythms match. My own lips part, and I move closer.

He repels with such force that he slams into the opposite wall. "Dandy," he says, "I—"

Above us, the solar door opens. I dash down the corridor to the main hall.

—

Henry leaves, taking Geoff with him.

My fingers twitch and limbs ache at the sudden loss. Geoff was here, now he's gone. When will I see him again? With the threat from the east, it might make sense for Henry to leave for Wales after all.

I fight the urge to run into the misty night, to chase Henry's entourage and find out if he plans to stay in London. I have more pressing matters: Thomas is upstairs in our chamber, waiting for me. My stomach roils and my feet drag as I climb the stairs.

Rhead streaks past me on his way down, and Joan waits for me on the landing with a steaming mug of tea. I wave her away. This is my problem; she needn't be involved.

"I can prepare myself for bed tonight, Joan."

"Are you sure, my lady?" She glances at the chamber door, apprehension etched on her pretty face.

"Yes, Joan." I force a smile. "I've gotten ready for bed alone for two and twenty years."

She gives a hesitant nod, then pushes the mug into my hand. "Your regular tisane, my lady."

I eye her. "My *regular* tisane, Joan?"

"Yes, the one you like before bed," she says. I lean down to the warm liquid and sniff. Parsley, artemisia, juniper, licorice. My eyes widen, and I take a step back. "It calms the nerves and aids with sleeplessness. Everyone knows that." She waves a hand, but something shines in her dark eyes. A shared secret.

I take a sip. "Thank you, Joan."

She bobs a curtsy. "Sleep well, my lady."

I lift the latch and push open the door.

Be a good wife.

"I am a good wife," I mutter. From the sideboard, Thomas's eyes jerk to mine.

"What did you say?"

"Nothing," I lie. He returns to glaring into his ale goblet.

The smell of his drink, mixed with the herbal concoction in my tea, makes my vision swim. Still, I force myself to take three gulps before he notices me.

Bad wife. Bad wife. Bad wife.

I give my head a little shake, and Maman's chiding dissipates. She's right. Ideal wives don't drink nightly tisanes to ward off pregnancy, but I'm not interested in her opinion. Maybe this is the best I can do, as far as being a good wife. Thomas need never know what's in my tea or wine.

However, the likelihood that I can ingratiate myself to this man, that I'll ever influence him, feels like it is growing slimmer each day.

He looks up again. "Why are you just standing there? Don't you want to come inside our chamber?" His cheerful voice raises the small hairs on my forearms.

I nod and move past him to my clothes chest.

Snatching my bruised wrist, he pulls me toward him. Hot tea splashes over the mug's lip and onto my fingers. I wince. He grabs the mug and slams it down on the sideboard.

"Why did the Earl of Derby come here tonight?" He squeezes me against the sideboard, gripping my sore arm with his long fingers.

"I don't know, Thomas."

"Bart told me your half-brother already visited you yesterday. I had no idea you were so close."

"We aren't." His brows pull together, and I draw a hasty breath, desperate to fix my error. "That is, we hadn't met before he came to Fobbing, the day I met you. However, we enjoy each other's company."

"Did you summon him?"

"I did not, lord husband. I would not."

"What did you tell him?"

"Nothing."

"Then why did he come?"

I glare into his cold, black eyes. We're the same height, so it's a simple thing to do. I itch to tell him to go boil his arse, but stay silent. With an effort, I content myself to letting my eyes shrink to slits of disdain. Maman would be proud.

"This afternoon"—his stare glints in the candlelight—"you were gone. Bart told me."

Ah, now at least I know the identity of one spy.

The notch of his throat works as he swallows. "I know where you were, wife."

My lips go numb, the roof of my mouth tingling. I see my plants, the new cuttings, arranged in neat, careful rows among the Tower's herb garden. If he knows I replaced those he destroyed, he won't hesitate to tear them out of the ground. I just hope he restricts his anger to me and doesn't punish Master Gardener.

"You went to see the Earl of Derby." Thomas yanks my wrist. He twists the bone, and I gasp as fresh pain sears. "Admit it."

Despite the pain, my relief is so palpable I almost sag. He doesn't know about my herbs.

I clear my throat. "I went to an apothecary, at Aldgate. Master William Burton. I needed a salve for my ear."

He releases me but doesn't move. After a moment, he shifts to look at the curtained bed with intent slowness. A block of ice settles at the base of my spine, but I reach to pull at my gown's lacings. I know what is required.

He plucks at the green fabric of my surcoat's sleeve. "Do you have nothing finer, wife? We're not in your little hovel anymore."

His jab renews my anger, his touch hot as cinders. I draw back.

"This wool is fine," I spit and smack his hand, "and cut by Essex's best dressmaker. There's nothing wrong with my clothes, husband."

Oh, Maman, I have failed again. It seems I cannot stay silent, cannot be meek. Thomas steps back and raises his hand, preparing to strike me.

My instinct is to cower. He's the stronger of us and can easily hurt me. Instead, I stand taller. I've already angered him; I might as well follow through. Plus, I can't forget Henry's words the day before. I have power. Although I'm a woman, and a bastard, I've brought Thomas his position and wealth. He wouldn't be the constable if not for our marriage. And I hold his secret. He's afraid I'll tell my powerful family he hasn't consummated our union. I square my shoulders and glare through the dim firelight.

Thomas freezes with his arm in a graceful arch. His chest heaves, and a dribble of saliva drips from his lower lip.

"Ha!" He barks a sharp laugh and lowers his arm. "It seems I can't raise a hand to you, even under my own roof. But don't worry, dear. Times are changing."

I lift a brow, unable to hide my curiosity.

"Oh, you haven't heard? King Richard isn't happy with the duke. And now these uprisings. The people want John of Gaunt dead. The tide is shifting for Lancaster."

He picks up his tankard of ale and pelts it at my trunk. It bounces off the wood and showers me with the stinking liquid.

Thomas strides to the door and wrenches it open. It slams behind him.

Chapter Thirteen

11 JUNE 1381

The next morning, I open my eyes to find weak sunlight streaming through the chamber's arrow slit. I rub my eyes with the heels of my hands. I've slept later than usual.

No wonder—I passed a fitful night, worrying over what Thomas said about my father, while trying to riddle out how I'd explain it to Henry. I must tell him our father is out of favor with the king, but don't want him to know my husband hates our family. After all, good wives don't gossip about their husbands.

I look at the other side of the mattress—his side. The coverlet and furs are pulled up; not a wrinkle has disturbed them.

I avoided paying my marital debt another night, but my reprieve cannot last. An unconsummated marriage is no marriage at all. If anyone discovers he hasn't done his duty, the results could be disastrous for Thomas.

I'm no fool, however. I know that if anyone learns Sir Thomas hasn't taken my maidenhead, my husband will make sure that I take the blame, not him.

On our wedding night, he called me a witch, more than once. In Fobbing, I overheard whispers about men burning witches on the continent. I don't think that's ever happened in England, but Thomas's harsh words, his accusations, still echo in my brain. I remember Eldridge's burned hovel, destroyed after her death. Tears threaten behind my eyes. I wish she was here.

Something makes me jump. I peek out from the bedcurtains and glance around the room. It's shadowy and dark, but I feel it. I'm not alone.

Something moves behind a trunk, and a piece of pottery thumps on the floor.

"Sweet Jesu," a voice murmurs. The form stoops to pick up the fallen cup.

"Joan?"

"Ah, my lady, you're awake." She bustles into the light, arms full of Thomas's tankard and the ale jug from the night before. "I'm sorry, I didn't mean to frighten you. I was just cleaning up."

"Don't worry, Joan. I thought you were..."

For a fleeting moment, sympathy shines in her eyes before she hurries away to deposit the crockery on the sideboard. There, she sees the empty tea mug, its cold contents dripping from the sideboard's edge.

She releases an annoyed puff of air from her nostrils and strides over to peer into my face. Satisfied with her inspection, she moves to my hands. The sight of my burned fingers, where Thomas splashed the hot tea, makes her give a little moan.

"It's all right," I say. "It's quite minor."

"Did you at least drink enough before he did this?"

"Not all of it, but..." I trail off and look at my fingers. Three angry boils bubble among old bruises. "It's all right," I assure her. "It will be all right."

With a sigh, she moves to heave the medicine chest from under the bed. "At least we got aloe at the apothecary. And from now on, I'll make sure the herbs are in wine, or that you get them at supper."

"Joan, you don't have to—" I cut myself short, and she looks up. I grimace. "I don't want you to get into trouble."

She shrugs. "I serve you, not Sir Thomas. You'd be surprised what herbal concoctions other wives take."

I sway a little, unsure what to do, then pad across the floor to the garderobe. Joan opens the medicine chest and digs out the aloe, before moving to my clothing trunk, all the while humming a liturgical hymn.

"The brown woolen gown, today, d'you think? I'm still laundering the blue surcoat, so you can't wear that."

"No, Joan." I lay my hand on the garderobe's door. "I don't think Sir Thomas will like that. He wants me in finer garments." I resist the urge to rub my temples as I tick off my clothing in my head—the green surcoat from last night, a brown houppelande, a simple rose-pink gown—each one not something my husband would approve of.

Joan blinks, clutching the brown woolen cloth. "Sir Thomas departed, my lady, before first light."

"Really? Where did he go?"

"To Windsor. A summons arrived late last night, from King Richard. Sir Thomas left straightaway."

I exhale a breath. "How long will he be away?"

"I don't know, my lady." Joan glances at the closed door. "Cook thinks the king summoned his men because of the peasant uprising. The villeins march to London as we speak."

"I see..." A tangled jumble of thoughts wrestle for space in my mind. Visions of time in my garden without Thomas breathing down my neck give me prickles of excitement. And tonight, I can sleep without fearing my husband will appear at any moment to demand payment of my marital debt.

But then there's worry. The king is so concerned about the insurrection that he's called his commanders to Windsor. What will happen to Fobbing's citizens? Is Maman safe? Henry and my father? The peasants want John of Gaunt dead. My heartbeat quickens, but I squeeze my eyes closed and breathe through my nose. I won't accomplish anything by staying here and worrying, so I resolutely push the worry away and open the garderobe door.

After I emerge and wash my hands, Joan dabs aloe on my burns and wraps them in soft linen. I sit for her to brush my hair.

"Hurry, Joan, I must leave, soon as possible."

Her hand, gripping the hairbrush, freezes in midair above my tresses. "Where are you going, my lady?"

"I must run an errand, on the Strand."

She throws me a questioning glance, but I ignore it. I don't intend to give voice to Thomas's threats for my father's safety, not to anyone but Henry.

I turn to peer out the wall's narrow opening as she tries to arrange my hair. She gives the smallest of sighs. I know I'm rushing her through her duties, but I can't seem to stamp out my panic and nervous energy.

"My lady, a thousand apologies." She tries, and fails, not to look annoyed. Her speech is muffled by the hairpins gripped between her teeth. "But I cannot plait your hair whilst you twist around."

"I'm sorry, Joan." I clutch my hands in my lap so they won't flap. "It's just...I must get to Lord Henry's house," I blurt.

"Ah, but my lady..." Joan places a simple headdress beside my hairbrush and pins. "The king called the Earl of Derby to Windsor, along with Sir Thomas. I heard your husband say it."

I flush. Stupid—of course the king summoned his cousin, the future Duke of Lancaster. I peek at Joan from beneath my lashes. Her face is smooth as she sorts through the pins. I'm glad. I don't want her to think I'm a foolish country girl.

However, I remind myself, my maid's approval doesn't solve my problem. Henry is gone, and I've no way to reach him. Writing is out of the question. I can't explain in a letter without incriminating my husband. Plus, it could be intercepted.

I know Henry's departure isn't the only source of my disappointment. Something else, someone, lurks at the back of my mind and heart.

—

Once dressed, I hurry out Constable Tower's front door, then halt. Joan almost collides with my back.

"My lady?"

I lift a hand, and she falls silent.

An eerie hush hovers over the Tower grounds. Yesterday's hordes of people have disappeared, and now only a few go about their business. A page boy gives me a furtive, scared look as he runs past. Across the inner ward, a sentry avoids my stare.

I shrug. It's a fine day, the warmest we've had this spring. The sun creeps into the sky, shining its soothing beams like the yellow of fresh butter. I'm determined to enjoy it. Near the Tower gardens, Rhead bursts out of a nearby stand of vegetable stalks to chase a rabbit. He disappears again almost before I'm sure it's him.

Joan leaves to find Gardener, a pottery crock full of powdered colchicum root clutched in her apron.

I stop at the edge of the herb garden and inhale, looking over the small plot of land. Freshly dug earth, water, and green things tickle my nostrils. I close my eyes, and for a moment, the dull thrum of noise emanating from London recedes; I'm back in Fobbing, behind Eldridge's cottage. The smell of the salt marsh floats toward me, permeating my skin and mixing with the familiar soil and growing plants of my home.

I'm no longer married to a man who frightens me, I'm not the Lady of the Tower. I'm just Blanche, an outcast in a small village, the daughter of a woman who sees her as a burden and a man she's never met. I'm a healer. I see strange things, do odd things, and no one understands me. Well, almost no one.

I open my eyes and push Geoff from my mind. The Tower's herb garden is still before me. This is my place now, where I belong.

Rows of fresh plantings stretch their slender stems up toward the sun. I kneel to inspect them, pleased with my work. They whisper to me in quiet murmurs. In hushed tones, they tell me they're well. They like their new home. A light coating of rain fell at dawn, feeding them. Their roots have already begun, just nubs on the cuttings, but the essence of them has sprouted. They're on their way.

I resist the urge to respond. No one else can hear the plants, so I must pretend I don't. This is what I've learned over the years. Pretend to be normal. You don't see pulsating, throbbing light when someone is in pain, and you certainly don't hear plants talking to you.

Frantic footfalls skitter behind me, and I turn to find a scullery maid, the one I met in the kitchens yesterday.

"Good morrow, mistress," I say, shielding my eyes against the sun. "How fares Master Gardener?"

She bobs a flustered curtsy. "He's well, m'lady. Not been nearly so peevish as usual since you helped him." She snaps her mouth closed and looks down.

I compress my lips to keep them from twitching up. "Do you need something, mistress?"

A moment goes by, then she shakes her head.

"Tell me. What's your name?"

"Aldith, m'lady."

"Aldith. A lovely name. Mistress Aldith, please. Look at me when you speak, and speak freely."

She peers up at me, gaze incredulous. Her skin, flushed and glistening with sweat, looks thinner than a sheaf of cheap parchment, with tight crinkles at the corners of her mouth. Her gray eyes speak of tiredness and worry, and wispy red hair flies out from beneath her coif. When she tries to push it back into place, her fingers shake.

"What can I do for you, Aldith?"

"It's..." she whispers. "It's me boy. Me son."

I try to hide my surprise. I'm not used to people coming to me of their own free will, and in the light of day. "Yes?" I encourage her. "What is wrong with him?"

"I...I..."

Joan returns to my side.

"Joan," I say, "this is Aldith, a scullery maid."

Aldith bobs a curtsy to Joan, who widens her eyes but says nothing.

"Aren't you going to say hello, Joan?" I ask.

"Um..." She coughs, but nods to the waif-like scullery maid. "Hello, Aldith."

"Aldith was just saying she has a son." I wave an encouraging hand to the maid.

"Yes, m'lady. He's...he's sick." She shoves her hands beneath her apron's fabric and twists.

"What are his symptoms?" I keep my voice soft, yet firm.

"A terrible cough, m'lady. Nothin' I do seems to help."

"Is there any fever?"

"No, m'lady."

"How old is he, and where is he now?"

"He's three, m'lady...and he's in me room in the servants' quarters, with me mum..."

"Bring me to him. I'm sure I can help." I look over my shoulder. "Joan, do you have the herbs? Yes, excellent. Aldith, lead the way." I make a strong forward gesture, but the poor woman looks terrified.

"M...m...m'lady, I couldn't...that is...I couldn't possibly bring you to me quarters."

I gaze at her calmly. "Well, it would certainly be easier for me to visit the boy there—what is his name?"

"Pate, m'lady."

"It's best for Pate if I see him in his own bed, instead of transporting him to my residence." I summon an imperious voice. "Show me the boy, Aldith."

She takes one last look at me before scurrying away. We follow, and I'm surprised when Aldith leads us to a part of the Tower complex I've yet to visit.

"The Salt Tower," Joan murmurs in my ear, "and the Well Tower beyond. They lead to the eastern entrance."

"Are we going beyond the Tower walls?" I ask over my shoulder.

"Yes, my lady. We must. To the Tower Hamlets, where the lower-level servants live."

"Beyond the Tower walls?" I turn to her, skirts swirling around my ankles. "Beyond London's *city* walls?" She nods. "What if the city is attacked?"

Joan doesn't answer, and I must hurry after Aldith, lest I lose her in the maze of towers, walls, and stairways.

Once beyond the eastern gate, Aldith takes us to a meandering sprawl of houses and outbuildings huddled in the Tower wall's shadow. Some of the dwellings, though cramped, are decently well-maintained. Smoke streams from their small chimneys, and savory smells drift toward us as preparations get underway for the midday meal. Many, however, are only huts. They look temporary at best, mere hovels to keep off the wet.

Aldith lives in the largest dwelling, but its daub plaster is crumbling away from the wattle framework, and the thatched roof is patchy.

"I can't imagine what the winters must be like..." I murmur to Joan. A crease has etched itself in the smooth skin between her brows, and she gnaws her lip when a filthy child scurries past, staring at us with wide, frightened eyes.

Aldith beckons us inside the crumbling building and up its rickety staircase. A rat darts by, and dozens more scratch and scrabble through the walls. The reek of humanity is overwhelming; I can't resist the urge to cover my mouth and nose. Unwashed bodies, filthy linen, sickness, and sadness flood the place like a shallow ditch, but when Aldith ducks through a tiny door, both Joan and I follow without hesitation.

She leads us inside what I initially think is a closet, tucked beneath the building's angled roof. Barely larger than Constable Tower's garderobe, one narrow cot is the room's only piece of furniture. On it, an older woman holds a small child. Sunlight dapples her cheek like a wound, sprinkled in from the ceiling's holes, and her stringy gray hair sways in the draft.

Aldith snatches a bucket from the corner and hurries to the window, throwing out its smelly contents. Her face shines bright with embarrassment.

There is no hearth. I wonder again about the winter months and feel myself shiver despite the warm, cloying air.

On the cot, Pate hacks with a whoop that shakes his narrow chest. When I remove his shirt, a soft glowing light pulsates beneath his scrawny ribs. I look into his mouth, nose, and eyes, and I listen to his heart and lungs with a hollow tube tucked in my medicine box. I let out a slight exhale. It's only his lungs, not his heart, nor a fever taking over his brain and the rest of his tiny body.

"Joan, I imagine there's a hearth downstairs. Can you boil water, and plenty of it?"

She nods and hurries out the door.

"The boy's humors are off," his grandmother insists. "We need to find someone to bleed him. Can you do it, m'lady?"

"No, mistress," I say. "That will only make him weaker. We must use herbs to relieve his cough and the inflammation in his lungs. Once it is relieved, he can rest, allowing his body to heal."

The old woman's face scrunches with disbelief. She opens her mouth to argue, but Aldith interrupts her. "Yes, m'lady."

"I'll make a tisane of agrimony, honey, and syrup of mulberries. He'll need to drink as much as we can get into him. And an ointment of mallow, saffron, and poppy spread on his chest will help him breathe."

"Yes, m'lady." Aldith bobs a quick curtsy. "I will make him drink it all, I swear."

I get to work grinding the herbs before steeping them in the boiling water Joan brings upstairs.

Aldith holds the cup to Pate's lips. She makes good progress, and he ingests a decent amount of the warm liquid.

I prepare the salve—goose fat and herbs, mixed in the mortar—and then Joan smears it on Pate's narrow chest while I make a tent from an old sheet. I set Joan to retrieve more boiling water and order her to place a bucket of it under the sheet.

We sprinkle herbs in the water, and soon the little cave fills with fragrant steam as Aldith rocks him.

I make quick work of cleaning up my supplies and repacking my herbs before peeking under the grubby fabric.

Sitting beneath the makeshift tent, Aldith's eyes fill with tears. The boy's coughing has ceased, and he sleeps in her arms. She clutches him tighter.

"I'm leaving some of the herbs for another tisane, and some ointment," I whisper. "Keep using them. The steam tent is the most important. I'll return on the morrow, but fetch me if there are any changes."

She nods and scrubs her eyes with her free hand, leaving a trail of dirt.

As I leave, another woman snatches my arm. She manages a wobbly curtsy. "I heard you was here seeing to Aldith's boy. Me own son has cut his leg in the stables, m'lady. Please, m'lady. Please..."

I give her clasped hands a squeeze. "Of course, mistress. Take me to him."

The cut is deep, running from the boy's knee to ankle, but the blood has clotted and rivulets of it have dried on his skin.

"What happened?" I ask.

The boy—James is his name—starts to speak, but his mother pinches his arm, and he falls silent.

"Nothing, m'lady," she says. "Just a normal injury in the course of a good lad's work. If James's master needs to discipline him, then more the good. Yes?"

I purse my lips. Although the cut is no longer bleeding, it could fester if not properly tended. People have died from less.

"When did this happen?"

"Yesterday, m'lady."

"And what of the Tower surgeon? Why didn't he see to this?" I ask James. His mother starts to silence her son again, but I raise a hand to stop her, gesturing for James to speak.

James watches his hands. "Master de Peel doesn't see to the likes of us."

I set to clean the wound and stitch it up, then make a poultice of marigold, aloe, chamomile, and agrimony to prevent infection. The mother thanks me profusely, but her son refuses to look me in the eye.

Before I reach the door, there's another young woman who needs help. She's successfully delivered her first baby but is so weak she cannot get the child to nurse. I make her a tisane of fenugreek, fennel, and blessed thistle. "To stimulate her milk production," I tell her husband. "And she needs food. A great deal of it." His brow furrows, but I pat his shoulder. "I'll send meat and vegetables from Constable Tower's kitchen later today."

When Joan and I finally make our way back to the Tower in the fading light, we find Master Gardener stalking between the rows of his vegetable garden. He whistles, swinging a basket of spring onions.

"Lady Prescott!" he cries, before dropping into a hasty bow.

"How are you feeling, Master Gardener?"

"Remarkably well!" A flock of birds flies out of the plantings, startled by his shout. I watch them disappear into the darkening sky with sharp cries of admonition. Gardener dips his chin, embarrassed. "I mean, it would seem yer potion helped, m'lady. I thank you."

"Excellent." I pause and glance up to measure the daylight, then realize it doesn't matter. With Thomas gone, I'm my own mistress. I look back down to give Gardener a level stare. "In the servants' village, a boy mentioned that the Tower's surgeon doesn't care for them."

Gardener's face falls. "Indeed, m'lady."

"I found their conditions deplorable. Filthy. Dwellings in need of repair. And the location—how can they be safe if London is attacked? We are at war, with France and the Scots."

Gardener shifts his feet.

"Has it always been this way?" I ask.

"No, m'lady. Not in the old king's time..." He clears his throat.

"Tell me," I say.

He lowers his voice and leans in. "When King Edward reigned, defense were a priority, and the Tower got more money fer upkeep. The plan was to extend the upper servants' quarters inside the walls. But now..." He trails off and looks down, engrossed by his basket of onions.

Another reason to ingratiate myself to my husband. My mind wanders to my nightly potion, but I push the thought away and press on.

"I will speak to Sir Thomas. I'm sure he's unaware, and will want the Tower's staff better watched over." My voice sounds more confident than I feel. Gardener smiles. "Sir Thomas will likely not return to the Tower for a few days, at least. But when he does—"

"Oh," Gardener interrupts, "have you not heard?"

"No, what is it?"

"The constable is due back on the morrow, with the king 'imself."

My stomach hollows. "King Richard is coming to the Tower?"

"Yes, m'lady. Arriving by evening."

"Why the hurry?"

He looks over his shoulder, but no one is nearby.

"Is something wrong?"

He leans forward to whisper over the cacophony of ravens flying over us. "It's the peasants, Lady Prescott."

"From the east?" I can hardly breathe.

"Yes. They're coming."

"To London?"

His head bobs like a duck paddling through the waves.

"When will they arrive?"

He shrugs. "At least a week, I'd say. They've no horses, and progress will be slow. But when they get here, the king must be at his strongest fortress."

"The Tower," I say. Joan and I share a look.

"Aye."

"Are there really so many as they say?"

"A couple thousand, from what I hear," he says. My sharp inhale whistles between my teeth. "Led by three men—Jack Straw, Wat Tyler, and Thomas Baker."

My vision wavers. "Thomas Baker?"

"That's the name." He chuckles. "But I can't imagine a noble lady like yerself knows such a man?"

"No, of course not." My chest burns from my deception. What does Gardener think? That I was raised in some castle by loving and generous parents? No, I'm from a village in the middle of nowhere, more peasant than lady. I grew up down the street from Thomas Baker. His wife, Avice, sold us our daily bread. Then there was their daughter, Cecily. I hope she's staying out of trouble. Eldridge is dead and I'm in London, so there's no one to make her another potion should she fall pregnant again.

I hear Gardener speaking, and with an effort, I pull myself back from the past.

"Many Londoners do be in accord with the villeins," he says. "The mood in the city is dangerous."

"What do these rebels plan to do?"

He leans in closer, voice hushed. "Word is that the king sent them messages, asking jus' that. They said they want to rid him of his traitorous advisors."

"Traitorous advisors? Who?"

Gardener looks down at the dirt and kicks a pebble with his boot.

"Tell me." I leave my imperious tone unchecked. Maman would approve. I hear Joan step closer behind my shoulder. In our brief acquaintance, she's only smelled of soap and sunshine, but now I pick up freshly reaped hay, stacked in the field in the early summer sun.

He watches as more ravens fly over us. "I'm sorry, Lady Prescott," he continues, "to be the one to tell you, but it's lucky the Duke of Lancaster is in Scotland. Those peasants want to string him up."

I press my hand against my chest. "And what of the Earl of Derby, Henry?"

"He's with the king, m'lady. Riding to the Tower."

I worry he'll see my heart pounding through my tunic and surcoat. If the peasants find my brother on the road, they'll kill him without a second thought, and Geoff would likely die protecting his master.

I hurry back to Constable Tower as the evening's sudden cloud cover turns to rain, its droplets pelting with no concern for whom they might strike.

—

The next day, I rise early and make my way to the gardens, where I find Gardener limping among his rows of vegetables. In a complete reversal, he gratefully accepts the powdered colchicum root, while bowing his thanks and praising my abilities.

"I'll see to my other patients, Master Gardener, and then make my way to the apothecary shop for more colchicum root, along with some other herbs I need. My plants are not yet large enough to serve all our needs."

"No, m'lady!" Gardener cries, spreading his arms. "You canna. It's not safe in the city, not now." He wrings his hands. "I've heard that many of London's citizens are roused by these radical ideas. The mood in the city is dangerous. Strike a flame, and the whole of London will burst into a fireball."

"Well, I don't intend to strike a flame," I argue.

He blinks at me, then repeats his previous statement.

The argument continues, and I'm surprised when Joan takes Gardener's side. She flatly refuses to allow me outside of the Tower, as if she's my mother.

"All right, all right." I throw up my hands. "I need to see my patients anyway."

"I'll send one of my lads, m'lady," Gardener says, his eyes kind. "Just tell him what you want, and he'll get everything, without fail."

I request parchment and a quill and write instructions for the boy along with a quick note to Master Burton, asking if he's heard news of the rebellion.

Gardener raises an eyebrow at my scribbling but says nothing, just hands the parchment to a young under-gardener who promises to hurry back with everything I need.

My patients are doing better today. Pate's color has improved; he only has a slight cough, and the women report he slept well the night before. I still see the light shining from beneath his ribs, but it's faint.

"Continue administering the herbs," I instruct them. "If he keeps improving, tomorrow we'll take him outside for some fresh air."

"And you still don't think we should bleed him, m'lady?" Pate's grandmother asks.

"No." I manage a smile. "No bleeding."

Aldith folds something into my hand with a shy smile. "I didn't have much time, m'lady, but I managed to make this for you."

I open my palm to find a pastry, folded into a delicate bow, brushed with egg whites and baked until golden and crispy.

"Apple with almonds, m'lady."

"My favorite," I say. "Thank you, Aldith."

She stands taller, her eyes shining.

I visit the boy, James, who cut his leg. The wound is clean and isn't swollen or foul-smelling. I apply another poultice and tell him he can go back to work if he keeps it clean and covered.

As I leave, Master Gardener's assistant returns with my herbs and a note from Master Burton. Outside one of the ramshackle homes, well away from a ditch containing unknown liquids, I rip the package open, desperate to see if Burton sent word of the rebellion from within the city.

"What news?" Joan squints at the page from over my shoulder. She can't read and seems deeply suspicious.

I scan the parchment. "I don't think he's heard anything we don't already know."

Joan lets a puff of exasperated breath escape her lips, clearly unsurprised. How could anything useful come from a letter?

I read aloud. "He says: *The peasants have gathered followers in Canterbury. They are loyal to the king, but seek to remove his traitorous advisors.* Ah, but this is new, listen: *They're demanding an egalitarian society.*"

"What does that mean?"

"They want their freedom." I look back at Burton's note. "*They want to see all the classes below the king abolished.*"

"What?" Joan's face takes on a ghostly sheen.

"Burton says that they're chanting..."

"What? What are they chanting?" Her words are barely audible.

"'*When Adam delved and Eve span, who was then the gentleman?*'"

Chapter Fourteen

12 JUNE 1381

That evening, a richly dressed child enters the Tower complex, lurching in his saddle at the head of a long, winding column of warhorses.

"Ah," a woman sighs, crowded beside me in the White Tower's inmost ward, "'tis the king."

"He looks like a child," I mutter under my breath. "I thought he was fourteen."

Behind me, Joan sucks in a sharp breath. I take a small step back so I'm even with her.

"Did I say that out loud?"

"Yes," she speaks out of the side of her mouth. I grimace. "Hopefully no one heard," she continues. I lean toward her, expecting to smell rotting fruit and other refuse, but no. Joan smells like soap and summer, like always. She offers me an encouraging smile.

I give a little one-shouldered shrug and turn back to watch. I can't go blurting whatever wafts into my head. Not anymore. I have a husband to upset, a bunch of courtiers listening in, and now the king's here. I suppress an absurd urge to laugh.

Richard's hair is thick and shiny, like his cousin Henry's, but there the similarities end. Everything about Richard is childlike—from his golden curls and spindly legs to his minute hands. He looks like a beautiful doll, not a king. He wears a surcoat of the finest samite, fastened with a jeweled belt. The purple fabric glints in the fading light, along with the hammered gold circlet on his shining curls and the gemstones hanging from his neck and glinting on his fingers.

Behind him, Richard's chancellor Simon Sudbury, Archbishop of Canterbury, sits astride his own courser, his blue coat of arms emblazoned on nearly every inch of the massive beast's ornate saddle and bridle. The archbishop, who inspired hatred over the despised poll tax, is a great bull of a man. He dwarfs his horse with legs like beef shanks, a massively creased forehead, and a bulbous nose. His hand trembles on his reins, ready to reach out and save the little king if he falls.

Behind Richard and the archbishop, I count at least a dozen noblemen. When I recognize the shining hair of my half-brother Henry, a smile stretches my features.

I glance at the back, looking for Geoff, but my gaze lands on Thomas instead. He holds his horse's reins with one hand, the other resting on his thigh. I watch the long fingers, displayed in their arrogant beauty, as if they're only inches from my face.

I force myself to look away.

The king dismounts with the help of a dark-haired nobleman. He walks past us without a word or glance, striding up the White Tower's stairs and through its door like he's the only person in the world.

His noblemen file in behind. When Henry passes me, the corners of his lips twitch up in greeting. I almost smile back, but the smell of rose oil stops me. Thomas is right behind him. Bile rises in my throat, and I resist the urge to wipe my mouth with the back of my hand.

Thomas's eyes harden like chips of flint when he sees me. He gives me the slightest bow, then offers his arm.

On the White Tower's top floor, the kitchens have prepared a feast in the grand dining hall. Against one wall, a huge fire roars inside the biggest fireplace I've ever seen. A metal dome covers it, keeping the smoke out of the room. I wish we had something similar in Constable Tower.

Trestle tables line the large room. A tall dais stands at its head, with the high table. Thomas leads me to the dais to stand behind our seats, only a handful of chairs away from the king's. Richard is no doubt waiting in an antechamber to proceed inside once everyone is assembled.

"Where's Joan?" I ask.

"Who?" Thomas grunts. "Your maid?"

I look at him but say nothing. His putrid aroma makes me long for Joan's fresh, clean aroma and reassuring presence. Without her, I feel alone and vulnerable, even in the hall's overwhelming noise and chaos.

"She'll sit at the back of the hall, or in the kitchen." He grips the back of his chair and stares out into the crowd. He doesn't bother to hide his derisive snort. "I see you're still behaving like a villein. I've half a mind to tell your father."

My cheeks go cold. He looks at me, and I know my face has paled. I hate that he sees my fear, so I look away and press a hand to my belt pouch.

Hundreds crowd onto the benches. The din of voices, dishes, and cutlery echoing and bouncing off the walls makes me want to cover my ears and run away.

Everyone falls silent. I almost close my eyes and sag with relief, but then the king processes inside, eyes straight ahead and chin up. He mounts the dais's three steps and makes his way to the throne-like chair at its center. The canopy of state, made of shimmering cloth of gold, ripples above him.

Next to his courtiers, Richard's childlike features and demeanor are enhanced. He's a beautiful boy, like a cherub, but kings are supposed to ride into battle. This child, my cousin, doesn't appear strong enough to lift a sword, much less joust or command an army.

Disappointment, with its reek of vinegar, emanates from the courtiers lining the hall's lower tables.

My half-brother, Henry, is a few seats down from the king. Though only nine months older than Richard, he stands over a head taller and must be two stones heavier. Already he is an established contender in the tiltyard, his skill at the joust celebrated. The natural comparison between the two cousins is unfortunate for Richard.

Everyone sits, and the hall rings with talk as minstrels play in the gallery. Henry speaks to the man beside him, the dark-haired nobleman who helped King Richard dismount his horse.

Without warning, the dark-haired man turns. Our eyes lock, and a shiver runs down my spine. He's handsome, with arched brows, an elegant nose, and a strong, angular jaw. His mouth, however, is set in what seems to be a permanent expression of disdain. He looks like he's smelled something distasteful and finds the world and everyone in it disappointing.

My eyes narrow on his signet ring. Maman made me memorize every noble house's coat of arms. An arduous task that seemed stupid at the time, but now I'm thankful. I recognize the shield of Oxford—red quartered with gold, framing one white star. He dips his head to me, even as his frown lines deepen.

"Lord husband," I whisper. Thomas grimaces. Maybe I didn't whisper after all. I lower my voice. "Is that Robert de Vere, the Earl of Oxford?"

"Indeed. Married to your *cousin*"—his sneer twists the word into irony—"Philippa de Coucy."

His eyes dart toward a young woman sitting beyond de Vere. I lean forward to get a better look.

I barely suppress my flinch. She's a child, no more than fourteen years old, married and living with a husband. I'm reminded of Emmote Thatcher, her immature figure too small for childbearing. I grip my skirts beneath the table.

Philippa's eyes are so light as to be almost colorless, the irises sparkling like pale aquamarines, some secret lurking beneath their shallow depths. She's sumptuously dressed in a red velvet kirtle and blue surcoat with a high collar, adorned with precious jewelry. Her headdress consists of a simple veil, exposing the front of black hair curled in tight tendrils around her face.

"She seems quite lovely," I say. "De Vere is fortunate in his marriage, to be sure."

Thomas snorts. "Don't tell him that."

I look back at the young woman with inky hair. When de Vere faces away from Philippa, she stares at him, and I recognize her expression; it's the same way I look at Thomas.

I purse my lips and turn away. This feast's gloom isn't limited to Philippa. A pervasive dread hangs over the assembly. Each laugh is a little forced, the attendants' finery is inexplicably wilted.

Behind their hands, the courtiers whisper. "At this very moment," an old woman in a dreary gray gown gossips to her neighbor, "an army of the king's own people marches on England's capital."

"Look at the head table," a knight grunts out of the corner of his mouth. "The peasants want every one of their heads."

The first dish arrives—roasted peacock redressed in its plumes. The king turns up his nose. "Disgraceful," he says, his high, childlike voice ringing. The crowd falls silent. Richard may be small, but his timbre commands attention. "Take it back, and tell Master Cook I expect better."

Everyone makes a show of talking to their neighbor or removing their belt knife, determined not to watch the servants struggle with the giant platter.

Within moments, the servants line the head table with meat, eel, and fish pies. No one touches the pies, not even me; instead, we crane our necks to watch the king take the first taste.

Richard seems not to notice the crowd's collectively held breath as he dips one slim white finger in the meat pie, pops the digit in his mouth. He pauses. Wrinkles his nose. "Send them all back."

My tender ears take in the courtiers' puffs of frustration and the growl of their stomachs. My own grumbles. I hope something—anything—remains long enough for us to eat, and that what the servants can't consume is given to the city's poor. I must remember to speak to the White Tower's cook.

Three more men carry in a ponderous sturgeon, blocking the pies' progress back out. I lean forward to inspect the fish. Displayed on a silver plate, it's been cut into thirds and either roasted, fried, or boiled, before being sewn back together.

I envision the cook sewing the fish like I stitch a wound, and a bubble of mirth grows in my belly. Are we supposed to pretend the fish was born this way? I must have made a sound because Thomas turns to glare.

The servants and courtiers sigh with relief when King Richard tastes the fish and signals his approval. Then he sends it, with a wave of his tiny, jewel-encrusted hand, toward us.

"A gift to my new Constable of the Tower, Sir Thomas Prescott," Richard pipes. "A wedding gift."

Some of the courtiers tap their hands together in muted applause, and Thomas nods. I tremble and close my eyes, cringing as his cold fingers wrap around mine in a harsh grip. Even in the safety of darkness, I feel the eyes on me. The noise of the hall, the thrum, grows to a rumble. Then a roar.

The applause dies down and I open my eyes again. Everyone else looks expectantly at the king, but at the back of the hall, I can still feel one gaze trained in my direction. My focus narrows, and I see Geoff at the last trestle table with a tankard of ale clutched in his fist.

Geoff and I lock eyes, and I smell gingerbread and horse feed. The tightness in my chest loosens. Geoff sees me, knows me better than anyone, yet still likes me. I remove my hand from Thomas's grip and rest it back on my belt pouch.

I watch the king, so unphased by hundreds of curious onlookers. I don't know how my cousin stands it.

You're illegitimate, a cruel voice taunts, rattling inside me like dead leaves blowing on the battlement's cold stones. *You're no cousin to the king.*

The truth hurts. It always has. In Fobbing, the villagers didn't think I could hear them, but everywhere I went, whether in the marketplace or on the streets, it was the same: *She's a bastard. Just a bastard. Plantagenet blood may run through her veins, but it's tainted.*

Richard knows he deserves old King Edward's blood in his veins more than the rest of us. He's a king, not a bastard.

I look back at him, the king, and our eyes meet. I know I should avert my gaze, but I don't, can't. I brace myself for the onslaught of jumbled scents. But there's nothing. Not so much as the smell of fine Castilian soap. He gives a bland smile, and I dip my chin.

Robert de Vere leans forward.

"Lady Prescott, my thanks for helping my servant the other day." His eyes flick to Thomas, and his lips curl into a sneer. Thomas glares, smelling of spoiled milk.

"Of what do you speak?" Richard's voice, at least an octave above anyone else's, rings like a clear bell. An eerie hush spreads over the company.

Everyone stares. I entwine my fingers beneath the table and say nothing.

De Vere looks at Richard, his movements slow and languorous. "Lady Blanche here seems to have a gift." His smile reveals a row of sharp, white teeth. "She's a healer. One of my grooms cut his leg in the stables. Stupid accident by a stupid boy."

My nostrils flare, remembering what the boy's mother had said to me: *If James's master needs to discipline him, then more the good.*

"James," I whisper. Thomas's gaze flicks to me. "His name is James."

My husband's eyes flash, but I ignore it. My insides feel like a lit taper. Coiling tighter and tighter, and fraying fast.

De Vere isn't listening to my mumbles. "...so they sent for the bride." He waves a hand in my direction. "She stitched him up and gave him a concoction to keep the wound from festering. I've never seen an injury healing so clean, and all because of Lady Prescott's herbs." De Vere's words smell like they're tipped with steel. He's pretending at admiration; I sense his malice.

A flicker of interest lights up Richard's sapphire blue eyes. "Really?" he asks.

"Yes, yes." De Vere twirls his knife on the table. "The lad's already back at work."

The air around Thomas quivers with rage, and he reaches beneath the table to squeeze my knee. His long fingers press, drawing blood to the skin with such alacrity I see the bruises bloom in my mind's eye.

"Is this true, Lady Prescott?" Richard's cold stare doesn't waver, and his confident voice allows no refusal. I must respond.

"Yes, Your Grace." I bow my head. "I've always enjoyed working in the herb garden, and I dally in the healing arts."

Thomas squeezes harder, but I keep focused on Richard.

"Excellent!" The tiny king claps his hands with delight. "I must keep you close by, cousin. There is no greater calling than healing a king, is there?"

A shocked gasp ripples through the crowd, and my face burns. He called me cousin. Thomas releases my knee. I feel his hand hover above my leg, unsure what to do. Will he pat me?

He pulls away to cut his fish, but when I glance at him, he looks pleased.

Chapter Fifteen

My temples throb with pulsating misery, and my heart flutters like a caged bird. Thomas said nothing when he accompanied me home after the feast, but now we're back at Constable Tower. His silence can only last so long.

Joan prepares me for bed as I drink a goblet of wine infused with my nightly herbs. When Sir Thomas enters, she hurries out, taking the empty goblet with her.

He blows out the candles, leaving only the fire's ashes, then unlaces his sword belt and tosses the weapon aside. To my ears, the sword hilt's *thunk* is deafening.

In the semi-darkness, he pulls off his boots, hose, and braise. He downs a tankard of ale in one gulp before turning to where I stand beside the bed in my shift. The muscles of his exposed legs are tightly coiled. He moves as though to slam the tankard back on the sideboard, but places it with infinite gentleness on the wood. I flinch nonetheless.

"Husband," I begin. "I must speak with you." My heart threatens to burst from my chest, but with the horde marching to London, there's not a moment to waste. I step from foot to foot, my bare toes cold. "I must address the safety of the Hamlet residents. They're not—"

"I told you no healing." He glares at me.

"I know, but there's something more important just now. The Tower's lower servants, they're in danger."

"Fuck that." He spits in a corner. "I decide what's most important, not you, little laundress. Why'd you stitch up a servant, and de Vere's, no less?"

"I couldn't refuse de Vere's servant. How would it look?"

"How did they know you could heal?"

"I don't know."

His approaching figure forces me against the mattress. I smell his putrid breath and squeeze my eyes shut to retreat into some corner of myself. There, I see the petals of a rose—pink with brown rot at its edges. I reach out, pluck the flower from its stem, and throw it to the floor's wooden planks, in a faraway shadow.

"Look at me."

"No, husband."

I feel his low chuckle pressing against me, even as I arch backward to get away from him.

"You're lucky the king was pleased."

I nod.

He presses harder and sticks his hand between us, rubbing himself.

With an angry grunt, he snatches my hand, squeezing my wrist where old bruises still glow. He thrusts it onto his groin, rubbing his body with my palm.

His smell changes. Putrid body odor and the strong scent of old fish mask the rose oil.

He steps away.

"Go to sleep," he growls, "and say nothing. If you tell anyone, I will kill you. I—"

Below, someone pounds on Constable Tower's front door. Thomas freezes and strains to listen as Bart greets the visitors.

"Can't hear a word," he grumbles. "Too many floors."

"It's Simon Sudbury, Archbishop of Canterbury. Along with Robert Hales, Lord High Treasurer," I say. His eyes flash in the dark. "They say they're here to see you, lord husband."

"You're lying, wife. There's no way you can hear them."

I can't resist goading him. I lift my chin and stare. "Believe me or not, there's only one way to find out."

He grunts as he struggles to dress. He's still buckling his sword belt when he strides out the door.

Rhead slinks from under the bed and rubs against my legs. I hold him to my chest, inhaling his familiar combination of dust and fresh air.

Through the floorboards, I hear Thomas's solar door open right below me. Across my chamber, a narrow beam of dim light shoots from the floor—someone's lit the room's tapers.

I tiptoe over the cold floorboards, still clutching Rhead. He purrs. Used to sneaking through Essex's marshes, I'm light on my feet. I won't be heard.

At the beam, I kneel and inspect the floor. The crack is not big, only the width of my finger, but it expands all the way through the floorboard. It's at the edge of the room, where floor meets rough stone wall. Thomas won't see me, even if he looks up.

Rhead settles beside me to lick his toes, and I press my eye to the crack and watch Bart leave the room.

Thirty seconds later, three sets of footsteps pass through the door Bart just exited.

One, burdensome and slow, is the archbishop. The second man, Lord Hales, walks into the constable's solar with a light, energetic step. The two men, so different in build, smell alike. Even through the floorboards, they're like an old room gone too long without fresh air or rushes. I don't know what that means.

Behind them, a third set of footsteps is punctuated with Thomas's ringing spurs.

I hear the rustle of fabric as Thomas bows. "Your Excellency, Lord Treasurer. Please, sit." The two men settle into seats before the fire. Thomas picks up a pitcher from the sideboard and pours three goblets of wine before handing one to each of his guests and sitting with his own.

"What news, Sir Thomas?" The archbishop takes a gulp of wine.

"The horde should arrive no earlier than Sunday. Probably later."

"Four days."

"Yes."

"How many people?"

"My sources say ten thousand. Though I believe it's less."

Both ministers mumble and sigh. My back twitches with pain, so I sit up, content to listen.

"How can there be so many? How did this happen?" The voice is high and reedy. It must be Sir Robert Hales.

"It happened, Lord Treasurer, because you didn't make the peasants pay their taxes."

"But...I..."

"Stop blubbering, Hales," Sir Thomas continues. "You should have stomped this out when it first started."

"They beheaded my men!"

"Yes, and?"

"Gentlemen," Sudbury's deep, cool voice intercedes, "this isn't helpful. Sir Thomas, the Tower is fortified and ready?"

"Of course. The fortress is impregnable—it can withstand any siege, much less a bunch of untrained villeins. But..."

"But what?"

"With respect, Your Excellency," Thomas says, "there's no army. Outside of the Tower, London is defenseless."

"Don't the lords have men? What of Derby, Salisbury, Arundel, Warwick?" Hales whines.

"They've brought what men they have, Lord Treasurer, which is few. In total, we have six hundred people in the Tower, including women and children."

My chest tightens. One of those men is Geoff. If it comes to fighting, he'll be in the heart of it, against his fellow citizens and villeins.

Thomas stands to refill their goblets, and there's silence as the men drink. Rhead saunters closer and rubs my thighs, purring.

"Where is the king's mother?" Sir Thomas asks.

"On a pilgrimage to Canterbury, thank Jesu," Sudbury replies.

"Really?" Hales cuts in. "That's ironic. I wonder if the horde passed her on the road." He chuckles, the sound like a wobbly chair scraping across rough floorboards.

"Wherever she is," Sudbury says, "I'm glad it isn't here. The woman's a menace. Worrying incessantly over the boy. Makes everything more difficult to control." He takes a sip of wine, sifts it between his teeth, and swallows. "It's fortunate we don't have to deal with Sir Simon Burley, either."

"The king's tutor is a great asset," Thomas responds. "Richard values his opinion."

"Indeed," Hales says. "Don't know why the man had to run off to Bohemia."

"Someone has to escort England's future queen to her new home."

Hales huffs. "Penniless future queen. I still don't understand why Burley insisted on her."

"She's the sister of the Holy Roman Emperor," Thomas growls.

"She doesn't have a dowry," Hales counters.

"She—"

"Lord Constable," Sudbury interrupts, "an exalted match though it may be, it's also an unpopular one. Mark me, it's no coincidence this rebellion started mere weeks after the marriage negotiations concluded."

"It's an investment in England's prestige on the world stage," Thomas says.

Hales snorts. "An investment using money we don't have."

"What's done is done. Anne of Bohemia will be Richard's queen." Sudbury's words carry an air of finality. "Let's focus on the problem at hand, gentlemen. If the threat demands we leave the Tower, there's only one option."

I lean closer and press my eye to the floorboard.

"What's that?" Sir Thomas sets down his goblet.

"The king must rally the Londoners to fight."

Hales laughs. "You say that like we're dealing with King Edward, not his grandson Richard. Edward would have marched out, looking every inch the conquering king, and the Londoners would have begged to fight for him. For that matter, Edward could just have ridden out and told the rebels to go home. They would have paid their taxes, thanked him, and trotted off." Hales takes another drink. "King Richard is another thing entirely."

"He's only fourteen," Sir Thomas murmurs. "He'll come into his own."

"I'm an old man, Constable," the archbishop says. "I remember when Richard's grandsire, King Edward, was crowned. At 'only fourteen,' as you say." He sighs. My back twinges again, and I sit back up. "Edward was, from the day his wicked mother Isabella placed the crown on his head, a leader and a warrior. Lord Hales is right. Even when King Edward was *fourteen*, he would have guided England through this crisis. Richard isn't Edward."

Thomas grunts.

"But," Sudbury continues, "he's all we have."

"In Richard's mind," Hales says, "kingship is his divine right. He believes the people can do nothing but obey him, that it's a villein's duty to listen, as it is his to be their king. That's what Burley's taught him since he was four years old."

Sudbury gives an audible *humph* while I knuckle my lower back. "Well, in this Burley is right. Between us, though..." He lowers his voice, too low for anyone other than me to overhear. "The issue is, it's not Richard's life they're calling for. They're shouting for *our* heads, not his. I don't think Richard cares."

"You'd think he would," Hales puts in, his own voice almost a whisper. "They want to kill his lords. Among them his own family members."

"Most of all, Sir Thomas," Sudbury interrupts, "they want your father-by-law, John of Gaunt." Suddenly, I'm back to pressing my eye to the floor before I even realize I'd moved. "You—"

"It's lucky, I suppose," Thomas cuts in, his voice harsh, "that Gaunt is in Scotland."

He doesn't sound like he means it. A muscle twitches in his cheek.

"You know what they'll do instead," Sudbury says. "Given the chance, they'll tear Gaunt's son to bits with their bare hands. He must be protected. After all, he's second in line to the throne."

Thomas takes another swig of wine. My hands start to flutter and my ears buzz. I shuffle on my knees, trying to creep back to the bed. Then I hear the knock of another visitor at the front door.

I slink back to the crack in the floorboards, trying to smooth my heart's erratic rhythm while quieting the roaring in my ears. In the solar, the archbishop and Hales are wishing Thomas farewell, and the archbishop's deep, resonant voice stops me from ascertaining the new visitor's identity. Etiquette will require Bart to keep the new arrival in the Great Hall until the archbishop departs, so I assume I'll have to wait at least a few minutes. Thomas would be furious if anyone—besides the king—interrupted a meeting with the Archbishop of

Canterbury. Not only is Canterbury the most powerful member of England's clergy, he's also King Richard's chancellor.

I'm therefore shocked when a sharp knock raps on Thomas's solar door. I press my eye back to the crack, but a puff of smoke from the hearth has wafted past, and my view is obscured. I'll have to content myself with listening.

"What the—" Thomas strides to the door, and it squeaks on its hinges as he wrenches it open.

"M'lord," Bart wails. "Please, m'lord, I tried to stop him."

There's a short bark of laughter.

"De Vere." The archbishop's voice is sharp and angry.

Crushed velvet crackles in my ears as someone makes a deep bow. I try to look again, but my eyes burn and smoke continues to cloud them.

"My lords, Excellency." This new voice is silky, sophisticated, yet cold and calculated. "Good evening."

"What are you doing here, de Vere?" Thomas asks. "As you can see, I'm meeting with the archbishop and Lord Hales."

"We were just leaving," Hales whines.

The archbishop's heavy tread and Hales's light one move together toward the door.

"Lord Constable," the archbishop says, his voice echoing in the stairwell, "let's hope your Tower is as impregnable as you claim."

The two men leave.

De Vere laughs. "That seemed fun."

"Interrupting the Archbishop of Canterbury?" Thomas thunks his goblet down on the sideboard. "What's wrong with you? You know Bart would've gotten you a drink while you waited. He always does."

I press my eye to the crack. The smoke has cleared. De Vere pours himself a goblet of wine.

"It's not like I'm a peasant." He throws himself into a chair to drink. "I'm an earl, dammit. And the king's favorite."

"One of these days you're going to get yourself in trouble." Thomas sighs, and someone raps on his door. "Enter," he says.

"Ale, sir." Bart deposits the drink on the sideboard with two tankards, then leaves without even a glance at de Vere, much less a bow.

Thomas pours himself a tankard of ale and sits, sighing deeply once again. The sound is different this time, satisfied and relaxed. "So, why're you here?"

"I've news." De Vere taps his fingers on the arm of his chair.

"Unless you're here to tell me you've discovered an army willing to fight for the king, I doubt it'll be useful to me right now."

"I think you'll want to hear this." He leans forward in his chair, letting the wine goblet swing lazily between his knees.

"All right. What is it, then?"

"The king is considering naming you Master of His Horse."

Thomas sits up straighter. "Really?"

"Really."

De Vere gulps his wine as Thomas watches him, silent. The fire crackles in the central hearth. Thomas swirls his ale and he shifts his gaze to watch the amber liquid.

Another uncomfortable twinge makes my back seize. I sit up and stretch.

"Do you want it, Thomas?" De Vere's voice is low, melodic.

Thomas leans forward, his sword scraping the floor. "The appointment?" There's a smile in his voice, and I smell something sticky and harsh, like camphor.

"Yes, that's what I said."

"Yes."

"Then you must come and get it." De Vere's chair creaks.

After an awkward pause, Thomas's spurs ring on the floorboards. He flips the latch of the door, walks back to de Vere. Then, it sounds... I tilt my head, trying to focus. It sounds as if...

The noises are moist and rhythmic; somehow, I recognize them as indecent. My skin prickles.

The rational voice in my head screams to go back to bed. Nothing can be gained by watching my husband right now. I should leave it alone. I turn, about to creep away.

De Vere groans.

Ignoring the pain in my back, I press my eye to the floorboard. Thomas kneels between de Vere's widespread legs, while the earl, hose pulled down in front, holds his goblet in one hand and presses the other to the back of Thomas's flame-haired head. Jaw hanging slack, de Vere throws back his head and moans as Thomas moves his mouth up and down, up and down, on his—

I jerk upright and stifle a gasp with the back of one hand, then hurry to my bed, praying the men don't hear me stumble. I clamber onto the mattress, curl up with Rhead, and clamp a pillow over my ears, shutting out the sounds of de Vere's pleasure.

Thomas comes to bed an hour later, smelling of costmary, lavender, and the rich satin of a fine doublet.

Chapter Sixteen

13 JUNE 1381

Hours later, something startles me awake.

I jerk upright to find Rhead gone and Thomas sleeping beside me. The room is dark. The fire is smoking ash, and cold dampness surrounds me.

My innate sense of the darkness tells me it's the hour before dawn.

A persistent hum penetrates the Tower's thick stone walls, and I strain my ears to listen. It's voices, the sound of hundreds—no, thousands—of voices. And feet, marching boots, moving our way.

I scurry out of bed with a pounding heart and sneak to the door, then throw my cloak over my shift, grab my belt pouch, and hurry down the winding stairs, shoes in hand. I almost collide with Joan at the bottom, carrying an oversized water pitcher through the dining hall.

She gasps. "My lady, why in heaven are you up this early?"

"Do you hear it, Joan?"

"Hear what?"

"The voices...the marching."

"No, Lady Blanche, I hear nothing."

I chew my lower lip, but not for long. If there's ever been a time to give Joan an order, it's now.

"Joan, go to the Earl of Derby's lodgings." I bend down to put on my shoes. She steps forward to help, but I wave her away. "He'll be housed near the king, in St Thomas's Tower. Bring him to the Salt Tower."

She sets down the pitcher and hurries out the door.

I follow her and stand on the battlements. In the inner ward, a handful of servants go about their early morning duties, and sentries watch at various stations along the walls.

My hair hangs loose, and I close my eyes, letting the breeze pull and twist it around my shoulders. The air feels like a living thing this morning, a persistent presence that refuses to be ignored. It blows from the west, but the sounds, the thrum of voices and marching feet, come from England's opposite coast, from Essex and Kent.

The Tower sits on the easternmost point of London, by the city's Postern Gate. I breathe in, letting the fresh air move into my lungs. I envision it moving into my brain.

Turn toward the east, Blanche. The voice whispering in my ear is Eldridge's.

I obey, holding the breath within the cavities of my head. I exhale.

The wind picks up and shifts, carrying the sounds to me.

They ride the wind's back, soaring atop a flock of wild geese. The birds take me as the wind whips cold in my eyes, my ears. I spread my arms like wings; I'm one of them.

The voices and marching come from two places. I look to the northeast and listen to the first group. With my eyes still closed, I see their feet, tired and caked with mud, yet strong. They trample the earth. They've come so far, united by a determined purpose. They have some horses, but not many. They don't need them.

"Three miles," I whisper.

How many people? Eldridge asks.

I close my eyes and cock my head.

"Twenty thousand, maybe five and twenty," I tell her, eyes still closed. I turn to the southeast. It's harder to hear. "This group is farther away."

I breathe in, as before, and out. The wind shifts so that it blows directly from the noise, carrying the thrum of human beings.

Entranced, I walk to the Salt Tower at the southeastern corner of the wall. The wind builds and my cloak flies behind me, hair whipped in a mad tangle.

"Eight miles," I say.

The sky lightens to violet at the horizon, trimmed with deep blue. At the very edge of my vision, stars still wink and sparkle. I look out over the river, my river, as it rolls in the wind toward the sound.

"They're over the river."

Yes, Blanche, yes. Eldridge's voice, old and cracked, echoes in the wind. *How many?*

I close my eyes to listen, but then—

"Blanche!"

The wind drops to nothing more than a breeze, and I turn.

Henry's boots ring atop the stone wall. A second figure runs a step behind, a taller, older man dressed in royal livery. He overtakes Henry.

"Geoff!"

"Blanche!" He grips my forearms. "What's wrong?"

He pulls me to his chest. My heart jolts as his warm body presses against mine. Henry skids to a halt beside us and stares, eyes wide with shock. Geoff releases me and steps back with an embarrassed cough.

I look down at my cloak, gaping open to expose my thin shift. I gasp and draw it closed before tugging the hood over my hair. I must look like a madwoman.

"Lady Prescott," Henry cries, "are you all right?"

"Yes, my lord."

"Why did you summon me? What's wrong?"

"Do you hear it?" I ask him.

"Hear what?"

"The marching."

He listens. Beside him, so does Geoff. They both shake their heads.

"They're coming, Henry, the rebels. I'm sure of it. They're right outside the city."

"That can't be, sister." Henry's voice is gentle. "They only left the eastern counties two days past. There's no way—"

"You said it yourself. They march with united purpose. Sometimes that can mean more than experienced leadership or horses."

"But—"

"I know what I hear. They'll be here soon. Anyone outside the Tower walls is in grave danger."

"Lady Blanche has always had sensitive hearing, m'lord," Geoff puts in.

"You two know each other?" Henry looks from Geoff to me.

Geoff's face reddens, and he looks at his boots.

"We grew up together, in Fobbing," I answer. "I've known him all my life."

"I see," Henry says. "What precisely do you hear, my lady?"

"Voices, and marching."

Both men tilt their heads to listen.

"Do you have any sense of where it's coming from? Just an estimate?" Henry asks.

I look out at the river. "There are two groups."

"Really? You're sure?"

“Yes, without a doubt. The first is to the northeast.” I point. “Three miles away.”

Henry’s brows shoot up, almost to his hairline. “I don’t think any scouts have returned,” he muses. “I wish we knew how many there are.”

“That first group has about five and twenty thousand,” I say.

Geoff smiles, but Henry only stares. Joan trots up behind them, panting and holding her side.

I face southeast, away from the two men.

“The second group is smaller,” I say over my shoulder, “and farther away. Eight miles to the southeast, over the river.” I point again.

“How many?” Henry asks.

“Fifteen to twenty thousand.”

“Two groups,” he mutters and runs a hand through his ruddy hair. “A total of five and forty thousand. Five and forty thousand? The scouts estimated it was only ten.”

“I imagine they’ve picked up followers on their way. I know they gathered quite a crowd in Canterbury,” I say. “And their numbers will only swell once they enter London.”

“God’s blood, Blanche, you sure are full of surprises.”

Behind him, Geoff nods in agreement.

“Geoffrey, go to the king’s council,” Henry says. “We must warn them—”

“No,” I interrupt, “we must get the people living in the Hamlet to safety. They’re beyond the walls, soon to be surrounded by almost fifty thousand angry rebels. They could be hurt, or worse.”

“What? What Hamlet?”

“The Tower Hamlet. It’s where the Tower’s low-level servants live.” I point toward the small thatch-covered dwellings nestled at the base of Tower Hill.

“Really? They live outside both the Tower *and* city walls?”

“Ye’ve not noticed, my lord, when you approach London from the east?” Geoff asks.

Henry shrugs. "No, I haven't."

"I need your men to bring all the residents into the Tower complex," I say. "We must keep them safe."

"Where are we going to keep them?"

I sweep my arms toward the inner ward. "We have plenty of space, look. There's only six hundred people in residence as it is. There's room for them in the soldier barracks."

"How do you know how many people are in the Tower?"

I pause, hoping Henry doesn't learn that I eavesdropped on my husband's meeting with the king's ministers. "I counted."

He gives a sudden grin. "Wouldn't put it past you."

"Henry, please, you must help." I fold my hands before me. "It's mostly women and children. It's my duty to protect them." Behind me, Joan smells, again, of freshly reaped hay.

Henry's eyes shine and he nods. He looks at Geoff. "Wake the rest of my men. We'll bring the Hamlet residents inside the Tower complex. There's no time for delay."

"Wait," I interrupt. "You yourself cannot leave the Tower walls." He starts to say something, but I raise a hand to forestall him. "You must go to the king's council and tell them what we know about the horde's location and numbers. Only you can do this, not one of your men."

He nods, and my chest loosens a fraction. Although it is vital that the king's advisors are forewarned, I also don't want my brother outside the Tower's walls, not for any reason.

"London is defenseless," I continue. "The Tower is fortified, but the king must try to rally the Londoners to fight for him. This needs to be done much quicker than the council planned, before they do anything else."

"Yes." He runs a hand through his hair again and grins. His excitement over a potential fight makes my stomach clench.

"But, please, don't tell Sir Thomas how you learned this information."

"Why? Your skills are useful. You have a gift, Blanche."

The sight is a gift, but no one can know.

"He won't see it that way."

Henry pauses. "It's your decision."

I nod.

He looks at Joan. "Can you escort Lady Blanche back to Constable Tower?"

She nods her head in vigorous agreement and takes a step toward me, but I look away and grip Henry's elbow.

"Henry." I widen my eyes, remembering our conversation about the early death of his mother, my namesake. "You must take care. The rebels want our father dead."

"I know." He sighs. "It's fortunate he's not here."

"Yes, but they'll...they'll kill you in his stead."

"I'll take care."

"And..." I pause and take a deep breath. "I overheard someone say our father has fallen out of the king's favor."

His nostrils whiten and flare. "Someone? Who?"

"I didn't recognize the man. It was one of the nobles," I lie. I can't tell him it was my husband, can't divulge the terrible things Thomas said about Lancaster.

"Why?" he asks. "What has our father done to make the king angry?"

"I don't know."

He glances toward where the first group of rebels march. "Can you try to find out?"

I stop myself from grimacing. Has Henry seen through my ruse? Does he know my informant's identity? If so, he doesn't know what he's asking of me. Still, I don't want to let him down, or our father, so I nod. "I'll try."

"Thank you." He starts to turn away.

"Henry?" I call. He looks back. "Remember, don't tell my husband."

He arches a brow. "I'd think he'd be proud of you."

"He won't be."

"Very well." He gives a quick bow and trots away. Geoff holds my stare for a lingering moment, then follows his master.

—

The thrum of marching feet continues as we hurry back to Constable Tower. I'm about to make my way to my residence's front entrance, but Joan grabs my hand and pulls me down a narrow stone stairway I've never used. Her light steps become a run, and we ascend another flight on the opposite side of the tower.

"The servants' entrance." She doesn't look over her shoulder as she leads me.

I exhale, grateful for her foresight; I had neglected to consider what Thomas would do if he saw me running about the Tower grounds in my chemise.

The servants' door enters directly into Constable Tower's small yet bustling kitchen. Bart stands at the large hearth, spinning a haunch of fragrant venison on the spit and whistling between his teeth, while Meggy, the chamber and scullery maid, washes a pile of dishes and cookware in a steaming copper basin set atop a table in the corner. From the room's central table, Cook shouts orders to them both over the sounds of bubbling kettles and ringing pots and pans.

The door closes and Cook looks up, beads of sweat glistening on his brow as he kneads the day's bread dough. His eyes widen and he clears his throat. The others go silent.

I stand just inside the door, my cloak's hood pulled up and its front wrapped tight around me to hide my thin shift. I nod and smile.

"Everything smells wonderful, Master Cook," I say. "I went for a morning walk, and thought I'd come in the kitchen entrance to check your progress. Everything is, just as I expected, in perfect order."

He bows. Joan makes her way to a door across the room, and I follow, determined not to squirm beneath the pressure of the staff's eyes. When she opens the door, we both hurry through without another word.

We're standing in another narrow stairway I've never used. Joan places a finger over her lips in a silent signal.

Light from a solitary arrow slit gives scarce illumination. Unlike the tower's main stairs, these don't just ascend; they also go down to a subterranean level I've never seen. I guess the bottom floor houses food storage, and possibly servant quarters.

After one flight, I see the door that must lead to the back of Thomas's solar. A second door, so small as to be almost indiscernible, is built into the opposite wall.

Joan brushes the smaller door with the tips of her fingers, then places her hand on her chest and mouths, "Mine."

The warmth of recognition spreads through my chilled limbs. She's shared something precious with me, but I can't speak. I nod and squeeze her hand.

She tugs my arm upward, but I shake my head and press my ear against Thomas's solar door.

Inside, someone moves, probably Thomas. He rifles through papers before stoking the fire and gulping down a drink. Ale, I imagine. No wonder he always smells of the stuff. I roll my eyes and turn away. Together, Joan and I scurry to the top floor and stop to listen at my own door. No one stirs within.

I nod to Joan and lift a hand toward the latch, but she pushes me behind her so she can open the door first.

When she swings the door out into the hallway, I stifle a gasp. The opening is blocked by a black panel. Joan pushes the fabric aside with one finger to peek in.

"Empty," she whispers, pulling the flap open. She enters behind me and the door shuts with a satisfying click.

She lets the tapestry fall back. It's the shabby one depicting a battle scene, which I've tried not to look at since arriving on my wedding night. I didn't know it concealed a door. What else is there still to learn about my new home?

When we stride into the room, Rhead bursts from underneath the bed and attacks my cloak with a playful pounce. Joan squeals and jumps so high I'm sure she'll bang her head on the ceiling, before clutching her chest and muttering something under her breath.

I giggle, until Joan's red cheeks make me clap a hand over my mouth. She purses her lips, but then a burst of her own merriment escapes, and for a suspended moment, the two of us double over in silent laughter as Rhead rolls on his back among my skirts.

Composing herself, Joan wastes no time.

"Let's get you dressed, quick." She pulls off my cloak and hangs it on a hook. Hurrying my arms into the sleeves of a rose-colored tunic, she makes a soft clicking sound between her teeth when the fabric snags, then jumps when the floorboards creak beneath my feet. Behind us, Rhead meows, and Joan gives another start.

"Don't worry, Joan," I say, voice muffled in the garment's folds. "It's nothing. Thomas is still downstairs."

"How d'you know, my lady?" She yanks the surcoat's fastenings.

"I can hear him."

She sniffs, but doesn't slow her fingers from pinning my hair in neat coils around my ears. She secures my headdress and wimple. "There you are." She pats a coil as if giving her blessing, her expression serene.

"I'd like to check on the Hamlet residents right away. Will you join me?"

Joan nods, and after she grabs my cloak and medicine chest—without my asking her to do so—we head downstairs.

As we hurry past Sir Thomas's solar, its door almost smacks me in the face. I halt, hardly able to breathe. Then I straighten and attempt to school my features into an expression of innocence.

"Where were you?"

"When?"

"When I woke up, you were gone."

My hands tingle, beginning at the tips of my fingers and spreading to my still-bruised wrists. I try to concentrate on holding them steady, but can already feel my fingers tremble. Behind him, the details of Thomas's solar come out of the periphery, jumping into focus. The sideboard, where Bart had placed the wine and ale. The chairs, one for Thomas, one for de Vere.

He stares at Joan. She drops her eyes, and I forget all about what I heard the night before.

I move to block his view. "I went for a walk."

"A walk? Before sunrise?" He stalks onto the stairs, forcing me to step down.

"Yes. Joan came with me."

He glares over my shoulder at her. I step to the side, obscuring her once again and forcing him to stare at me.

"Is this a common practice for you, wife?"

"Yes, of course," I blurt. My face heats. Why, why, *why* must I always say the first thing that floats into my mind? My new husband already thinks I'm mad. There's no need to tell him I'm used to rising before dawn to forage through a salt marsh.

My skin pebbles with the memory. The salty air, the water creeping to meet my bare feet. The damselflies fluttering in my face. Rhead—

"I don't have time for this." Thomas steps back inside his solar.

A bubble of victory swells in my belly, and I hurry down the stairs.

"I'll see you—" Thomas is saying, but I intentionally block out his words, listening only to the clatter of my shoes on the steps.

Chapter Seventeen

Some of the Hamlet's people make loud complaints about leaving their homes, but I stay firm and insist they shelter within the Tower's walls. I remind them that the rebels might attack if they come near the Tower. This puts an end to the objections, but not the nervous glances. They've brought their livestock with them—only about a dozen chickens and one scrawny cow—but must worry they'll return to burned and destroyed homes.

The barracks are well-equipped, and there is plenty of room for everyone. Without much to do, I seek out my patients.

Pate is playing with another boy, so like a normal child that it makes me grin. I still give Aldith and her mother a fresh tisane and more of the ointment, but tell them to only use them at night.

"And there's no need to continue the steam tent," I tell Aldith. "The focus now is for him to get plenty of sleep and healthy food. The kitchen will continue sending meat and vegetables. Make sure he eats some stew, not just bread."

She nods vigorously and smiles.

I find Betsy, the young mother whose newborn baby wouldn't nurse, housed in a cell adjacent to Aldith's. Her face, which was gray and shadowed before, is now flushed pink around the cheekbones. She's eaten the vegetables and meat I had Bart deliver, and the herbs I prescribed seem to have helped. She tells me—with distinct pride—that she's nursed her baby for the last day; I could swear the child herself has doubled in size.

I take my leave of Betsy and her child with the promise to visit them again soon, and to send more meat and vegetables.

I can't find James, the groom who cut his leg, but his mother, a seamstress, assures me her son is recovered and back to working in de Vere's household.

"He must keep the wound clean," I say, "and I'll still want to check its dressing tomorrow at the latest, before removing the stitching in about a fortnight."

"Yes, m'lady." She bobs up and down in a series of awkward curtsies. "Of course, m'lady."

I'm about to leave when she gives me a small square of delicate linen, embroidered with Lancaster's entwined esses.

"I made it for you, m'lady."

"Thank you, Goodwife. I've never seen such a lovely thing." I pause. "Um...for what is it used?"

"The king uses 'em." She puffs up her ample bosom with pride and leans in to whisper, "A *handkerchief*, he calls it. He wipes his nose with 'em, instead of using his sleeve." She chuckles. "We made a dozen yesterday, in preparation for his visit."

"Really?" I stifle a giggle and deposit the token in my sleeve. "Thank—"

My words die in my mouth as her jovial expression changes. She looks stunned, then horrified. All the blood has drained from her face, and her jaw hangs slack. "Goodwife, are you all right?"

Before she can answer, someone seizes my arm and spins me around.

Thomas's enraged face lurches into view from the barracks' shadowy darkness.

"What are you doing?" he asks.

I lift my chin and straighten my spine. "I'm helping these people settle in," I say. "I tried to tell you last night. They were, until this morning, housed in the Tower Hamlets, beyond the walls. They—"

"Why weren't you there?" He's almost screeching, and despite myself, I flinch.

"Where?"

"At Mass!"

I give my head a little shake, trying to understand him.

"It's the *Feast of Corpus Christi*!" he cries, voice rising even higher. "The king heard Mass in the chapel, with the court! You should have been there!"

"I had to see to these people," I say, waving my hand feebly in the woman's direction. She curtsies and hurries away. "Besides, haven't you heard there's a horde of rebels marching on London? They'll be here soon. They—"

"Yes, I heard. Apparently, the Earl of Derby caused quite a fuss this morning, storming into the council chambers and announcing that *somehow* he's been made aware that the rebels are on our doorstep."

"And the king went to Mass?" I don't bother to lower my voice.

"It's...a...feast...day." Thomas enunciates each word with care, like he's conversing with a simpleton.

I press my lips together until they hurt. I will not tell my husband I had no idea it was a feast day, and that I don't care. I'm proud of my newfound restraint, but don't have much time for the sentiment to linger.

"Come." He grabs my elbow. "We can discuss this somewhere more private."

He steers me out of the barracks, almost dragging me across the inner ward, Joan scampering behind with my medicine chest.

I assume we're headed for our residence—my heart grows leaden with each step—but am surprised when Thomas turns to face me in the shadow of the White Tower. In my periphery, I see Joan waiting several yards away.

"You have obligations." His voice is a low grumble. "You're my wife, whether I like it or not. Your place is by my side, especially when the king is here."

I drop my eyes. "I know, husband. It won't happen again."

"I don't have time to impress upon you the importance of this."

Through my lashes, I see his eyes burn with anger. My fingers tremble, and I hide them behind my back.

"I'm sure it will be fine." I try to make my voice soothing, like how I speak to patients when they're in pain. "I'm sure the king will still name you Master of His Horse."

My eyes bulge, and I clamp a palm over my mouth. *Stupid, stupid, stupid*. Thomas's expression goes blank. His jaw dangles and his eyes hood over, his scent passing through a remarkable progression: vinegar, garlic, burning ash.

"How do you know about that, wife?" He pulls me a few steps further away from Joan. My heart sinks lower with each step.

"I...I..."

"You listened at my door, didn't you?" His smell intensifies to a burning fire, then to the sulfur of a pestilence.

"No, no, of course not." I shake my head. "I'd never."

"You little slut."

"Thomas, I don't know what you're talking about."

"Just like a Lancaster. Just like *him*."

Suddenly, his scent shifts again, to spoiled milk, so strong that I know Thomas isn't just embarrassed, he's mortified.

"What else did you hear?" he asks.

"I heard nothing. I wasn't listening."

"You were. No one else knows the king is considering making me Master of His Horse."

"Well, you must be wrong. A White Tower scullery maid told me, so clearly word has gotten out."

He stares at me and then looks over his shoulder, as if worried someone is listening. With a jolt, I realize he can't—won't—simply ask me if I heard him pleasuring de Vere with his mouth. He'll never admit his guilt. Such a crime—two men together—is punishable by death. It doesn't matter if one is an earl and the other the Tower's Constable.

So, I don't plan to tell him what I heard, nor anyone else. Not even Joan. If I did, if word got out about Thomas and de Vere, they could be killed, executed because they're different.

That would make me a widow. *Don't I want to be rid of Thomas?* I ask myself, and I realize: Yes, I do. But not like that. I can't end my marriage—end Thomas's *life*—because he has a secret, because there's something about him that makes him an outsider. I've been ostracized my whole life. I know how it feels to be unlike the others, and I can't fault Thomas for that, much as he's ruining my life.

He takes a deep, shaky breath, then exhales through pursed lips. "Look. You're going on the royal barge. In one hour. You can't wear this." He flips his long, elegant fingers at my sleeve, the gesture dripping with disdain.

I'm too relieved he's changed the subject to be angry. "What? The royal barge? Why?"

He sighs, pinching the space between his brows. His shoulders slump, and for a strange moment, I find myself wanting to reach out and comfort him. Now that I'm over the shock of seeing two men together, to know the truth is almost a relief. Although my marriage will never be a loving one, maybe we can form a partnership. Two outsiders, holding our secrets against the harsh glare of the world.

"What is it?" I ask again.

"The councilors have decided there's no choice but for him to meet with these rebels."

"Him? The king?"

Thomas doesn't answer. He releases the bridge of his nose and glares at me. I wait for him to respond, knowing he won't. Knowing I'll have to carry on as if I didn't ask a question.

Sweet Jesu, I was wrong. I hate him. There's no hope for this marriage.

"And they're going by barge?" I say at last.

"Yes. The hope is that it will be safer. Our scouts have confirmed the rebels have no river craft."

"The priority should be rallying the Londoners to the city's defense. There are at least five and forty thousand rebels. Without the help of London's people, we don't stand a chance."

"I've advised the king that Henry of Lancaster's report can't possibly be correct. There can't be that many peasants—we should be fine, whether the Londoners fight with us or not. The rebels won't even have decent weaponry."

"Henry's numbers are correct, Thomas. He got them from..." I swallow. "...a reliable source. If the king can't count on London's citizens, we're lost. And you'd be surprised what kind of weapons—"

Thomas growls deep in his throat. "I don't care about Lancaster's sources."

I suppress the urge to run to the king and tell him what I witnessed between my husband and de Vere. God's wounds, I could never be so cruel, but it's fun to consider. I take a slow, calming breath before opening my mouth to speak. "Fine. The king is to speak with the rebels. I still don't understand why I must go."

"Your cousin the king has asked for you. He wished to see you after Mass, but we couldn't find you." He grits his teeth. I dip my chin, playing the penitent bride. "He wanted to speak with you about an intestinal complaint. He's quite interested in your healing and wants you with him, in case he has need for it."

"Are you going?"

"Yes." His eyes cut toward Joan. "Take your lady to Constable Tower and dress her. You must hurry, and make sure she's in her finest robes."

Thomas strides away without another word.

After Joan and I rush back to my chamber, she dresses me in the bright yellow tunic and green surcoat I wore for my wedding.

"I think this is fine enough, even for Sir Thomas," I say, smoothing the shiny satin under my fingers while she pins a veil atop my coiled braids.

Joan opens her mouth to respond but is interrupted by a commotion from beyond the arrow slit.

I lunge forward to peer out. Joan clucks her tongue but moves with me, struggling to keep my veil from snagging on the hairpins.

"Lower the drawbridge!" The shouted command echoes across the ward.

"Men are running toward the east," I say to Joan.

"Someone's entering from the eastern gate?" She leans down to squint through the opening. "That's odd."

I nod, looking at her as I listen.

Another voice rings from the eastern side of the Tower complex: "Make way for the king's mother!"

Joan's dark eyes widen.

"The Dowager Princess of Wales?" I ask.

"It can't be." Joan shakes her head. "She's on a pilgrimage to Canterbury."

Chapter Eighteen

I hurry toward the king's water gate, lugging a leather bag full of ground herbs and other medicinal supplies. Joan trots behind, trying to hold up the hem of my ornate surcoat, but we both know there's no way to save it from the Tower's constant dust and grime. The sun beats down on us, and an uncomfortable trickle of sweat runs between my shoulder blades.

Shouts reverberate through the otherwise quiet inner ward. Based on the racket coming from the eastern entrance, no one expected Joan of Kent, King Richard's mother, and her arrival isn't going smoothly.

A squire with a hooked nose and freckles runs by, heading away from the gate. I grab his sleeve.

"What's happening, boy?" I ask. Joan skids to a halt behind me.

"The king's mother, the Fair Maid of Kent, she's here!"

I keep holding onto him so he can't dart away. "Do you know why she's here?"

"Why yes, m'lady. She wants to be with her son, with the rebels marching, so she jumped in her whirligig and rode straight here." He puffs up his chest with pride after his little speech.

"Well, what's with the commotion?" I let go of him as Joan stands on her toes, trying to see the water gate.

"She rode through the rebels' encampment at Blackheath, m'lady."

"What?" Joan and I cry in unison.

"Yes, m'lady!" His chest expands further. "'Twas the fastest route. They seized her, and—"

"They'd never hurt the Princess of Wales!" I gasp.

"Nah, m'lady. They just kissed 'er!"

"No." My bag slips off my shoulder, and I let it fall to the dust. Beside me, Joan's jaw drops.

This boy must be joking or misinformed. It would be an epic scandal if rebels hurt the king's mother. But to *kiss her*? I'm not sure I'll ever recover from the shock of it.

A gurgle of laughter swells in my middle, and I press a fist to my mouth. Even with everything consuming my mind—fear for my brother's safety, anger over the disastrous state of my marriage, the perilous safety of the Tower's people, a desperate need for Geoff's company—for a brief instant all I want to do is run to my chamber and write Maman. This is a story she needs to hear.

I must have heard him wrong. "The peasants kissed the king's mother?" I ask, eyes watering.

"Aye." The squire nods, suddenly solemn. "The world's gone topsy-turvy."

"On her mouth?"

The boy scrunches his nose. "Well, I assume so, m'lady."

He turns on his heel and scampers away. Joan and I watch him go, both of us silent.

When I look at Joan, I burst out laughing. She shakes her head. "I don't believe it, my lady. Not for a minute. Even Kentish rebels would never do such a thing, not to a great lady like the king's mother."

I fan myself with one hand and look around. Men scurry toward the water gate, and Joan and I watch them, still unmoving.

"I doubt we have much time, my lady," Joan says. "It's been nearly an hour." Nevertheless, she doesn't move. After a weighty pause, she grips my sleeve. "Do you have to go? Maybe the king will change his mind."

My heart flutters. "Surely the rebels won't harm the king. I'll be safe. But you must stay here."

She shakes her head and the corners of her mouth tremble. "I'll go with you, my lady."

"No. Sir Thomas will be on the barge too. Stay here, Joan. Someone needs to make sure the Hamlet residents are settling in."

She nods and takes my arm in gentle fingers. Within moments, we're swept up by the crowd rushing toward the royal apartments. Ahead of us, I see my husband, Sir Thomas, followed by the Archbishop of Canterbury, Sir Hales, and the Earls of Oxford, Salisbury, Warwick, and Arundel.

When we get to the top of the outer ward's steps, the men stop abruptly.

"Princess," my husband murmurs, bowing to the tallest woman I've ever seen. Around him, the other men bow, and Joan and I sink into deep curtsies.

I straighten, fast as I dare, because I'm desperate to see her, the most powerful woman in England.

Joan of Kent, Princess of Wales, became a widow when her husband, Prince Edward of Woodstock, died of a wasting sickness. Their only surviving son, Richard, was nine at the time.

The Prince of Wales—my uncle—was a famous warrior and renowned leader. Before he contracted the illness that killed him, while fighting alongside my father at Nájera in Castile, he conquered much of France and even captured its king, imprisoning him here in the Tower.

He was supposed to be king right now, and I can't help but think we'd be safer with him at the helm. At only sixteen, he led the vanguard in the Battle of Crécy, was unhorsed, and fought for his life beside his men. When his father, King Edward, was told his son and heir was in danger, he laughed and refused to send a single soldier to assist. He said, "It's time my son earned his spurs."

And he did. Edward of Woodstock won a glorious victory for England that day.

We're in a different time now, with a different king. King Edward and his prince are both dead, and Richard sits on the throne, barely big enough to balance the crown upon his golden curls.

I gaze at the Dowager Princess. Standing above the men, her clothing is luxurious, if rumpled. A berry-red surcoat drapes her voluptuous frame, and gemstones of every color decorate her fingers and neck. Her violet wimple covers her from forehead to chin, and her face, although clearly once beautiful, is pinched and strained. Blue eyes, like her son's, flick back and forth with nervous energy, deep-set under fair eyebrows.

In her youth, she was reputedly the loveliest woman in England, but one plagued by scandal. Before marrying the Prince of Wales, rumors say she was wed to two men at once.

Right now, though, the Dowager Princess looks more like a middle-aged, nervous mother than a noble temptress. She stands anxiously watching the stairs, no doubt waiting for her son to appear. The nobles around her try to speak, but she acknowledges none of them.

"Where is my son, the king?" she speaks over their fluttering voices, and silence falls.

"He's on his way, Your Grace," the archbishop says, bowing again.

"Was this your idea, archbishop?"

"It is the council's plan, Your Grace." Archbishop Sudbury, the largest man I know, seems to shrink before the Dowager Princess.

She sniffs. "I can't help but think it would make more sense, and be safer, for my son to meet with London's aldermen, and the leaders of its guilds. With support from the guilds, he'd have all London behind him. The rebels wouldn't stand a chance."

"*We* feel he first needs to meet with the rebels," Sudbury growls. "Once they see him, once they speak to your noble son, their king, they will know their duty and return to their homes."

"Securing London's citizens, to make sure they don't side with the rebels, must be the priority."

I take a step toward her. This woman's talking sense. Surely the king will listen to his mother if she has a chance to speak to him.

"I am told you planned for ten thousand rebels, arriving three days hence," the princess continues, her tone that of a hostess bemoaning the rude behavior of a dinner guest. "Yet here they are, today, fifty thousand strong with ranks swelling by the moment. How can I trust your plans, given your past performance?"

"I...I'm sure, Your Grace—"

"How can you ensure my son's safety?"

"He'll be in a barge, out of the peasants' range. They have no boats. Besides, they won't harm him, we're certain." The archbishop clasps his hands before him.

"But you plan to land on the shore and have the king talk with these people, do you not?"

"He...well...I suppose..."

The Dowager Princess seems to grow taller. "Yes or no, archbishop?"

"Yes, Your Grace, that is the ultimate plan. But if there is any sign of danger—"

"I will accompany him."

She moves toward the boat, and Sudbury and the other councilors shift from foot to foot.

"Your Grace," he says, "we fear that if you do, your—ah—*luminosity* will distract them and infringe on the king's negotiations."

"She'll take over, is what he means," I hear the Earl of Salisbury mumble to the Earl of Warwick, who stands beside him. "Richard is next to useless on a good day, but with his lady mother nearby, he becomes a bona fide mute."

Warwick grunts his assent. His eyes meet mine, but he looks away after a moment, unaware I can hear.

"No, no," the princess is arguing with the archbishop, and I drag my attention back to her. "If I'm not there, how can I guarantee his safety? He's just a boy. He needs a woman there to care for him."

Sir Hales steps up beside Archbishop Sudbury and bows. "Lady Prescott is to accompany him, Your Grace. She is family, after all, and a skilled healer. She will be responsible for his safety."

The blood drains from my face with a cold rush. I've gone from provincial outcast to Lady of the Tower, to the woman responsible for the King of England over the course of a week.

The princess glances around. "Lady Prescott? Who is she?"

I step forward, feet leaden with dread, and sink to my knees. "I am here, Your Grace." I try to keep my voice steady, but it trembles along with my fingers. I hide them in the folds of my skirts. "I am Sir Thomas's wife, and the Lady of the Tower."

"The natural daughter of John of Gaunt, Your Grace," the archbishop murmurs in her ear.

"Ah, I see." Her expression warms. Despite my father's treasonous reputation among the commoners, rumors say the Dowager Princess loves the Duke of Lancaster like a brother. She takes my hands in her own and raises me up. Her fingers are soft, yet cold.

She keeps hold of me. "And you are a healer, my lady?"

"Yes, Your Grace."

"Are you a mother?"

"No, Your Grace."

I can almost sense the crowd leaning forward, expecting my next words. For young, newlywed women, there's only one answer to this essential question: *Not yet.*

But for me, the words curdle on my tongue.

That's what I'm supposed to say, to think, to *be*. But I can't. No matter how much I may try to be a good wife, I will never be a mother. So, I allow myself a small rebellion, and say only, "I will watch over the king as if I am."

I look into her eyes, azure and bright as a cloudless sky. I've never met a woman who stood taller than me, and I'm not sure I like the experience. She holds my gaze for what feels like five minutes. I try not to fidget.

At last, she nods. "I will stay here," she announces to the group, as if it were her own idea, "and await my son's return."

She looks back at me. "I trust you, Lady Prescott, with my son and king."

I nod, but apprehension rushes through my veins like sudden poison. I'm considering this oppressive weight of responsibility, wondering if I've made a massive mistake, when everyone sinks to their knees, even the princess. The suddenness is startling, and my head reels, but Joan yanks me down before anyone notices.

The young king walks by, his golden surcoat, trimmed in ermine, floating on the wind behind him. Beneath it, he wears a long tunic of green damask, the pattern resplendent with little R's topped by a crown. His circlet rests on his curls. Both the gold of the crown and of his hair shine, even though there isn't much sun. The crown's uncut emeralds and diamonds wink at me, and a ruby the size of a pigeon's egg hangs from his neck.

From my knees beside Princess Joan, I watch Richard's eyes land on his mother. He looks at her with a half-lidded gaze, gracing her with nothing more than a nod. Her shoulders hitch slightly.

I rise along with everyone else and face the Dowager Princess. She nods to the barge. I follow King Richard without another word as Joan watches from the river gate's steps, wringing her skirts in tight fists and clenching her jaw. I know Thomas is right behind me. I can smell him.

The large, flat-bottomed boat is red and white, its sides and stern are embellished with dancing, roaring lions made of carved wood. Covered in gold leaf, each lion's head is encircled with a wreath of laurel and roses. Fat angels, naked but for light golden fabric draping their loins, lounge upon the lions' backs and flanks. Cloth-of-gold curtains hang from a canopy over the royal seats, lined with red tassels and pinned back with blue pennants of Saint George.

Four additional boats bob behind us, without bright decorations or gold leaf. They're full of soldiers for the king's protection.

Most of the king's nobles and ministers are present, but not Henry. Our father is so widely detested that everyone knows it's too dangerous for his son to leave the Tower. His height and red-gold hair make him too recognizable.

Beneath the royal canopy, Archbishop Sudbury waits on a red satin cushion. His smile looks more like a grimace. He gestures to us. "Please, Lady Prescott, sit." He waves to the cushioned seat to Richard's right. "The king wishes to keep you close, my lady."

Richard doesn't glance up when I approach. I wonder about his choice of attire. The common people want to admire their king, true, but he could achieve that without the circlet or ruby. These people can't feed their children. They work for a manor lord who owns them, directing every aspect of their lives. Sometimes manor lords even force villeins to marry. Children mean more workers for their fields, more money in the lord's pocket.

Now, the king wants to make the peasants pay a poll tax of one shilling per person over fifteen years old. A plowman or a shepherd earns about thirteen shillings a year, so if that man has a wife and five children, he'll pay over half his income to finance a decades-long war in France. Then there's the rent due to the manor lord, along with any other taxes. And all the while their king drips in velvet and jewels. One stone from his finger—one stone—could feed Fobbing's peasants for heaven knows how long. A year, maybe more.

The memory of Hawise Groom, Geoff's mother, swims before my lowered lids. I see her face, wan and angular after that rainy, cold summer. Starved, along with her husband, Ceadda, and son. When Hawise and Ceadda died, the manor lord demanded Geoff pay him another tax. How do these people expect the villeins to survive? How can anyone live under such injustice?

Beside me, Richard absently twists a ring around his index finger.

Last night at the banquet, I overheard Sudbury argue that the tax is for everyone. The lords also pay one shilling per person. However, that shilling is a minuscule percentage of their overall income, earned on the backs of other humans.

Robert de Vere sits on the king's left-hand side, eyes half closed with boredom. He and Thomas have not made eye contact.

Most of the men here know nothing about the common people. I, however, have lived among them, delivered their babies, and healed their wounds. Yet no one asks for my opinion. I'm just a woman.

The last noble seats himself, and the oarsmen push off from the wharf, dipping, pulling, and thrusting their oars to the rhythm of the drummer's steady beat downriver to Rotherhithe. Some of the men start to chatter, their low voices hidden beneath the foam of the waves and slap of the oars—hidden to anyone but me.

"They're saying the nobility isn't ordained by God. That our class system is a creation of men," the Earl of Salisbury murmurs to the Earl of Warwick, clenching fists in his lap.

Warwick picks at an invisible piece of lint on the blue sleeve of his fine woolen surcoat. "More about Adam and Eve, and how they were spawned or some such?"

Salisbury stifles a chuckle with a belch.

From the seat behind them, the Earl of Arundel leans forward. "It's no laughing matter," he whispers. "They want to kill the nobility. All of us."

"The king will calm them and send them home," Warwick mumbles back.

I look at the four boats following us. The sun peeks out, and the men's weapons glint across the water: long swords and pikes on one boat, long bows on the second and third, and crossbowmen, ready and attentive, on the fourth. A chill runs up my arms.

Contrary to what these earls and the archbishop think, the rebels aren't in awe of the nobility. The men on this boat with me think the rebels want to bask in the glory of their king, just like they think I'm nothing more than a bastard daughter who is thankful for a good marriage.

The nobility can't imagine anyone like us would fight for a better life, not even when we're pushed into an impossible situation with no options. The rebels will see the armed men behind us and think we mean to hurt them. They'll fight to defend themselves. However, once we provoke them with these few shiploads of soldiers, we can't back up our threats. The king has yet to secure the Londoners' support. We're defenseless against these hordes; our soldiers are elsewhere.

I glance sideways at my husband. He's still puffed up with pride. I look the other way, across the king to Robert de Vere, who stares at the shore. They don't appear worried that we'll frighten the rebels into a fight, only to find ourselves outnumbered and backed into a corner.

A new thought snatches my breath, exploding like a dandelion puff in my brain. If the peasants abolish the nobility, everything in our world changes. What will stop me from leaving Thomas then?

"We've arrived, Your Grace!" Sudbury's shout brings me back to the real world.

Every head turns to the riverbank, and every jaw drops. The rebels are shoulder to shoulder, men and women both, not wearing the tattered, dirty clothing I'm sure the noblemen expected, but dressed in clean—if plain—clothes and standing in orderly lines. We gaze at their colorful pennants fluttering in the breeze and their banners of Saint George, but soon, most eyes move to their gleaming armor and weapons. Just like the men crammed into the four barges behind us, the rebels' clothing is covered with hammered armor and their gauntlets grip swords and pikes in work-hardened hands.

"Armor? Swords?" a nobleman whispers to his neighbor.

"Yes," the other man responds. "And their ranks...organized. How did they do it?"

"And it would appear they brought their wives."

I squint, trying to see the women's faces. They're carrying weapons and wearing armor just like their male counterparts. Are there women from Fobbing among them? Has Avice Baker come with her husband? Is Cecily here? It seems the squire was right; the world has gone topsy-turvy, and in this new reality, anything seems possible.

"Your Grace." Thomas leans past me to speak to the king. "There are only ten thousand. The Earl of Derby's report of up to fifty thousand must be incorrect."

I grab my husband's sleeve. "No. Henry—um...the earl, I mean—wasn't wrong." Thomas glares at me, reeking of disdain. "Don't you see?" I shake his arm, still gripping his sleeve. "The riverbank is too small for all of them. The other forty thousand—maybe more by now, with the Londoners joining them—"

Thomas's jaw drops, and behind us, the other men gasp; I guess I wasn't supposed to bring up the Londoners' duplicity in front of the king.

I plow on. It's his fault for not meeting with London's aldermen before boarding his gilded barge. "The other rebels are surely preparing to take the Strand, the city, the Tow—" I gulp. Even I can't bear the suggestion that the rebels could take the Tower. "All while we sit here, rocking on a boat."

Thomas stares at me, face pale with rage and lips pressed into a thin line.

"I'm sure Sir Thomas is correct," Salisbury says to the king. "There must only be ten thousand."

The other lords nod in agreement. I suppress a groan.

De Vere leans forward. "Your Grace," he murmurs, "the rebels' numbers are irrelevant."

I open my mouth to argue, but Thomas grabs my sore wrist and squeezes.

"The point," de Vere continues, "is that you cannot disembark. It's too dangerous."

Richard's eyes dart back and forth nervously. "But...I...I..." he stutters.

Sir Thomas begins to stand. "Let's go."

"No," Richard says.

Each and every one of the barge's occupants—even me—stares at our child-king, open-mouthed. Ignoring us, Richard stands and moves to the edge of the barge.

The rebels recognize him in an instant. They emit an inhuman roar, like the Tower's lions, and bang their pikes and standards on the ground, yelling themselves hoarse with glee. Richard takes a minute step back. I resist the urge to clap trembling hands to my ears. To anyone, the sound is deafening. To me, it's torturous.

Richard raises his hand, and the rebels fall quiet.

"Sirs," he calls out. Though high and childlike, his voice is clear and strong. I am impressed and take in a breath that feels like the first of my life. He raises both hands. "Tell me what you want."

They scream their demands. It's a jumble of vocal humanity, and I can't make out one syllable from another. Richard looks at de Vere and the Earl of Salisbury, who's moved to stand beside him. No one utters a word.

The crowd grows quiet as one man moves to the water's edge; the river laps at his leather boots, more finely crafted than anyone expected.

"Your Grace," the man shouts, "'tis I, Wat Tyler, the leader of this humble group of English commons."

The nobles shift in their seats for a better view, and a few mumble to their neighbors. Tyler isn't tall, but he is strong and wearing good, stout woolen garments that are clean and well-cut. He removes his green felt hat and presses it to his heart before sinking to the ground. His tunic is soaked in moments.

The other rebels follow suit and drop to their knees in the water and mud.

"We wish you to land," Tyler shouts, "where we will remonstrate with you and tell you more at our ease what we want."

Salisbury scoffs. "Gentlemen," he calls, "you are not properly dressed, nor in fit condition for the king to talk with you."

The rebels' hushed silence buzzes in my ears. I stifle a sob. Any hope of diverting violence is gone.

The silence only lasts a few moments. Salisbury has hardly stepped back from the railing before the horde releases a frustrated, guttural yell. They raise their pikes and swords and thrust them in the air, calling for the ministers' heads. They make a chant of it: Archbishop Simon Sudbury of Canterbury, Sir Robert Hales, and most of all, John of Gaunt.

The rich scent of terror emanates from our barge, overpowering anything from the Thames.

"Depart!" Archbishop Sudbury calls to the oarsmen, his pudgy face devoid of color. "Row!"

The drummer pounds his sheepskin membrane, and the oarsmen make one stroke before—

"No!"

We all stare at Richard. He stands at the barge's edge, looking over the water toward the rebels. I grip the edge of my cushion, knuckles white. We can't wait here; every second of indecision and confusion will enrage them more.

The boat floats, water lapping like a lazy dog against its hull, while the king opens and closes his mouth, silent. The rebels fall silent too, but after a full minute, they renew their calls for his ministers' heads.

"Give us the traitors!"

"Traitorous advisors! Sudbury...Gaunt...we have no king named John!"

"Give us Gaunt's son—Henry of Lancaster!"

Bowstrings tighten on the neighboring barge, but the rebels' shouting only increases. They bang their longswords on trees or against their shields, anything to make a racket, and take up a propulsive rhythm, chanting, "Traitors! Traitors! Traitors!" over and over. The sound of metal on metal rattles my blood. Unable to bear it, I cover my ears.

I watch with terror, sure that at any moment a rebel longbowman will take my young charge through the chest. I picture the Dowager Princess's pastel blue eyes, gazing into mine with the possessive pleading only a mother can master.

With my hands still on my ears, I watch de Vere murmur something in the king's ear. He caresses the king's shoulder, his embrace intimate.

Richard gives a quick nod.

"Row!" de Vere calls. "Return to the Tower!"

We set off as the rebels scream and run along the shore, heckling and shouting curses all the way.

"Sweet Jesu," I murmur, feeling nauseous. The smell of fear, pungent as overripe manure, threatens to overwhelm me.

"Don't fear, wife." Thomas grips my arm, his face drawn and pale. "We'll be back at the Tower soon."

His concern for my well-being only makes my stomach churn more.

Chapter Nineteen

Our landing at the Tower's water gate is sloppy and rushed. Thomas stands before we stop, intent on helping the king disembark, but when the bow bumps against the wharf, he stumbles, falling with a muffled curse. He pops back up, doublet wet and wrinkled, then hurries the king off the barge before the hull even scrapes the water gate.

What was this morning a steady and measured royal progress is now a frenzied hustle inside. Although everyone is intent on first getting Richard within the Tower walls, once he's through, men pour out of the barge like rats fleeing a flood. Not a single nobleman stands aside to let a friend go first. Although I'm the only woman, I'm allowed no priority, and slip in haphazardly toward the back of the group.

The last man's eyes dart over his shoulder as he slams the gate behind him. It's quite unnecessary—the men-at-arms still haven't disembarked from the four additional barges—but terror is nonsensical.

The smell of low tide is punctuated by putrid fear. This morning's conceited nonchalance and entitlement have transformed into outright panic. I'm dragged along in the tide of bodies, propelled by no will of my own as they surge up the water gate's stone stairs, the Thames nipping at their heels like an incessant dog.

Thomas's red velvet chaperon bobs through the crowd, but I lose sight of it when I'm shoved to the side by Robert de Vere. I stumble and almost fall, but no one, not my husband nor any of the earls, glances over their shoulders.

I'm alone by the time the king's soldiers leave their barges and surge up the steps, moving toward me like a wall of metal armor and weaponry.

It's as if my skin retracts. My heart closes, my lungs too. Afraid they'll overtake me, I gasp for breath, hands flapping. I can tell my body is overstimulated and about to shut down.

A large hand closes on my elbow, and before I can spin around, I'm scooped up and carried out of the soldiers' path. I smell sugary marchpane and Fobbing's salty air.

The rush of voices recedes.

"Don't worry, Dandy," Geoff rumbles against my ear. I breathe deeply and envision a field of dandelions along Fobbing's marsh. The yellow carpet changes to soft white puffs until they explode in a riot of seeds, scattering on the wind.

I let out a long breath and close my eyes, content to stay silent until we get to wherever Geoff is carrying me.

"Lady Blanche," another man—Henry—says, trotting along beside Geoff. "I'll take you to my chamber."

"No," I say. Geoff stops moving. "Where are we?"

"On top of the inner ward's wall," Henry says. "Outside St Thomas's Tower."

"Set me down." I pat Geoff's chest, then my face heats and I snatch back my hand.

Geoff does so with infinite gentleness. I brush my skirts and straighten my veil, careful not to meet his eye.

It's relatively quiet. Everyone is inside the ward, except for the guards stationed along the walls and roof of the White Tower.

"Let's walk to Byward Tower," I say. "I hear the rebels moving. Maybe from there, I can tell where they're going."

Geoff and Henry exchange a glance, and Henry nods.

I turn on my heel, and they hurry to follow me.

"My lady," Henry begins, long legs easily matching my pace, "can you tell me what happened?"

I look at him, assessing his intent. "Of course." I gnaw at my bottom lip. "However, I must ask—why didn't you go with the other nobles and the king to the White Tower? You could hear the story from them."

"I would think it obvious," he says.

I pick up my skirts, allowing for a faster pace.

"With the king there," he continues, "they'll stroke his ego and lie to him. Combined with the obvious panic overtaking the party, I doubt I could get an ounce of truth from that lot. De Vere will do all the talking. It's been that way, lately." He smacks a fist into the other palm. "I've always loathed de Vere, since childhood."

I'm glad we're hurrying. My cheeks are already flushed from exertion, and Henry can't possibly notice my discomfiture. I long to tell him what I witnessed on the boat, the odd intimacy between de Vere and the king. Coupled with what I overheard last night in my husband's solar, I'm starting to wonder if maybe the king wouldn't demand an investigation if I went to him about my husband's late-night activities. What's worse, instinct tells me de Vere is taking advantage of the king's youth and inexperience, that there's a sinister and inappropriate explanation behind the earl's recent influence. But I can't voice this. I hardly understand my suspicions myself.

"Besides," Henry continues, "over the past days it's become clear that you, Blanche, have more rational thoughts on your worst day than the king's councilors collect in their entire lives."

I turn back, still walking, and examine his eyes. I expect to see laughter in them, but he stares back, frank and serious. "I'm flattered"—I look forward again—"but I don't think you'll like my report."

"Tell me everything."

Despite my hesitation, once I start telling Henry about the royal barge's journey down the Thames, I can't stop. Words rush from my lips like water under London's bridge, and I hardly take a breath until Henry interrupts me.

"How many were there?" he asks, after I tell him about the horde of rebels gathered at Rotherhithe.

"Only ten thousand," I say. We walk up the stairs of Byward Tower. "There wasn't room for the rest. They're preparing to take the city, I'm sure of it. I told my husband and the king—"

"You did?" He grins.

"Yes. But they didn't listen. My husband..." I trail off.

"What, sister?"

We stop at Byward Tower. I feel Henry and Geoff's eyes on me, and I sigh, unsure where to begin. However, when I open my mouth, the words flow out easier than I ever would have expected. "Thomas said he thinks you were wrong when you reported the horde's numbers this morning. The archbishop, de Vere, and the other nobles agreed and advised the king that there must only be ten thousand rebels." Henry grunts. "But I'm certain. There are more rebels elsewhere in London, and they're preparing to attack."

"I don't doubt you..." he murmurs.

"I think the nobles were also surprised by how the rebels presented. They didn't look the way the earls and archbishop expected."

Henry's head tilts.

"I wasn't surprised," I say, spreading my hands. "I lived with these people, in Fobbing." I tap my index finger against my upper lip and search for the right words. "I think the earls expected bedraggled, starving villeins who can hardly put two words together."

I peer into Henry's blank face and resist the urge to roll my eyes up toward the sky.

"Many of them are starving, to be sure. They can't pay the king's taxes, their manor lords' rents, *and* feed their families. However, they have pride, and they're from the coast. The *east coast*. Which means they have cellars full of weapons to fight off the French, should they invade. They've had their stores ready, and have been training for the eventuality of war for generations."

A soldier hurries past and bows to me and Henry. I wait until he's well clear before I continue.

"It's like you said. They're united in purpose. They love their country, and their king. But they're not base, stupid. They're tradesmen, and women," I add. Henry's ruddy brows shoot up. "Yes, there are women among them. Every single one work-hardened and experienced, and here to fight. Furthermore, they're better organized than us, with better leadership. Wearing armor, with pikes and swords."

"How did we not realize?" He paces back and forth on the stone walkway. "My grandsire—*our* grandsire"—I blush and look at my feet—"sent weapons to the coastal and northern peasantry, instructing them to train for battle with the French and Scots. They're prepared."

I nod.

"But...armor?" His face is drained of color. "Pikes?"

"Yes, and longbows. Thank Jesu they didn't use them today." He opens his mouth to speak, but I go on. "Standing in neat rows. Each division had a pennant to signify their town or village."

He shakes his head with disbelief. When I tell him about Salisbury's choice of words when speaking to the rebels, Geoff scoffs. Henry turns to blink at him. Geoff clears his throat, unsure, but Henry gestures for him to speak.

"M'lord," Geoff begins, "what he said was quite offensive, and..."

"He looked and sounded like a puffed peacock, resplendent in its plumage, yet ridiculous," I finish, ignoring Henry's answering gape. I envision the peacock from the feast the night before, sent back to the kitchens by King Richard, and an unexpected bubble of mirth bursts forth. I give a squawking giggle.

Henry shakes his head again, confused. I tell him of Richard's indecision and the ministers' fumbling retreat, and he sighs.

"I'm not surprised," he says. "What did they think would happen?"

"Exactly," I mutter.

We're standing at the edge of the parapet, gazing out over Middle Tower, with the Lion Tower and moat beyond. A prickle of unease climbs my spine as I think about that particular structure's inhabitants, but I push the sensation away.

Further on, the jagged and irregular roofs of London stretch upriver. I rest my hands on the stone wall, sniffing the wind like a hound.

It's a clear, bright day, and I can see for miles. London Bridge's drawbridge is raised, barring entry to the city. In the heart of London, the spire of St Paul's Cathedral dominates the view. Beyond it, on the Strand, is my father's palace, the Savoy.

"Where did Tyler's men go after the king left?" Henry asks. "And where are the others, Jack Straw and Thomas Baker's men?"

I close my eyes and listen to the men marching, and screaming with rage. "There are still two groups." My eyes fly open. I can hear them by the bridge, but a mist has drifted over the water to block my view.

"Where are they?" Henry's hands, balled into fists, press atop the crenelated wall.

"They're trying to force their way into the city."

His gaze snaps around. "How d'you know?"

"I hear Tyler's group, at the bridge. They want it lowered."

"The aldermen won't do it," Henry declares. "They're loyal to the king."

I click my tongue.

"What?"

"When you went to the king and his council this morning, did you tell them they must meet with London's citizens, right away?"

"Yes, but it was decided not to be a priority. The aldermen will stay loyal to Richard, as will the guilds. What other choice do they have?"

Behind him, Geoff coughs.

"Speak, Groom."

"M'lord," Geoff begins, "the Londoners despise the royal court. They'll support the rioters. Richard should have met with the aldermen and the guilds, right when we knew the rioters were arriving. He could have convinced the guilds to help, or even cut them a deal. Lower taxes, incentives, something. Now...I'm not sure there's hope for their support. I think it's too late."

Henry grunts and looks away from Geoff, but I can't. Am I imagining it, or is my friend's rural accent already changing to that of a wealthy merchant or upper-level servant?

Everything's moving too fast. It's only been a week since Geoff left the only home either of us has ever known. Now he's standing atop the Tower of London's battlements, discussing its defenses with Henry of Lancaster. I'm happy for Geoff. This is what he wants. But a part of me misses the lanky villein whose greatest adventure was leaving dandelions on my front stoop.

I breathe in and give my head a shake, then walk to the other side of the tower. "While Tyler's group met with the king on the Thames, Jack Straw and Thomas Baker led theirs the opposite direction, likely to Aldgate. Tyler's meeting with the king was a distraction. While the king and his soldiers were parading around the river, the rebels have entered the city. The aldermen must have opened Aldgate as well. They're surrounding the city, then coming inside its walls."

I force my gaze back to the river, where the mist has lifted. "Look."

Both men squint and lean over the crenelated barrier.

Geoff shakes his head with frustration. "I see nothing."

"They're lowering the bridge," I say. "Tyler's group. They're coming."

"Where will they go?" Henry looks at me with wide, sparkling eyes.

I watch the river and give a dry cough. Surely that was a rhetorical question? It's obvious where Tyler's men will go first. With our father in Scotland, his grand palace is virtually unguarded. All those rich tapestries. The floor-to-ceiling stained glass. The jewels, the gold plate. The rebels won't pass up the opportunity to plunder or destroy it.

Henry sighs. "The Savoy," he says.

"Yes. I'm sorry, Henry."

He draws a deep breath and stares toward the bridge, then closes his eyes.

I pull his sleeve. "Is Lady Swynford still at the Savoy?"

His eyes fly open, like two windows overlooking a perfect sky. "I don't know." He turns to the right, takes one step, stops. Then he paces to the left, running a few steps before skidding to a halt.

He moves back to the wall, looking as if he might punch it.

"Henry." I seize his right hand in mine. "You cannot go." He opens his mouth to argue, and I place two fingers over his lips. "I know you want to. But you can't. Lady Swynford will be safe. They won't harm a woman. But you...the house of Lancaster depends on you. You're the only male heir." I swallow down my blatant disregard for the duke's three illegitimate sons with Lady Swynford. They don't matter, just as I don't.

Henry throws up his arms. "How can we find ourselves at the mercy of the king's own subjects?"

"He should have joined forces with the city's tradesmen, should have negotiated with the aldermen. But forget that. We can go even earlier in England's parade of bad decisions. King Richard's council shouldn't have forced a tax the peasants could never afford; the king shouldn't be overspending money he doesn't have refurbishing his castles and showering gifts on his favorites." Henry says nothing, so I continue. "Now it's too late. The rebels are here. We're all in danger, but no one more than you, Henry. You need to focus on your own safety."

He sighs. "They can't breach these walls. We can survive here for years, maybe forever."

His rationale is sound. However, although I can't say why, I don't agree. Maybe I'm just used to feeling vulnerable and afraid.

But if London's people will open the city's gates to the rebels, raise the bridge's drawbridge for them, how protected can we really be in a fortress guarded by the very same citizens?

I say nothing.

Chapter Twenty

By dusk, the air hangs thick with black, acrid smoke. The growing darkness is punctuated by the cookfires of a hundred thousand souls, blinking and dancing on Tower Hill.

I find Joan back at Constable Tower. After a quick meal, we return to the outer wall to watch the Savoy's smoldering remains spit smoke into London's skyline.

"Is it really…" I trail off.

"Yes," Joan says, "the Savoy is destroyed. Gone."

"All of that splendor," I murmur. "Finer than Westminster Palace, they said."

"The king will be happy."

I stare at her in shock. She bites her lip and looks down. I take her hand and squeeze.

"You're right, of course. I hadn't thought of that." Silently, I wonder if that's the reason my father has fallen out of the king's favor. I guess it doesn't really matter. "And now it's just smoking rubble." I clutch my hands to stop their trembling.

"Lady Katherine is well, my lady," Joan says quietly. She places a light and reassuring hand on my forearm. "Rumor says she took refuge in an abbey with her children."

I exhale, slumping. "That's one piece of good news. We must make sure Henry knows."

"Gossip says the rebels took nothing. They burned the furniture, or threw it into the river, and ground the jewels to dust underfoot. When one rebel tried to steal a gold plate, Tyler threw him into the fire."

I shiver. "What else?"

"They burned the mayor's brothels, and the houses and businesses of the wealthy. But nothing owned by commoners. Many Londoners have joined them."

I rub my temples. A hundred thousand are camped outside the Tower's walls, and I wish I could block out the din of their celebrations.

"The Temple is destroyed, razed to the ground," Joan is saying. I wrench my attention from the peasants' voices.

"What is the Temple?" I ask.

"London's lawyers' quarter. They killed the lawyers..."

"Why?" I wrap my arms around my waist. Although the night air is still warm, I suddenly feel cold.

"They wrote the laws of feudalism, and the rebels want to destroy those laws. So, they burned the records and killed those who wrote them."

"You said your father's a lawyer." My words are rushed. "Is he all right?"

She peers at me. "Did I tell you that? I didn't remember."

I look away. Joan had mentioned her father's profession in passing the morning we prepared a healing salve for my bruises. I was only half listening, worried as I was that she might be my father's spy, but I still recall every detail of the conversation. I can't seem to shake those kinds of things from my mind. Yet, I've learned that other people, even good, kind ones like Joan, don't remember things like I do. What a blessing it must be to get rid of the clutter.

She shrugs. "There's no way to know. I haven't had any messages from home."

I examine her pensive face. Lined and shadowed, with dark smudges beneath her eyes, it's as if she's aged years in the week since we met. I imagine we all look like that tonight.

I turn again toward the Savoy. Clouds of thick, black smoke billow from where the Lancastrian palace once stood.

She points at London Bridge, upriver and to the west. "They say there are eighteen heads on the bridge."

"Eighteen?" I take in a deep breath, but it rattles in my throat and I choke, both on the smoldering air and the sorrow. Guilt tickles the back of my conscience. Did I wish for this? I thought that if the rebels changed the world, I could leave my husband, but I never wanted this.

"Don't go outside the Tower again, my lady." Joan grips my arm. "I was so worried for you today, when you were gone."

I give a little shrug, but smile. "If Sir Thomas tells me to go, I have no choice."

She opens her mouth but shuts it as we hear a commotion at the White Tower.

We scurry to the inner ward to watch King Richard, along with his ministers, leave the keep and make his way to the eastern wall. My husband's red chaperon bobs along behind. Henry is beside him. It seems like every living soul, from the lowliest scullery maids to me and Joan, emerges from the Tower's buildings to follow.

"He must plan to make a proclamation," Joan says as we walk up the crowded stone steps of the outer wall.

The wall is packed with every one of the six hundred Tower residents. They all seem to push past us for a better view. I suck in a ragged breath.

Joan grabs my elbow and pulls. "Make way for Lady Prescott!" she yells while using her other hand to clear a path.

Within a minute, I stand beside my husband, not far from the king.

I give Joan a grateful nod, but as she steps back, I wonder if I shouldn't have acknowledged her efforts. I'm supposed to be an imperious lady, not Joan's friend. I'm just not sure I could live a life that way: detached, alone, above it all.

Thomas looks at me, and I stifle a gasp. His face is more careworn than ever, with deep creases at the corners of his scowl and dark circles beneath his eyes. He exhales through his nose, and for a moment, I pity him.

From our vantage point on the outer wall, we look out over hundreds of cookfires dotting the landscape.

"Bloody fools," Thomas growls so low that only I can hear. "A few volleys of fiery arrows into their camp would solve this problem."

My pity evaporates like mist.

The thousands of singing and shouting voices begin to quiet when they see the king, and the rebels hurry to the wall, carrying their torches.

Richard hasn't changed his clothes since this morning. A shame. The ermine and precious gems were poor choices earlier; the passage of a day hasn't rendered them more appropriate for calming the rebels.

Richard looks out over Tower Hill, the torches and campfires reflecting off his blue eyes. The diamonds and emeralds on his coronet sparkle in the firelight, and the ruby, which had been his father's, flashes red like fresh blood. He stands on a large box. Without it, his head wouldn't top the Tower wall.

He places both hands on the stone, not gripping, but with gentleness, as if playing an instrument. With his lips pressed into a firm line, he lifts both hands with the elegance of a dancer.

An eerie hush spreads, and I rise on tiptoe to see. Robert de Vere stands beside Richard, along with the king's mother, the

Dowager Princess. I could swear they're both poised, balanced on the balls of their feet, ready to catch Richard's collar should he topple over the wall.

As I stretch my neck toward him, a sharp pain strikes my right temple. Instinctively, I shut my eyes.

But I still see Richard.

With the flicker of a foreign and sudden light, the others disappear as he lifts his hands. The glow of his ruby intensifies until his robes, his hands, his face, the very stones of our fortress radiate crimson light as if drenched in blood.

Richard lowers his head then, and his crown, with its diamonds and emeralds, topples over the Tower wall.

My body convulses, and I open my eyes. Richard still stands with crowds of people around him. His coronet rests on his head, and Thomas, along with everyone else , still stares at him, waiting for him to speak.

I glance at my husband, terrified I might have revealed what I saw by some gesture or sound. He ignores me; it's like I don't exist. I exhale. The vision was for me alone, but my mind still whirls.

The blood and the crown—falling, falling, falling.

Was it Richard's blood, or another's? He could grow into a great warrior, despite early ineptitude. In the future, this king could defeat the French, slaughtering thousands.

I suppress another shiver.

But the crown. A king's coronet slipping from his head can only mean one thing.

I push the thought away. Right now, Richard is king. My one choice is loyalty.

The flames tremble and flicker, the only sounds. Here and now, it's like we are all standing on tiptoe, waiting to hear what Richard has to say.

He opens his mouth, and the rebels inch closer, as if he breathes them in, inhaling. They hang on his every word before he even speaks. Scribes stand with parchment and quill, ready to copy his message, and criers clutch their bells and wait.

Just when I think he'll speak, he instead breathes out. The crowd exhales as well, disappointed. When he inhales again, I pray that this time he'll speak, that he'll say something, anything, to fix this.

Even after the destruction of my father's palace, after mourning the eighteen heads posted on London Bridge, a dark, secret part of me still hopes for a rebel victory. I try to deny it, try to ignore the pervasive thought that seems irrational, but can't. I can't stop thinking about how my union with Sir Thomas remains unconsummated. Could I gainsay my father and revoke my bondage, like the villeins have? If they have the power to rewrite the social laws, why can't I?

I give myself an inward shake. My marriage isn't about happiness. It's about my father's wishes, my family's needs.

"We thank you, good commons," Richard begins at last, his voice a pure bell, "for your loyalty. We pardon you for all your illegal offenses. But we wish every man and woman to return home."

A muffled rumble starts in the crowd and spreads, faster than the plague.

"Once home, set down your grievances in writing," Richard continues, "and send it to us. By the advice of my lords"—the rumble grows to a murmur, and with alacrity, a drone of discontent—"we will then provide such remedy as will be profitable to ourselves, our commons, and the whole realm."

The horde erupts, a cacophony of rebellion. Rage floats on the playful wind, as confusion and frustration buzz within the fortress.

I want to throw up my hands. Richard just told a crowd of illiterate subjects to go home and write him a letter. Insulting. Placating words that lead nowhere. The people are tired, and this speech was a meaningless attempt at appeasement without substance. They love their king, but his inaction is eroding their trust like the constant brush of river sand against stone. More of this, and Richard's life will be in as much danger as Henry's.

My illegitimacy has always felt like a misfortune, a cross I had to bear. Now, I think about my upbringing in Fobbing differently. Thomas, Henry, and Richard have never lived among the common people. To them, Richard's speech might have seemed acceptable, generous even. To me, who has straddled the worlds of commoner and lady, it is clear how much harder the nobles need to try.

Robert de Vere comes up behind the king, caressing his shoulders and urging him to step down from the box. The dowager princess stiffens before trying to pry his fingers away. De Vere's grip tightens. I watch Richard's mother whisper in his ear, only to be pushed away. The king turns to de Vere, takes his hand.

De Vere eases Richard down from his platform and guides him past us. The Dowager Princess is left alone. I catch her eye, but she looks away, back out over the rebel camp.

Thomas leaves to follow the king and de Vere back to the White Tower.

Below, Tower Hill erupts with jeers. I lean over the parapet, watching the rebels, who seem to dance with rage.

Inside the Tower walls, the crowd jostles and shakes. Although the fortress isn't close to capacity, every one of its occupants has crammed near the king, and now there's a stampede to get away. My breath rushes with terror. Will I be trampled? I look for Joan but can't see her. I can only hope she's safe. I stumble and gasp, but then a hand wraps around my waist.

When I turn, I find myself nose to nose with Geoff.

My chest rises and falls in rapid succession. Geoff places his other hand, the one not wrapped around me, palm-down between my breasts. My heart pounds against his touch.

I've never been healed before, never needed it. Eldridge used to say I was too busy healing others to get sick. But now,

Geoff—in one simple gesture—pulls the fear from my heart, smooths the irregular beats, and cures me of an ailment I didn't know I had.

This is very wrong, yet everyone else has receded. A second before, hundreds of bodies pressed into me, thousands writhed below. Now, all I feel is Geoff.

"You're here," I say, our lips so close they almost touch.

"Dandy," he answers. "I have you." He pants, steals my breath as I struggle to manage each inhale and exhale.

I taste the slightest hint of him, the sweet smell that's always identified him since childhood. Wherever Geoff lives, he befriends the cook. Even now, there's sugar on him. Our mouths don't touch—in reality, I'm sure he's inches away—but I sense him, taste him. The strangest sensation of marchpane invades me. I'm sure he hasn't eaten it today, what with rebels running through London, but still, there it is.

The crowd screeches. I want to ignore them, want to pull Geoff closer, to feel his mouth on mine. A soldier rushes past, ramming into his side. Geoff keeps his grip on me, but the jolt revives my senses and I lurch back.

My face burns as I gasp, afraid, just a moment after I'd felt nothing but relief in Geoff's arms. If we were seen, if Thomas or one of his men witnessed what just happened...

I look past Geoff's shoulder and see Joan. Her hands are raised, beckoning me. I look back over my shoulder. No one of consequence remains. Everyone has followed the king.

But Geoff is still here, watching me, Joan at his side. They want to protect me. Why, I can't say. My actions, my very existence and the odd things I do put them in danger. I harm anyone who loves me, just by being me.

But this...whatever is happening between me and Geoff...this is beyond any other bad idea I've ever pursued. This isn't foraging with Eldridge, isn't skipping a "lady lesson" with Maman to play with my kitten in the marsh. I'm married now. To a powerful man with reputation, position, and wealth at stake. A man with a terrible secret to protect. One misstep, and I could doom Geoff to return to a life of poverty, or worse.

And me? Where I'd be doomed to go, I can only guess.

Chapter Twenty-One

14 JUNE 1381

Thomas stays with the king's ministers, and Joan and I return to Constable Tower. All night, I stare up at my bed's tester, Rhead sleeping beside me. The moon moves across the sky, from matins until the bell of St Peter ad Vincula's chapel tolls prime, the shadows shifting across the sagging green fabric. Still, I don't move.

Screams carry on a light wind from the rebel camp. I try to close my ears to them, to block out the words, but as the moon's slanted wedge reaches its pinnacle in the western sky, I give up. Exhausted but unable to sleep, I lay there, hands folded over my throbbing heart, listening.

They demand the heads of every one of the king's nobles and ministers, but there's one name they shout louder than the rest: "Death to Lancaster!" I flinch. "We have no king named John!"

Then, the calls for Henry's head begin. They chant, "Give us Derby, give us Derby!" I weep with frustration. My brother is just a child, but to the rebels he's a fair substitute for our father.

Henry is housed further away from the rebel camp, in the royal palace at St Thomas's Tower. I pray he can't hear the screams punctuating the night air, but there will be no such respite for myself. I wish they'd take me instead of my brother, but such an offer would be futile. My bastardy and femininity keep me safe and useless.

At last, moonlight is replaced by sunshine, bright and cheery, in sharp contrast to how I feel.

I rise and walk to the arrow slit, where I rest my hand on the cold stone and stare out. I am still there when Joan tiptoes in through the door. Her feet crunch on the rushes, and I hear the light thump of crockery as she sets a water basin on the sideboard. I turn and watch as she bends to scratch Rhead.

"What news, Joan?"

She compresses her lips. "The king and a small escort are getting ready to leave the Tower, my lady."

"Where are they going?"

"To Mile End, to meet with the rebels." Joan bustles around the room, straightening my bedding and setting out the items for my morning toilette: a fresh chemise, my brown woolen gown, a simple white-veiled headdress, my hairbrush and pins, and a clean towel for washing my face and hands.

"Why are they going to Mile End when the rebels are here?" My voice is sharp. Though none of this is Joan's fault, I can't seem to help it.

"I don't know, my lady."

Sighing, I pad across the floor to use the garderobe. My business complete, I wash my face and hands, then turn to find Joan near a stool, holding up a hairbrush in invitation.

I flop onto the stool and crumple my nightgown in my fists. Joan starts to brush the snarls from my hair. She grunts, struggling with a particularly stubborn knot at the back of my head. Her hand twists but can't find a way through the snarl.

"Ouch!" I swing around to face her. "What was that for?"

"Nothing, my lady!" She flinches as though I might strike her.

Ashamed, I lower my chin. "Forgive me, Joan. I'm just so fearful... The rebels..."

She steps closer, pats my shoulder. "There's nothing to forgive." She untangles the snarl and sets down the brush to separate my hair into sections for plaits.

I spread my hands on my lap to stop fidgeting. I can't tell Joan the truth, that although I am worried about the rebellion, my sharp words were about what happened with Geoff the night before.

Fear, shame, and confusion fill my head to the point of bursting. I shake slightly, and Joan clicks her tongue.

I wince. "Sorry, Joan..."

She pins one braid and begins on another. I lift a hand to feel her work. It seems she's attempting a more intricate style than normal. She takes my hand and gently returns it to my lap. "I thought we'd try something more ornate today."

I give a little smile, then it falls. "Joan," I ask, "have you heard anything about your father? After the rebels attacked the lawyers' Temple? Is he safe?"

She shakes her head, but says nothing. As she works, Rhead lays on his back and plays with the hem of my chemise. I don't press her for more information. I wish that, instead of responding with sharp words, I dealt with the pressure by taking on more work and trying to improve my labors, like Joan. I must do better by her. I've never had a servant like Joan, someone I can trust.

She's pinning the final plait when I jump at the sound of the front door thumping shut.

"What is it, my lady? Did I hurt you?"

I press a finger to my lips and mouth. "*Thomas.*"

Rhead hurries beneath the bed. I try to listen as my husband speaks to his squire, but his words are covered by the jumble of noises from the rebel camp.

"I think he said he's going with the king," I whisper.

"Where—"

I hold up a finger to silence her. "He's coming upstairs."

My words hardly escape my lips before we're flying around the room. She grabs a gown and flings it over my head, lacing it as I frantically pull on a headdress.

It's only when his footfalls ring on the top steps that I wonder why we're doing this. What is wrong with my husband seeing me in my shift?

Thomas enters, and Joan curtsies before leaving through the servants' door without another word.

He doesn't look at me. It's not easy to feel sympathy for him because I hate him, but the feeling does sneak its way in. He must be exhausted—he's spent all night with the king's ministers—but every time I see him now, I also worry someone has discovered the secret of his relationship with de Vere. The thought makes my guts clench.

He goes to his clothing chest, flips it open, and pulls out a fresh tunic and hose.

"Husband." I give a shallow curtsy. "Shall I fetch some water?"

He shakes his head. "I'm going with the king to Mile End, along with de Vere."

"De Vere?"

He shoots me a tired look. God, I wish our marriage was different. We don't need intimacy. He doesn't have to love me, even like me. But I want him to trust me. I could help him, could let him know his secret is safe.

"Why...what..." I don't want him to leave yet—as an experienced soldier, he dresses fast—but I have no idea what to say.

He shrugs me off like I'm a toddler. "I don't have time for this."

He hurries to the door, but I grab his sleeve. "Why are you going to Mile End? Why not meet with them here?"

"Isn't that obvious?" He stops, looking at me with disdain. "The rebels don't want to hurt the king. They want his ministers, the nobles, and the lawyers. Not Richard."

He pauses to see if I understand. I say nothing. Thomas rubs a hand over his face, his smooth fingers rasping over his whiskers, rough after not shaving for two days.

"By going to Mile End, Richard lures the rebels away from the Tower. That way, the lords and archbishop can escape," he says. My nostrils flare, and I open my mouth to ask a question, but he interrupts me. "We will promise the rebels whatever they want to get the nobles and archbishop to safety. Then, the rebels will go back home. The king can always renege on his promises."

My face heats. "Is that really—"

"Do you ever think twice before speaking?"

I sigh. He sounds like Maman. "Just don't hurt them."

"Who?" His hand settles on the door latch.

"The rebels."

I'm about to touch his shoulder, but pull away when he turns and lifts a quizzical brow.

"Why do you care?" he asks.

Clasping my fingers under my breasts, I drop my eyes to the floor. "They're my people, husband. Some of them are from Fobbing... I cared for them."

I blink as new scents waft my way. The spoiled milk of embarrassment is nothing new from my husband, but the pungent sulfur of onions? I can't explain his disappointment.

"Cared for them?" His lip curls, and he growls deep in his throat. "Don't tell me you had a lad among them."

I freeze and my lips go numb.

"Did you?"

I shake my head.

He leans closer and looks me up and down. "I'd assumed you were a virgin."

"Of course I am."

"If you're not, if I find out you're lying, there will be hell to pay."

"I'm not lying."

"I'll hunt that man down. Skewer him."

I make a choking sound. My vision swims, but I can just make out my belt pouch over Thomas's shoulder, still hanging on its hook by the door. I'm desperate to touch it, to smell the dandelion inside. But there are no scents of earth and yellow sweetness for me now, only the sour, spoiled smell of Thomas's uneasy defeat. I cough, and Thomas turns back to the door. As he lifts the latch, awareness surges back into my body, and I leap in front of the door to block his way. I have to make him see that the king must not hurt his own people.

He huffs. "Move."

"No. Thomas..." I look into his cold, black eyes and search for something to say. "You've never been someone's property. You were born...free." The corner of his mouth jerks in a sneer. "Don't you have any compassion?"

He barks a mocking laugh. "How would you know what it's like to be someone's property, wife? You, too, were born free. The daughter of the kingdom's wealthiest noble."

His black stare wanders back to the door, but I follow his eyes with my own, demanding he meet them. "I'm not free, Thomas, and you well know it."

His mouth presses into a tight line, and I hold his gaze for a moment. Without another word, he pushes me aside, opens the door, and walks through.

"Do whatever you can to help the lords escape, my little peasant," he calls over his shoulder.

—

Once he's gone, Joan hurries back through the servants' door. "Let's go out and learn what's happening," she urges, a hand on my arm.

I almost agree. I need to get to Henry, need to help him escape.

But I pause. "No." I pull my stool to the arrow slit and sit down without another word. Rhead leaps into my lap.

Joan's features go slack with surprise, but she recovers herself quickly and fetches her own stool to sit. We're silent—me staring out the window and Joan knitting—as shouts ricochet outside. Unlike last night, I shut out the din from the rebel camp. I need to focus on what's happening inside the Tower, need to know the exact moment King Richard leaves.

It takes a long time to prepare a king and his entourage, however. An hour passes.

"My lady," Joan says at last, resting her knitting in her lap. "Shall we go outside now?"

I shake my head. "I don't want to see the Dowager Princess of Wales."

"Why not?"

"I don't want her to force me to accompany Richard to Mile End. I need to be here."

Joan's eyes widen, but she nods and takes up her knitting once again. I bite my lower lip, determined not to waver. If the Dowager Princess were to demand I go with Richard, I wouldn't be able to refuse. And my focus must be on Henry's safety. And Geoff's. The further they both are from London, the better.

Unable to sit still, I rise and pace the floor.

Outside the Tower walls, the crowd chants the same demands and taunts as the night before: "We have no king named John!" and "Give us Derby! Give us Derby! Henry of Lancaster!"

I squeeze my eyes shut and focus on the shouted commands from inside the castle compound.

"Ready the horses..."

"Lower the drawbridge!"

Joan starts to speak, but I hold up a hand and keep listening. The voices are growing further away.

"Make way for the king! Make way for King Richard!"

"They're gone." I sigh. I wish I didn't have to seek out Geoff, but I have no choice. "I need to find my brother."

Chapter Twenty-Two

The inner ward is abandoned. Every door is barred, all the windows shuttered, and a stagnant quiet tiptoes around every corner.

Constable Tower is just one of thirteen identical towers within the Tower of London's complex. There are also multiple stables, barracks, outbuildings, kitchens, the chapel of St Peter ad Vincula, and the White Tower keep in the center of it all. In such a massive place, even a limited search takes over an hour, but I'm determined to find my brother. His words ring in my head: *Your skills are useful. You have a gift, Blanche.*

Henry must get out. Must get away from the rebels, and I can be of use to him. I must find him.

"Maybe he's already escaped." Joan pants as we tramp back to the royal palace's main door after searching the whole building.

"And taken Geoff with him, with any luck," I mumble.

She looks at me quizzically, but says nothing.

"I—"

A destrier's sharp bugle interrupts me, followed by the shouts of multiple men. Without another word, Joan and I follow the sounds, careening into the White Tower's nearby stable yard to find Henry in a cloud of dust and a swarm of panicking servants. He's surrounded by the country's highest-ranking men: the Earls of Salisbury, Arundel, and Warwick, the Archbishop of Canterbury, and Lord Robert Hales. They sweat as if they've just run a mile, and their woolen traveling cloaks are rumpled and dirty.

The courtyard is in uproar. Soldiers mill around, unsure where to go, grooms rush to saddle horses, and frightened servants peer out from nearby kitchens and towers, desperate for news.

Joan and I stop behind the lords, both of us panting and holding our sides.

I see Geoff at the edge of the yard, holding the reins of two saddled horses. I refuse him eye contact but sense his gaze while I squeeze my way through the group to stand beside Henry.

I grab his arm. He turns with wild eyes. "What happened?"

He shakes his head. "We tried to escape," he says, "in a boat. Tried to get away, but the rebels left behind a small party. They came after us, and we had to turn around."

I puff out my cheeks, then exhale the air in a frustrated rush. Of course, the lords assumed the rebels were stupid enough to leave no one behind, and of course the opposite was true. Henry means a great deal to me, and I think he's a good person, but he has much to learn about England's people before he inherits the Duchy of Lancaster.

"What now?"

He shrugs. "Supposedly the remaining guards are going to escort us out the gate. I'm not sure how they plan to do that, though. The rebels are watching every exit."

A soldier trots to the little group and stands before Simon Sudbury, Archbishop of Canterbury. In full armor, he struggles to kneel, metal rubbing and clashing while his broadsword, sheathed at his hip, digs into the ground. He grimaces as the plates pinch. "Your Excellency," he murmurs.

"Rise, Captain Crawford," Sudbury says. His jowls quiver and his beady eyes dart around the yard with alarming speed, first toward the gate to the outer ward, then the White Tower, before at last settling on the soldier before him. Sudbury pulls him up by his elbows with surprising strength. "Tell me, through which gate shall we ride?"

"My apologies, Excellency." Crawford's eyelid twitches. "It's not possible."

"*What*?"

The captain's eyelid twitches again. "I'm sorry, Excellency, but there are rebels stationed outside of every gate. You'll be ambushed. Killed..." His voice trails off, and he looks down, closing his eyes. The offending lid keeps twitching.

"Isn't there some sort of secret exit?" the archbishop insists. "A secret means of escape?"

"Sir...the Tower is a prison. The best in the world. It's built to be inescapable."

"What do you mean?" He grabs Captain Crawford by the shoulders and shakes him until his helm rattles.

Lord Hales steps forward and wrenches the archbishop's beefy hands away from Crawford. "Your Excellency, calm yourself!" He peers at Sudbury and lowers his voice. "We'll stay here. The rebels cannot break into the Tower."

Sudbury gives a frantic series of nods, flabby jowls shaking.

Hales looks back at Crawford. "Lord Constable Prescott went with King Richard, yes?" He continues before Crawford can even nod. "Where is his lieutenant?"

The soldier's face reddens. "He'll be back soon, m'lord. He's escorting his wife downriver. He was anxious for her safety, and wanted to send her away, like the other lords and officers."

I sense rather than see Joan's furtive glance. I look around and shudder. Other than a sprinkling of servants, we're the only women here.

Hales groans and smacks his thigh with his riding gloves, like a thwarted child. So much for calm. The reek of rotting fruit—my old friend, fear—wafts on the breeze. I suppress a gag, and my eyes start to water.

"Where's the Dowager Princess of Wales?" I mutter to Henry out of the corner of my mouth.

"I believe she's in her chambers, in St Thomas's Tower."

"Good. Hopefully she'll stay there." Something about a mother's terror is harder to bear than that of half a dozen noblemen fearing for their lives. And I can't forget what I saw last night. The vision of King Richard losing his crown, drenched in blood. I don't want to think about it, but somewhere deep down I know that nothing the princess does can protect that boy.

"Now what?" I grip Henry's arm.

He looks around as if trying to find a way out. He's like a rabbit, crouched on its haunches and ready to jump at the slightest sound; he's being hunted and he knows it.

At last, he looks at Geoff, still standing with the horses. I look away—at the ground, the stable, at Joan—anywhere but at Geoff.

Henry gives a little wave to the horses. "Put them away."

I still feel Geoff's eyes on me, but refuse to look up.

"Gentlemen."

Everyone in the yard turns toward Archbishop Sudbury's booming voice. He stands in the middle of the packed dirt, right beside a pile of horse shit. He flicks his long red robes to avoid trailing the costly fabric through it. After his exchange with Captain Crawford and Lord Hales, the archbishop has composed himself, and his face is all regal calm.

"Come, gentlemen." He nods to me and smiles. "And ladies. Everyone..." He spreads his hands, palms up. "Come to St John's chapel, in the White Tower. I will say Mass, and we will pray."

The nobles and many of their servants move to hurry up the White Tower's outer staircase. It is narrow, but people rush to get inside first. Everyone—squires and earls alike—push and shove. People fall, and the others step on or over them. Painful squeals and angry shouts reverberate. Henry grips my arm as we fight our way through the crowd. No one cares that I'm the constable's wife, nor that Henry is second in line to the throne. I clutch Joan's hand, determined not to lose her.

"What about Geoffrey?" I shout over the din.

"He'll make his way inside once he unsaddles our horses," Henry says, nodding. "I'm sure of it."

A minute ago, I dreaded being in the same fortress as Geoff, but now I'm desperate to have him in my sights. I stifle a sob in my growing confusion.

"Don't worry, my lady," Joan whispers in my ear, "he'll be safe."

I crane my neck to look at her. "Oh, I know. It makes no difference, I just wondered." I give a sloppy shrug as Henry hauls me up the stairs by the hand.

It's hard to see inside the dark interior of the White Tower's entry hall after the bright courtyard. As the smells of woodsmoke and incense tickle my senses, I understand how the king and his ministers, sequestered in this isolated bubble of quiet, could have no concept of the real world. Many Londoners would give much for just one of the meals served from the Tower's kitchens, much less the nobility's lifetime of feasts and banquets. Every time the king eats, here in this very building, at least half the food goes untouched. Meanwhile, England's peasants, even some of its tradesmen, go hungry.

Henry pulls me and Joan up the three stone steps at the back of the hall into St John's chapel.

The Archbishop of Canterbury is already there, preparing for Mass at the front of the narrow, tunnel-like nave. He waves the incense, sets out the chalice, and dons his vestments.

Henry and I kneel on the cold stone floor at the front of the chapel, and the Earls of Salisbury, Warwick, and Arundel hurry in beside us.

The chapel feels like a cathedral, with its tall columns and arched ceiling made of forbidding white stone. How many pounds of it sit around us? Hundreds? Thousands? I have no idea, but somehow, imagining slows my heart's panicked rhythm. A little, at least. My eyes flick over the nave's austere, white brick columns, and I count them, striving for calm. One, two, three, four of the same structures extend around and behind the altar at the semicircular front of the room. I strain my neck to look up. The ceiling stretches up two stories with unmolded arches, extending to a gallery on the building's top floor. It's not a large space, nothing like nearby St Paul's Cathedral, but it makes me feel small and insignificant just the same.

Sunshine streams through three stained-glass windows as the archbishop opens his sacred text, thumbing through with trembling fingers. Despite my fear, the colored light—flecked over his white robes—takes my breath away.

The rustle of Joan's stiff woolen tunic crackles in my ears, and I flinch away from the tinted sunshine as she settles behind us. I crane my neck to make sure she's close enough to touch, only to see Geoff kneel beside her. Sweat streaming down his face, his brown eyes lock with mine. A foreign scent wafts from him—not the sweet sugar or horses of my childhood friend, but the rotting fruit of pure, unbridled terror. I twist my torso toward him.

"What is it, Geoffrey?" I whisper, heart thumping.

Geoff swallows, and his eyes flick first to me, then to Henry's back.

Henry turns. "Speak, man. What's happened?"

"As I put away the horses, m'lord," Geoff whispers, "I heard the most recent news from London."

A hush falls over the chapel as everyone listens, even the archbishop.

Geoff's eyes dart from person to person. He dips his chin and drops his voice even lower. "The king—"

"Speak up," Sudbury booms. "We all need to hear."

Geoff clears his throat. "The king was stopped by several commoners as he rode to Mile End. They demanded he give them the heads of...of..."

"Go ahead, lad."

"Of the archbishop and Lord Hales." Geoff looks like he might vomit, and his words come out jumbled and rushed. "The king told them they might do as they please with any traitors."

Silence falls on the chamber's cold white stone, and it's like frost blooms beneath our feet. I wrap my arms around my middle and shiver.

After a few suspended moments, someone mutters from the back of the room. "The king gave them permission to take his ministers?"

We look at the archbishop. His mouth works, but he says nothing.

My own mouth is dry. Geoff clears his throat again. I turn back.

"There's more?" I ask.

He nods. "At Mile End, King Richard agreed to free the villeins." Scoffs roll through the little crowd. Geoff's voice lowers to nothing more than a tremor. "After that, Wat Tyler left Mile End—they say with the king's authority—for the Tower." He looks to the earls and the archbishop. "They're coming for you."

A collective gasp sucks the air from the room.

"They want their heads," a servant whispers at the back of the chapel.

"The executioner's block," another voice murmurs. "That's what waits for 'em."

Splotches of gray dance at the edges of my vision. I turn to Henry. His skin gleams pearlescent, like an angel's might, and his jaw hangs slack. He brushes the skin of his neck with one hand.

The shadowy blush of youth's first beard, red-gold and patchy, lays across his face. I close my eyes as tears threaten. He's my brother, fifteen years old. I must protect him.

I reach to touch his hand. "The soldiers won't let them in, Henry."

He looks at me. "Are you sure?"

I say nothing. I can't lie; danger creeps up the chapel's center aisle like a panther, and we both know it. I close my fingers around his instead.

The archbishop spreads his arms. "Children," his weighty voice rings, "let us pray."

Drenched in colored light, Sudbury recites two full Masses. I watch through lowered lashes, my knees aching. He chants the litany of *Our Lady of Seven Sorrows*, the story of the virgin as she stood at the foot of her son's cross to watch him die.

"*Ave dulcis, Mater Christi.*"

I close my eyes and I'm back at Fobbing's parish, a frightened child hiding behind Maman's sleeve. I see the church's statue of Mary.

"*Natum lugens inclytum.*"

In St Michael's, seven daggers, representing Mary's seven sorrows, pierce the effigy's wooden breast. Painted blood runs over her blue robes. I press my eyelids tighter to release the image. I don't want to see her, don't want to watch her lose her boy.

"*O quam tristis quaesivisti, triduo iam perditum.*"

Eldridge used to whisper that the statues were just blocks of wood, and that the saints were made up. I hadn't possessed the courage to admit it at the time, but I'd believed her. I still do. Instead of turning to God, I sought solace and guidance from the marsh and surrounding forest.

Yet now, as I think of Mary bleeding, of her mourning her only son, I grab Henry's hand. Wetness seeps out from behind my squeezed eyelids. I see myself in her: a woman covered in wounds. I try to escape the captivity of men, yet I'm consumed with a love that ensnares me.

"*Huius memor o doloris! Christum fac inveniam, et inventum per amoris nexum semper teneam.*"

This is a funeral service. My brother, a boy I only just found. His mother is dead, his father is in Scotland. I'm the only family he has, and I must save him.

When I place my hand on the fine green wool of his surcoat, he turns, one ruddy brow raised in question.

"Henry." My voice cracks as I whisper. "We—"

Shouts and then screams erupt from the inner ward, interrupting me. Everyone leaps to stand on anxious, bouncing legs. A page runs inside and skids to a stop at the back of the chapel.

"They're inside the fortress, Yer Excellency!" he cries. "The rebels!"

Everyone groans.

"How did they get inside?" the Earl of Arundel demands, huge fists clenched at his sides.

The boy's face, splotched with acne, flames. "The soldiers let 'em in, m'lord."

We stare at the page, unable to speak. He turns and runs back out the door, his felt boots padding like a cat as he bounds down the chapel steps.

Outside, the rebels swarm the inner ward, their shouts ricocheting off stone and their swords splintering wood. They whistle as if to a pack of dogs, calling out for their prey with the singsong voices of a town bully.

"Sudbury! Sudbury! Where's the archbishop?"

"Hales, Lord Hales!"

"Legge, Legge, John Legge!"

"Lancaster, Lancaster, Henry Lancaster!"

Amid this chaos, the stone chapel's only sounds are the candles' flickering flames and the occupants' rattling breaths.

"What will we do?" the Earl of Warwick moans.

His voice seems to release the congregation, and movement ripples through the chapel. Some move to the door, others toward the back of the room.

The archbishop raises two fingers. "Stop," he says, silencing the whispers and shuffling feet. "I will hear the confessions of anyone who finds it necessary."

My lips tremble. Sudbury doesn't need to say more. The church teaches that dying unshriven, unpardoned by a priest, means an eternity in hell. I watch Lord Hales step forward; he's resigned to death, to what's about to happen. All he can do now is go to God with a clean soul. It's always seemed irrational to me, confession, but as I watch Hales, it's suddenly clear. In the events leading to this, the end of his life, he's lost control. But by approaching the archbishop to engage in this ritual he's known his whole life, Hales maintains control, dignity.

Lord Hales and the archbishop huddle in an archway behind the altar. In my head, I count the stone columns over and over, determined not to eavesdrop. After the archbishop absolves him, Hales hurries back to kneel among the crowd.

"Run, Dandy," Geoff whispers in my ear. His breath makes my veil tremble, and gooseflesh pebbles my neck. "You and Joan. There's a servants' door."

His chin, rough after days without shaving, brushes my shoulder when he jerks it toward the chapel's rear. I suppress a shiver.

"I'll try to keep 'em from you," he continues, oblivious to my squirming.

"They don't want us," I mutter. "They only want the men."

He exhales a frustrated breath on the tender, exposed skin of my neck.

Unable to stand it any longer, I spin around and push him by the shoulder, forcing him back to kneel beside Joan. "*I won't leave Henry*," I grind out through clenched teeth.

I turn back to the front of the chapel to watch John Legge, creator of the hated poll tax, give his confession, followed by Friar William Appleton, my father's surgeon and lawyer, the man who perfromed my wedding Mass.

When Appleton returns to kneel beside the earls, Henry stands.

"No," I hiss and grab his wrist. I pull, trying to force him back to the floor. "You don't need to confess. You'll be spared." I tug again, but he pries my cold fingers away and shakes his head, mouth set in a firm line.

He walks to Sudbury and delivers his confession in muted tones. As before, I refuse to listen.

After Henry receives the archbishop's blessing, Friar William Appleton returns to the altar to hear the archbishop's confession. My throat squeezes.

I clasp Henry's hand, pulling it to rest in the folds of my skirt. He smells of determination. Fingers warm against my chilled skin, he lowers his eyelids but holds his chin high.

When I close my own eyes, a pain strikes behind them. I see Henry dressed as a warrior in armor, galloping across a battlefield on a white horse. Even through a dense morning fog, the horse shines, glows, and I see Henry's full beard. He's a man, not a child. It's winter; the horse's hooves spray silver frost from the grass as it races, the sound ringing in my ears like bells.

Kneeling in the White Tower's chapel, I'm certain that what I've seen will happen. I'll watch him ride across that battlefield.

I almost wail when the archbishop pulls me from my vision with another funereal Mass. I wanted the sight—my gift—to tell me more.

During the *placebo*, Geoff leans forward once again.

"Dandelion, listen." He squeezes my shoulder. I try to swat his hand away. "They won't kill you." His whisper smells of simmering rage. "They'll...rape you, Blanche. You're the Lady of the Tower, after all. They'll want that...from you. And Joan too."

My bones turn to water, and a shudder dies in my throat.

"Run." He slips a dagger into my hand, and for the briefest moment, I see a dandelion instead, white and puffy in late summer. It sheds its seeds and lets them float away.

Gripping the dagger's hilt, I nod and start to pull Joan with me toward the servants' door.

The crash of the keep's main door makes the chapel walls shudder, and thunderous footfalls burst inside the building.

"They're here!" someone screams.

"*Omnes sancti, orate pro nobis,*" the archbishop intones. He must shout to be heard over the din. The stained-glass beams cover him from head to foot. Blood-red.

The chapel door flies open, banging against the white stone with a crack like cannon fire. I swallow a scream as the air erupts and armored rebels storm inside, brandishing their great swords and pikes.

"We've found 'em!" one man calls, his sweating face red and triumphant. They stream toward the archbishop. Other men seize Hales and John Legge, along with Friar Appleton.

I drag Joan toward the exit but stumble and fall, taking her down with me. From the ground, I catch a glimpse of the men hustling the nobles and the archbishop toward the main door.

Behind us, I hear a rebel strike Henry with the back of his sword, and I turn to watch as Geoff lunges to help his master.

"I have Lancaster!" the rebel cries, twisting Henry's hands behind him. He works to tie them despite Henry's struggles. Geoff draws his sword.

"Geoff, no!" I scream. There are more rebels than he can fight, four for every one of us.

Within moments, three men pull Geoff from Henry. One slugs him in the gut, while the other two hold him back. Henry, now bound, is pushed out of the chapel, and Geoff receives a backhanded blow across the jaw before they secure his hands.

"Leave the women alone!" Geoff shouts as they shove him through the door. "Leave 'em!" His screams echo as they force him out.

"My lady." Joan tries to haul me to my feet. "We must go, we must—"

Joan's words die in her throat when she's seized from the back of her tunic by a hulking rebel with immense shoulders. From my place, sprawled on the stone floor, I want to spit at him.

"Who's this?" He peers down at me while Joan's legs dangle like a poppet. She kicks and flails, trying to strike him. He laughs. His protruding eyes and thick lips make him look like one of London's wild pigs.

"Put my woman down." I stand, then see the look in Pig Face's watery gray eyes. I could kick myself for not disguising my French vowels and educated, upper-class accent. *Just because you're brave doesn't mean you're smart,* Maman once said.

"It's a lady!" he crows, triumphant. In his excitement, he gives Joan a little shake. She clamps her mouth shut and moans through clenched teeth.

The other rebels cock their heads, watching us.

An older man, heavyset with dark hair greased back against his scalp, takes a step toward me. "Whose wife are you, lady?"

At this point, I've no choice but to play my rank. "I am the wife of Sir Thomas Prescott," I say, "Constable of the Tower." I'm betting they've no idea the constable's wife is also the Duke of Lancaster's daughter. That connection won't help us. I tilt my chin, staring at Pig Face. "As I said, release my woman."

He places Joan on the floor. A sliver of the despair pooled in my chest evaporates. Pig Face let Joan go because of me. Maybe they'll let us slip away, to hide in Constable Tower. I grab Joan's hand and give it a reassuring squeeze.

"What do we do with 'em? Can we..." Pig Face grins, an uncomfortable glint in his eye as he leers at us. My stomach drops with sickening speed.

"Take 'em to Tower Hill," Greasy Hair says. "We'll have to ask permission first. Tyler said to leave the common women alone...but he said naught about the wife of the constable."

My guts contort as they laugh, but I don't release Joan's hand. "We have nothing to do with this conflict!"

"Nothing to do with it?" Greasy Hair raises his voice, mocking me. "Tell me, m'lady, where'd you get the wool for yer fine surcoat? And who earned the coin to pay the craftsmen who sewed it, and yer pretty shoes and headdress?"

A block of ice settles on the base of my spine. He's right. I can't claim innocence. I exist because of England's villeins. My clothes were purchased by my father from income raised by his many properties. Hundreds, if not thousands, of villeins toil in his fields. They pay him rent for dilapidated homes. My husband's income from his manor in Suffolk pays my allowance, which subsidizes anything I need, including Joan's earnings.

Everything I have is because of people like Hawise and Ceadda Groom.

When one of my father's villeins dies, does he make their child pay a heriot, like Hereford did to Geoff?

Greasy Hair ignores my horrified expression and addresses his friends. "If Tyler says yes, you can have the lady." He grabs Joan's wrist and pulls her to him. "*I* like 'em little, and young."

They laugh.

I lunge at him with Geoff's dagger, which I'd concealed in my skirts. A third man seizes my waist from behind. Pig Face snatches my wrist and bangs it against the wall. I cry out, and the dagger clatters to the floor, useless as a wooden sword.

Chapter Twenty-Three

They're about to drag us across the drawbridge when one of the menagerie's feline occupants roars directly below us.

"God's bones!" Greasy Hair cries. His two companions scream and almost run away. "What the fa' was that?"

I glance at the stone beneath our feet, but say nothing.

"A wild beast!" Pig Face shouts.

"Hurry, run!"

My own reaction couldn't be more divergent. My heart doesn't race—no more than it already does—and I don't gasp with fear. I feel only apathy toward the beasts. Perhaps I'm used to them, already accustomed to my new home at the Tower of London and its contents. Or, maybe I simply have no capacity for extra fear. Human men are more terrifying than any wild beast. Either way, I barely remember the young woman who trembled and cried when she first arrived at this place, only a week ago.

If I'd hoped the rebels' terror might induce our release, I'm disappointed. If anything, Pig Face's grip only tightens as he hauls me across the drawbridge and toward Tower Hill.

The green expanse is covered by a riot of yellow dandelions. I gasp and dig in my heels, forcing my captor to give a sharp yank on my wrist.

"The dandelions!" I cry, attempting to point, but he's still holding me.

He barks a sharp laugh. "Dandelions?" he calls to his friends. "The Lady of the Tower's been captured by the likes of us, and now she wants to talk about flowers?"

They roar with laughter, but I can still hear Joan softly crying.

There are men and women everywhere, trampling the yellow flowers into a pulpy disaster. They scream triumphant declarations and wave their swords, some clutching charters of freedom in blood-stained hands.

In the green's center stands an executioner's block, a hooded figure waiting beside it. His ax's handle is as long as I am tall. A female rebel stands beside the executioner, gesturing and clearly giving directions.

The smell of the place makes my eyes water. Although I see no blacksmith, it reeks of molten steel and burned, smoking iron, along with the tangy sweat of overworked men. It's a bright spring day—neither too hot nor too cold—but to my senses, the air around us cooks like a forge threatening to burn itself to ash. It soaks into my mouth, like blood on the tongue, so pungent and forceful that my vision swims with bright pops of color.

It's rage I smell, and a righteous search for justice that won't be satiated until everything, and everyone, is dead and gone. It smells of scorched earth.

Walking beside me, Joan's black eyes are wild. Her tunic is twisted and ripped at its hem, and her linen coif is gone, revealing snarled and unkempt black hair. Without her austere cap, I'm reminded how young she is.

I clasp her hand. I squeeze once, twice. Finally, she squeezes back.

Our captors prod us in the back with their sword hilts, and we shuffle toward the block, still holding hands. Beside it, Archbishop Sudbury, Lord Hales, John Legge, and Friar Appleton wait in a ragged line, their faces a mixture of shock and terror.

The scent of burning metal is strongest here, yet my breath catches and unexpected hope blooms in my chest. I don't see Henry. Perhaps he escaped. Better yet, maybe the rebels realized he's too young to be held culpable and let him go.

A rebel shoves the line forward, and my optimism plummets. Appleton's shifting frame reveals my brother, last in line and with his hands tied behind his back, eyes downcast.

I lurch toward him, but Pig Face seizes my right arm and twists it painfully behind my back. I yelp. Henry looks up. Our eyes lock, but he whirls to address someone behind him before I can manage even one strangled syllable.

A few feet beyond Henry, a pair of men hold Geoff, his hands tied like the other captives. A trickle of blood leaks from his split lip.

"Release my servant," Henry calls out. "Your quarrel is with me. My man was only following my orders."

"M'lord!" Geoff says. "No, I—"

"Quiet, man," Henry snaps. Through a mist of terror, I watch him jerk his chin in my direction. Geoff's eyes lock with mine, and his jaw sets with barely concealed rage.

When the rebels slice through Geoff's bindings, he runs to me and Joan without another glance at Henry. He grabs at his belt for his sword, only to find it gone, no doubt taken by the rebels.

Still twisted in Pig Face's grip, I give Geoff a frantic shake of my head. With thousands of rebels surrounding us, physical force is useless.

Greasy Hair leaves Joan and me with his companions and shoulders roughly past Geoff. As he passes the block, the rebel woman finishes her conversation with the executioner and faces the archbishop. I peer at her. Her clothes are soot-stained and burned, the fabric strained over her massive bosom and plump figure, and her hair, raven black, is slicked back from her face in a severe plait. Although her face is careworn and lined, I doubt she's much older than Maman.

And yet, even though the top of her head doesn't reach the executioner's collarbone, her every gesture conveys authority. It's clear that she's in charge.

"Sudbury!" the woman cries. "You're first."

She gestures to the archbishop. He shrinks away, so she strides over and yanks his upper arm. When he still doesn't move, she kicks him in the shin.

A tall man with a nose like a hawk's steps up beside her. His tunic sleeves are rolled up to his elbows, revealing muscular forearms slashed with innumerable thin burns. His right arm, however, hangs limp and useless at his side. He moves toward Sudbury.

Greasy Hair attempts to block his progress, but Hawk Nose shoves the man back with his good arm, then yanks the archbishop forward. Sudbury stumbles. They've removed his mantel and surcoat, and he shivers, even though the day is warm and a cheery summer sun beats on our necks. He reaches up to remove his miter with trembling fingers, but the woman snatches the shield-like headdress and smashes it back onto his head, crumpling the precious silk and gold embroidery as if the sacred garment were nothing better than the cheapest homespun.

"You're to die with it on, *Your Excellency.*" The woman sneers and makes a deep bow. The rebels around her howl with glee.

"Wouldn't want anyone confusing which head is yours atop London Bridge, now would we?" Hawk Nose adds.

The screeching laughter overwhelms me, and my eyes almost roll back into my head.

Unintimidated, Greasy Hair reenters the fray, poking the back of the tall man's arm with one blunt, dirty finger. Hawk Nose turns away from urging the archbishop toward the block, anger etched on his harsh features.

"What is it, man?"

"Where's Tyler?" Greasy Hair asks.

"We're in charge here." Hawk Nose gestures to the woman, who is now heckling Hales and Legge. "Why do you need Tyler?"

"This lady"—the heavyset rebel throws a hand in my direction—"is wife to the Tower's Constable. And she's got her maidservant. We want—"

"The constable's left his wife behind?" Hawk Nose emits a harsh bark of laughter. "What was he thinking?"

Greasy Hair laughs and shrugs. He opens his mouth, but Hawk Nose interrupts him.

"Do whatever you want with them. We're busy here."

Greasy Hair hurries back. I shudder as his thick hand closes around my wrist, pulling me away from Pig Face. The first man tugs back, and for a moment I wonder if they plan to split me in two.

When the ax thuds, however, they both release me.

The Archbishop of Canterbury, Simon Sudbury, lies facedown on the block, his thick arms outstretched to each side. The executioner, face hidden by a black hood, has lodged his iron ax into the back of the archbishop's thick, creased neck. Blood spurts from the wound, but the tendons and bone aren't severed.

My scream pierces the air. I cover my mouth with the back of my hand.

Or was it Joan's scream?

No, it's Sudbury who screams and writhes, two rebels pinning him down by the arms. His fellow prisoners, including my brother Henry, watch with white, horrified faces. Geoff, lingering nearby, wrings his hands together, fingers twitching for his nonexistent sword.

With a sickening squelch, the executioner hefts the ax head out of the wound and prepares to lodge it once again in the back of Sudbury's neck. Sudbury lets out another blood-curdling shriek as the second blow lands on the same spot.

Still, it doesn't sever his head.

He screams and wrenches, soils himself as the female leader orders more men to hold him down, trying to keep him still while avoiding the executioner's next strike.

I scream along with Sudbury now. My nostrils burn with the acrid smell. I use my free hand to cover first my nose and then my ear, desperate for any relief from the onslaught of smells and sounds. But it isn't enough. I turn and vomit, and the men holding me and Joan drag us away. I sense Geoff hovering nearby, unable to help but unwilling to leave.

Our captors don't go far—they want us to stop screaming, but still want to watch the proceedings.

It takes seven swings of the ax to kill the archbishop. While they remove his body, I squeeze my eyes shut and pray the others will die faster.

My eyes fly open. The others. Henry is in that line, and he must not die. He can't; my vision told me that someday he'll ride a white horse on a battlefield. I must make that happen.

I count the men in front of him. Hales is already stepping to the block, careful not to slip on the quagmire of Sudbury's blood and reeking effluence. John Legge and Friar William Appleton wait behind him, followed by Henry at the rear.

I've never seen my brother look more childish. He holds his head high, determined to die a noble death, like our father would. But his skin is pale, his cheeks smooth, the light facial hair invisible in the bright sunshine.

I close my eyes again and breathe in, like yesterday when I listened for the rebels' army.

Sweet Jesu, was that only yesterday?

The melee of the execution yard shrieks around me. The shouts of men and women ring, joyous and raucous, as Hales dies, blessedly easier than the archbishop. The rebels raise their fists and scream for more, more death. They want the blood of the lawyers and the nobles, want Tower Hill's green grass and gold dandelions to run crimson with it.

I shut the sounds out, trying to listen for the voice inside, Eldridge's voice.

Open your eyes.

I see a crystalline light in the air above the men's heads. It sparkles like sunshine through a cut-glass goblet; it pops and burns, twists as it grows and changes. It pulsates, throbs along with the rhythm of my heartbeat, the blood that pounds in my ears.

I squint and take a step closer. The crowd—moments ago a solid, screaming surge of sound—dims to a dull throb. My captors, no doubt assuming I want a better look at the executions, walk behind me. They drag Joan.

We move to the front of the crowd as John Legge, the lawyer who first introduced the poll tax, lays face-down on the block. He stretches his arms, indicating he's ready to die, and I hear the thudding clunk of the ax. I step around the last of the spectators, expecting to find the light shimmering over Legge's corpse as the angels take him to heaven.

It isn't there. The sky above the block, its wood filthy after three bloody deaths, is a clear, light blue. Wisping clouds float by, too small to blot out the sun.

I shield my eyes against the sunlight and see the ethereal light once again. It sparks, forms tendrils that twist and entwine through the rebels' hair. It travels from person to person, as if it is searching for something or someone. They don't notice. Only I see it.

Watch it, watch where it lands.

"Eldridge?" I ask.

No, Blanche. This voice is yours. It's you.

The burning presence changes as it rolls through the crowd, pauses above the heads of different rebels. At the first, it forms a candle flame, before it moves on and twists into a white horse charging into battle. It moves again, forming the crown of Saint Edward—the great crown of England.

Why is it moving and reforming?

See who will aid your brother, the voice says.

Still in the form of a crown, it settles over one man. Hawk Nose, the man who gave my captors permission to rape me. Unaware of the blazing light twisting above him, he doesn't flick his gaze away from the executions. He's hungry for every drop of blood.

I push away the dregs of my terror and stride toward him, forcing my captors to trot along behind me.

"Sir," I say. Hawk Nose jerks his head away from the chopping block, where two men drag John Legge's headless body away and a third tosses the head into a basket.

"What?" he snaps. He looks back at the pile of corpses. One rebel, a boy no older than thirteen, dips the heads in tar. Someone has nailed Sudbury's miter to his head so no one can mistake it when mounted on London Bridge, like the rebel woman promised.

"Sir, I need to speak with you."

"Ah, really, *my lady*?"

I keep my voice firm, like I speak to my patients. "You must spare Henry of Lancaster."

His eyes widen. They're gray, flecked with silver. Although his hair is almost white at the temples, I doubt he's over five and forty. He's a tradesman, a Londoner, based on his accent and clothing—clean, if plain.

"What's your name, sir?" I ask.

He chuckles. "John Ferrour of Southwark. Blacksmith. Leader of London's Craft Guild and its rebel tradesmen, along with my wife, Johanna."

He gestures to the woman, who is currently leading the crowd in a chant: "When Adam delved and Eve span, who was then the gentleman?" Johanna Ferrour, joined by tens of thousands, screams and pumps her fist in the air.

John Ferrour gives me a mocking bow. "At your service, *my lady*."

"Henry of Lancaster is only fifteen years old," I say. "He's just a boy. You cannot execute him, no matter the actions of his father."

He laughs and lifts his hand to push me away. I step aside, and he stumbles.

I know what I must do, but still, I'm afraid.

I push the emotion away.

Just because you're brave doesn't mean you're smart.

I breathe in, about to take the biggest risk of my life.

"I will make you an offer, Master Ferrour," I say. He turns, eyes sparkling. I take a step closer and lower my voice. "I have certain...abilities...powers." I take a gulp of air; it shakes in my throat, but I swallow my terror and plow on. "You have a child, do you not? One who can't seem to thrive, who's always sick?" It's a great gamble, but almost everyone has at least one sickly child, don't they?

His gaze softens, and he sucks in a sudden breath. I must be luckier than I thought.

"My Matthew," he says, "my youngest boy. How d'you know about him?"

"I can help him." I ignore his question while straining to keep my eyes clear and steady, my voice imperious. "I will do everything I can to heal him, to make him strong. But—"

"And my wife," Ferrour interrupts, eyes darting to where Johanna leads the rebels in another cheer, this one about my own father. "She's with child...again...and at her age...it's dangerous."

I glance at Johanna's middle, realizing some of her bulk is the swell of pregnancy, five or six months along.

Ferrour shakes his head. "I fear for her life. I've been out of work, and we can't afford a midwife. The expense..."

His voice trails off. Despite the situation, his agony pulls at my heart.

"I am an experienced midwife," I say. "I can help your wife and son, can provide wisdom and medicines."

A smile twitches at the corner of his lips. "M'lady—"

"But *only*," I interrupt, holding up one finger, "if you spare Henry of Lancaster's life."

"What's this, husband?" Johanna Ferrour appears at her husband's elbow. Behind her, two rebels are attempting to clean the block, and the executioner gulps from a tankard, sweat streaming down his exposed forearms.

John's face goes slack as he looks down his hawkish nose at Johanna. He takes her arm to draw her further from the crowd. "This woman," he flutters his good hand to me and whispers, "claims she can help Matthew."

She refuses to look at me, just stares at her husband, a deep furrow between her black brows. "And how does she know about Matthew?"

"I...I, um..." he falters.

"I'm a—"

Johanna lifts her chin to look at me. My words die in my throat. Her eyes are the same moss green as Eldridge's. Close up, I can see her dark hair is threaded with strands of ash-gray.

"I'm a wisewoman," I say, voice flat. "A healer."

She moves so close that her protruding belly taps my skirt. "Who are you?"

I speak without thinking. "I am Blanche. Blanche Fitzjohn."

"Fitzjohn?"

"Yes. Daughter of John."

"A bastard?" She doesn't flinch, doesn't blink, just stares at me, green gaze penetrating until I think my kneecaps will give way.

"Yes. A bastard."

I could have given my married name, like I told her husband. I'm Lady Prescott, wife of the constable. In this moment, however, speaking to this strange woman, I can only be myself. I'm a Fitzjohn.

"You're clearly a lady," Johanna Ferrour jeers up at me.

"It doesn't matter," I say. "Lady or peasant, a bastard is a bastard."

She grins. "That's true, I suppose. And what do you want in return, Fitzjohn?"

"I want Henry of Lancaster freed."

She frowns and shakes her head so hard her chin wobbles. "No, never. Canna do that, m'lady."

"Johanna." John bends to speak only to her. "Not only will she help Matthew, but also you." His eyes dart to mine, then away in an instant. "She's a midwife."

Her scowl deepens. "I dinna need help."

"You do." He grips her elbow and leads her another step away from the other rebels. His voice drops to a deep rumble. I know the words aren't for me. It's not right to listen, but I must think about Henry right now. "You do need her help, wife. Please."

"No." She crosses thick arms over her chest and juts out her chin.

"Then what about me?" John presses her. "Can you accept her help for me? I canna do without you. *We* canna. Not just Matthew, but all the boys and me."

Johanna huffs. She eyes me sideways for a quick moment before looking back to John. "And give up Henry of Lancaster?"

"The Earl of Derby is only fifteen," I say as Ferrour glances over his shoulder. The executioner has finished his ale; we must hurry.

Johanna chews her lower lip.

He tugs her sleeve. "Think of Matthew, my love."

She sighs, then taps his finger with one knuckle. "Only for him. And you."

The scent of leather and spun sugar hits me like a tidal wave, and I look over Johanna Ferrour's shoulder to meet Geoff's gaze. His face is drawn and white, streaked with blood.

Without another word, Johanna nods, then hurries away to the executioner as another rebel forces Friar Appleton to the block.

John Ferrour starts to turn toward Henry, but I grab his sleeve. "And you'll make these men release me and my woman."

Ferrour nods and shifts his gaze to our captors. "Let them go."

Greasy Hair opens his mouth to argue, but Ferrour shoves him hard before striding toward Henry.

Friar William Appleton lies prostrate on the block, and Johanna hovers above him while the executioner readies his ax. He whispers a prayer in a rasping voice, and the executioner waits for his signal.

I hold my breath as Ferrour makes his way to Henry. He grips the young earl's upper arm and speaks to the rebels flanking him.

As Ferrour pulls Henry away from the block, my knees buckle. I lean on Joan for support.

The rebels holding Henry protest, but I can't hear their words over the din of cheering voices. Appleton has stretched out his arms; the executioner is ready. Ferrour pulls Henry toward me as the executioner raises his ax and drops it with weary force. He misses, striking Appleton in the shoulder. The crowd groans. Appleton's screams fill the air.

Ferrour shoves Henry in my direction. My brother is weak with terror, and with his wrists still tied, he stumbles and almost topples me and Joan to the blood-soaked grass. Geoff snatches his master's torso and holds him up.

"Take him and go," Ferrour says, "before I change my mind."

Behind us, a rebel slices through Henry's bindings.

"I'll come to you, at Southwark," I say.

Ferrour nods and turns away to watch the executioner's final, fatal stroke.

Chapter Twenty-Four

We run. Geoff grabs Henry by the upper arm and half-drags him. Joan and I pick up our skirts and follow, up Tower Hill before the rebels question why Henry, the Duke of Lancaster's only heir, was spared.

We sprint instinctively back toward the Tower's drawbridge. We don't have time for reflection on the absurdity of it—seeking shelter in a fortress just infiltrated by rebels.

By the time we reach the drawbridge, Henry leads our little group. Geoff has dropped back. Before he crosses the bridge, Henry stops to wait for us. Bright patches of pink flare on his cheeks and his chest heaves; his auburn hair stands on end.

I resist the urge to throw my arms around his neck and hold him. We're not safe yet.

"Wh—" Henry can't finish the question. He's winded, not only from our sprint up the hill, but from the sheer panic of facing the surety of his own death, only to escape by the width of an eyelash. He doubles over and grips his knees, panting and coughing. He looks at me out of the corner of his eye.

"I know where we can go." I pull him by the arm and lead the group across the drawbridge. All the gates stand open—the Tower of London is abandoned.

"We can't trust the guards," Geoff shouts from behind. "Once they come back, any one of them will find us and give us away, no matter where we hide."

I skid to a stop and look around. "We'll be somewhere they won't dare go."

We stand atop a semicircular barbican, about to cross the causeway to Middle Tower and Byward Tower beyond. I pull Henry down a small flight of stone steps on the tower's outer edge, heedless of my filthy skirts billowing around my legs.

Joan takes one step before realizing where we are. She grips the stone wall, plants her feet, and shakes her head.

"No," she says. "I'm not going in with the lions."

"Joan, we must." I try to keep my voice gentle, but it shakes with urgency. "The rebels will be too afraid to follow. It's the only place we'll be safe."

"The lions are caged," Henry adds, still panting. "Everyone's scared of them, but really, there's no danger. Blanche is right. It's a genius idea, actually." He gives me a smile, and I feel my cheeks heat.

I ease Joan's hands off the stone wall and coax her down one step at a time. When we arrive at the door—at last—Henry lifts the latch, and we exhale with relief. It's not locked.

We hustle inside and slam the door.

Somewhere in the tower, something growls. My hair stands on end, and I ram my back against a cold, damp wall. Joan shies away from the sound as well, bumping into me. I wrap my arms around her, and she turns to cry softly into my hair.

"Shush, Joan, shush." I rub her back. "It'll be all right. We're safe."

I look around. We're standing in an entry hall; one iron sconce illuminates its stone walls, bare of any other decoration, even arrow slits. I strain my ears, but hear nothing. The tower seems abandoned, except for the animals. Their keepers must be on Tower Hill.

"Come on." Henry touches my arm, and I jump. "I've been here before. They're this way." He gestures toward a closed door on the narrow chamber's opposite wall.

"They?" Geoff asks.

"The lions. The closer we get to them, the safer we'll be."

He strides toward the door, Joan following close behind. Terrified though she was to come inside, now she seems intent to get away from the door—and the rebels above.

Henry takes her hand and leads her through the door and into the darkness beyond. I move to follow them, but before I can cross the threshold, Geoff pulls me back.

The door slams behind Joan, and Geoff buries his face in my neck.

"Dandy." His voice cracks as he wraps his arms around me, beneath my cloak. "I thought they'd..." He presses the hard bridge of his nose into the soft bend of my flesh. "I'm so sorry. I...I couldn't stop 'em."

"Geoff." I take his head between my two hands and look into his eyes. "Don't apologize. Henry couldn't stop them. Henry, the future Duke of Lancaster, was powerless. We all were."

His eyes burn into mine. In the dark, his pupils are dilated, growing out into the iris of brown like a puddle in a rainstorm. Even in the shrinking color, I see little flecks of gold intermingled with the brown. I've never noticed them before.

I realize I'm still holding his head, fingers laced through his sweat-damp hair.

"What did you say to that rebel?" I feel his lips on mine as he whispers. "Why did he release Henry?"

"It doesn't matter," I breathe. His lips are featherlight, soft. I taste them against my own. There's blood, from where the rebels struck him, and for a minute I remember what's happening above us. But then, I don't care. I relish the feeling, the other flavors of him. Sugar and saddle leather. So much closer, so much better than last night on the Tower wall. Finally.

He presses his mouth to mine, only soft for a fraction of a heartbeat. Then, he nudges it open with his tongue. It should be absurd, I should pull away, I must. But it's not, and I don't. I let him tickle my tongue, let him press his mouth to mine hard and deep. I release my strain and worry in his embrace. I'm limp; all the fear and the bruises, the hatred from Thomas, dissolve.

His hands climb my back and pull my loosely coiled braids free. His fingers are in my hair, on my face, my neck, my chest. They're tangled in mine, in my dress's fabric, in my belt. He squeezes my bottom, a growl rumbling deep in his throat. Pleasure spikes through my middle. I give a little gasp as he presses me to the wall and grinds his pelvis into mine with an urgency that highlights what was missing with Thomas. He bites my earlobe, then kisses along my jawline back to my mouth. He sucks my lower lip between both of his, until I moan and clench his forearms, digging my nails into the fabric of his red-and-white coat.

The pressure of his body lifts me onto the tips of my toes. I'm no longer limp, but tense as a coiled spring. I run my hands through his damp hair, and use my own tongue, returning his nips with my teeth.

He breaks our kiss with a gasp, then tilts my head back with the bridge of his nose on my jaw. A desperate mewl escapes me as he kisses down my neck. He pushes me against the wall again and nibbles at the neckline of my bodice, tickling my skin and palming my breast with one hand.

"Dandy...my Dandy," he whispers, his voice gruff and muffled against fabric and skin.

I cry out as his tongue dips under the bodice's trim, grazing one nipple. Then he tugs my bodice down and takes my breast in his mouth. I press the back of his head, urging him on. He pulls up my skirt. His hands are on my hips, my thighs, the backs of them. He hoists me up against the wall, and I wrap my legs around him.

When he touches me, we both inhale, as if realizing what just happened. He snatches his hand back. "Dandy…" he groans through gritted teeth.

I grab his fingers and thrust them back between my legs.

I shudder beneath his touch. I know Henry could return at any moment, could come back to find me, to find us. Like this. Henry wouldn't hurt Geoff, nor me, not like Thomas would. But he would dismiss Geoff, send him back to Fobbing. Whether my brother likes Thomas or not, I'm married. This is wrong. Very wrong.

But I don't want Geoff to stop, can't let him stop. The bodies, the blood, come rushing back to my memory as he strokes me, touches me while we kiss, deep and hungry and hard. I still taste blood on his mouth. I push my pelvis to meet him as he slides one finger inside. The violence, the smell of it still permeates our bodies. But I want this. This right now is what I want. What I need.

Another finger. He's moving in and out of me; I hear the slick sound of my wetness, and it makes me gasp and squirm. My hands are flat on his chest, pressing, urging, as if he's an animal I can command. His lips are on my cheeks, my ear, my mouth, my eyelids. Everywhere and nowhere. Pinned against the wall, my legs wrapped around him, I reach down and grab his wrist, holding him inside me. My thumb presses his wrist bone; my fingers can't make it all the way around. I cry out with my face pressed to his cheek, rough with stubble.

It's as if wild chaos was there one moment, then all that energy and mania is concentrated into one, tiny speck. It lives in me, in my most secret sex, pulsating in one minuscule part of my desire and pleasure. I think I might cry, then scream in jubilation. Like I'll never be happy, or like I'll be happy for the rest of my life. I think for a moment that I'm dying, then I think myself immortal.

He's panting, heart racing against mine. Then he whispers it in my ear. Those three words I've never heard, not from anyone.

He pauses, then rushes ahead. "I thought, when the rebels took you, that I would never get the chance. This chance. So now, I need you to know."

I say nothing. I don't know why. Why I can't say it back, because I know I feel it. But I can't. Something stops me, grips my voice. My body yearns for his. I want to tell him to take me, here on the wall of a prison, to take all that I have. But I can't tell him those three words.

I am a coward. Thomas might be dead. I know it's true. In this wild new world, where peasants kill the Archbishop of Canterbury, anything could happen. But until I know Thomas is gone, he's still my husband. He could hurt Geoff for loving me, could even kill him. I can't tell Geoff I love him—it would give him some kind of permission, some access to me that's just not possible. Not yet.

He misreads my silence.

"I'm sorry." He pulls away, but I snatch his torso and nuzzle into his neck, enjoying the sharp pain of facial stubble against my cheek.

"No, I—" I freeze.

"What?"

"Henry." I grab my dress's bodice, which is pulled all the way down, revealing both my breasts. "He's coming back."

Geoff sets me down and darts back, wiping his hands on his surcoat. I've just pulled down my skirt when the door opens.

"What are you doing?" Henry asks. Joan peeks out from behind him, eyes glistening with unshed tears. "Your maid and I got all the way to the bottom of the building before we realized you weren't there. I had to convince her to come back. It took a while."

"Joan," I say. "I'm so sorry. We...we got lost."

Henry looks me up and down, my hair loose, my dress rumpled and askew. He looks at Geoff, standing hunched over himself, arms crossed over his broad chest.

"Right," Henry says. "Come on, then."

He gestures, and we follow him back down the stairs.

When the door shuts behind us, there's no light on the stairway. Henry takes my right hand and leads the way. Joan grips my left until my bones crack, and Geoff takes up the rear, placing a hand on Joan's shoulder. Our little caravan snakes down two flights of narrow, winding stairs, shuffling our feet as we all breathe in short, ragged gasps.

The air smells dank and tired, like urine, sweat, and feces. It presses in, and the euphoria of those stolen minutes with Geoff ebbs away, replaced with the terror of where we're going, of what we escaped on Tower Green.

The sound of dripping moisture punctuates the air, and we all jump when we hear odd slithers, shuffles, and growls from the open doorways we pass.

The smell intensifies. My empty stomach flips and twists, and I gag. I can't cover my nose, as Henry holds one hand and Joan the other, so I let my jaw dangle, determined to breathe through my mouth.

When the stairs end, we step through a doorway and into a chamber. I blink as the sudden sunlight streams through arrow slits, then gasp. A few feet away, a row of three wooden cages is built along the semicircular room's flat wall, each no larger than ten feet long and six feet deep.

A low growl prickles my senses, and I back against the wall, pressing myself flat and sucking in my stomach. Beside me, Joan, Geoff, and even Henry do the same.

On the other side of the closest barrier, two giant yellow eyes watch us. Their owner crouches behind the wooden boxes strewn about its cage. Its paws are the size of dinner plates, and its long, golden-yellow tail swishes soundlessly. It takes one step, its low, threatening growl so resonant that the stone behind my back vibrates.

"That's one of the females," Henry mutters.

She prowls closer, one careful, elegant step at a time.

My breath catches. She's so like Rhead that I want to stretch out my hand and touch her, even though my heart pounds so hard I think it might break me.

She must be eight feet long, with sinewy flesh that ripples with each step, even as bony shoulder blades protrude from her back. She's golden, like sunlight on the marsh, like a dandelion flower.

In the cages flanking her, a second, smaller female and a beast that must be a male, with a mane of yellow-red hair, step into the light.

"She's spectacular," I say.

Henry chuckles. "Do you dare to touch her, Blanche?"

I resist turning to him with a smile. It's such a relief to hear him sounding like my fifteen-year-old brother.

"I wish I could," I murmur. "I only wish I could."

Geoff sucks in a horrified breath. Joan is frozen, pasted like paper against the wall.

"I've never seen anything so beautiful." I take a step closer. The lioness freezes, teeth bared. She doesn't move from the tip of her tail to whiskers.

"I heard the keepers complain about this one," Henry says. "She's a fearful beast, they say, full of malice. They can't let her near the others. It's as if she doesn't know how to act around her own kind."

She watches me with yellow eyes that glow like two suns in the sky. I read her with one glance, and she reads me, too. *I don't know how to be with my own kind either.*

"She's unhappy, Henry. She's a prisoner." I cock my head and she starts to purr, a low rumble deep in her throat. "No one wants to be held captive. Everyone, no matter who they are, craves freedom."

The menagerie's foul air dissipates, replaced by the golden sunshine of a field, the kind of place I know she wants to roam, where she deserves to be. A wild part of me longs to open her cage, to release her onto the Tower Green where she can race through the yellow flowers. For her, I smell them: green, aromatic shafts of fresh-cut hay, musky cream interspersed with pollen and a fresh, sweet dribble of honey. Bright, crisp air, full of puffy seeds.

"*Dent de lion*," I breathe.

"Dandelion?" Henry asks.

I don't answer, just repeat the French words. "*Dent de lion*."

My mother tongue's expression for a dandelion flower: lion's tooth.

The lioness and I stand there for a few minutes, silent and staring at one another while the other beasts pace back and forth.

At last, Geoff gives my wrist a gentle tug to pull me back against the wall. Soundlessly, the four of us slide down to sit in a crumpled heap on the floor. Geoff sits to my left, Henry on my right, and Joan beyond him.

Geoff slips his arm around my waist, hidden by the stone wall and my skirts. His strong fingers pull me close, and I rest my head on his shoulder.

Above us, blood and terror reign, and it frightens me. Yet, the promise of a new world beckons. My old life, when I was either the outcast illegitimate daughter of a great man or a battered wife trapped in a loveless marriage, is no more. My eyes close, and I wonder, again, if Thomas is dead. The rebels want those in power gone, and next to the king, the Constable of the Tower is the most powerful man in London.

My breath grows even, and the calm blanket of darkness beckons. Within minutes, I'm fast asleep.

Chapter Twenty-Five

15 JUNE 1381

The shuffle of boots on stone makes me stir.

I rub my eyes. Then yesterday's memories—and the fear that the rebels have discovered us—jolt me awake.

Bright light streams through the windows. I blink, shrinking back. I see rough boards, built to keep something out. Or something inside? The flick of a golden tail. A low, tight growl.

Turning my head, I find Geoff beside me, asleep. His breath—in and out, in and out—stirs the little hairs around my face. He smells of the lingering incense of St John's Chapel, and of...me. I feel my face heat.

His face is peaceful, not unlike that of a child, and the corners of his wide mouth curve into a smile. I look to my right. Henry's there, Joan beyond him, both still sleeping.

Another shuffle makes me face forward, and as my eyes adjust, the figure of a man solidifies. He's silhouetted against the sunlight, its strength and cheer a contrast to my turbid thoughts.

Despite my fear, a yawn threatens to crack my jaw. I'm so tired. But there's nothing for it; I must talk to this man and see what I can learn.

"Who are you?" I ask. I stifle another yawn with my fist.

"Who'm I?" He scoffs and bends down. "Who are *you*?"

His breath smells of onions and day-old porridge. I long to cringe back from his stench but lean in to get a closer look at him. A rangy man in his middle years, he's thin, scrawny even, but with an odd impression of strength. His colorless hair and nondescript features don't help identify him, but his tunic, emblazoned with the lions of England, does—he's a royal servant.

I open my mouth to speak, but stop.

Many of the king's servants support the rebels. They let them into the Tower. Will this man drag us upstairs and hand us over to the bloodthirsty horde?

A nearby squeak of fear draws my gaze to Joan, who is awake and staring at the strange man before us. She tugs Henry's arm, and his eyes fly open. He stands, while on my other side, Geoff pops up and runs a hand through his hair.

Henry unfolds to his full height, at least a hand above the rangy man. The Lancastrian heir is filthy and wrinkled, but still well-dressed, and the collar of his house's golden esses shines on his neck.

The servant shrinks back and yanks off his felt cap.

"I am the Earl of Derby." Henry's voice is calm and measured. "This is Lady Prescott, my sister and wife of the Tower's Constable."

The man bows while Geoff helps both me and Joan to our feet. My body aches and my head pounds, but I try to match Henry's imperiousness in stance and expression.

Joan cowers against me, refusing to even look at this man who has discovered us.

"Tell me, man," Henry says, "what's going on above?"

The servant sighs and shuffles his feet, crumpling his red cap in his hands. I peek around him at the lions. He seems unconcerned by them; I imagine he's their keeper. Only such a man could appear so nonplussed around the powerful, lamp-eyed lioness and her two companions. With his back to them, no less.

Henry looks out of the arrow slit. "What time is it?"

"Midmorning, m'lord," the man croaks. "The king..." He clears his throat. "...went to meet with the rebels this morning, at Smithfield."

"Again?" I ask.

"Aye, m'lady." He bows and wrings his cap so tight I fear it might tear.

"And?" Henry asks.

"Wat Tyler was killed."

"Really?" I ask, incredulous. "Did the rebels riot?"

"No. The king had asked Tyler to meet with him across the field, away from the rebel forces. When one of the king's companions stabbed Tyler in the neck, the rebels couldna tell what was happening. They thought the poor sot was getting knighted."

I stroke Joan's hair and murmur something soothing, unable to watch as the man continues his story. There's no rebuke in his voice, but he must think the king's actions dishonest at best, treacherous at worse.

"When Tyler's horse came back riderless, they knew." From beneath my lashes, I watch the man wave his hands about, the red cap flopping. Behind him, the lions pace back and forth and growl. He ignores them. "They notched their bows and prepared to fight, but the king himself galloped across the field, beseeching 'em to parlay."

Henry's jaw drops. "Really?"

"Aye. And they did, of course. He apologized for Tyler's death. Said it was an accident. He agreed to their demands, and they marched home, clutching their papers of freedom."

I shake my head. "Just like that?"

The man bobs his head.

"How many nobles were killed yesterday?" Henry demands. "How many ministers?"

The man shrugs. "Not sure. I only saw those they pulled out the White Tower's chapel." His face turns bright red, and he looks at his feet, avoiding Henry's gaze.

"What of Sir Thomas Prescott, the Tower's Lord Constable?" I ask.

He looks up, and I smell preserved fish. Pity. "Dunno, m'lady. Haven't seen him, but haven't heard he was hurt or killed neither."

My heart thuds in my ears. The man's pity is wasted on a wife like me. I want my husband's death. With it comes my freedom.

Geoff grips my arm, and my heart skips a beat. "We need to get upstairs, m'lord," he says to Henry. "It seems we're safe."

"Indeed." Henry gives a curt nod to the lions' keeper, then departs.

I steal one last glance at the lioness. Much as I want fresh air, I resist. My fingers twitch, answering the absurd urge to open her cage.

"She deserves to be free," I murmur, the loose hairs around my face swaying in the breeze from the unglazed windows.

"What?" Geoff asks.

I shake my head and compress my lips. The lioness should be outside, with sunshine on her golden fur, not locked on the bottom floor of a stone tower. She gazes back, unblinking.

There's nothing I can do, not for her.

Geoff squeezes my arm and gives a minute tug toward the exit. I ignore him.

Losing his patience, Geoff pulls me to the door. I sense the lioness's yellow eyes on my back all the way up the stairs, and still feel her watching me as we emerge from the top of the Lion Tower, blinking in the bright light of day.

I return to the den of a king who lied to his subjects, who feasts on their labors and tricks them into submission. I'm a complacent participant in this calamity, and I sense the lioness's judgment.

Chapter Twenty-Six

We emerge into a flurry of activity. Pages rush past, messages clutched in their sweaty fists. Builders erect scaffolding against damaged walls, and soldiers mount horses in preparation. Children rush across the drawbridge, followed by anxious mothers.

Henry hurries toward the Middle Tower and the outer ward beyond, but when I try to follow him, Geoff's fingers encircle my wrist. I pull away.

"Dandy," he whispers in my ear.

"Shush," I say through gritted teeth. I notice Joan huddled by the stone wall, fearful eyes darting at every man that rushes past.

"What're you going to do?" Geoff asks. "What're we—"

"I have to figure out what happened to Thomas."

"Do you want me to—"

A soldier trots by on a shining destrier, and I notice he's staring. At me. At Geoff. At me with Geoff. At Geoff holding my elbow.

I wrench away. "*Have a care,*" I hiss.

"A care for what?" He closes the distance between us with one long stride.

"For your safety."

Smells of rotting garbage float on the wind. My old friend disdain. The smoldering fire of anger.

The soldiers know I'm the Lady of the Tower, and this unnamed commoner, this Lancaster soldier, is daring to speak to me. To *touch* me. This is not permissible for the constable's wife. The constable's widow? I must find out the truth. I must locate Thomas, dead or alive.

My only hope for a future with Geoff—albeit a private one—is as a widow. If Thomas lives and discovers an affair, he'll kill Geoff.

I grab Joan's hand and hurry away.

Geoff's heavy footfalls follow close behind, but I don't look over my shoulder. I can't stand the prospect of seeing him. Up ahead, a small crowd mills around something slumped on the paving stones.

"Is that..." Joan pants.

"Yes." I pick up my pace. "A body."

"Is it...is it missing..."

"Yes." The corpse is headless, but I don't say that word. Not to Joan.

I push through the crowd. Joan hangs back, away from the stench of death, but I can sense Geoff behind me. My stomach twists. I've seen plenty of death in my life, but I've never felt like this before, not while approaching a corpse. Hopeful.

"Who is he?" I ask a woman holding a child on her hip. She shrugs.

The dead man's clothes are so coated in blood that they're virtually unrecognizable, but I can tell by the crimson-stained stitching and leather boots that they were once well made, like a successful merchant's. Or a high-ranking military officer. The body has been stripped of anything valuable: weapons, belts, jewelry. If he'd been a knight, whoever killed him would have taken his golden spurs. I stare at the boots, trying to remember those that Thomas had pulled on as I watched him dress, before he went with the king. But for once, my memory fails me. I can't even recall how long ago that was. It couldn't be only a day—it seems like a lifetime ago that King Richard left the Tower and we sheltered in the chapel, only to be hauled out by the rebels.

A cart, pulled by a mule, trundles up beside us, and a soldier picks up the headless corpse and tosses it on top of two other bodies, also decapitated.

"Who is this man?" I demand of the soldier, pointing to the body. "Is it Sir Thomas Prescott, Constable of the Tower?"

He draws back, surprised. "Why no, m'lady. 'Tis Wat Tyler, leader of the rebels. His head is going to London Bridge. His body...well, I'm not sure where that'll end up."

I gape at him. "His head will go on the bridge? But I thought the king gave the rebels what they wanted. He said Tyler was killed by accident."

The soldier flushes and looks away.

An understanding of the king's deceit is beginning to form in my mind, but I push it aside. Thomas. I must find Thomas.

"And those men." I gesture to the cart. "The others. Who are they?"

He shrugs.

"Have you heard any news of Sir Thomas Prescott, the Lord Constable?" I ignore the sound of Geoff breathing behind me.

The sharp scent of preserved fish emanates from the man, and I wrinkle my nose, my annoyance at his misdirected pity tempting me to say something I'll likely regret. "Dunno, m'lady. Haven't seen him."

I hurry away, unable to bear the reek of sympathy.

Joan and Geoff follow me into the inner ward. The king is probably in the White Tower. Thomas is either with him or someone there will know his fate. I run across to the ward's crenelated wall and up the great keep's steps.

I burst inside the White Tower's cold, shadowed great hall, hand flat on my heaving chest. Joan and Geoff slide through the door before it closes.

It seems an eternity before my eyes adjust to the gloom. Voices echo, whispering and booming at the same time. It's as if some are in the next room, some down a long corridor, while others shout in my ear. My hands tremble, but I hide them in my skirts. Even in this large, airy room, the walls seem to move, pressing in as the sounds threaten to overwhelm me.

I breathe in the cold air, reminding myself that I'm in a massive hall. Walls don't move, not on their own. I take in the details of the place, trying to calm my racing heart.

An iron candelabra, suspended by a thick chain, hangs from the high ceiling, and the floor is almost entirely taken up by an enormous table, littered with faded maps and letters. Half a dozen men sit around it, talking. At its head sits the king.

Henry sits with the Earl of Warwick, their faces thunderous. Beside them, I recognize the Earl of Salisbury. I'd expected the chamber to be packed, but it isn't. I only wonder where everyone is for a split second.

The king's top ministers: the Archbishop of Canterbury, Lord High Treasurer Hales, John Legge, Friar William Appleton. I watched them die. Terrible, grisly deaths.

"There will be many open positions," I hear a baron, whose name I don't know, whispering to a friend as he walks past. "The king will need to replace those that perished. Could be a good opportunity."

My cheeks go cold.

The king is speaking. I force myself to listen.

"...issued in haste," he's saying.

"In haste, Your Grace?" a scribe asks, quill held frozen above his parchment.

"That's what I said, isn't it?" The child king's voice is hard and remote, and I absorb his words as if from the other end of a tunnel. "Their charters of freedom were issued in haste. Declare them void. Once the horde gets back to their manors, of course."

"Y-y-yes, Your Grace. Of course."

The young man scribbles. Sitting around the table, no one says anything. I try to scan the men's faces, to look for Thomas, but the king's words ricochet through my brain. I can't focus.

"Tell them..." Richard grins, like a brilliant idea just came to him, then glances at the scribe to make sure he's keeping up. "Tell them, 'You have been and are villeins; in bondage you shall remain, but incomparably more debased than before!'" He waves a tiny, bejeweled finger in the air, waving it and smiling with each word.

"Liar," I hiss between my teeth.

A cool hand closes around my wrist. I jump, but when I turn around, I find Joan's pensive face instead of Geoff's. She holds one finger to her lips.

"He lied," I whisper. "All those lives wasted, and for what?"

She shakes her head, but says nothing.

"And hunt down their leaders. Execute them on the spot," Richard says. Joan's fingers tighten on my wrist. "Jack Straw, John Ball, Thomas Baker. Bring their heads to London. It's London Bridge for them."

"No trials?" the scribe asks.

"No. Traitors' deaths: hung, drawn, and quartered." The king seems to relish the prospect.

"And extra prayers for the dead?" Salisbury asks.

"Who?" the king responds.

"The archbishop, Hales. Your loyal ministers..." The earl trails off.

"I've ordered their heads removed from the bridge. That's enough."

Bile surges into my throat as someone groans. The baron and his friend, still standing nearby, stare at me. At the table, the king's ministers turn.

Joan tugs my wrist. "Shhh, my lady..." she whispers.

"Lady Prescott?" one of the earls asks.

I look toward the voice, trying to identify each man at the table. The last man, seated beside the king, stands.

His black eyes meet mine.

"Wife."

Sir Thomas's glare sucks the air from my lungs. Still, he stands and stretches out an upturned palm. I walk to him on stiff legs. He takes my hand, his fingers cold and sterile, like the day we met in Fobbing.

"I'm pleased to find you safe, lady wife."

I nod, remove my hand from his grip, and hide it behind my back.

On the king's other side stands Robert de Vere. I feel his eyes on me, and for an odd moment, we're frozen in a tableau: my cousin the king, Thomas, Robert de Vere, and me.

Through the hall's murk, I see stones, glittering and precious. Set by the continental masters. Pearls, gold, silver. And de Vere at the center of this wealth, smiling like the panther that stalked my brother's life. He *is* stalking my brother's life, I realize. My brother and my father. Then there's water. Gushing water. My river, my tidal Thames.

The tide is coming; I see it in my mind's eye. But as I make to pick up my skirts to run away, a stagnant calm floods over me, one that can only be due to my sight. The tide's not hunting me. Its prey is de Vere, the man standing beside the king of England. The Thames will come if I wait long enough. My river will come for him, and for Thomas.

"Are you well, wife?"

I open my eyes and see Thomas: his pale, tired face, features drawn and puffy with exhaustion. He looks a decade older than yesterday.

"You've had quite the scare," he continues. "Go back to my residence. Rest."

Chapter Twenty-Seven

16 JUNE 1381

I awake in my bed with no memory of how I got there. A weight rests on my stomach. It shifts, purrs.

I pull Rhead to my face and inhale his comforting scent. For a moment, I think we're back in Fobbing. It's early morning—I can tell by the purple light shifting through the bedclothes. I smell the briny salt of the marsh. I hear its birds, feel the damselflies flit through my hair. Blades of seagrass brush my bare shins as I run beside Geoff, two children through the salt beds. I cut knotted hedge parsley with my belt knife. Eldridge lives. There is no Thomas. The jangling call of a yellow bunting makes me smile, and I breathe in through my nose, deep, to soak it in. I'm back at home. I'm safe.

I close my eyes for the space of a heartbeat, then open them and sit up.

Instead of the small, shuttered window of my cottage, I see a cross-shaped arrow slit. Outside, sheets of rain pour off the inner ward of a fortified castle.

It all rushes back with painful accuracy. The rebellion, Henry's near-execution, my near-rape. Then, what happened in the lion's den.

I rub my face with both palms. Suddenly everything hurts. My shoulders, my back, legs, and my feet. I'm exhausted and want to go back to bed. I glance around. I'm alone. Thomas must be in the barracks or the White Tower. Or with de Vere. I shiver.

I hurry to my trunk and grab my simplest gown: the brown wool. I dress in a hurry, lacing everything myself with no trouble, then throw on my cloak and shoes. I leave my hair in its loose plait. With the rain, I'll keep my hood up.

I must check on my plants. It's been two days. Then, I'll go find my patients and the other Hamlet residents. There's also John Ferrour, the rebel who freed Henry, whose wife and son need my care. I've no time to waste.

I creep down the twisting stairs, listening to Constable Tower's morning sounds. The cook and his small staff are in the kitchen, preparing the daily bread. Two mice scamper in the dining hall's rushes as the rain continues to pour outside the walls. Joan is likely somewhere nearby. This morning, though, I want to be alone.

I'm almost to the front door when it opens, letting in a blast of cold air, a shower of rain, and Geoff.

"Geoff." I take a step back. "What are you doing here?"

"I wanted to see you," he whispers.

My stomach grows leaden, then churns.

Geoff steps inside and eases the door closed. Sopping wet, he stands there in a puddle of water, blinking at me. He gives a little shrug, shaking away his thoughts. "I've something to tell you."

My cheeks heat as Rhead brushes my skirts, purring. When he sees Geoff, dripping wet in the doorway, the cat freezes and stares.

"Hi, Rhead." Geoff waves a big hand.

Rhead lifts his nose and sniffs, moving to push open the swinging kitchen door with one paw. He drifts inside with his tail standing stiff and straight, like a pennant. The door slams behind him.

"He seemed eager to leave," Geoff says with a low chuckle.

I scoff, and his brow creases.

"Dandy."

Tears threaten at the corners of my eyes. I know I should open the door and force him out. Instead, I give him a pointed look. "You said you had something to tell me?"

He nods and shoves wet hair back from his forehead. "The earl's freed me."

My mind goes blank.

"I'm *free*," he says again.

"He gave you papers of manumission?"

"Aye." He reaches into his belt pouch and pulls out a small roll of parchment. His words rush and tumble over one another. "I canna read, you know that, but I'm sure it's what the earl says it is."

I grab the parchment and unroll it. "Yes, Geoff." I look up. "You're a free man. No one can make you go back to Fobbing Manor, not the countess, not the king himself."

"And there's more," he says.

"What could be more than this?" I shake the parchment beneath his nose. Laughing, he tries to snatch it. I giggle and draw the parchment back just in time. He laughs again.

"Keep it for me, Dandy," he says.

"What?"

"It'll be safer with you." He pushes the papers away with both hands, palms up. "Hide it in the secret compartment at the bottom of Eldridge's medicine case."

The fine vellum seems to chafe my fingers, and I'm seized with the urge to open his belt pouch and shove the document inside. It's personal, deeply so, and I'm not his wife. I have no right to hold this for him.

"No, Geoff, take it."

He resists again.

His smile broadens, deepening the creases lining his eyes and mouth, and warmth spreads through my chilled limbs. I give a slow smile and place the parchment in my own belt pouch with infinite care. My fingers brush the dried dandelion, the one he gave me when I left Fobbing.

I pat the pouch. "I'll protect it with my life."

He nods.

"What," I say, taking a step closer, "was the other thing you mentioned? You said there was more?"

"Henry's promoted me, to captain of his personal guard."

"Oh, Geoff. I'm so happy for you."

The corners of his mouth curve up, and he shakes his head like a dog. Droplets of water come loose from his hair, spraying in graceful arcs toward me. I see each one; they descend with exaggerated slowness and land on my cheeks and eyelashes.

I blink the rainwater away and try to refocus.

Before I can, his mouth is on mine, his palm on my cheek. He opens his mouth, and I feel his tongue on my lips. My limbs loosen. I want to be with him, want to do this. To open to him, to love him. But I am married. Married. To Thomas.

I push him away.

"Geoff," I whisper, "this...this..." I spread my hands. "This can't happen."

He grips the sideboard and pants, raking one hand through his wet hair. "It *is* happening. It's already happened. Remember—"

"Leave, Geoff. Go away." I bunch my cloak in my fists and wrap it around me, angry and bereft and heated all at once.

"Blanche, please—"

I hurry across the room, desperate to put the trestle table between us, to douse this fire.

"Dandy—"

After skirting the table, I stop by the stairs and face him.

"Dandy." He hunches over, places his palms on the table, and leans in. "I love you."

I draw a ragged breath. The ache returns to my limbs.

Maman said my father would love me if I married Thomas. But I know he doesn't. He won't.

Maman doesn't love me either, not as a mother should. I know that. I can admit it to myself now, no longer a child.

Eldridge is gone. My husband loathes me.

I want to cling to Geoff, but I can't. His declaration puts him in greater danger than he ever was as a simple villein, destined to live out his days destitute and enslaved. I know how I feel, and that means I have to keep him safe.

"How do you think this could possibly work?" I ask. "I'm married, Geoff."

"I have no idea." His arms hang limp at his sides, water dripping from his coat cuffs to the floor.

I shake my head.

"So you don't love me?" he asks.

"Geoff, if we were discovered, and you know we would be, Thomas—"

"Yer father and brother would protect you."

"Yes," I say, voice flat, "but who would protect you?"

"I don't need protection."

"Yes, you do, Geoff."

His own parents loved him in a way I'll never experience. But they're dead, just like Eldridge. The only person left to protect Geoff is me. What would happen if Cook, or the serving boy, or Thomas himself walked in right now? What about sixty seconds ago? Geoff may not be a villein anymore, but I'm still the constable's wife. Thomas could ensure Geoff lost his position with Henry, then make it impossible for him to find another. It might not even come to that. In his fury, after discovering another man could sleep with his wife when he couldn't, Thomas might draw his sword and kill Geoff, right in our dining hall.

And he'd get away with it. He's one of the king's favorites.

I'll do anything to make sure that doesn't happen.

"Dandy." His voice is a deep rumble, in counterpoint to the rain lashing against the wooden door. "Please."

"I'm not Dandy anymore, not to you."

His expression darkens, and something compresses my chest.

He opens his mouth, but thinks better of it and sets his jaw. Rain drips from his hair onto his shoulders.

"I'm Lady Prescott and you're the captain of my brother's guard. Nothing more." I lift my chin and try to ignore the stark pain in his eyes. Fumbling with my belt pouch, I pull out the rolled parchment. "Take this." I try to shove his manumission papers across the table, but as I do, the dried dandelion falls out and snaps in two.

I stare at it, broken on the table. Bits of the yellow petals are ground to dust and scattered across the rough wood.

I crumple the flower's remains in my fist, then look back at Geoff and blink away my tears. "You're just another soldier. I can't be responsible for your things."

"I see," he says.

We stand, each on one side of the oaken table, right where I first realized he'd come to London. The table seems wider than that night, back when he was a villein. Now he's free, but an even more insurmountable distance separates us.

He stares at me, eyes dark. My knees go weak with want. I brace myself against the wall and make to grab the paper back, but he snatches it up, gritting his teeth. I square my shoulders.

"My father—"

"I know what you think yer father expects."

I take a shaky breath and set my jaw. "Go away, captain. Please." I pull my cloak tighter. "Just go away."

He turns, opens the door, and leaves.

Silence roars in my ears. There are no rats in the walls, no staff in the kitchen, no fire crackling in the grate. There's no one here but me.

"I love you," I say to the empty room.

Outside, a worker's hammer strikes the White Tower's limestone wall, repairing the rebellion's damage. Soon, it will be as if it never happened. England, and all our lives, will be just like before.

I'll be someone's property, beholden to Thomas's every whim just as Geoff is to Henry's. Eventually, Thomas will take my maidenhead, will force me to become his wife not just in name but in deed. I can only avoid that eventuality for so long. He wants me—needs me—as a vessel for his seed. A mother for his child and heir. I haven't been given a choice about that.

I open my fist to find the crushed dandelion, now nothing more than green-and-yellow powder, like the tansy and hellebore Eldridge used to end Cecily's pregnancy.

Only last month, that young woman took control of her own fate. I wonder what Cecily is doing now, if she's learned her father is destined for execution. That she, her mother, and her siblings will have to run the bakery without their patriarch. That is, if her eldest brother can afford the heriot.

"My lady?"

I spin around to find Joan standing beside me.

"Sir Thomas left an hour ago for the White Tower," she says, "but he bid me tell you he'll dine at home tonight."

I nod, a grim ball of dread settling in my stomach. I move toward the door.

She grabs my elbow. "Also, my lady, I know I've been remiss the last few days, what with everything that's happened."

My brow raises. "Joan?"

"Your nightly tisane," she continues. "You haven't had it in days."

"Oh."

"I'll have it ready tonight."

A surge of something blooms in my chest, gone in an instant, yet unmistakable all the same. Hope, agency, and control over one aspect of my future.

"Thank you, Joan."

"Of course, my lady."

I tip my still-open palm, letting the green-and-yellow remnants of the dandelion slip away. "Parsley, artemisia, juniper, and licorice," I murmur, watching the powder disappear in the floor rushes.

"I won't forget."

"Neither will I."

Epilogue

SEPTEMBER 1381

John Ferrour stands in the corner, dry-washing his hands and working his jaw.

It's been three months since the rebellion. Three months since he, Johanna, and the other rebels stormed the Tower of London. Since they forced their country into a new social order, a new balance of power, the possibility for a real future.

That was the intention, at least. For a day, for a few hours, he'd thought he changed the world. He'd been wrong.

Johanna screams and he's returned to the present.

Crouched at the foot of the bed, Lady Prescott presses one hand to his wife's belly and inserts the other between her legs, from where his child is trying to emerge. Johanna's belly seizes with a contraction. Lady Prescott grimaces, but says nothing. Her dingy work tunic's sleeves are rolled up, and her forearm tenses, her teeth clenching as Johanna's pelvic muscles tighten around her fingers.

The lady's maid steps forward with another clean towel. "My lady, are you all right?"

"Yes, Joan," she says through gritted teeth. "Fine."

The young maid's pretty face is lined with concern. "Is all well?" she mouths.

Lady Prescott removes her hand and wipes it on the apron, streaking his wife's blood across the white linen.

"All will be well," she assures. "Give her more of the groaning ale."

The lady moves to Johanna's head as her maid fetches the cup. When she tips a swallow into Johanna's mouth, John can smell the dark ale. Stronger than any other brew, it's laced with the usual flavorings: cinnamon and nutmeg. But Lady Prescott added new spices they'd never tasted. Ginger—imported from the far east—in addition to Aristolochia and beta minor. *They'll help with the pain more than spices will*, this strange and unexpected midwife had told them before Johanna's pains began.

Now, she takes his wife's hand and whispers in her ear. "The babe is healthy, I believe"—her voice is soothing and melodic—"but is emerging feet down."

Johanna groans.

"Is that a problem?" John asks.

"Yes." Lady Prescott seizes Johanna's other hand as she's wracked with another contraction. "Try not to push," she leans over and whispers. "Not yet."

"You can fix it?"

"That's why I called you. I'll need your assistance."

His stomach flips and bile crawls up his throat, but he nods and takes Johanna's hand from Lady Prescott. On the other side of the bed, the maid uses a cloth to bathe the tears and sweat from his wife's face with fragrant lavender water, brought from the royal palace.

"Tell me what to do," he says.

"When I signal, push here." She places her hand on Johanna's swollen belly. "Push *hard.*"

Her eyes bore into his, and he nods without hesitation. In this moment, if Lady Prescott told him to set his wife's hair on fire, he'd do it.

For all that he'd thought joining the rebellion would ensure a better life for his wife and children, his only good decision that week had been to free Lord Henry. In exchange, Lady Prescott has visited them regularly for three months, just as she promised. His son, Matthew, is stronger than ever. Since she gave them an aromatic salve to help him breathe and showed them how to make a steam tent, his wheezing fits have decreased. When they do happen, he recovers faster. He coughs less and is growing, thanks to the meat and vegetables delivered from the Tower. Before, he'd looked more like a four-year-old than a boy of seven and could only speak a few words. Now, he could pass for a small six-year-old and speaks more each day.

"Joan, fetch the block from my medicine chest." Lady Prescott takes the cloth from the maid and dips it in the lavender water. "On the next contraction, I'm going to place my hands inside, and will attempt to turn the child."

She wipes Johanna's face and kneels on the dirt floor to look into her eyes. Johanna's green gaze is clouded with pain, and her gray-streaked hair flies in wild shocks around her face.

"Don't push, please don't push," Lady Prescott whispers to her. "I'm sorry to say this is going to hurt." The maid fetches the birthing ale and holds it to Johanna's lips once again. "Drink deep, Goodwife." After Johanna can drink no more, the maid gives her a small wooden block, lined with teeth marks on both sides. "Bite down on this, for the pain."

Johanna is two and forty, malnourished, and overworked. Just like everyone else in Southwark. Now the baby isn't coming out right.

John watches Lady Prescott move back to the foot of the bed. She sits on a stool and prepares to turn his child around.

This woman can't be the constable's wife, he thinks to himself, for what must be the hundredth time. Where did a lady learn such skills? Her husband can't be aware that she's coming here to help them—the family of two known rebel leaders. He and Johanna should both be dead. The king had all the other leaders killed. Their rotting heads still decorate London Bridge.

A few weeks after the Tower's siege, over five hundred peasant-soldiers were slaughtered at the Battle of Billericay, the peasants' final stand in Essex. His sister, Mary, had begged both him and Johanna not to go. "Think of your children," she'd said. "You could both be killed. Then what will happen to your three boys?" He'd agreed and commanded Johanna to stay home as well. She hadn't wanted to listen, had tried to sneak away. He'd physically restrained her.

The rebels hadn't had a prayer. The king's soldiers, returned from Wales, even killed those who took shelter at Ramsey Abbey. It's a crime against God, a mortal sin to kill a man who has sought sanctuary in a holy place, but apparently the rebels deserved no such protection.

John Ferrour knows the only reason he and Johanna are alive is because of the woman who's now trying to save his wife and child. She told her brother, Henry of Lancaster, what Ferrour had done, and Lancaster has protected them ever since. Such is the power of wealth. Lancaster can make anything happen, but John knows it's really all due to this young woman kneeling between his wife's legs. He owes her everything.

In the end, the rebellion did change his life, just not as he'd planned. It brought this unusually tall woman, with her Plantagenet nose and royal blood, to help his family.

When he agreed to help Henry of Lancaster, he hadn't realized Lady Prescott was John of Gaunt's illegitimate daughter. Although she'd told them she was a Fitzjohn, in the chaos of the moment, he hadn't pieced the facts together. John's a common name. Christ, it's his own name. This woman could have been the illegitimate daughter of any number of men.

No, when he accepted her offer and freed Henry of Lancaster, Blanche Fitzjohn was the constable's wife. That was all.

It was only last month that a passing soldier told his eldest son that Lady Blanche Prescott was the Duke of Lancaster's daughter. Although the relation makes sense, in that it explains her fervor for saving the duke's only legitimate son, John can't reconcile this in his mind. For the constable's wife to heal with herbs and deliver babies is odd. For such a woman to traipse up to an executioner's block and demand a prisoner's release is unusual.

But for *John of Gaunt's daughter* to do such a thing?

"It's coming," Johanna says, a terrible shudder rippling through her body. The maid thunks down the ale goblet and grips her hand. John takes the other.

Johanna bites on the block and presses her chin to her chest. Lady Prescott slips one hand inside his wife, straining against what appears to be a fierce pressure. Johanna wails into the wood, the sound muffled and like a wounded animal.

She won't survive this, she won't survive this. Visions of caring for three children alone swim in John's mind. A world without his loving, generous, hardworking wife. Matthew will die without her tender care during his wheezing spells. The other children will starve; John has no idea how to cook. Johanna also mends linens in the evenings for extra money, which they use to pay their second son's apprentice fee. He tries to catch her gaze, but their mossy green irises flit about the room, unable to settle as she cries into the wooden block.

"Now, Ferrour!"

He hears it on the edge of his senses. "Please stay with me, my love," he murmurs. *Please, Mary, Mother of God, let this woman stay with me.*

Someone smacks him on the shoulder. He looks around; the maid has begun to push down on Johanna's belly, as Lady

Prescott instructed. He drops Johanna's hand and joins, pressing his good hand against his screaming wife's body.

"Harder!" the Lady of the Tower cries.

He pushes with all his strength, going against his instincts, basing his judgment only on what this woman says. Johanna screams. She's crying. He's never hit his wife, never made her cry, unlike some men, and he can't bear the sound of her pain. The block falls from her mouth, and she begs God to kill her. He feels tears on his cheeks; he hasn't cried since he was seven years old, when his own mother died trying to give him a brother.

He glances at Lady Prescott. Both her hands are inside Johanna. Blood extends up her tunic sleeves and has drenched her apron. Johanna keeps screaming. Then, there's a sudden shift. The hard plank of his wife's belly rumbles and rolls, a life moving within it.

"Yes!" Lady Prescott cries. She flings herself backward, panting and crying, her own hair loose around her shoulders. In an odd moment of clarity, John notices it's cut unusually short.

"It's flipped?"

She nods. "Yes."

Johanna's entire body trembles. He wraps his arms around her torso, holding her as she weeps. Lady Prescott settles back onto her stool for only a moment, wiping her hands on the towel handed to her by the maid before tossing it back. She spreads her hands just in time for the baby to slip out, headfirst and screaming.

"Here she is!" Lady Prescott cries.

"She?" John asks.

"Yes." She cleans mucus and blood from the infant's mouth and nose, then rubs its skin with an apron. The baby cries harder. "Yes, yes, little girl." Lady Blanche grins, cradling the baby in her arms before lifting her up for her parents to see. "Listen to those wonderful lungs! A beautiful girl."

His heart compresses as he watches his daughter, red-faced and furious, yet large and seemingly healthy. They've lost two in the past. One stillborn and another gone before her first birthday. This one seems to have a thirst for life, with black hair like both her parents. A thick cord of sinew stretches from the infant's stomach to his wife's womb, but Lady Prescott seems unconcerned, so he tells himself not to worry.

Lady Prescott places the baby gently on Johanna's chest, and his wife's eyes flutter open. The cord stretches, still connecting mother and child.

"My baby?" Johanna asks.

"Yes, yes!" Lady Prescott declares. "A perfect baby girl. Ten fingers, ten toes."

Johanna gives a tired smile, caressing her daughter's face, ears, hands, bottom, and feet. John cradles the girl's head in his palm and kisses her tangled mass of wet hair.

As Lady Blanche returns to her stool, Johanna grunts with pain. The lady reaches to massage her belly.

"What's happening?" He grips Johanna's wrist with one hand, the other placed protectively on the baby's back.

Lady Prescott shakes her head and smiles. "Just the afterbirth. Don't worry, it's normal."

A minute later, a dark bundle of blood and fleshy meat slides from between Johanna's thighs. With brusque efficiency, the lady cuts the cord—attached to the bloody mass—ties it, and lets the maid take the afterbirth outside with instructions to bury it.

John tries not to look.

Johanna eases the baby to her breast. The infant takes it and sucks. She is strong and lusty, but drifts asleep after only a few minutes.

Lady Blanche takes the baby from Johanna with gentle hands and carries her to the table. There, she washes the baby with lavender water and wraps her in a clean white cloth.

"When shall she be christened?"

"Today," John responds.

"Will you attend, my lady?" Johanna asks.

Lady Prescott looks at them, surprised. "Well, if you wish it, of course."

"I'd like you to be her godmother. We'll call her Blanchette, I think. For the lady who saved her."

Lady Prescott stares. Her mouth works open and closed, then she clenches her jaw, picks up the baby, and returns her to Johanna. "Are you sure?" she asks at last. "I've...I've never..."

John cocks his head. There is no reasoning with this strange woman.

"It's a lovely name," Johanna says. Lady Prescott pulls a clean quilt over her legs and torso, covering Blanchette as Johanna shifts her to the other breast. "Fitzjohn is as well. Named for your powerful father."

Lady Prescott nods but doesn't look pleased. "Blanche Ferrour is a much finer name."

A pit hollows in John's stomach. He shakes his head. "There's no future for her. She'll be just like me, just like all those born into this." He waves his hand, the gesture taking in the shabby home: one room for six people. His children sleep on the dirt floor. His eldest son, Gerald, is his apprentice and will grow up to work in the forge. The best he can hope for is to shoe a rich man's horse. His second is apprenticed to a tanner. He has no idea how they'll afford the apprentice fee for Matthew, or if the boy will even be strong enough to work.

Now, this daughter, Blanchette. Another hungry mouth, and they hadn't enough food before. Since he injured his arm two years prior in an accident at the forge, he's been unable to take on much work. Until Gerald is old enough to take over, bringing in a solid income will be difficult. Plus, since John's injury, old customers now go somewhere else. Building the business back up won't be easy, especially when the king is constantly levying new taxes for the war with France.

"You don't know that, husband," Johanna says, voice growing faint. There are dark smudges of exhaustion beneath her eyes.

Lady Blanche covers his wife's hand with her own and brushes a lock of dark hair from her face. "Rest, Goodwife."

Johanna shakes her head and squares her shoulders. John knows she's trying to look strong, healthy. Acting as if she didn't just birth a human being. He grins. Some things never change.

Lady Prescott goes to the table to gather her tools.

Johanna looks up from the now-sleeping Blanchette to gaze at her husband. "We came close to changing history before," she whispers, her words meant for him alone. "Maybe change will come for us sooner than you think."

His eyes widen, and he glances over his shoulder. Lady Blanche is depositing her herbs and mortar into the large chest her maid hauled in. He doubts she heard Johanna's statement. Still, when he turns back to his wife, he fixes a stern expression on his face. "I'd never rebel against the king, wife. *We'd* never. Not again."

"I know." Johanna smiles and tucks the blanket tighter around the baby. "I just—"

She stops suddenly as the lady returns to her side with the goblet of groaning ale. "I agree with your wife, Master Ferrour." She holds the cup to Johanna's lips and lets her drink. "You don't know that to be true."

"Know what, m'lady?" he says, a little louder than he intended, fear warping his insides. If the lady heard his wife's words, will she tell her brother, or her cousin the king?

"You don't know what the future holds for your daughter."

The tightness coiling inside him loosens a little. "Respectfully, m'lady, I don't think you understand what it's like, for the likes of us."

"Because I'm a lady?"

"Yes."

“No one knows what it feels like to be another person, that much is true. I don’t know how it is to walk in your shoes. But remember what I told you on the Tower Green. I’m a bastard. Whether a lady or a peasant, that never changes.”

He shrugs.

Johanna takes Lady Blanche’s hand. “You’re right. Who knows what the future holds for Blanchette, for you. For us.” She nods her chin to John.

“Blanchette will be bound to a life of servitude,” John replies. “To her king, to her husband. Her children. Such is the way of our world.”

“What about servitude to her father?” Lady Blanche asks Johanna with a smile.

Then she faces John. In the blink of an eye, her gaze suddenly becomes intense and serious. He yearns to flinch away from it, but something holds him to her.

“More opportunities will arise, Master Ferrour,” she says, voice gentle despite her expression. “Opportunities for change. And when they come, we must take them. We must keep trying.”

“How do you know?” he asks.

“Women like me,” she whispers, “sometimes we just know things.”

—

The figure of a tall, lean woman wanders the marsh, searching through the reeds and sea grass. Her eyes shine, her spirit soars. There’s a hope in her, alongside her sadness. Beyond it.

She sees a future. The possibility for more.

A woman is meant to be subservient. Submissive and meek. She should have no wants, no real needs beyond pleasing her husband and raising her children. She toils. She serves, and she gives, expecting nothing in return. The world happens *to* her; she does not mold it to her desires.

"Not always," the woman of the marsh whispers, just before disappearing into the mist.

Author's Note

Blanche Fitzjohn's story—my version of it, at least—began over a nice dinner in London. I'd recently finished my first novel and was trying, unsuccessfully, to get it published. As the waiter brought our wine, my husband asked if I had any plans for my next story.

He didn't know it, but that was just about the scariest thing he could have asked. Really, what's more frightening than jumping off a second cliff when you're still falling from the first? But the truth was, I had begun thinking about my next novel. I couldn't help it; there was an idea niggling at my mind that wouldn't go away.

"What if I wrote about an autistic character in medieval England?" I asked.

"Sounds interesting," he said, "but it also sounds kind of sad."

"What if it wasn't?"

What if questions are the building blocks of historical fiction, especially for characters like Blanche Fitzjohn. I first learned of her existence in one of my all-time favorite novels, Anya Seton's *Katherine*. Blanche occupies a mere sentence in John of Gaunt's backstory, but after a deep dive into contemporary historical sources, my what if questions kept coming.

What if Blanche's differences went beyond her illegitimacy? What if her abilities manifested as magic? What if she established a close friendship with her half-brother? Did she loathe her husband? What if she was in love with someone else? Could she be the reason her brother Henry survived the Peasants' Revolt?

The answers to these questions, as I've decided to write them, formed the *Fitzjohn* duology. The story started with a framework of historical facts, followed by author's conjecture and creativity.

Very little is known about Blanche, and uncovering her history meant hunting for clues in the lives of others, primarily her father. What I was able to find—her name, her approximate date of birth, her mother's identity, her husband's name and their year of marriage, her husband's occupation and property, her dowry—all came from Gaunt's financial records.

But in the end, my task as a novelist is to fill in the gaps. In this novel, although historical accuracy was always a priority, my first responsibility was to tell an authentic human story.

Although Blanche's character began with my question about autism in medieval England, I've shied away from any diagnostic labeling. In the fourteenth century, there were no neurologists, no testing, no diagnoses. Blanche was inspired by my own son, who has autism and ADHD; my daughter, who has ADHD and epilepsy; and my own experiences as a neurodiverse woman. However, I want to be sensitive to the fact that Blanche would never have understood these labels, so they're not relevant in this setting. Also, as I'm not a neurologist, I'd never try to diagnose Blanche.

Another important historical note pertains to Blanche's husband, Thomas. A quick Google search will tell you he wasn't actually named Sir Thomas Prescott. Why did I change the name? The real Thomas Morieux was, in the basic ways, just like the fictional Sir Thomas Prescott. He was the Constable of the Tower of London and Master of the King's Horse. He hailed from Suffolk and had a sister named Elizabeth. He was in his late twenties when he married Blanche. In fact, I wrote the entire novel's first draft using the name Thomas Morieux. Then I realized I'd created a truly heinous villain, who in the second book gets even worse.

As with Blanche, historical documents tell us nothing about Sir Thomas Morieux's personality and day-to-day activities. Unlike historical figures such as Robert de Vere or King Richard II, for whom historical facts verify their questionable choices and evil deeds, I created Thomas's character in the service of a fictional narrative.

The real Thomas Morieux might have been a perfectly nice guy. Maybe he was a good husband. The fact that he was an actual person is important, and I want to honor his memory. For this reason, and out of respect for the Morieux family, I changed the character's name to Sir Thomas Prescott.

My goal was to write an authentic medieval setting in a compelling, modern voice. Therefore, some of the words and phrases I've chosen weren't typically used in the Middle Ages. Please note that this is a deliberate, stylistic choice. I wanted Blanche's story to be accessible and relatable. I also made some minor changes in the service of continuity and ease of reading. For example, when Blanche's brother, Henry, was a young man in the fourteenth century, he would have been known as Henry of Bolingbroke. However, historical novels' vast array of characters can quickly become confusing. Therefore, I chose to refer to Blanche's brother as Henry of Lancaster, or Lord Henry. Other noblemen's and noblewomen's names were similarly simplified.

In this same vein, the Peasants' Revolt of 1381 was a complex event with a complicated timeline. To avoid confusion, I chose to focus on the events affecting Blanche. *Uprising* tells the rebellion's story through the eyes of one person, in real time, as opposed to a historical account with the benefit of hindsight.

Historical sources give conflicting accounts of both John and Johanna Ferrour. Some historians even believe they were the same person. As can be imagined, contemporary sources weren't always reliable, especially when it came to documenting common rebels. It's impossible to know the truth of who these two were, but we know they existed in one way or another, and that they saved the future King Henry IV. Furthermore, I like to think their characterizations reflect the spirit of the rebellion for which they fought, and honor their memories.

Toward the end of *Uprising*'s long publication journey, I started to wonder if Blanche's story would ever be published. Maybe it just wasn't good enough. But what made me do one last rewrite, what induced me to send off yet another batch of queries, was the memory of the real Blanche Fitzjohn. Her name has been virtually unspoken for over six hundred years, and it's time for that to change.

My Blanche is a fictional character. We don't know what she was really like, and never will. But, at least through this book, readers will know she existed. The goal of my writing will always be to shed light on the experiences of women, particularly those who are different. Blanche lived through, and survived, some of the bloodiest and most consequential events of medieval English history. Given her proximity to power, it is only rational to believe she influenced and changed history.

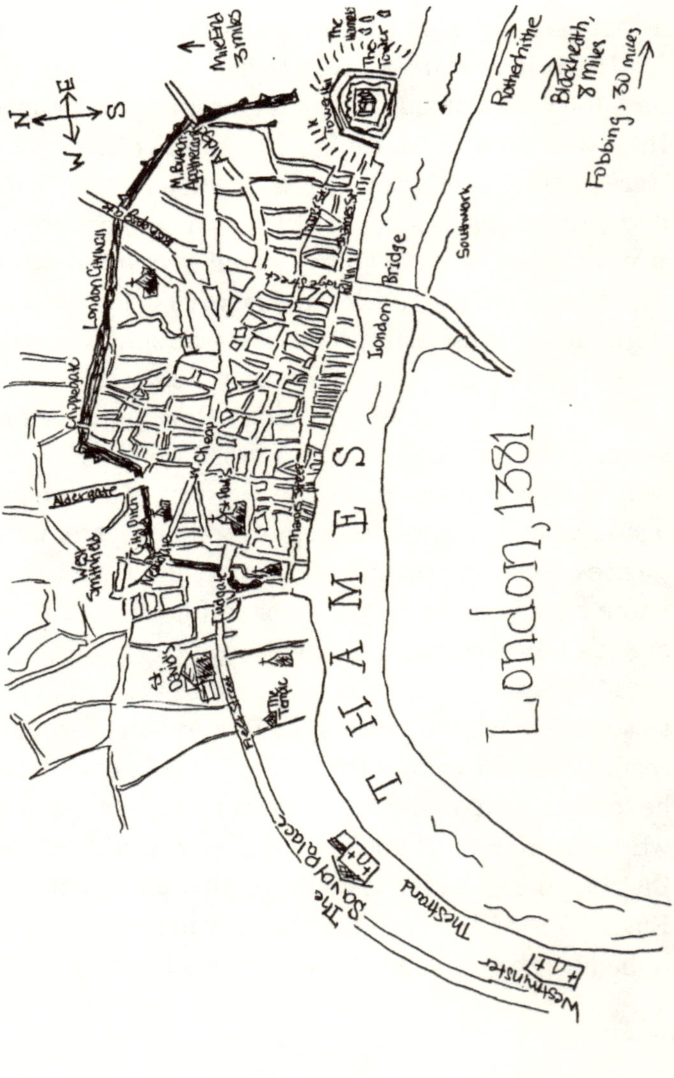
London, 1381
THAMES
London Bridge
Southwark
Rotherhithe
Blackheath, 8 Miles
Fobbing, 30 miles
Mile End 3 miles
London City Wall
Cripplegate
Aldersgate
West Smithfield
City Ditch
Newgate
Ludgate
Fleet Street
The Temple
W. Cheap
St Paul's
Aldgate
Tower Hill
The Strand
The Savoy Palace
Westminster
N
E
S
W

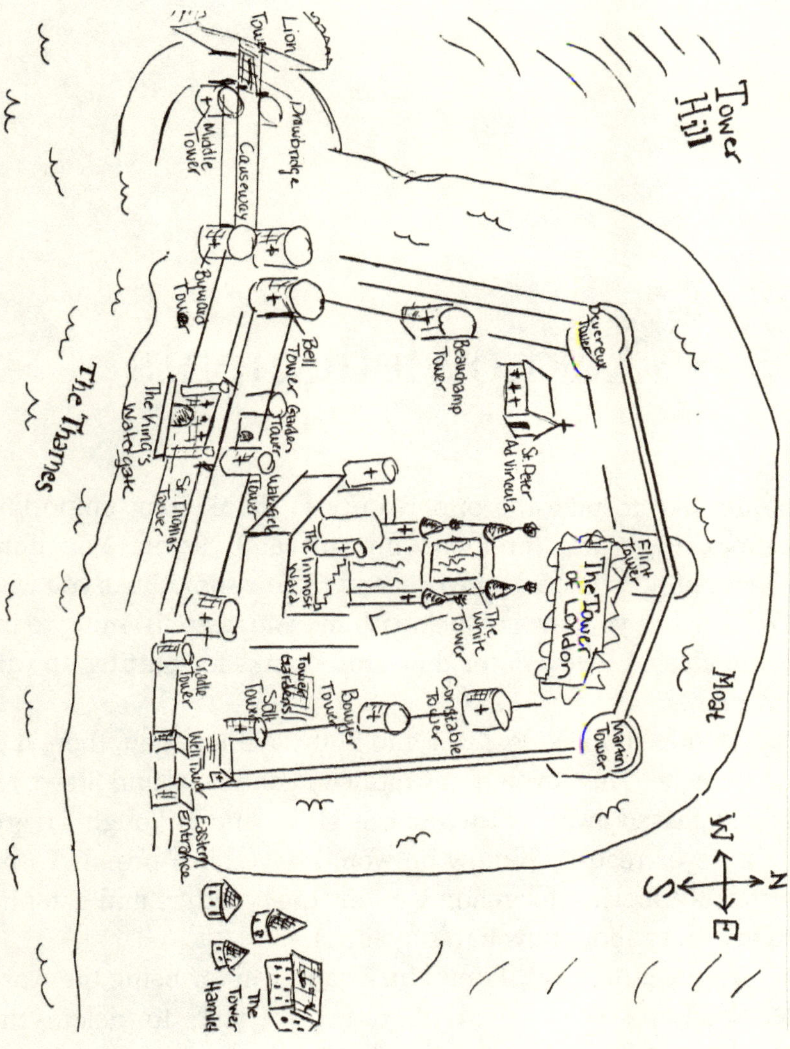
Tower Hill
Moat
The Tower of London
The Thames
Lion Tower
Drawbridge
Middle Tower
Causeway
Byward Tower
Bell Tower
Beauchamp Tower
Devereux Tower
St. Peter Ad Vincula
Flint Tower
The White Tower
The Inmost Ward
Garden Tower
Wakefield Tower
The King's Watergate
St. Thomas Tower
Cradle Tower
Tower Gardens
Salt Tower
Bowyer Tower
Constable Tower
Martin Tower
Well Tower
Eastern entrance
The Tower Hamlet
N
E
S
W

Acknowledgments

I'd like to take the opportunity to thank some important people. First and foremost, my husband, Kevin. You don't always understand why I write, and I know sometimes you wish I'd stop, but you always stick with me and keep listening to my crazy ideas. I love you for that. And thanks for putting up with my plants.

Thanks to my kids, Lizzy and Sully. Without you, there'd be no Blanche. Thank you to my mom and dad, Suzi and Steve. My father passed away as I wrote this story, and although I regret he'll never read it, I know he would have been proud. To my sister, Kimberley, for reading all my query letters and listening to my rants about how hard my life is.

To my ginger cat, Pumpkin. Thank you for being the worst feline. I'm still so mad at you for trying to delete this manuscript. Twice. I wrote the absolute best of you into Rhead, and even though you repay me by lying in wait with murderous intentions, I still love you.

Sincerest gratitude to my critique partners, Wendy and Claire. To my editor, Jennica, thank you for taking a chance on *Uprising* and for having the best ideas. All the rejection led me to you, and for that I'm grateful.

Lastly, thank you to Blanche Fitzjohn. Imagining what might have transpired in your life has changed my own forever. You've existed in my brain for years now, and I have a feeling you're not going away any time soon.

About the Author

J.E. Rizzo is a life-long history fanatic and writer of historical fiction, and her work can be found in *Vanity Fair*, *The Boston Globe*, *The Guardian*, *The Tudor Times*, *Tudor Life Magazine*, *Scary Mommy*, and *Ultrarunning Magazine.* Rizzo's debut novel, *Uprising*, Book One of the *Fitzjohn* Duology, is forthcoming from Literary Wanderlust, and tells the story of Blanche Fitzjohn, a fourteenth-century neurodivergent woman whose perceived disabilities become superpowers during England's peasant uprising of 1381.

Rizzo won Manuscript Academy's Agent Choice Award in 2024, and her article *Past and Precedence: Abortion Law in the Middle Ages and Its Use to Overturn Roe v. Wade* won *History Inquiry*'s Medieval History Writing Challenge.

By day, Rizzo works in Human Resources—a field offering more than ample opportunity to observe the follies and fancies of humankind. Before her career in HR, Rizzo worked as an opera singer, a professional baker, and a dog walker. These days, when not writing she can be found running ultramarathons through the forests and mountains of New England, knitting, reading, sewing, baking, or performing any number of (what some might call) old-lady hobbies. She also keeps busy caring for her two children and forty-seven houseplants, making her husband carry heavy things and cook her gourmet meals, and rehabilitating her rescue dog and semi-feral ginger cat.

Read more about her at www.jennifererizzo.com.

www.ingramcontent.com/pod-product-compliance
Lightning Source LLC
Chambersburg PA
CBHW050004090926
51161CB00031B/518
* 9 7 8 1 9 5 6 6 1 5 6 4 7 *